ROBERTA KRAY was ~~born~~ ~~in~~ ~~London~~ and worked in publishing and ~~journalism~~ for fifteen years. In early 1996 she met Reg Kray and they married the following year. Her bestselling first novel, *The Debt*, was published by Constable and Robinson last year. She currently lives in Norfolk.

Praise for Roberta Kray's *The Debt*

'*The Debt* paints a vivid and frightening picture of the criminal class. For a debut novel, Roberta Kray steers the twisting plot with steady hands; injecting the right amount of humour and suspense.' *Shotsmag*

'No doubt about it, British crime fiction is getting sharper and tougher . . . *The Debt* convinces on every page – not only about the gangster world but also as a portrait of a woman whose life has been changed by forces beyond her control.' *Chicago Tribune*

Also by Roberta Kray

The Debt

THE PACT

ROBERTA KRAY

ROBINSON
London

Constable & Robinson Ltd
3 The Lanchesters
162 Fulham Palace Road
London W6 9ER
www.constablerobinson.com

First published in the UK by Constable
an imprint of Constable & Robinson Ltd 2007

This paperback edition published by Robinson,
an imprint of Constable & Robinson Ltd 2007

A copy of the British Library Cataloguing in
Publication Data is available from the British Library.

ISBN: 978-1-84529-499-1 (pbk)
ISBN: 978-1-84529-411-3 (hbk)

Printed and bound in the EU

3 5 7 9 10 8 6 4

Chapter One

In a room full of men, Terry looked distinctly out of place. Small and skinny, his skin pale as porcelain, he seemed scarcely old enough to buy a drink never mind serve a prison sentence. Like some half-starved Dickensian waif, a pair of wide grey eyes dominated a delicate heart-shaped face. It was a face that was dangerously close to being pretty.

Except today – she stopped dead in her tracks – there were marks on that pale flesh, a large mauve bruise encircling his left eye, a vicious reddening around the jaw.

Hurrying forward, Eve grabbed hold of his arm. 'Jesus! What happened?'

'Nothing.'

'It doesn't look like—'

He shrugged her off, glancing furtively around. 'It's nothing,' he insisted again. This time it was more like a warning than a reply. As if to close the exchange, he quickly sat down, putting his elbows on his knees, and staring at the floor.

'Terry?' She sank down on the chair beside him. She knew they were being watched, examined. The hairs rose up on the back of her neck. And she knew what they were all thinking – the cons, the visitors, even the screws – it hardly took a genius to work it out. Inmates were always being bullied, being harassed, being . . . She stopped, swallowing hard. She could hardly bring herself to articulate the thought and so settled on the word *abused* instead. It didn't help much.

Her stomach heaved.

Eventually he raised his eyes and forced a smile. 'What are you looking so pissed off about?'

'What do you think?' Anger burned into her cheeks. His injuries were worse close up; there were other bruises staining his neck, purple marks on his slender hands and wrists. She flinched. 'For God's sake.'

'Leave it,' he insisted. 'Just leave it, okay?'

As if she should just accept it, as if it was perfectly normal to see your little brother with half his stupid cupid face smashed in. Not to mention whatever else had . . .

'Tell me, tell me who did it? Who did this to you?'

He gave her one of his full-on incredulous looks. 'I'm not some bloody grass,' he swore softly. 'You know the score, Evie. You want to get me fucking killed?'

'Seems like you're doing a pretty good job of that yourself.' She scowled. 'Anyway, it's *me* you're talking to, not the bleeding Governor.'

He dropped his head into his hands. 'I'm not listening.'

Eve released a low frustrated sigh. That was the trouble with Terry, he never *did* listen. He never had. He'd had the best teacher in the world, their own smart, smooth-talking swindler of a father, but had never had the patience to absorb a single sentence. 'Now' was the only word he'd ever understood. Everything had to be here and now, instant success, instant cash, instant gratification, which was why he'd ended up in this lousy godforsaken hellhole of a place.

And why *she'd* been left with the thankless job of picking up the pieces.

'You could get me a brew,' he said sulkily, 'if it's not too much trouble.'

'Sure.' She got to her feet. 'Whatever.' There was no point pushing him. Perhaps, when he had space to think, he might confide in her. Although the odds weren't great; twenty-one years of stubborn stupidity were unlikely to dissolve in the few minutes it took her to get to the counter and back.

Stumbling across the room, she blindly swiped at the tears in her eyes. She bit down hard on her lip. Damn! She wasn't the crying sort and blubbing like an infant wasn't going to change anything. Although, come to think of it, what was?

For the first time in his life, Terry was well and truly on his own.

It's only six months, she repeated like a mantra, trying to reassure herself, *six months, six months*. But, hell, it didn't take six minutes, never mind six months, to wind up with a noose around your neck.

Lost in the horror, she bumped into the edge of another con's chair and almost fell.

'Careful, darling,' he said, extending a hand.

Quickly she snatched her arm away. 'Sorry.'

'No need to apologize.'

She might only have glanced at him, glanced and moved on, but there was something about his voice, its shifty provocative edge, that caught her attention. Eve raised her head and stared. A pair of dark assessing eyes returned her gaze before quite blatantly sliding down her body to view whatever else might be of interest.

'No point rushing,' he grinned sleazily into her breasts. 'I'm not going anywhere.'

She glared back at him. Great, this was just what she needed, some low-life piece of scum reviewing her assets in the middle of a prison visiting room. As if she didn't have enough to deal with. Spit in my face, why don't you? At any other time, in any other place, she might have drawn her claws and prepared for a fight – but not today. She had more important things to worry about.

'Fuck you,' she murmured.

He laughed as she walked away.

Later, thinking back, she'd claim this was the moment that everything changed. But it wasn't entirely true. It was only while she was in the queue, grinding her teeth and quietly seething, that the idea slowly began to take form.

She bought tea and snacks, took a more circuitous route back to the table and clattered the tray down. As if he hadn't eaten for a week, Terry snatched up a bag of crisps and opened them.

'What's his name?' she asked, glancing over her shoulder.

'Who?'

'The one with the attitude, the one I bumped into.' She was sure Terry would have been watching her, probably trying to think of some yarn to spin, some tall story to get her off his back.

He hesitated again, his lips pursing to ask why, but then clearly thought better of it. This line of inquiry was preferable to her last. 'Cavelli,' he said. 'Martin Cavelli.'

'Yeah, I thought so. I thought it was him. Is he on your wing?'

He nodded.

'Did he do that to you?' she asked, gesturing towards the bruises on his face and neck.

'What?' He had just raised the plastic cup to his mouth. A stream of hot brown tea spluttered out across his chest. 'God, Evie, what—'

She didn't give him time to finish. 'Or have *anything* to do with it?'

'No!' he insisted, scowling and rubbing ineffectively at

the stain on his shirt. 'Shit, look what you've made me do. I'm going to have to wash this now.'

She sat back in her seat and smiled. Good. At least that was one question answered. Terry could lie for England – he was the quintessential blond-haired angel – but on this occasion she was certain he was telling the truth. Settling back to sip her tea, she sneaked a glance at the man called Cavelli, caught his eye and held it for a few lingering seconds.

She'd taken the opportunity for closer scrutiny while she was waiting to be served: an experienced con, she was sure, late forties, maybe a touch older, tall, broad, and with the kind of over-developed shoulders that came from too many hours in the gym. His dark hair streaked with silver was receding from his forehead, and his eyes, sharp and sly, were the shade of wet slate. But it was his mouth that she recalled most distinctly, the wide narrow lips that had mocked her, the mouth that was built to curse.

Yes, all things considered, he might not do too badly.

'Give him my number,' she said, 'ask him to ring me tonight after seven.'

Terry stared at her dumbfounded. 'What?'

'I need to talk to him.'

'Why? Why do you—'

'Because I know him,' she said, lowering her voice. 'I've met him before. Just tell him to call. He'll understand.'

It wasn't exactly a lie. Eve had met a hundred men like him before. At a glance she could spot those who were powerful and those who were not.

Terry frowned at her. 'How do you know him?'

She widened her grey eyes and smiled. 'It's a long story. But if you're prepared to tell me what happened to *you*, I might just consider . . .'

'Forget it,' he said.

She shrugged. 'Fair enough.'

For the second time she gazed deliberately, almost seductively, over her shoulder.

The man called Cavelli glanced up again, his gaze hovering briefly on her face before slowly slipping down. He had that look in his eye: appraising – was that the word? Only something a little nastier than that.

Chapter Two

Unlocking the door, Eve stepped cautiously inside her father's flat. Even after all these weeks she still felt it was a liberty to walk straight in without knocking first, without giving him the opportunity to hide an over-generous glass of brandy or stub out a forbidden cigarette.

She strode across the room and swung open the french windows that led out on to a rusty iron balcony. Some fresh air to sweep away the mustiness, the lingering memories.

'What's wrong?' Sonia asked, sauntering in uninvited behind her. 'Where have you been? I thought you'd be back hours ago.'

Watching out for her then, like she always did, probably with her nose pressed against the glass. A spurt of irritation made Eve's voice tetchy. 'Well, I'm here now. You don't have to worry.' But as soon as she snapped she was sorry. 'I went for a walk,' she explained, 'I needed some fresh air.'

Sonia snorted. 'That's what those places do to you. Is your Terry okay?'

'He's fine,' Eve said, turning her back and walking into the kitchen to fill the kettle. 'He's coping.'

Sonia heard the lie but let it pass. She'd made enough prison visits herself to recognize the glib response. 'That's good.'

Eve didn't want her there. She wanted to be alone but there was no chance of that until she'd had a brew and a chance for a gossip. Better get it over and done with before the call came through. *If it came through*.

'So what's new?' she asked resignedly.

Sonia dropped her denim-miniskirted backside on to the nearest chair and sighed for England. She stubbed out her cigarette in a saucer. 'The old bastard's still saying he won't give me a divorce. You should have heard him. Ranting and raving he was, screaming down the phone. Said he'd see me burn first. So I told him that'd be nothing new; every day with him was a living hell anyway.' She paused briefly for breath, coughing up her animosity. 'And he's only doing it to spite me. It's not as though he gives a shite. You know what he's like.'

Eve did, although only through her neighbour's colourful updates. She had never, thankfully, had the pleasure of meeting the demonic Peter Marshall face to face. Placing two mugs down, she slid one across the table. 'You only have to wait. Be patient. You'll get it eventually. It's not as though you're in any hurry to get hitched again.'

But Sonia wasn't appeased. 'It's the principle, love. What if I come up on the lotto? Be just my luck to still have that bloody millstone round my neck. Be entitled, wouldn't he? The idle son of a bitch would be entitled to a share.'

'Not necessarily,' Eve replied, a smile creeping on to her lips for the first time that day. Sonia's ability to create imaginary obstacles to her future peace and happiness was a talent in itself. '*You're* entitled to a quick divorce but that doesn't mean you're going to get it.'

'True,' she muttered thoughtfully. 'If me numbers come up, I can always leave the country, can't I? Hop on a plane and disappear.' At this heart-warming prospect she cheered up considerably. 'Yeah, that'd teach the bastard . . .'

Still grinning, she reached down and picked a carrier bag off the floor. 'Got something here you might fancy.'

Eve shook her head despairingly as a selection of expensive cashmere jumpers spilled out across the table. 'Christ, Sonia, how old are you now?'

For a second she looked aghast, as if stunned by the question. 'Forty-seven,' she eventually declared huffily, lowering her heavily mascaraed eyes and flattening out the creases in her tiny skirt. 'Why are you asking?'

Nearer fifty-seven, Eve suspected, absorbing the deep lines, the crow's feet and the harshly dyed black hair, but she had the good grace to look convinced. 'I mean, do you really want another stretch inside?'

They both stared down at the stolen sweaters.

Sonia paused for a moment, pulled a face and then started to laugh. 'Blimey,' she chuckled, rocking back in her chair, 'who rattled your cage? You found God or somethin'?'

'No,' Eve riposted, grinning back, 'but I don't want to end up visiting *two* of you. Terry's more than enough.' She buried her face in the steam from the tea. It wasn't the crime that offended her, only Sonia's susceptibility to getting caught. She'd been nabbed twice in the last three weeks and only escaped charges by the skin of her teeth.

Sonia flapped her left hand in a vague dismissive gesture while with her right she lit another of her endless cigarettes. Inhaling deeply, she blew out the smoke in a long narrow stream. 'Oh, don't worry about me, ducks. I can always talk me way out of a tight spot.'

And that might be true. If there was one thing to be said, she could certainly spin a yarn, a touching tale to melt the hardest of hearts. On the last two occasions, she'd probably had the manager and all the staff crying

13

in the aisles – but she wasn't going to get away with it indefinitely.

Good luck, as Terry had learned to his cost, didn't last forever.

'I mean it, Son, you have to be more careful.'

'I *am* careful,' she insisted over-brightly, missing the saucer and flicking her ash all over the cloth. 'It's been fifteen years since I did a stretch. Clean as a whistle, I am. Just trying to make an honest living.'

Eve smiled as she turned over one of the jumpers, her fingers drawn towards the soft warm wool. It was a classy black number with a row of pearl buttons along one shoulder. Black always looked dramatic against her hair. And dramatic might come in useful if she was going to . . .

She glanced up at the clock on the wall and noticed the hands moving gradually towards a quarter to seven.

Would he ring?

He must. *He had to!*

Frowning, she looked back down at the jumper, still in two minds. If she bought it, wouldn't she be encouraging Sonia to keep on with her mad kamikaze shoplifting expeditions? But if she didn't, she'd only be condemning her to endless nights down the pub trying to flog the goods to someone else.

She gazed up at the clock again.

Sonia, thinking that she knew a hint when she saw one, rose reluctantly from her seat. 'I'd best get back. Val's coming round with the kids.'

Eve raised her eyebrows. More like Val was coming round to *dump* the kids; her daughter used Sonia as an unpaid babysitting service, dropping off her sprogs and frequently disappearing for days on end. She glanced back down at the jumper. 'How much do you want for this one?' While she waited for an answer she rummaged in her purse and took out forty quid. It was half of what it was worth but twice as much as she'd get for it down The Bell.

'That'll do lovely,' Sonia said, her eager hand briskly palming the notes. Before any change might be considered, or even worse demanded, she quickly turned away. 'See you later, sweetheart.'

As she heard the front door click shut Eve released her breath in a sigh of relief. It was almost worth paying just for the silence. She was fond of Sonia, amused by her, but if she was being brutally honest she was as much an unwanted legacy as the space she was currently sitting in. Standing up, Eve wandered through to the living room and gazed around. The dull walls, once a pale shade of moss, were stained with age and nicotine. She'd only come here to clear the place, to pack up her father's belongings, and to hand the keys back to the landlord. And if it hadn't been for Terry she'd have done exactly that.

'You *can't*,' he'd declared, his wide eyes becoming tearful. 'Please, Evie, don't do it without me. I want to be there.'

She had never taken him for a sentimentalist but then prison did unusual things to people. It wasn't as though there was even much to sort – only the clothes in the wardrobe, the untidy desk with its overflowing papers, the rows of orphaned books. But Terry had been so insistent that she'd eventually agreed. Why not hang on? It was only for a few months and the rent was cheap enough.

So now she was stuck, at least for a while. The flat was in a small shabby block, uncared for and neglected, tucked away in the back streets of Norwich. Anonymity at least was guaranteed. She still missed London but for all her reservations she had to admit that there were some advantages to living here. It was closer to the jail, a leisurely fifty-minute drive rather than a three-hour haul. And, all things considered, she was better off staying away from London, keeping her head down until that unfortunate business with Henry Baxter's family had subsided.

But that didn't mean she was happy. Far from it. She missed the city she'd grown up in, missed its familiar streets and distinctive smells, missed her friends, her routine, her sense of belonging. She was a stranger here. Most of all, she missed her father. It wasn't easy living with a ghost. Everywhere she turned he was lurking, a regretful shadow at her shoulder.

Would he approve of what she was about to do? A sharp uneasy breath escaped from her lips. She ran her fingers across his desk as if from that dull scarred surface she might absorb some psychic inspiration. He had always been braver than her – but never reckless, never too careless of the consequences.

She glanced at her watch. It was already past seven.

Was Cavelli making her wait, making her sweat, or was he not going to ring at all?

Turning away, she hurried back to the kitchen. She snatched open the cupboard door and took out the bottle of brandy, poured a generous measure, added ice, and for a moment stared intently down into the glass. As she slowly drew it to her mouth, she wondered what she would do if she didn't hear from him. No, she didn't want to think about that.

Instead, Eve thought about her father. She had no idea what she'd been doing when he had filled his pockets full of stones and walked into the river. Something mundane, she imagined, like making coffee or watching television. Why hadn't she realized? It tore at her conscience that she hadn't felt anything profound, that the event wasn't marked by the instincts of a sixth sense, by a soaring, a sinking, not even by an inauspicious prickle on the back of her neck.

It wasn't right.

She still couldn't quite accept that he was dead. The fact lay like a cold leaden weight in the pit of her stomach. That he was *dying*, yes, she'd understood quite clearly, but that had seemed a distant prospect, a tiny cancerous dot looming on the horizon, threatening but not yet close enough to be truly menacing.

Eve walked back into the living room and touched the desk again. Aimlessly, she tidied some of the papers into a pile, trying not to stare too hard at his neat sloping script. Notes. He was always making notes, mainly about the authors he admired. His tastes were eclectic: Hardy, Forster, Fitzgerald, Chandler . . .

She slid his slim silver mobile, discharged and blankly grey, into a drawer. Then she picked up three packs of playing cards, still wrapped in cellophane, and placed them neatly in a cubby hole. He might have hankered for more but games were what her father had excelled at. Especially poker. Especially *cheating* at poker. Perhaps, when she was feeling up to it, she might lay out a hand or two . . . but not tonight. She wasn't in the mood for any final goodbyes.

Then, as she was about to move away, she noticed the edge of a small green slip of paper lodged between the pages of a magazine article. She pulled it out but might not have given it a second glance if it hadn't looked so oddly familiar. A few days ago she had come across a similar green square in the cutlery drawer in the kitchen. That one, as her father had a tendency to leave his notes everywhere and anywhere, she had virtually ignored – in fact, in some vain attempt to pretend she was coping, she had actually screwed it up and dropped it in the bin. But this scrap, identical in every way, she took some time to study. It was three inches square and in its centre, written in bold black ink, was what she was sure was the very same sequence of letters and digits: W1/267/32/BC/8PR.

Eve gazed long and hard, her brow furrowing as she tried to make sense of it. Not a phone number. Or the number for a safe. Or a bank account. She reached for her brandy again and sipped it. Maybe some kind of postal address? Her eyes instantly lit up. Now that seemed plausible – W1 covered Soho, her father's old hunting ground, and the scene of many a triumphant con.

Then she scowled. It was nothing. Why was she even thinking about it? She was only grasping at straws, hoping for some message, some hidden mystery, something that might bring her father back to her. Stupid! But still she carefully folded the piece of paper, over and over, until it was the size of a fingernail and she could thrust the tiny package deep inside her jeans pocket.

Then she sat back down and waited for the phone to ring.

And waited . . . and waited.

It was after eight before it sprang into life. Eve jumped, her anxious fingers hovering, doubt biting at her nerves. Should she? Shouldn't she? Eventually she snatched up the receiver and yelped, 'Yes?'

'Martin Cavelli.'

Short, sharp and to the point. She waited but he had nothing more to add. Her heart was thumping, thrashing against her ribs. She was tempted to fall back on politeness, to thank him for ringing, but instead swallowed hard and took another swig of brandy. 'I need to talk to you.'

'You *are* talking to me,' he replied drily.

She frowned down the line. 'Face to face,' she insisted. 'Can you send me a visiting order?'

'Why should I?'

'Why shouldn't you?' she retorted smartly. If there

were two things she had learned about men it was never to let them walk all over you . . . and never to explain.

'What's this about?'

She sensed his curiosity and smiled. 'I'll tell you when I see you.'

'I can always ask Terry.'

'Ask away, but you'll be wasting your breath. He doesn't know anything.' She lowered her voice confidentially. 'This is between you and me.'

There was a short electric pause before he replied. She could almost hear his thoughts ticking over, could almost feel his eyes roaming slyly over her body again.

'I'll think about it,' he murmured.

'You do that,' she said, 'but don't wait too long . . . I'm not the patient sort.' And before he had a chance to respond, she abruptly hung up.

Her hand was trembling, jittering against the sides of the glass, as she lifted the drink to her lips again. Her palms were damp. Tiny drops of perspiration leaked on to her forehead. Now it was done she felt more afraid than she had before. If she blew this, if she lost her nerve, Terry would be the one to suffer.

'Well?' she asked aloud to the empty room. 'You got any better ideas?'

But there was only a resounding silence.

She spent an anxious week, worried at first that he would send the visiting order, then fretting that he wouldn't. Her hopes were beginning to fade when the envelope finally slid through the door. There was no message inside, only the stark official slip. Well, that suited her fine. She liked to keep things simple.

She rang and booked a visit for Wednesday.

Today was only Monday. What to do in the meantime? She fancied a trip back to London, lunch with a

19

friend, perhaps even some retail therapy, but decided against it. Best to stray on the side of caution. But unable to stand being stuck inside – the walls of the flat were starting to close in on her – she grabbed her coat and headed for the street.

There was a chill breeze and she walked with her head down, her chin buried in the front of her coat. It was fifteen minutes before she reached her destination, the gateway to the old cathedral, and she spent a moment gazing up at the tall golden spire before suddenly deciding not to go in. It might hold too many memories of her father. Instead, she cut through the side streets to the main city square and took temporary shelter from a shower in the covered market. Perusing the book stalls, the clothes and the jewellery, she felt glad to be amongst people again, to be gently jostled by the crowds.

Once the rain had eased she set off along the quaint winding alleys, exploring the surrounding shops. She stopped by the window of a recruitment agency. It was a gruesome thought but she really ought to consider a job, some temp work to keep her ticking over. There was still money in the bank – Henry had been generous with her severance pay – but it wasn't going to last indefinitely.

Eve smiled at the memory of him, his grey head bent over his desk in the dim and dusty basement, looking industrious but his mind somewhere else, thinking . . . thinking of what? And for a second as she gazed blindly at the rows of white cards, at the endlessly tedious 'job opportunities', she wished that she was back there with him, that she could step once again into the closeted safety of that calm and quiet room.

There would be no Cavelli to think about then.

She shuddered, resenting the invasion of his name, and tried to think of pleasanter things.

There was plenty she had liked about Henry Baxter, not least the way his eyes lit up whenever he saw her. She could see them now, brightening, turning from pale brown to gold, as if they were lovers – although they were not. Had never been. It wasn't sex he had wanted from her; he had made that quite clear from the beginning. No, that was not his motivation. And even now she couldn't claim to know exactly what it was, could only sense it vaguely, as if she were a door he might walk through, an entrance or an exit, some portal anyway that would take him temporarily from this slim unsatisfying world to another of more generous and interesting proportions.

Perhaps, like her father, he had only craved escape.

And maybe, for a while, he had found it in their late lunches, their dinners, their stolen Sunday walks and rambling conversations. She frowned into the pane of glass. What had they talked about? She had told him more than she should but was not afraid of repercussions. All they had said had been spoken in confidence and Henry Baxter's lips, she was certain, were sealed as tightly as her own.

The rain had started again, splashing around her feet and seeping into her shoes. It was the beginning of May but still felt more like November. She raised her gaze to the grey forbidding sky. It had been inevitable, of course, that it would all come crashing down. Good things didn't last. And people gossiped, especially those with nothing better to do. A respectable, ageing, married businessman 'out on the town' with his much younger secretary was naturally cause for comment – especially when she was a slender, cynical, dangerous redhead!

Still, those seven months they had shared had been good. She looked back on them now with an increasing sense of loss. And it struck her with a sudden and almost aching ferocity that she had *loved* Henry Baxter, loved him in that way that people never talked about, with a feeling that had nothing to do with lust or sex but everything to do with another kind of nakedness.

But she had lost him as surely as she had lost her father.

Not that they were similar. Not at all. Alexander Weston had been witty, extrovert, a man of the world. Henry was cast from another mould. Quiet and retiring, his charm was of an entirely different character.

Overtaken by weariness, she turned for home. It occurred to her, as she sloshed through the puddles, that there was nothing to stop her from calling him. But there was. Once something was over, it was over.

You couldn't resurrect the past.

Eve woke on the Wednesday morning with a feeling of dread. When she got up, she made coffee and toast and smoked a cigarette. Now all she had to worry about was what she was going to wear and, more importantly, what she was going to say . . .

By one o'clock she had driven to the prison, found a parking space and booked in, but still had an hour to kill. First she went to the bathroom where she stared at her reflection beneath the unforgiving fluorescent light. A thin worried spectre returned her gaze. Perhaps she shouldn't have worn the black jumper; it made her face seem even paler than it was. And her red hair even redder, which was fine if he liked redheads but a major mistake if he didn't. She had twinned the jumper with a cream linen skirt, short enough to reveal her long legs but not so short as to make her look available. A pair of expensive high heels completed the outfit. She'd been aiming for cool and professional, with just a hint of the seductive, but she frowned into the mirror unconvinced that she'd pulled it off.

It was not the clothes that were at fault, only her attitude.

Where had her confidence gone?

She clenched her hands into two tight fists and tried to will it back, to lure it from whatever miserable corner it had taken refuge in.

Think of Terry, she urged.

But that just made it harder.

Were those shadows under her eyes? The skin looked bluish against the ivory of her cheeks. She had not slept well last night, had tossed and turned, waking over and over to the sound of the rain battering against the window.

She shivered. She couldn't do this.

She must.

The door opened and a blonde girl came in, younger, in her early twenties. She smiled at Eve in the way that women often smiled at each other here, friendly but resigned, as if a sigh lingered always at the edges of their mouths. The girl dumped her bag on the counter, fidgeted with her hair and then started to apply a fresh layer of mascara.

'Don't know why I bother,' she mumbled faintly. 'All the appreciation I get . . .'

A gentle complaining seemed to be par for the course too.

'I know what you mean,' Eve replied sympathetically.

'Your old man the same, huh?'

She laughed. 'Aren't they all?' This was an easier character to inhabit, the part of the faintly disgruntled wife or girlfriend. Better anyway than . . . but she didn't want her thoughts to scramble off in that direction. 'Have you come far?'

Now the lip gloss was out. The blonde skimmed it expertly across her lips, pouting into the mirror. 'Essex. Romford. You know it? A real shitter of a journey too, takes me hours, but then what do they care about that. I reckon the bastards sit down with a map and *deliberately* send them as far away as possible.' She frowned hard into the mirror as if the authorities might have a secret camera hidden there. 'Bastards,' she murmured again.

Eve got out a comb and ran it through her hair. She felt a sudden urge to prolong this chance encounter, to hold on to this thread of semi-normality, this lifeline. Gradually her nerves were beginning to steady. What was she worrying about? What was the worst that could happen?

He could only say no.

'You're right,' she agreed. 'It's a liberty.'

The girl nodded, encouraged by the response. 'I'm Amber, by the way.'

'Eve,' she reciprocated.

And if they'd been men they might have shaken hands but women have a different code of conduct. Instead they simply exchanged another smile and returned their attention to the mirror.

'There are worse places, mind,' Eve offered, to keep the conversation going. 'I mean some jails . . .' She raised her brows as she let the sentence peter out.

Amber glanced sideways at her, making a sound in the back of her throat. 'You know what my Dan says? He says it's a shithole. He says it's full of nonces.'

The word settled like ice at the base of Eve's neck. *Nonces.* Men who preyed on the vulnerable, on children, on young teenagers, and if there weren't any of those available then . . . She thought of Terry and his bruises. By messing with her hair, by quickly twisting it up behind her head, she tried to hide the shivers that trembled through her body. 'Does he?'

Her voice sounded thin and strained but Amber didn't notice. She was too preoccupied with the more essential business of self-decoration. As she carefully applied yet another layer of lip gloss, she laughed and said, 'Still, he says that about bleedin' everywhere.'

Eve tried to laugh too but it took an effort to even force her mouth to move. *But is it true?* she wanted to ask. *Is Hillgrove full of . . .* But she couldn't quite find the courage.

Amber tilted her head and stared intently at her own reflection.

Eve scrutinized it too. Perhaps she was even younger than she'd thought. She gazed at the wide blue eyes and bleached blonde hair. She wasn't beautiful but she had that fresh-faced glow of youth, that inner vibrant light. And above all else – Eve felt a vague sense of loss as she recognized it – she still had *hope*.

Amber packed her cosmetics back into her bag. 'Fancy a coffee?' she asked.

Eve took one last glance at the mirror. 'Sure,' she replied. 'Why not?'

It was just after two o'clock when the numbers were called and they gathered at the desk, collecting their forms, before trudging through the rain to the main building. Here they waited again, compliant as sheep, before being herded into a small lift-shaped box and crammed in tight until the doors behind them could close.

It was at this point Eve always experienced a momentary panic. Trapped in the overly warm and claustrophobic space, the delay between one set of doors closing and the next set opening felt like an eternity. She took deep steady breaths, in and out, in and out, too aware of the crush of bodies around her. The seconds ticked by. Gradually, an uneasy hush descended. Even Amber ceased in her relentless monologue and eventually fell silent.

Then suddenly, thankfully, they were all spilling out into the fresh damp space of an inner courtyard. A babble of freed voices drifted up towards the sky. Eve gulped in the air as she walked, filling her lungs with oxygen. Usually that would be it, the worst part over, but now she had another ordeal to face.

Cavelli was only minutes away.

Amber's chatter rolled over and around her as they entered yet another red brick building. She nodded automatically in response, murmuring, making tiny sounds of deaf acknowledgement as they climbed the flight of stairs.

Confidence was a state of mind. Eve thought of everything her father had taught her. She imagined him outside, waiting in the car, his fingers tapping restively against the wheel. She couldn't let him down. She couldn't let Terry down. Adjusting her posture, pushing back her shoulders and straightening her back, she tried to prepare herself.

As they entered the search area she could see the entrance to the visiting room.

She was less than ten steps away.

Usually, she couldn't wait to get the search over and done with but today she was in no hurry; if they'd asked her to take off all her clothes she'd have readily agreed. Anything to delay what lay ahead. Typically, even the drugs dog was absent, the snuffling inquisitive brown Labrador that usually held up proceedings for a few extra minutes. Perhaps he was on holiday. She laid her purse on the table for the screw to root through. He went through it too quickly, too carelessly, before handing it back. *Slow down*, she wanted to insist, *take your time*.

Propelled by the queue, she was pushed relentlessly forward again.

Now she was only feet from the door. A female screw smiled faintly. Without waiting to be asked Eve assumed the familiar pose, extending her arms while the woman ran her expert hands swiftly and efficiently over her body, skimming her hips, the length of her legs, examining her belt and skirt pockets. It wasn't pleasant but she'd known worse. Once she had been to a jail where they peered inside your mouth, a procedure that had felt more intrusive, more disturbingly intimate, than any fleeting pat of her breasts or buttocks.

It was over in a minute. And she was cleared, declared clean and summarily dismissed.

Free to have her visit.

And there was no retreat now unless she screamed or fainted or a flash of lightning split through the window and cut them all dead.

The open door loomed ominously ahead.

She took a deep breath and before she could change her mind, before her courage might fail her, raised her chin and stepped boldly forward. Quickly, she glanced around. The men were already in there, already seated, impatiently waiting for their visitors.

She saw Cavelli instantly. He smiled, if that vague quiver of his lips could be called a smile, but didn't bother rising from his seat. Instead, he lounged back and watched as she strolled across the room.

And there was something in that gaze, such overt arrogance, that even as she approached him her fear was beginning to dissolve. It was gradually being replaced by a different impulse, a need, a desire, a determination *not* to be beaten.

She swung her hips provocatively.

It was only when she arrived, hovering for a moment above him, that he finally moved . . . and then it was only to intimidate. Rising to his feet, all six feet plus of mulish masculinity, he used his height to look down on her.

'Nice to see you again,' he said, without even a hint of sincerity.

'You too. You haven't changed a bit.'

There was a thin brittle silence before he waved his hand towards a chair and sat down again.

Eve lowered herself graciously on to the padded turquoise seat, sliding her legs to one side and neatly crossing her ankles.

He gazed at her with a faintly chilling scrutiny.

She let him. She let his eyes roam over her body, from her forehead to her toes. And while he blatantly studied her, she took the opportunity to stare back. Was he exactly as she remembered? Not quite. His eyes were colder, darker and more brutal. Oh God, had she made a mistake, had she got it all wrong? No, she couldn't think that way. She mustn't go traipsing down that road again.

'So?' he asked impatiently.

'So,' she repeated. 'What do you want?'

His wide brow burrowed into a frown. 'What do *I* want? You were the one who—'

'Tea or coffee,' she interjected, getting briskly to her feet again. She glanced over her shoulder. 'They're all coming in. If I don't go now, I'll be there all day.'

Cavelli hesitated. As if he'd been out-manoeuvred but wasn't quite sure how, he glared at her suspiciously. 'Tea then,' he eventually said, 'two sugars. And none of that dishwater shit.'

'No dishwater shit,' she echoed, just to prove that she was paying attention. 'Would you like anything else?'

'No.'

No, *thank you*, she was ludicrously tempted to correct, just as her father had always done when she was a child. *Common courtesy costs nothing, Evie.* But sensibly, although the idea made her grin, she simply nodded and set off for the kiosk.

The queue was short and she was there and back in a matter of minutes. Placing the plastic cup of hot strong tea in front of him, she settled back down in the chair. She could see from his expression that there wasn't much point in wasting time on small talk. Best to cut straight to the chase before her courage sprang another leak.

'I'm here, Mr Cavelli, because I need you to do something for me.'

His eyes flew up warily but he kept his silence.

Eve cleared her throat and, after a brief hesitation, continued. 'I want you to look after my brother Terry. I want you to stop him from getting hurt again.'

Whatever he might have expected her to say, it clearly wasn't that. He gave what could only be described as a snort before he shook his head and growled, 'And why the hell should I do *you* any favours?'

'I'm not asking for any favours,' she quickly snapped back. 'I'll make it worth your while.'

Now that hit the target. A glimmer of interest swept across his face. He leaned forward, splaying his powerful hands across his thighs. 'Meaning?'

'Meaning exactly that.' She shifted forward too and lowered her voice so that no one around them could hear. 'You tell me how much you want – within reason – and I'll pay you. A straightforward *private* business deal.'

She watched as he thought about it, could almost see him mentally processing the proposition. Why had she chosen him? It was mainly down to chance but then she had a healthy respect for the vagaries of fate. It was down to that original collision, to the way he had looked at her, to her instant recognition of his vile male arrogance. A bully maybe but she didn't care – just so long as he protected Terry.

It was a while before he replied and it wasn't the response she'd been anticipating. 'If this is some kind of fucking set-up . . .'

His tone was softly vicious. Eve heard the implicit threat and inwardly shuddered. She could feel her heart starting to pump. By an effort of will she forced herself to meet his gaze.

'Jesus,' she replied defiantly, 'what do you think I am? You've seen him. He's not going to survive five minutes in here. And I'm not going to sit back and let that happen. Either you help me to protect him or I'll find someone else who will.'

He lifted his chin, gave her another long hard look but finally seemed to relax. His mouth curled into the semblance of a smile. 'Well, you've got a fucking nerve, I'll give you that.'

'I'll take that as a compliment.'

'Take it how you like,' he shrugged, 'but before you get too excited, there's something you should know – I *never* do business with women.'

Eve sighed despairingly. She'd only just got over one obstacle and now she was being bludgeoned with another. Great! So along with all his other endearing qualities, Cavelli had to be a small-minded prehistoric chauvinist as well. Still, she'd come this far. She wasn't giving up without a fight.

Smiling sweetly back, she asked, 'And why is that precisely?'

'Why do you think?' He barked out a laugh.

'I've no idea,' she replied, all wide-eyed innocence. In a stereotypical female gesture she lifted a hand and swept back her long red hair. What she was going to say next was a risk but it was make or break time. 'Because you're worried they might be smarter than you?'

And it certainly had an effect – although she wasn't sure if it was the one she'd been hoping for. As if he'd been hit by a brick his smug expression disappeared. The temperature dropped a further few degrees.

He glared at her. 'You've got a pretty high opinion of yourself.'

'Unlike you,' she retaliated, gently raising her eyebrows.

He scowled back.

In an agony of doubt, she held her breath. Had she gone too far? There was suddenly every possibility that she'd not only messed up Terry's future but might also be leaving this jail with a price on her own head.

But then, thank God, he actually laughed. The suspicion fled from his eyes and just for a moment, a brief fleeting second, he seemed almost human. He sat back in his chair and folded his arms across his chest. 'Your brother's a stupid little fucker.'

'Well, no one's arguing with that – but it's hardly the point.'

'Of course it's the fucking point,' he insisted. 'I don't need the grief. I don't need some pathetic kid constantly dragging me into his rows.'

By which he meant, she was sure, that this was all going to cost her a damn sight more than she expected. But she could deal with that. She'd find the money somehow.

'Oh, don't get me wrong,' he continued, staring intently at her breasts, 'I'd love to help, sweetheart, of course I would. But as I was saying, I don't do business with women. They can't be trusted. They act on their emotions and not with their brains. They're unstable.'

'Really,' Eve replied, resisting the urge to stand up and slap him hard enough to prove his point. But there was more than one way to skin a cat. Slowly she started to gather her things together, her jacket and her purse.

He frowned. 'What are you doing?'

'Going,' she replied, throwing him a dismissive glance.

31

'You've made your position clear and I appreciate your honesty. I don't want to waste your time – or mine.'

But Cavelli, as she suspected, was enjoying himself too much. He was the type of man who liked to be in charge – especially of women – and this visit was rapidly slipping out of his control.

He twisted in his chair, unfolding his arms and shifting towards her again. 'Out of interest,' he said, 'just how much are we talking about?'

Eve laid down her purse. 'How much do you want?' She had spent the last few days wondering about it. What *was* the going rate for protection in prison? She didn't have a clue. A hundred quid a week? Five hundred? A thousand? Whatever it cost, she'd find a way to pay it.

Cavelli's lips widened into a grin. 'You can't afford me.'

'You don't think so?' Eve deliberately glanced down at her clothes: the cashmere jumper, the designer skirt, and a pair of heels that had cost over a week's salary. She looked the part even if it was an illusion. 'Just name your price.'

His grin grew even wider. 'The thing is, love, I'm not some piss-poor con in search of a few quid. I don't need the aggro and I don't need the money.'

'So what *do* you need?' she snapped back.

As if genuinely considering the question, he raised his eyes and looked at her. But then he slyly shook his head. 'No, you can't help.'

'Anything,' she insisted.

Sheer frustration had sprung the word from her mouth but now, as she met his loathsome gaze again, she had the feeling she had walked straight into a carefully laid trap.

'Anything?' he repeated softly.

Her voice faltered as her heart made a violent leap. 'Yes.'

'Well,' he said, 'I suppose, under *those* terms, we might come to an agreement.'

Like the devil he was sitting there with one almighty smirk on his face. She could almost feel her soul being valued for auction.

Chapter Three

Henry Baxter took off his glasses and placed them carefully on his desk. He screwed up his eyes as he peered at the stranger in front of him.

'DS Shepherd.' The man flashed his identity card. 'If I could have a few minutes of your time?'

'And this is concerning . . .?'

'Eve Weston. I believe she used to work here.'

At the mention of her name, Henry's usually placid demeanour became more animated; his brows lifted and a twitch invaded the corners of his mouth. He half-rose from his chair. 'Has something happened? Has she—'

Shepherd raised his hands in a flat-palmed gesture of reassurance. 'No, it's not that.'

'So what's the bitch done now?' Richard interrupted from where he was still loitering by the door. 'Tried to con some other poor sucker?'

'Thank you,' Henry said tightly, 'but I think I can deal with this.'

'But—'

'Really,' he insisted. 'I don't want to keep you.'

Richard, for a moment, looked determined to argue the point but then had second thoughts. Instead he merely grunted, threw a meaningful glance at Shepherd, and turned on his heel. He shut the door with rather more force than was necessary.

The sergeant, helping himself to a seat, looked smugly pleased by the exchange. 'I take it your son has some *issues* with Ms Weston.'

'It would appear so,' Henry concurred. He gave a small polite smile but conceded nothing more. While he waited, he examined the enemy. That he *was* the enemy there was no doubt in his mind at all. It had taken him over thirty years to realize that he didn't like his son but only thirty seconds to realize the same of DS Shepherd.

With due care and attention he scrutinized the features in front of him: a fleshy pallid face, its nose crossed with a maze of tiny red veins, the forehead slightly bulbous. The eyes were a dull shade of brown, the mouth sulky. In his early fifties, he estimated, a cynical and disappointed man, too used to the privileges – and abuses – of power.

Shepherd waited too, expecting clarification. When it became clear that this wasn't going to be forthcoming, his lips winced into irritation. With the kind of exaggerated tone he might use with a confused and elderly witness he said very slowly, 'I understand that Eve Weston was your secretary.'

'Yes.'

'But no longer?'

As if she might still be lurking in a corner, Henry glanced cautiously around the room. 'It would appear not.'

The sergeant paused, perhaps to allow time for further information but more likely to hide his growing impatience. He tried to keep his voice controlled. 'Perhaps you could tell me why she left?'

Henry paused too as if grappling with the depth of the question. In fact he was only considering his options. He could see where this was going and was in two minds how to proceed. The solicitor in him was tempted to raise the barricades, to shut him out, but that would hardly help Eve. If she was in trouble, then he wanted to know why. Accordingly, he gazed up at the ceiling and sighed. He raised a hand to his head and raked his fingers through his fine sparse hair.

'Of course,' he finally said, apologetically. 'The thing is, Sergeant . . . well, this is slightly embarrassing.'

Shepherd grinned as if he knew exactly how embarrassing it was going to be. It had taken a while but they were finally getting there. Old men and their secretaries – he'd heard it all before. 'It's all right, sir,' he urged reassuringly, 'we're both men of the world.'

'Indeed,' Henry replied, twisting his hands on the desk. 'Indeed we are.'

His interrogator shifted forward a fraction.

Henry tried to keep his own expression benign. 'Yes,' he declared, 'it's unfortunate but sadly my son made it impossible for Ms Weston to remain here. He was – how can I put it? – somewhat *enamoured* of her. Unfortunately, she didn't feel the same way. It made for . . . well, a certain awkwardness in the workplace.'

DS Shepherd fought hard to keep the irritation from his voice. 'But I understood that she was *your*—'

'My secretary?' he interrupted smartly. 'Oh, she was. That's right. She was. But we're a small unit here and it's pretty hard to avoid each other. If we had a little more space, perhaps, then it wouldn't have mattered but, in a building of this size . . .' He tilted his chin and frowned. 'She's not in any kind of trouble, I hope?'

The sergeant glared at him. 'If I didn't know better, I might think you were trying to protect her.'

'Protect her from what?' Henry asked innocently. And he felt a faint frisson of delight as he went up against The Law. He had spent most of his life devising ways to circumvent the minor inconveniences of the British legal system but this was a battle of a more direct kind. Face to face. It made for an interesting challenge.

'I understood from your son—'

Henry quickly interrupted again. 'My son's been upset, Sergeant, not acting altogether rationally. I believe it's what's referred to in common parlance as a mid-life crisis. A touch premature perhaps but then Richard always has been ahead of his time.'

Shepherd glanced down at his watch, a gesture specifically intended to convey how precious his time was. He hadn't come here for a biography of Baxter junior. 'But you knew Eve Weston well,' he persisted, placing his knuckles on the desk and thrusting his head forward. 'You were *close*.'

Henry leaned back in his chair, resenting the intrusion into his personal space. He resented the implication even more, the way he said *close*, the ugly leer on his face. As if Eve was nothing more than a piece of meat.

'She worked hard,' he replied firmly. 'She was a good secretary.' He wondered if Richard had filed a complaint against her, an accusation of theft or fraud or perhaps the more heinous crime of attempting to seduce a man over sixty. 'Look, officer, perhaps if you could explain what this is about . . .'

He noticed with distaste how his interrogator sat with his legs splayed open. An aggressively masculine pose. Like the men on the tube who took up two thirds of the seat, who always refused to relinquish an inch.

Shepherd frowned at him, releasing a clearly audible sigh into the room. 'Miss Weston is part of an ongoing investigation.'

'What sort of an investigation?'

But the sergeant shook his head and said, with the kind of stiff formality of a bad actor reading from a card, 'I'm afraid I'm not at liberty to disclose that information.'

'Ah,' Henry murmured.

Silence fell between them. In the background the clock ticked monotonously. Then the questions resumed.

'How long was Miss Weston here?'

Henry was tempted once again to bring the exchange to a close . . . but he had found out precisely nothing. Perhaps he should run with it for a while longer. Shepherd might inadvertently let something slip.

'Six – no, I tell a lie, *seven* months. She left several weeks ago.'

'And she left because . . .'

'I believe I've already explained that, Sergeant.'

'Ah yes,' he said drily, 'because she found the attentions of your son uncomfortable. And yet, she's a good-looking woman, isn't she? Used to the attention of men. Not the type, surely, to be fazed by a few unwanted compliments?'

Henry lifted his shoulders in a slight dismissive shrug.

'Would you say Miss Weston was a trustworthy person, Mr Baxter?'

'Very,' he lied smoothly. 'I'd say she was one of the most scrupulously honest people I've ever known.' Recalling their conversations and her intimate confessions, he felt an urge to snigger but wisely stifled it.

Shepherd snorted. 'Honest, huh?'

But Henry, refusing to rise to the bait, simply raised an eyebrow. 'I don't understand where this is going. Perhaps, if you could—'

'Did you ever meet any of her friends – or her family?'

'No.'

'Were you aware that her brother was in prison?'

'Of course,' he replied calmly.

Shepherd scowled, his wide forehead crumpling into waves. 'And that didn't bother you?'

Henry almost embarked on a short speech about the sins of the brother not being visited on the sister but thought better of it. 'I didn't see that it had any bearing on her position here.'

'Even though he'd been charged with armed robbery?'

The actual conviction, as Henry understood, was of handling stolen property. But now probably wasn't the time to get into that particular debate. 'What exactly are you suggesting, that *she* had something to do with it, that she—'

'No,' Shepherd retorted, as jumpy as a gossip in danger of a libel suit. 'No, I'm not saying that.' His mouth took a sly upward turn. 'Only that the family had something of a . . . reputation.'

A sudden thought came to Henry. 'Are you investigating her father's death?'

'Alex Weston committed suicide,' the sergeant replied, with a rather too obvious look of satisfaction. 'Why should we be investigating his death?'

'Why should you be investigating Eve Weston?'

But Shepherd wouldn't answer directly. 'Have you seen her since she left, met up, talked on the phone?'

'No.'

'So you have no idea where she's currently living?'

'No,' Henry lied for the second time that morning.

'And why exactly is that, Mr Baxter? You became *friends*, didn't you, spent time together? Odd that you no longer keep in touch.'

Again the barely disguised insinuation. Henry felt a growl roll over his tongue. His friendship with Eve was private. 'We worked together, had the occasional lunch. That's all.'

'Your son seems to believe that you were having a "relationship" with her.'

So Richard had been talking! Well, that was hardly a surprise. 'My son has a very active imagination.'

'So you're denying it?'

'Unless my personal life has some direct bearing on

your case, Sergeant, I really don't see that it's any of your business.'

As if he'd just confessed to the affair, a gleam came into the officer's eyes. He coughed. It was a noisy phlegmy sound that might have been covering a laugh. 'I see.'

Henry played with the papers on his desk, shuffling them from side to side. He didn't often get angry but his reserves of patience were rapidly running out. One more minute and he might just lose his cool. It was definitely time to pull the plug. Before he did something he might regret.

But Shepherd, fortunately, was already lumbering to his feet. He scraped his chair back and hauled himself into an upright position. 'Well, thank you for your time,' he said. 'We'll be in touch if we need to talk to you again.'

Henry felt that tyrannical 'we' like an implicit threat.

It was a while before he heard the sergeant's heavy tread on the concrete steps outside. Henry went to the window and peered up. He could only see the bottom of his legs, his creased dun-coloured trousers flapping over a pair of damp unpolished shoes.

Shortly, he was joined by another more expensively clothed pair of limbs. Richard's. The two men shuffled on the pavement. By bending his knees and cricking his neck, Henry could just see their faces. They appeared to be having some kind of an argument, or rather his son was arguing while Shepherd gazed back with stolid indifference, his hand occasionally rising to his mouth as if to stifle a yawn. It was only when Richard grabbed him by the arm that he briefly became more animated. As if swatting a fly he deftly brushed off the fingers and then leaned forward to hiss menacingly in his face.

Although Henry couldn't hear what he said, the words were enough to make Richard jerk back. His lips

40

straightened in anger, his nostrils flaring. But he didn't retort. He knew better than to provoke a man like Shepherd. Muttering under his breath, he clattered back up the steps and slammed the door behind him.

Henry saw Shepherd grin before he lit a cigarette and strolled off down the street.

Eddie Shepherd rolled his eyes towards the heavens and then spat down towards the kerb. What a pair! Couldn't wait to put the knife in. That was the middle classes for you. No sense of family loyalty.

He rounded the corner and slid clumsily into the passenger seat of a silver-grey Peugeot parked beside a meter. 'Jesus,' he muttered.

The driver turned and glowered at him. 'Put that stinking fag out. I've told you before. I'm not going to die of *your* fucking cancer.'

Reluctantly, he wound down the window and threw the half-smoked cigarette out. He sighed as it rolled into the gutter. At over five quid a packet, it was a diabolical waste.

'So?'

'It's like you said. The old guy was clearly screwing her but he's not going to admit it. Married, isn't he? Doesn't want his missus traipsing down the divorce courts. Claims he hasn't been in touch since she left.'

'You believe him?'

He shrugged. 'Maybe. Although he's hiding something. I reckon she left with a golden handshake – but not the kind that comes with vol-au-vents and heartfelt speeches. More like a farewell gift she helped herself to.'

'She ripped them off?'

'I reckon. But not to the extent where Baxter's prepared to get the law involved. He'd rather cut his losses than open that particular can of worms.' He looked out of the window at a tall good-looking blonde walking down the street, his gaze focusing on the tight stretch of her sweater over her breasts.

'And the son?'

He tore his eyes away. 'Oh, he's convinced she was always out to con them – but then he's bitter as hell and not the most reliable of witnesses. From all accounts, he spent most of his own time trying to get into her knickers.'

'You think she might have been sleeping with them both?'

Eddie thought about it but slowly shook his head. Richard was just a resentful shit, still seething with his failure to get her into bed. He wondered why a piece like Eve Weston had chosen to shag a dry old stick like Baxter – but then some women would do anything for money. 'Nah, she wasn't stupid. She went for the one who was writing the cheques.'

'Give me back the photo.'

Taking it out of his top-right pocket, he passed it over. 'You going to tell me what this is all about, guv? I mean, we're hardly the fraud squad, and even if we were this isn't exactly the crime of the century.'

'It's not about what she's done. It's what she might be planning to do.'

Eddie looked at him.

There was a short pause.

'She's been visiting Martin Cavelli – and I want to know why.'

Henry picked up his pen and started to write. *Dear Eve* was as far as he got. He screwed the paper into a tiny ball, hurled it into the bin and then instantly bent down to retrieve it. Shoving the crumpled note into his trouser pocket, he stood up, grabbed his jacket, and went through to the outer office. He smiled at the secretary Richard had so generously bestowed on him. 'I'm going out, Louise. I'll be back in an hour.'

'Yes, Mr Baxter.'

Then, quickly lowering her face, her fingers flew again across the keyboard.

He gazed down at her. Quite clearly, she would rather be with her friends on the more glamorous upper floors, brushing shoulders with the soon-to-be-divorced rich and famous, than consigned to the stuffy depths of the basement.

Poor Louise: pretty and efficient but undeniably dull. Donated by his son because he thought she was a safe choice, because he thought that the old man's libido could never be roused by such an uninspiring woman. And he was right. Although, just to spite him, Henry was tempted to treat her to a very expensive lunch.

But not today. He had more pressing matters to attend to.

Outside, the rain was falling in a cool drizzle. He turned up the collar on his coat and headed for his favourite place, an excellent bistro that he and Eve had once frequented. As he walked, he reviewed his interview with Shepherd. Was her past catching up with her? Was that why they were asking questions? *An ongoing investigation*. God, this was all she needed after the loss of her father. Or were Shepherd's words just a blind, a cover for something else?

Henry had almost walked past the entrance when he realized his mistake and doubled back. Pushing open the doors, he stepped inside and found an empty table by the window. He picked up the menu and stared at it.

A waiter arrived, a familiar man with a friendly smile. 'Good afternoon, sir. Would you like to order?'

He chose the 'dish of the day' and then, as an

afterthought, added a half-bottle of red wine. He could do with a drink.

While he waited, he took a notepad from his pocket and started to draft another letter. But again he got no further than *Dear Eve*. He stared down at the page and tapped his pen against his teeth. What was he doing? Why didn't he just call her? Except that would mean ringing either from the office or from home. He considered these two options but dismissed them both. The office walls were thin and he didn't trust Louise; her loyalty, he suspected, still lay with Richard. And as for home, well, Celia rarely let him out of her sight; she watched him with the concentration of a hawk, her bright eyes constantly searching for further signs of infidelity.

The waiter arrived with the bottle.

'Thank you.' Henry nodded and waved him away.

He poured himself a glass of wine.

There was always a phone booth but he shied away from having such a private conversation in public. For the first time, Henry could see the advantage of a mobile. Until now, he had viewed them with suspicion, almost with contempt, not understanding why anyone should *choose* to be at the beck and call of those demanding metal boxes. On the train, on the bus, even on the street, they constantly shrieked for attention.

But perhaps he should take the plunge. There was a shop down the road, a place he passed every morning, its window filled with a glittering display, small phones, skinny ones, pink, black and silver ones. If he bought one he could ring from a quiet spot, maybe even the archive room. He could talk to Eve and tell her what had happened. He wouldn't be able to take it home, however. If Celia found it, she would be suspicious. It would have to be locked in his desk at night. His heart sank. The thought of all that subterfuge, as if he were about to embark on an illicit affair, made him feel weary.

Henry's food arrived. He pushed his notepad to one side and began to eat.

He sighed as he chewed. If it hadn't been for Richard, he wouldn't be eating alone. And his life would not have returned to this dull monochrome. Eve had been the colour of his existence.

Gossip, that's all it had been. As if a man can't have lunch with a woman without . . . But in Richard's world perhaps they couldn't. He spent his working day dealing with betrayal and divorce, and his evenings with his mistress.

'People are *talking*, Father.'

'Let them talk. I've nothing to be ashamed of.'

How he had managed to produce such a hypocrite remained a mystery to him. And he still wasn't sure what had irked his son more: his belief that his father was betraying his mother, or that Eve had rejected his own advances.

'Dickie' she had always called him to his face. Henry smiled at the recollection. Richard had hated that slightly mocking diminutive, visibly wincing whenever she used it, but had never found the nerve to correct her. He was accustomed to women finding him desirable. He was used to his fawning secretaries, to the girls he picked up at parties, to the wives who came to his office, vulnerable and needy after their husbands' desertion. Eve's immunity to his charms had left him angry and bemused.

Was that why he had done what he had done?

Or perhaps it went deeper than that. Perhaps his son's anger had its roots in something more profound. The smile faded from Henry's lips, along with his appetite. He laid down his fork. Whatever Richard's motivation, telling Celia that he'd been having an affair was

45

unforgivable. How could he? His hands curled into two tight fists. He could still see the hurt, the frantic pain spreading slowly from her mouth to her eyes. He caught his breath. That had been one of the worst days of his life. There had been no shouting, no demands for explanations or apologies, only a long recriminatory silence. After thirty-two years of marriage, she had looked at him as if he were a stranger. And the more he had tried to refute it, the less convincing he had sounded. Eventually, his vehement denials had trailed off into whispers. She didn't believe him. Why should she? Richard had presented her with enough 'evidence' to damn even the most innocent of men. And although he *was* innocent – he had never gone to bed with her, never even thought of her in that way – he was still guilty of another kind of infidelity. His platonic relationship with Eve was more intense, more captivating, than any naked moment spent between a pair of sheets. And how could he explain that without . . .

The waiter came by and took his plate. 'Would you care for—'

'No,' Henry said. 'Just the bill. Thank you.'

He poured another glass of wine and gulped it down.

Later, he had tried to speak to Celia again but it had all gone wrong. Somehow the truth was even more incriminating than the lies she had heard. How to confess? His lunches with Eve, their long Sunday walks and intimate conversations, were harder to explain than some sordid little affair with his office secretary. He hadn't been able to find the words.

So it was accepted that he'd slept with her. Celia believed it. Richard believed it. The whole bloody world believed it.

He glared down at the table.

He thought of his son and shook his head. It was wrong to hate him. It went against nature. As his father, he must himself be partly responsible for whatever Richard was, whatever he'd become. But Richard had driven Eve away. He wasn't sure if he could ever find it in his heart to forgive him.

Henry made a decision. He picked up his pen and started to write.

Richard sat forward and listened to the phone ringing at the other end of the line. He smoothed back a lock of chestnut hair, exposing the frown on his forehead. He was still seething from his recent encounter. No one talked to him like that, especially not some jumped-up piece of authoritarian shit like Shepherd.

Fuck the police. He had a right to know where she was. The bitch had bailed out before he'd had the chance to confront her.

'Yes,' he said, when the call was finally answered. 'Put me through to Paul Clarke. It's Richard Baxter.'

There was a short pause.

'Paul? Yes, fine thanks. Listen, I've got a job for you. Woman by the name of Eve Weston. I think she might be in Norwich. I need her tracking down. It's important. I'll fax through the details.'

Chapter Four

Eve was riding a tentative wave of relief. In the two weeks since she'd made her secret pact with Cavelli, Terry had not just been surviving but positively flourishing. There were no fresh bruises and the old ones had started to heal. If it went on like this, there was every chance he would roll through his sentence.

But would it last? Cavelli, to date, hadn't asked anything more of her than a promise to visit every time he asked. But there had to be a greater price. She was still waiting for the final bill.

His second visiting order had arrived in the post a few days ago.

This time, as she walked through the doors, her nerves were dancing to a different tune. He was sitting on the far side of the room. As she negotiated the tables, she watched his cold slate eyes move to follow her.

He didn't stand up. Sitting forward, with his large hands resting on his thighs, he said sarcastically: 'Hey, you didn't need to get dressed up.'

She looked down at her faded jeans and T-shirt. 'Sorry, I didn't realize it was cocktails.'

'You don't think it's nice to make the effort occasionally?'

Eve shrugged. If he wanted dress-up, she would do dress-up. 'Next time,' she promised, sitting down beside him. She found her leg situated too close to his and casually shifted it away.

'So, have you seen Terry?' he asked.

'I came on Monday.'

'And . . .?'

She nodded. 'He's okay. Pretty good. What do you think?'

His answer wasn't what she expected. 'I think he's lucky to have someone watching his back.'

Eve swallowed hard. 'What are you saying?'

He lifted his large hands and slapped them down emphatically against his thighs. 'No one's ever a hundred per cent safe, love. Not in a place like this. All you can do is to try and keep the odds in your favour.'

Was he deliberately trying to scare her? That wasn't too hard when it came to Terry. He'd always been her weak spot, the chink in her armour. At twenty-one, he was thirteen years her junior and in many ways still worryingly childlike. The thought of prison had terrified him.

He added smugly, 'So, you keep to your side of the bargain, Evie, and I'll keep to mine.'

She had the feeling it was coming at any moment – payback time. She made a feeble attempt to change the subject. 'And how are you?'

He tilted his head and stared at her. 'Thirsty.'

Obediently, she got to her feet again and walked over to the kiosk. No sign of Amber. Not that many visitors at all. It was the weekends that were busy, the room always packed, the place swarming with kids. During the week it was quiet. Today there was only a low steady hum, a gentle wave of conversation.

She ordered the teas and carried them back.

As if she might have added cyanide, he slowly stirred the dark brown brew with a look of suspicion in his eyes. 'There's something I want you to do for me.'

'Sure.'

'I haven't told you what it is yet.'

'Whatever,' she replied firmly. She had to convince him that their contract was binding, watertight. 'We've got a deal, haven't we?'

As if the idea amused him, his mouth curled up at the corners. 'Apparently so.'

'So tell me.'

He sat back in his seat, stretched out his long legs and folded his arms across his chest. For a second she thought he might have changed his mind but then he leaned forward again and began to talk softly. 'I need some . . . some things picking up from a friend in London. I need them kept safe until I get out. Do you think you can manage that?'

'What kind of things?' she asked automatically and instantly wanted to bite her tongue. *Anything* was what had been agreed. 'No, it doesn't matter. Of course I can. That's fine.'

'A couple of packages,' he added ominously.

The word *packages* had the unpleasant suggestion of drugs about it. God, if she wasn't careful she'd end up serving a prison sentence herself. But still she smiled and nodded. 'Okay.' How far would she go for Terry? She reckoned the answer only just fell short of murder.

He let her sweat for a while before saying smugly, 'You don't have to look so worried, love. It's nothing bad. Just some stuff of mine, some clothes and papers. My friend – well, she's going abroad, doesn't know when she'll be back.'

'Your girlfriend?' Eve wasn't sure why she asked.

He ignored the question. 'Could you do it tomorrow? She's leaving on Friday.' He produced a slip of paper from his pocket and passed it over. 'Her name's Paula. These are the details. She'll be expecting a call.'

Eve looked down at the address. Hampstead. Well,

there were worse places to spend the morning. And as long as she stayed well away from Covent Garden . . .

'All right. I'll ring her when I get back.'

'Good,' he said. Then, as if the serious business was over, he picked up his tea and started to drink.

Eve wasn't sure what to do next. Barely fifteen minutes of the two-hour visit had passed. Was she expected to stay or go?

The decision was taken out of her hands.

After a short silence he said, 'You don't look alike, you and Terry.' He seemed to consider the uttering of this statement as a perfect excuse to blatantly scrutinize her body again. How exactly he expected to find similarities between Terry's chest and hers was a mystery – but it didn't stop his gaze from lingering.

'He's my half-brother,' she admitted. 'Same father, different mothers.'

'Ah.'

Seizing the chance to push Terry's cause, she continued, 'He's a good kid at heart. It's not been easy for him. He's had a tough time and—'

'Please,' he interrupted swiftly, raising his palm. His face had taken on a severely bored expression. 'Don't bother going there. I've heard enough sob stories in this dump to last me a lifetime.'

'I was only trying to explain why—'

'I'd rather that you didn't.'

She was clearly wasting her breath. 'Okay.'

'Why don't you tell me about yourself, instead?' That sly smile was playing round his lips again. 'I mean, we should get to know each other, now that we're officially *partners* . . .'

As if he'd just unexpectedly announced their engagement, she flinched. Immediately, she tried to cover it by crossing her legs, by fidgeting on her seat, and then by the gift of her widest smile. But it was too late. He'd

51

already seen the involuntary movement, the revelatory spasm of disgust.

'Of course we should,' she said, repentantly.

But like some bloke who'd propositioned her in a bar, and got a knock-back, he refused to meet her gaze. He shook his head. 'Forget it.'

Eve knew that she'd made a mistake. Men's egos, especially those confined within four walls, were infamously fragile. Anxiously, she stared at him, trying to think of a way to put things right. She searched for a subtle compliment but found herself at a loss. He wasn't a good-looking man: his dark eyes were too scathing, his cheeks slightly pock-marked, his mouth too cruelly knowing to be attractive. He did have muscles, however. She could trace the biceps of his arms through his striped cotton shirt. Flattery sprang to her lips: *I can see you work out*. But she quickly dismissed it. It was too bland, too obvious. Which only left his character.

And there was no hope of salvation there.

So she resorted instead to the old *It's not you, it's me* routine. She didn't even have to lie. 'Sorry,' she murmured, cupping her chin in her hands. 'I'm just on edge. It's been a tough few months. First Terry getting into trouble, then my father dying . . .'

Eventually he met her gaze again but his voice was hard with no hint of compassion. 'Yeah, it must have been a shock. What your father did.'

Eve frowned. How did he know about that? Not from Terry, that was for sure; he wouldn't even talk to *her* about it. She felt at first surprise and then a faint uneasiness. It wasn't as if his suicide was a secret but it was hardly common knowledge either. There was no reason why Cavelli should be aware of it – unless he'd made it his business to find out . . .

He finished his tea and crushed the plastic cup

between his fingers. 'Alexander Weston.' He rolled the syllables slowly over his tongue.

A shock of alarm jolted through her. 'You knew him?'

'No, I can't say our paths ever crossed.' He paused. 'He was a fraudster, wasn't he?'

She stared at him, her throat tightening. Her father had been called a lot of things: grifter, swindler, con-man, cheat. Fraudster was one of the more polite descriptions.

'Retired,' she answered grimly.

He gave a small indecipherable nod. There was a flicker in his eyes – amusement, perhaps, it couldn't possibly be sympathy – but it was fleeting, there and gone before she had time to interpret it.

'And *Eve* Weston,' he continued softly. 'What about *her*? Thirty-four years old. Born in Stepney on the third of March. Raised by her father. Lived – well, all over the place but mainly in London. Married Patrick Fielding, a small-time Irish hustler, at twenty-three. Separated two years later. No kids. As regards a career, well, how shall we describe it? Perhaps we'll just settle on financially rewarding. Most recently worked for Baxter & Baxter. Would you like me to go on?'

She didn't reply. Her mouth was too dry.

Then, as if the intervening monologue had never taken place, he murmured, almost reminiscently, 'Your father liked a game of cards. Poker. That was his game.'

She took a deep breath and tried to garner what remained of her crumbling self-assurance.

Their eyes met across the table.

Cavelli leaned forward with a low, almost menacing laugh. 'But what about you, Evie? Do you like to gamble too?'

* * *

She drove with her foot firmly on the accelerator. Hell, she'd never been more glad to get out of anywhere. Opening the window, she welcomed the cool rush of air. The rain slanted in, dampening her right arm and shoulder. Who did he think he was, reciting her life history, talking as if he knew *everything*? He didn't! Although he appeared to know a damn sight more than he ought to.

Eve turned the radio up loud and scowled.

What did it mean? She screwed up her eyes. It wasn't too hard to figure out. If he'd taken the trouble to do this kind of research, then he must have a reason for it – and some serious expectations. He might not want cash but that wasn't the only way to pay off a debt. And she owed him. She owed him big time. Their deal was a two-way agreement and her pick-up from Paula was just the beginning. If she wanted to keep Terry safe, there was clearly worse to come.

She wondered again how he'd managed to find out so much. About her. About her father. About how he'd died. Ever since it had happened, she'd been in a daze. Henry had sympathized, Sonia had fussed, Terry had clammed up, but she had just carried on. Coping – wasn't that what it was called? But how do you cope when your father fills his pockets full of stones and walks into a river in the middle of the night?

By just not thinking about it.

Eve glared at the road ahead. There had been no goodbyes. Not even a note. She slammed her palms resentfully against the wheel. How could he? How could he have left her like that? They'd always been close, always able to talk. Even about the cancer.

'Don't worry. I'm not ready to go yet,' he'd promised.

And she'd believed him.

What had happened to change his mind? And only days after Terry had been sentenced. Just when she needed him – when they both needed him. She didn't want to feel angry but she couldn't help herself. She wanted to scream and shout. 'How could you? How could you desert me?' But then she felt guilty for the rage and tried to suppress it, to drive it back into that dark hidden recess of her soul.

Eve groaned. Now she didn't even have Henry to turn to. Richard must be rubbing his hands with glee. She'd been driven away like a scarlet woman. Smarmy, charmless, Dickie had got his revenge. Well, at least she had the consolation of not having to look at *his* face every day.

That thought took her mind off Cavelli for a while. But not for long enough. By the time she was back in Herbert Street, his dark gaze had started to haunt her again. She could feel her heart banging against her ribs. What was it he *really* wanted from her?

She found a space fifty yards from the flats and squeezed between a grubby white van and a silver-grey Peugeot. It was only as she started to walk back that she noticed the cop car parked near the entrance. There was no reason at all to presume it had anything to do with her but as she traipsed up the stairs she began to experience a familiar sinking sensation: *there was trouble ahead.*

The lock had been broken and the door stood wide open. From the hallway, Eve stared at the wreckage inside. The flat had been trashed. All the furniture had been overturned, her father's desk ransacked, and his books pulled from their shelves and strewn across the threadbare carpet. The glass from two smashed framed photographs lay glittering at her feet. Stunned, she stood in silence. Only her eyes swept over the damage, absorbing what seemed like a cruel desecration.

A pair of uniformed officers, both wearing gloves,

were lethargically picking through the debris. But it was Sonia who saw her first and came dashing over. 'Sweetheart,' she said, grasping her arm. 'I'm so sorry.'

'What . . .?' But it was hardly a question that needed asking.

'I got home half an hour ago,' she said. 'Found the door like this and – I tried to call you but your phone wasn't on, and I didn't know when you'd be back so . . .' She lowered her voice. 'Well, I *had* to ring them.'

'Of course. That's okay.'

'Kids, probably,' she continued. 'You know what they're like round here. It looks bad but don't worry, we'll get it sorted. Soon have it back to how it was. I don't think they've taken much.'

Eve bent to retrieve a thin green paperback, dragging Sonia down with her.

An authoritative voice rang out from behind. 'We'd rather you didn't touch anything.'

Rising quickly to her feet, she turned and saw a stern fair-haired man in a suit.

'And *you* are?' he asked.

'This is Mr Weston's daughter,' Sonia replied, as if she wasn't capable of answering for herself. '*Eve* Weston. She's been staying here since . . .'

'Detective Inspector Raynor,' he said. He sighed and looked around the room. 'Bit of a mess, I'm afraid.'

'I don't understand,' Eve murmured. 'Why would anyone want to do this? I mean, it's not as if . . . it's not as if there's anything worth stealing.' Her father had never been one for material possessions. Oh, he'd liked the high-life all right, expensive hotels, champagne and all the luxuries, but when it came to his home he'd been careful never to accumulate more than could be thrown into the boot of a car.

Raynor drew a notebook from his pocket. 'Perhaps if I could take a few details?'

'Her father's only just passed on,' Sonia said defensively, tightening the hold on her arm. 'She's got enough to deal with, without this.'

Eve smiled, before gently disentangling herself. 'It's okay, Son. I'm all right. A cup of tea would be good, though. If you don't mind.' She looked at Raynor. 'Is that possible?'

'You finished through there?' he asked one of the officers.

The man nodded.

Sonia hesitated a moment before retreating. She didn't like coppers at the best of times and this particular specimen with his cool efficiency and smart grey suit wasn't about to alter her opinion. She glanced back over her shoulder. 'Don't worry, love. I won't be long.'

Eve smiled at her again but as soon as she was out of earshot, she turned and asked, 'Do *you* think it was kids?'

'Hard to say.' He shrugged. 'Perhaps you could have a look around, see if you can spot anything that's missing.'

She tried to concentrate. The most obvious things, the portable TV and the mini CD player, were still there, although both had been broken. The TV had a long crack running the width of the screen. His small collection of CDs were scattered across the floor. The focus of the attack seemed to be on his desk. It wasn't that long since she'd tidied it but now every drawer had been pulled out and emptied, the papers scattered. Had they been searching for money?

She frowned. 'I don't know. I don't think so.'

The spare room, the room she'd been sleeping in, had been barely touched. Not surprising as it was almost empty. She had learned to travel as lightly as her father. But the bed had been disturbed, the single mattress lifted to check underneath, and then carelessly dropped back down.

They progressed to the master bedroom where her father's clothes were lying, crumpled, on the bed. It was obvious that someone had been through all the pockets. There was one suit in particular that attracted her attention, a dark blue pinstripe that he had worn to Terry's trial. She felt a lump forming in her throat. Instinctively, she leaned over to touch it but then remembering Raynor's earlier instruction quickly drew back.

'Perhaps they were looking for something in particular,' he suggested.

'Like what?'

He shrugged again. 'What do *you* think?'

But she couldn't say what she thought. Now that the shock was beginning to wear off, it was being replaced by a different but no less disturbing feeling: a suspicion that this was something to do with Cavelli. Was it really a coincidence that on the day she'd gone to visit him, when he'd made it so perfectly clear that he knew too much about her, this had happened? She had a debt to pay. Perhaps this was some kind of warning or threat.

One of the officers put his head round the door. 'We're off now, guv.'

Raynor raised a hand. 'I'll see you back at the station.'

Then Sonia arrived with two mugs of tea. She passed one to Eve but dumped the other, unceremoniously, on the chest of drawers. She glared at Raynor. 'There's sugar, if you want it, in the kitchen. So, is that it? Can we get on with the clearing up?'

'I'm sorry,' he said, 'I just need a few more minutes with Ms Weston.'

Sonia put her hand on her hip and waited.

'In *private*,' he stressed.

As if Raynor might bring out the thumb screws as soon as she was out of sight, she shot a furtive glance at Eve. 'I can stay if you want.'

'No,' she insisted. 'It's fine. Really. And thanks for the tea.'

'I'll be next door when you're ready. Just give me a knock.'

They headed back to the kitchen although it wasn't sugar Eve was after. She needed a drink. Incredibly, although all the cupboards had been turned out, the bottle of brandy was still intact. 'There's the first clue,' she said, forcing a laugh. 'Our burglar's teetotal.' But her hand trembled as she reached for a glass. 'Would you like one?'

He sat down with his tea. 'Thanks, but no.'

She poured herself a large one and took a chair on the opposite side of the table. Compared to the living room, the kitchen wasn't in too bad a state. The drawers had been emptied but, as there hadn't been much in them, the mess was minimal.

'What time did you leave today?' Raynor asked.

She thought back. 'It must have been about half-twelve.'

'And where did you go?'

Eve frowned at him. 'What's that got to do with anything?' But then, seeing his brows lift, she decided to come clean. 'Okay. I went to Hillgrove Prison. My brother's serving a short sentence there. Terry Weston.' It wasn't a lie but it wasn't the whole truth either. Until she found out what was going on, she intended to keep Cavelli's name out of it.

Raynor didn't seem surprised by the information. He made a brief note in his pad. Then he flipped back a page. 'And this is your late father's flat, right? Alexander Weston.'

It seemed like everyone wanted to say his name today. She sighed into her glass. 'It's rented,' she explained. 'It's cheap and close to the jail. I thought I'd stay for a while.

59

Terry might want to take on the lease when he comes out.'

He sat back and looked at her, twisting the pen between his fingers. 'And he kept nothing of value here? No large amounts of cash or jewellery? No share certificates or bonds?'

Eve wasn't sure what alerted her, something rather too casual in his tone perhaps. But she was suddenly certain that Raynor, just like Cavelli, was well aware of Alex Weston's dubious past. Not that surprising – he was a policeman after all – but then again, her father was hardly on the list of Interpol's most wanted.

'Inspector, I can guess where this is going but you're way off the mark. He hasn't been in trouble for years. He was the kind of man, as I'm sure you're aware, whose fortunes tended to fluctuate.' Glancing over her shoulder, she made a loose sweeping motion with her hand. 'As you can see, he was hardly on an upward curve.'

'I wasn't meaning to suggest . . .'

'That he was involved in anything illegal?' She took a sip of brandy and grinned. 'Perish the thought.'

After a slight hesitation, Raynor's lips curled into a smile. 'Sorry,' he said. 'I'm sure this is the last thing you need at the moment.'

He had a pleasant smile. In fact, now she came to really look at him, he had a number of other quite favourable attributes: good cheekbones, a firm jaw, and a pair of rather compelling blue eyes. With his shock of blond hair, he reminded her a little of her ex-husband Patrick. Shame he was a cop. 'It's okay. You're just doing your job, right?'

'For my sins,' he replied.

'And you don't believe it was kids who did this, do you?'

He hesitated. 'It's doubtful. If you want my honest opinion, I'd say . . .' He paused again.

'Go on,' she urged.

'From what I've seen, I still think they were searching for something specific.'

Eve shook her head. That didn't make any sense. If there had been anything valuable in the flat, he wouldn't have left it for burglars to find. No, she was more inclined to go with her own theory – that Martin Cavelli was exerting his authority.

Raynor scraped back his chair and stood up. 'Well, if you think of anything that might be useful . . .' Digging in his pocket, he pulled out a wallet and removed a card. He dropped it on the table.

She saw him to the door.

He hovered on the threshold for a while. 'Are you sure you're all right?'

'I'll survive,' she said.

He nodded and began to walk off down the corridor. As he reached the stairs, he turned around and called back: 'Just make sure you get that lock fixed.'

Eve woke to the sound of the phone ringing. She flicked on the lamp, dragged her wrist out from under the duvet and peered at her watch. Eight thirty. Who was calling at this time? With all the clearing up, she hadn't got to bed until after two. With a grunt she buried her head back under a pillow. Whoever it was could wait.

Five minutes later it started ringing again. She ignored it.

Two minutes later it was going again. Groaning, she crawled out of bed, and stumbled into the living room. The curtains were still drawn. She had to fumble around the sofa until she eventually found the small round table. She scrabbled for the phone. 'Yes?'

There was a short pause. 'Eve?'

'Yes.'

'It's Martin.'

She muttered her incomprehension down the line. 'Huh?'

'Martin *Cavelli*.'

Eve was kick-started into consciousness. 'Oh, right.' And as if he could see her, she instantly stood up straight and gathered together the unbuttoned front of her night-shirt. 'Sorry. Hi.'

'Did I wake you?'

'No. Yes. Well, kind of. Bit of a late one.'

'Lucky for you,' he said. 'I was wondering why you hadn't rung Paula.'

Her jaw fell open. Oh God! Paula. She'd forgotten all about her. After the events of yesterday, she'd gone clean out of her head. 'Actually, there's a bit of a problem there.'

'A problem,' he repeated sourly.

She was tempted to make a snide remark, maybe one relating to the trauma of having your dead father's home turned upside down. But she kept it civil. 'The flat was broken into.'

'What?'

He sounded surprised but she wasn't convinced. He'd had all night to work on that innocent one-word response. 'They wrecked the place,' she said, 'while I was out visiting you. So, I can't see any way of getting to London today.'

'Why not?'

She glared down into the receiver, inwardly noting how he hadn't asked, *Did they take much?* like any normal person would. But then Cavelli was hardly 'nor-mal' and there was every chance he already knew the answer. 'I'm still clearing up. And it's not safe now, is it? I thought you wanted your things to be secure.'

'Don't worry about that,' he said.

'I am worried. I don't want—' But the phone line was

already dead. She put it back in the cradle and waited. A minute passed, then two. When it became apparent that he wasn't going to ring again, she went through to the kitchen and put the kettle on.

Sitting at the table with a strong mug of coffee, she replayed the conversation in her head. Well, she had the minor consolation of knowing that if he had been responsible for the break-in, he'd just shot himself in the foot. She smiled. But then again, if Cavelli wanted his 'packages' so badly, why would he do that? Her moment of satisfaction soon faded. No, it didn't add up. Nothing added up about this break-in. She hadn't been able to find a single item missing. Lots of stuff broken or damaged but that was all.

By nine thirty she was washed and dressed and starting to get anxious. It was an hour since she'd last heard from him. Why hadn't he called back? Pacing from one side of the living room to the other, she raked her fingers through her hair, regretting her earlier decision. She shouldn't have been so hasty. What if he saw her failure to go to London today as breaking her side of the bargain? He didn't strike her as the type to accept *extenuating circumstances* as a reasonable excuse.

She found her jacket, rooted in the pocket and pulled out the number for Paula. It wasn't too late to change her mind. The flat could wait. With Sonia's help, she had cleared the worst of the mess. It still needed a good clean but other than that there was only her father's desk left to sort and the books to line back up on the shelves. And she could survive without the TV for another night. Except that wasn't really what was bothering her. It was more the idea of going out and leaving the place empty again. What if she got back and found . . .

Well, she'd have to take that chance.

Eve dialled the number and listened. The phone rang five times before switching to an answering machine. A sultry voice said invitingly: 'Hi, this is Paula. Leave a message and I might get back to you.'

She listened to the beeps but then hung up. What was the point? Cavelli must have already rung to tell her that she wasn't coming. Then, as quickly as she'd made the decision, she instantly revised it. Paula could be in the shower or just screening her calls. She had to leave a message. That way, at least, she could honestly claim that she'd tried.

Eve raised the phone to her ear again but was interrupted by a series of short sharp knocks on the door. She jumped. Who was that? Definitely not Sonia. For a few nervy seconds she stood holding her breath. Then, giving herself a mental shake, she replaced the receiver. What was the matter with her? It was hardly the hour for any would-be intruder to come calling.

She strode across the hallway and opened the door to a short apple-cheeked man with a bulky holdall at his feet. 'Hi. Miss Weston, is it?' he said cheerily. 'I'm Barry.'

She smiled faintly.

'Come to sort the locks,' he said. 'Not too early for you, is it?'

Eve looked at the brand-new mortise that had been fitted the night before. 'Are you from . . .?' She tried to recall the name of the company she had called yesterday but couldn't. They were just a random number she'd plucked from the directory. 'I'm sorry but I think there's been a mistake. You've been out already. It's been fixed.'

'Fixed?' he said. He gazed down at the bright new lock. After a brief examination, he made one of those sounds redolent of all British workmen, a kind of low despairing sigh that formed in the back of his throat and slowly leaked out through his lips. 'I wouldn't say that exactly.'

She frowned at him.

He shrugged. 'We're hardly talking Fort Knox here.'

Eve was beginning to wonder if she'd ever actually woken up this morning. Perhaps this was one of those insanely mad dreams where you kept on thinking you were awake when you weren't. 'I'm sorry, but I don't understand why—'

Before she had any further chance to object, he'd already stepped forward, placed himself securely in the hall, and whipped out a tape measure. 'It's not the lock that's the problem, you see. It's the door.' He rapped his knuckles smartly against the wood. 'You hear that? Flimsy as shit – if you'll pardon my French. You can put as many locks as you like on this, love, but it's not going to make a damn bit of difference.'

She took a step back. 'Look, I don't—'

'It's okay,' he said. 'I know you're busy. Martin told me what happened. You just get on with what you need to do. Don't worry about me.'

'Martin,' she murmured.

His rosy cheeks bunched as he gave her a smile. 'Yeah. He did tell you I was coming, didn't he?'

Eve faltered but then turned away. 'I'll make you a brew.' She didn't want Barry to see her face, to catch the conflicting emotions passing over it. There was too much to read. She felt relief that Cavelli hadn't called off the deal, anger at his presumption that he could fortify her flat at will, and fear that he felt the need to. What was really in those packages? Nothing illegal, he'd said, but that was beginning to seem doubtful.

Going through to the kitchen, she put the kettle on again and waited for it to boil. Although she wanted to pace, she forced herself to stay still. Perhaps she should have stood her ground and sent Barry away. But then where would that leave Terry? No, she didn't have a choice. For the time being she had to stick with the cards she'd been dealt.

From the window she could see the alley that ran between this small block and the next, a dank litter-covered passage that led eventually to the supermarket car park. She looked down on a man's head, on the bald ring in its centre, a perfect circle like a monk's tonsure. He was walking carefully, side-stepping the puddles. She idly followed his progress until he was out of sight.

When Eve went back into the living room, she found that another two guys had arrived. She wondered how Cavelli had managed to conjure up a trio of workmen at sixty minutes' notice, but preferred not to ask. A new door, so heavy and solid that it might have come straight out of HMP Hillgrove, was propped up in the corridor.

'That should do the trick,' Barry said, grinning. 'What do you reckon?'

She reckoned it was the kind of extreme defence that worried gangsters favoured – but that it was also wise to keep her opinion private. She smiled. 'Looks good to me.' She passed him his mug of tea.

'Lovely,' he said. 'Ta.'

She was about to politely extend the offer of refreshments when a voice stridently demanded: 'What's going on here? What are you doing?'

Sonia suddenly appeared between the three of them, squeezing her way through. 'Oh, Eve. You're here. Thank God!' She laid a hand against her breast. 'I thought . . . I didn't realize. I heard the noise and—'

'It's okay. They're just fixing the door.'

Confused, she stared at her. 'But you only had a new lock put on last night.'

'Yes, but . . .' Eve tried to think of a rational explanation as to why she was apparently erecting an anti-riot barricade but failed to come up with anything feasible.

Instead, she smiled broadly at the newcomers and said: 'I guess you two wouldn't mind a brew either?'

'Wouldn't say no,' one of them answered.

'Come on, then,' she said, grabbing Sonia by the arm, 'let's get out of their way.'

Back in the kitchen, she refilled the kettle and took another three mugs from the hooks on the wall. 'Would you like one?'

'What's going on?' Sonia asked again. She had taken a seat but was still glancing over her shoulder.

Eve kept her back to her, busying herself with the mugs and the tea bags. She wanted to tell her the truth but she couldn't. 'Oh, I don't know,' she shrugged. 'I'm just being paranoid, I guess. They had a special offer on – new door, cheap price, a bit more security, and after yesterday, well, I just thought . . .'

Sonia sighed sympathetically. 'Oh love, you didn't have to do that. It was only kids. I'm sure it won't happen again.'

Eve wished she felt as confident. But she didn't. 'Yeah, I know.' She went to the fridge and got out the milk. Before she might be tempted to confide, she hurriedly made the extra teas and rushed them through to the room next door.

When she came back there was a small pile of mail sitting on the table.

'Sorry,' Sonia said. 'I brought it up yesterday when . . . I forgot to give it to you.'

'I'm glad you did,' Eve replied, wincing as she flicked through the envelopes. 'There's only so much bad news you can take in a day.' The first three were bills, final demands. It was only the fourth that caught her attention. She recognized the handwriting. *Henry's*.

Quickly, she tore it open. She read it once and then again.

Her heart sank.

Chapter Five

Cavelli stretched out his legs on the hard skinny bunk and put his hands behind his head. It was twelve o'clock, lunchtime lock-up. He gazed up at the ceiling. Barry should be there by now, doing his job, shoring up the defences. This was working out better than he could ever have imagined. He smiled. Five bloody years he'd spent inside – and now he could get what he wanted without moving a muscle. It was all so easy, so simple. Thanks to Eve Weston.

And with due thanks as well to the Reverend John Miller. It could hardly be a coincidence that he'd seen him coming out of Terry's cell last week. *Divine intervention* was how he liked to think of it.

All he'd had to do was to invite him in and look suitably anxious. 'We're all worried about Terry,' he'd said. 'After what's happened.'

It was common knowledge that he'd been to his father's funeral a few weeks back. But, after that first visit by Eve, when she'd made her unusual proposition, Cavelli wanted to find out more. He had tried to talk to Terry but the kid had clammed up. Mad little fucker he was. On the dope most of the time, three sheets to the wind. Although after what his papa had done, that was hardly surprising. He should have felt pity but he didn't. Pity was weakness and you couldn't afford weakness in here.

'Take a pew,' he'd said, not intending the pun and trying not to grin as soon as it came out of his mouth.

A more worldly priest would have seen straight through him, would have easily shrugged him off, but Miller was a new boy in the jail, still finding his feet. He didn't have a clue about the bastards he was dealing with. In his late thirties, he reminded Cavelli of a crow: a long sharp nose, beady eyes and thinning oiled black hair.

'How is he?' he'd asked. 'Is he okay?'

And Miller, mistaking his curiosity for genuine concern, had soon spilled the beans. In five minutes flat he'd got the information he wanted: old man Weston had given up the ghost and drowned himself in the river Wensum.

Cavelli hadn't been sure why the information was useful; it was just that old gut instinct coming in to play. Maybe it was because it made Eve Weston more vulnerable, more desperate. If her father had taken his own life, it wasn't beyond the realm of possibility that Terry might do the same. Was there a genetic predisposition towards these things? Perhaps it was a Weston family trait.

He might have left it there but his interest had been piqued by the tall sexy redhead prepared to take risks. He asked around, made a few calls, and the more he found out, the more interested he became. Alex Weston had been a conman and a good one too by all accounts. However, like most of his breed, he had managed to squander his various fortunes: some on women and high-living, but most at the card table. He was a good poker player but the odds always got you in the end.

And what about his daughter? She'd had a few run-ins with the law but still had a clean sheet. There were rumours but nothing concrete. Hard to say for sure whether she was a chip off the old block or if she'd found an easier way to make a living; with that face and those legs she wouldn't have too much trouble in persuading gullible old men to part with their money.

Well, he wasn't going to rush anything. No point scaring her off. He'd reel her in slowly, very slowly, until she was so tight on that hook she'd never be able to wriggle free.

'Will we see you in chapel on Sunday?' Miller had asked.

'I don't think so, Father.'

What was the point? In Eve Weston, he'd already got the answer to his prayers.

It was almost half-twelve when the second knock came, a deeper and more resonant sound thanks to Barry's installation. With two mortises, a Yale, and three heavy bolts, it would take a party of storm troopers to break down the door.

She opened it to discover a tall curvy brunette, impeccably dressed in a tailored suit, but with a pronounced scowl on her face. A pair of flashing chestnut eyes surveyed her. 'You Eve?' she asked shortly.

When she nodded, the woman thrust two long black garment bags into her arms. 'Here. The rest of his stuff's in the car.' Abruptly, she turned away.

Eve threw the bags over the back of a chair and quickly followed her along the corridor. 'You must be Paula,' she said, when the penny finally dropped.

As if the comment was superfluous, Paula ignored it. Clearly less than overjoyed at being forced to play delivery girl, she clattered down the stone stairway, her stiletto heels echoing. It was only as they hit the second flight that she deigned to speak to her again. 'You ever thought of living someplace with a lift?'

70

'It's only two floors,' Eve retorted, bristling at her tone. She had been on the verge of offering an apology – it was *her*, after all, who should have been driving to London – but instantly changed her mind. 'Good exercise,' she said instead.

Paula snorted.

Just outside the entrance, a gleaming blue BMW sports was parked. Paula paused for a moment, perhaps to admire its sleek low-slung beauty, but more likely to check for malicious scratches. Then she opened the boot and passed over a heavy cardboard box. 'You take this and I'll bring the rest.'

The 'rest' appeared to consist of one much smaller box and a handful of shirts still in their cellophane wrappers. Eve gave her a withering glance but didn't object. The sooner they got this over with the better.

Gritting her teeth as she lugged it up the stairs, she tried to judge from the size and weight what might be inside. It was about eighteen inches square and securely sealed with wide dark red tape. It felt as heavy as a ton of bricks – or books. Books? From what she knew of Cavelli, that didn't seem likely.

'What's he got in here?' she puffed.

'I didn't ask,' Paula replied, in such a way as to suggest that she shouldn't be asking either.

Eve was out of breath by the time she reached the flat. Perhaps there *was* something to be said for a lift. She dumped the box unceremoniously on the floor. 'You want a coffee?' she asked, more out of politeness than any desire to prolong the encounter.

But as Paula stepped over the threshold, she stopped to stare intently at the door. Raising her perfectly plucked eyebrows in a blend of surprise and curiosity, she asked, 'You expecting company?'

And she didn't need to spell out what kind of company she meant.

Eve sighed, wondering if this was the reaction she was going to get from every visitor. That door was just too . . . extreme. 'I've already had it. I was broken into yesterday. Didn't he tell you?'

'Oh, he never tells me anything, love. Just gets me running around like a blue-arsed fly. Won't take no for an answer.' For the first time, Paula extended her wide scarlet mouth into a smile. 'Still, I suppose you know all about *that*.'

She didn't – although she'd had an inkling of his obstinacy this morning when she'd told him that she wouldn't be going to Hampstead. She smiled back, sensing a thaw in their, to date, rather icy relations. It suddenly occurred to her, after Cavelli's unwelcome revelations yesterday, that this could be an opportunity to do some research of her own.

'Grab a seat. I'll get the coffee.'

Paula hesitated, glancing first at the battered sofa and then at the two overstuffed and mismatched armchairs. From the dizzying heights of her spiky four-inch heels, she gazed down on the choice as if weighing a no-win option between the devil and the deep blue sea.

Eve's intention to do some subtle digging was supplanted by a surge of indignation. This had been her father's home and, okay, it might not be a Mayfair penthouse or a luxury flat in Hampstead, but it *was* clean. After the break-in she and Sonia had spread enough disinfectant to kill the most malevolent of germs. And she'd even spent the rest of this morning, after Barry had left, dusting and polishing. Mr Sheen would be proud of her. Who was Paula to peer down that supercilious nose and pass judgement? Without attempting to hide her irritation, she snapped, 'Look, it might not be the Ritz but don't worry, you won't catch anything.'

Surprisingly, Paula laughed. 'I wasn't thinking that.'

72

'Right,' Eve murmured disbelievingly, before retreating to the kitchen. She refilled the kettle and flicked it back on for what already felt like the hundredth time that day. Slamming a couple of mugs down on the counter, she turned around to find Paula watching her.

'You're kind of touchy, aren't you?'

Eve glared at her. 'This is my father's flat. He died recently. So, yes, I suppose I'm kind of touchy.'

'Sorry, I didn't realize.' Paula placed one hand on her elegant hip and sighed. 'To tell you the truth, I've been in a filthy mood all morning. Well, ever since Martin rang and told me you weren't coming.'

'I'd never have guessed.'

Paula grinned. 'I shouldn't have taken it out on you.'

Eve, prepared to call a truce, nodded back at her. 'I would have driven down tomorrow. I tried to call.'

'It doesn't matter. I couldn't take another day of Martin hassling me. It's worth the trip just to get him off my back.'

'Have you known him long?' she asked, trying not to look too interested. She poured the water carefully over the coffee.

'Too long,' Paula replied, but didn't elaborate.

Back in the living room, she slumped down on the sofa and kicked off her shoes. She leaned down to massage the arches of her narrow feet. 'You're not his usual type.'

Eve forced a smile. 'I'm sorry?'

'Not another dumb blonde at least. That's a step in the right direction.'

'I'm not his girlfriend,' she retorted, a little too smartly. 'I'm just . . .' Just what? She tried to think of something suitable to describe their association. In the end, defeated, she murmured, 'I'm just a friend.'

As if Paula had heard *that* a thousand times before her mobile eyebrows made another tiny upward shift. 'Oh, don't worry about me. No skin off my nose. He's none of my business any more, hasn't been for years.'

'So you used to . . .'

'He didn't tell you, did he? Typical of Martin. Still, you'll get used to it.' She laughed, exposing both rows of her pure white teeth. 'I'm his wife, love – although not, thank God, for much longer.'

Eve sat back in her chair, genuinely surprised. She couldn't imagine them together, this tall striking woman and the uncouth Cavelli. Like a bizarre re-creation of Beauty and the Beast.

'And before you ask,' Paula added, although Eve hadn't been going to, 'I didn't dump him when he went inside. I'm not *that* much of a bitch. We'd already split.' She played with a thread on the arm of the sofa, winding it around a blood-red talon. 'Three months, that's all we lasted. Not what you'd call a mighty success.'

Sipping her coffee, Eve studied her over the rim of the mug. She had the feeling that condolences weren't exactly in order. So she offered instead, 'Short and sweet?'

'Well, half right.' Paula's lips pursed into what might have been bitterness or regret. 'Personally, I don't much care for always being second best.'

'Second best?'

She turned her dark eyes on her. 'He really hasn't told you anything, has he?'

Eve couldn't argue with that so she simply lifted her shoulders in a shrug.

'Living in the shadow of a ghost,' Paula explained. 'The beautiful Nadine. Let me give you a piece of advice: never get attached to a man with a dead first wife, especially one he's still in love with.'

Eve wondered why she was telling her all this – a kindly warning or a deliberate attempt to undermine her

74

'relationship' with Cavelli? Either way, she didn't much care. 'So why did you get together in the first place?'

'For the usual stupid reasons. You know . . .'

Eve had an inkling. 'I was married once,' she volunteered, 'a long time ago. We staggered through two years, but he preferred pool rooms and whisky to me.'

'Tough competition.'

'Too tough.' Where was Patrick now? Still hustling, probably, still living off his wits. If they hadn't been pickled in alcohol. For all his utter uselessness, Eve still felt a lingering ache whenever she thought of him. 'I won't be rushing there again.'

But Paula just laughed. 'Some men can be very persuasive.'

If she was referring to Cavelli, she didn't have to worry. Eve was still trying to work out how he'd managed to persuade one woman to walk down the aisle with him, never mind two. Which reminded her of something she needed to ask: 'What happened to Nadine?'

As if she hadn't heard, Paula glanced pointedly at her diamond-studded watch and stood up. She slipped her feet back into her shoes, smoothed down her skirt, and made a small unnecessary adjustment to her hair.

'Paula?'

Eventually, reluctantly, she looked back at her. 'She left him, didn't she? Found some piece of scum, divorced Martin, and headed off into the sunset with the latest Mr Right.' She hesitated, doubtful perhaps as to whether she should go on, but then cleared her throat and continued. 'The shit dumped her of course. No big surprise there. A few weeks later she took an overdose.'

'God,' Eve murmured, swallowing hard. She couldn't help but be reminded of her father.

But Paula, unaware, gave an impatient flap of her hand. This time there was no disguising the bitterness in her voice. 'Oh, don't feel sorry for her. She ruined her own life and then wrecked Martin's as well.'

And *yours* too, Eve thought, although she had the discretion not to say it out loud.

Quickly, as if she'd already revealed too much, Paula headed for the door. 'Look, sorry, but I have to go. Thanks for the coffee.'

'Hey, thanks for saving me a journey.'

As she crossed the room, Paula inclined her head towards the boxes. 'Whatever you do, don't open them. Martin's paranoid about his stuff. He likes to keep it private.'

'Of course,' she replied, trying to sound dismissive. Trying to sound like the type of person who wasn't even remotely curious about their contents.

Paula stepped into the corridor but then turned as though she might have something more to add. She gave Eve a long hard look. It was hard to tell just how friendly it was. But in the end she smiled. 'Well, good luck,' she said, and without waiting for a response began click-clacking her way towards the stairs.

It was only after she closed the door that Eve began wondering if those final words had some greater significance. *Good luck*. Was it just one of those casual things that people said or a direct reference – and she really hoped that this wasn't the case – to the two mysterious boxes? Frowning, she prodded the larger one with her right foot. It was solid as a rock.

She walked over to the window and stared down at the street. Paula emerged a few seconds later. She didn't look back or look up. With the ease of a supermodel, she coolly poured herself into the driver's seat. Eve felt a pang of envy: what she wouldn't give to be getting as far away from here as possible.

Unfortunately, that option wasn't open to her.

She stood watching until the BMW slid around the

corner. She realized that she hadn't even asked her where she was going. Back to London first but then . . . Perhaps it was better not to know. Anywhere had to be more desirable than here. There were some other questions she would have liked the answers to, most essentially what Cavelli was serving time for – but then again, she could hardly have inquired about *that* without revealing that she barely knew him.

With a sigh, she turned back towards the room.

Eve gazed at the boxes. It had been easier to think of Cavelli as totally alien, as a man she could never relate to. Now, in the worst possible way, it transpired that they had some common ground. She screwed up her eyes. Her fingers curled into two loose fists. *Suicide*. Recently, that word had taken up permanent residence in her mind, a sad sloshing word that revolved like a piece of dirty laundry. She could put it through the wash a thousand times but it was never going to come out clean.

Her father had killed himself.

And *she* hadn't known that he was going to do it.

She sank down on to a chair and lowered her face into her hands. Naturally, there had been an autopsy. They'd found a cocktail of booze and pills, plus all the evidence of his deadly creeping cancer. The coroner's verdict had never been in doubt: Alex Weston had taken his own life. And she wasn't arguing with that.

But why had he chosen to walk out of the warmth and comfort of his own flat and into the bleak desolation of the river? Perhaps the answer was simple – to save Sonia from the joyless task of discovering his body. She would have knocked, as she always did, the following morning. And if she'd got no reply, eventually would have used her spare key and opened the door to find . . . She sighed. He had spared her that at least.

So, although she might just about be able to comprehend his motives for the midnight stroll, she still couldn't grasp why he hadn't left a note. Not a word of explanation. No goodbye. Nothing to help ease the pain of her loss. How to understand, how to forgive, that her father – who had spent his entire life scribbling notes – had failed at the final most important moment to put pen to paper?

DS Eddie Shepherd shuffled the papers on his desk and growled. In the past week, there'd been two post office robberies, a violent assault, three muggings and the usual quota of thefts and burglaries. So why was Raynor still obsessing over Eve Weston? Maybe she *had* conned some old codger out of a few quid but who gave a flying fuck? She was just a classy tart with an eye to the main chance.

Raynor was like a terrier, biting and snarling, refusing to let go. Eddie was sick of it. He had better things to do. It wasn't as if it had happened – *if* it had happened – on their patch, not even in their county. And, okay, there'd been that break-in at her old man's place, but so what? There were plenty of low-lives roaming the streets. And so what if she was visiting Martin Cavelli? It didn't mean they were planning the heist of the century. He smirked into his coffee; more likely she got paid to talk dirty to him!

No, Raynor had got it all wrong this time. But then that wasn't surprising; he might be smart but he didn't have the experience; it took years to develop a real copper's nose. These fast-track graduates got on his nerves. Promoted almost as soon as they'd pushed them through Hendon. One minute they were still wet behind the ears, the next they were running the bloody show. Although he had a grudging respect for the inspector's tenacity, he couldn't say he liked him much. With his fancy suits, silk ties and fanatical health habits, he didn't fit in with Eddie's idea of what a copper should be. It didn't help, either, that half the female relief worshipped the ground he walked on.

Muttering under his breath, he opened the file on Martin Cavelli and started to read. It made for slim pickings. Before the trial, fifteen *years* before, there had been a few minor incidents, mainly of affray, a couple of cautions, a few fines, but that was all. Nothing to indicate the ferocious violence he'd later unleash on Jimmy Reece. That he hadn't killed the guy was a miracle. Still, it hadn't been through lack of trying. Anticipating his lunch, Eddie didn't look too closely at the photographs.

Cavelli had started as a bouncer, working the clubs, dealing with the pushers and the drunks, before wisely moving into the more glamorous and lucrative world of personal security. Back in the mid-nineties he had launched a small but elite bodyguarding business. By employing only the cream, ex-SAS, ex-Marines, he had soon built up a reputation, as well as a healthy bank balance.

How exactly he'd raised the start-up capital – a high-interest loan from the bank or a more imaginative approach to borrowing – wasn't revealed in the papers in front of him. Eddie had his suspicions. Anyway, whatever the means, that was how Cavelli had come to meet Jimmy Reece, or rather James Archibald Conway Reece as he'd actually been christened. He snarled. He had about as much regard for aristocratic playboys as he had for fast-track coppers. But Jimmy Reece had been on the up then, a favoured 'celebrity'. His face had been splashed across all the tabloids. He'd made a couple of films, nothing special, but his good looks, background and nightclub antics were rapidly launching him into the stratosphere. He was never seen without a different girl on his arm.

But the female species, as it turned out, was to be his downfall.

Or, more to the point, one woman in particular. When Jimmy Reece set his sights on Nadine Cavelli, he was making the worst mistake of his life.

In Eddie's long career, it had never failed to amaze him as to just how many men were brought down by the fairer sex. They should have learned their lesson by now – but that would be the day hell froze over. All it took was a flash of cleavage, a sultry look, and their cocks took charge of their brains. On the inauspicious day that Jimmy had waltzed off with Cavelli's wife, he may as well have slit his own throat.

Eddie impatiently shoved that file aside and opened the next. It was only as he flipped through the report on the Weston break-in that something promising leapt out. The person who'd reported the incident was a neighbour called Marshall, *Sonia* Marshall. For the first time that morning, his eyes lit up. Now if that was a coincidence . . .

He lumbered to his feet and pulled on his jacket. It was years since he'd last seen her but it had to be the same one; he could feel it in his water. And although breaking and entering was hardly Sonia's modus operandi, her fucker of a husband was more than capable. Yeah, the more he came to think about it, Peter Marshall sat very nicely in the frame.

Eddie drove all the way to Herbert Street with a grin on his face.

When he arrived, he couldn't find a space and was forced to circle twice before parking the car several streets away. Whether it would still be there in half an hour was a matter of debate. A spillover from the adjacent red-light district, this wasn't the most salubrious of areas. It had a downbeat, downcast air as if its residents expected nothing – and knew that they were more than likely to get it.

He walked swiftly back, past a few dilapidated shops and an almost empty café. The cool steady rain put a dampener on his mood. This wasn't improved by the two flights of stairs that loomed up before him as he swung through the glass doors of the entrance.

It was a while before he reached the top landing and by then his breath was laboured. He was sweating too, the clammy perspiration on his shirt leaking through to meet the dampness of his outer layers. A purplish red stain lay like a bruise across his nose and cheeks. He paused to light a cigarette.

As on the other floors, there were only two flats to choose from. He raised a fist and rapped on number six. There was a short delay before he heard a rustling sound followed by silence. Sure that he was being viewed through the spyhole, he got a faint prickling sensation on the nape of his neck.

Eventually, a bolt was drawn back and the door was opened.

It took him a moment to connect this woman, knocking on sixty by the looks of it and dressed in a burnt-orange tracksuit, with the young tom he'd regularly arrested all those years ago. But Eddie's fleshy mouth gradually shifted into a smile. 'Hello, Sonia, love. Long time, no see.'

She didn't seem to have the same problem on the recognition front. 'Not long enough,' she replied smartly. 'Eddie Shepherd. What the fuck do *you* want?'

'Charming as ever. Aren't you going to invite me in?'

As if she'd rather take a walk through a glade of poisonous snakes, she glared at him. 'You got a warrant?'

'What would I want one of those for?' He shook his

81

head. 'I'm only here for a chat, love. About the break-in, across the way.'

'I've already given a statement.'

'And I've got some more questions.'

Sonia continued to glare for a few seconds longer but then, as if the effort of her contempt was too much to sustain, she released a lungful of air and reluctantly stood aside.

He brushed past her into the living room. It wasn't exactly spacious. The proportions of the flat were mean; the whole block had been cheaply squeezed into too small a space and it showed. The flamboyant flowery wallpaper, a riot of unnaturally large blossoms, brought the walls even closer. He felt like he was being drowned in petals.

'I suppose you want a brew,' she grumbled.

'Two sugars,' he said.

He settled himself down into the nearest chair, glad to take the weight off his feet. While she fussed in the kitchen, her tea-making accompanied by a series of soft disgruntled noises, he watched her through the open archway. He flicked his cigarette towards an overflowing ashtray. She'd got older, all right, older and a damn sight wider. Fuck, if he'd passed her in the street, he wouldn't have known her.

She came back and dumped a mug on the small cracked table by his elbow.

'You haven't changed,' he said.

Sonia slumped down on the sofa. 'And you're still the same lying bastard you always were.'

He sniggered. 'It's been a while. What have you been up to?'

'I thought you were here to talk about the break-in.'

'I am,' he said. He cocked his head and stared at her. 'Thing is, Sonia, I've got a little problem . . .'

She scowled suspiciously at him. 'Oh yeah?'

'Yeah. One of those problems that keeps nagging away. You know the sort? I just keep wondering what exactly *you* were doing yesterday.'

Abruptly, she shifted forward. 'What?' Her chin jerked up, an angry pink flush invading her cheeks. 'Oh, that's your bloody game, is it, trying to pin it on me? You think I've started breaking into other people's homes? You must be bloody desperate! Alex Weston was my *friend*. You really think I smashed down his door and wrecked the place?' She stopped to scrabble for a cigarette, her hand shaking with indignation. 'I was out, *out*. I didn't get back until going on four . . . For God's sake, *I* was the one who rang you.'

Eddie calmly sipped his tea while she vented her fury. That was one thing that hadn't changed about her. Sonia Marshall was still as loud and bloody-minded as ever. She'd be pleading her innocence if she was caught standing over a corpse with a knife in her hand. Not that he thought she was guilty, not of this at least, but he was pretty sure that she knew more than she was letting on.

He gazed around nonchalantly. 'Your Peter not here then?'

'No.'

'You know where he is, sweetheart?'

She glowered. 'Ten feet under for all I care.'

'What are you saying?'

'You're the bloody copper, you work it out.'

'He's moved out then?'

She curled back against the sofa. 'Got it in one, Mr Shepherd. I haven't seen him for over a year.'

Eddie glanced around but there was no evidence to refute the statement. A bottle of vodka on the sideboard but that was probably hers. And no man, in his right mind, could possibly live with *that* wallpaper. 'You got an address?'

'I've told you. We're separated.'

'And you never talk?'

She shrugged. 'We've a kid, grandkids. Course we talk.'

'But you don't know his address?'

'No, I don't know his address. I don't have a bloody clue. You think he'd bother telling me?' She pulled her brows into a frown. 'Find some poor sad cow who doesn't know any better and you'll find him in her bed.'

Eddie grinned. 'Did you tell him about Alex Weston?'

'Why would I want to do that?'

'Just asking,' he said.

She directed that full-on glare at him again. 'Well, ask away. I don't care what you think. This has *nothing* to do with me. You just try and prove otherwise. And nothing to do with Peter either. I've told you – he's not around.'

He nodded, rising slowly to his feet. 'Okay, no need to blow a gasket. Where's the bog?'

'Over there,' she said, waving a hand. She managed to restrain herself until he reached the door. 'What's the matter, Eddie? The old prostate playing you up?'

As it happened, she wasn't far wrong. He was pissing for Britain these days. Although that wasn't the only reason he wanted to go to the bathroom. After he'd flushed and zipped up, he opened the cabinet and swiftly rummaged through the contents: women's deodorant, perfume, and a ton of fuck-knows-what. He fought a path through the cosmetics. There was a good supply of tranks as well, a bottle of aspirin, even some disposable razors – but nothing specifically male. If Peter Marshall had been living here, he'd been pretty efficient at covering his tracks.

He went back into the living room and sat down heavily in the chair.

'Feeling better?' she mocked.

Taking a notebook from his pocket, he flicked through the pages for a minute or two. Then he looked up and gave a small unpleasant smile. 'So, how are you keeping the wolf from the door these days, Sonia?' He presumed she wasn't still turning tricks; even the sex-starved punters of Norwich couldn't be *that* desperate.

'What's it to you?' she snapped defensively.

He waited, tapping the thick fingers of his hand against his thigh.

She held out for a few seconds but eventually, sulkily, admitted, 'I've got a job, haven't I? Part-time. At the cash 'n' carry down the road. There's where I was yesterday – working. I told that other one, your mate, *blondie*. Check it out if you don't believe me.'

Eddie scribbled a note in his book. 'Does Peter still have a key to this place?'

'You think I'm stupid?'

'He could have come round when you were out.'

She barked out a laugh. 'What, and broken in next door and taken sod all? The day he walks off with his pockets empty they'll declare a national bloody holiday.'

Eddie couldn't dispute that. But he still had a few avenues to explore. 'Who said nothing was taken?'

Caught off guard, Sonia's black-rimmed eyes widened a fraction. 'What do you mean?'

'Perhaps they took something that you don't know about.'

She stopped to think about it. 'Like what?' Then, as if she guessed he was only on a fishing expedition, she abruptly waved the suggestion away. 'No, they couldn't. Alex had nothing worth nicking. He was broke, never had two pennies to rub together.'

'He liked to gamble, didn't he? Maybe he got lucky.'

Sonia wasn't having any of it. 'Yeah, right. Lucky enough to go throw himself in the river.'

Eddie nodded. She had a point. In all likelihood he was wasting his time – even if she did know anything she wouldn't dream of sharing it – but he was reluctant to leave. At least it was warm and dry in here. He might as well stay until the rain eased off.

'So tell me where you think I might find Peter.'

But Sonia's well of cooperation, never overflowing at best, had just run dry. In a gesture that might have been down to impatience or anger, she stubbed her half-smoked cigarette out in a saucer. 'Look, what's going on here? What's with all the questions, the bloody inter-rogation? You lot can't usually be arsed to turn up at a break-in, never mind come back for seconds.'

Her mouth clamped into a tight thin line and Eddie knew that his interview was over. He could carry on pushing but it wouldn't be worth the effort. Never mind, it wouldn't take him long to find Marshall. He was a man of regular habits and limited imagination; if he wasn't in the bookie's, he'd be in the pub.

By the door he turned and took her chin in his hand. Leaning forward, close enough to kiss her, he whispered his stale breath into her face. 'If I find out you've been lying to me, Sonia, I'll have you fucking hung, drawn and quartered.'

Chapter Six

Henry's letter was sitting on her father's desk. As too was Sonia, her backside perched on the edge as she passed her the books one by one. While they talked, Eve dutifully placed them on the shelves, distractedly shuffling them into alphabetical order.

'What do you think he wanted?'

'Nothing good,' Sonia said. 'That Eddie Shepherd's a piece of shit. Believe me, love, whatever he's after, it's nothing to do with victim support.'

'And he came round yesterday?'

'I tried to let you know.' There was an edge of huffiness to her voice. 'I knocked on the door but you were out.'

Eve smiled guiltily. It was true: she *had* tried, about five times if she recalled correctly. And she hadn't actually been out at all, just curled up on the sofa with a bottle of red wine, two sealed boxes at her feet, and a desperate yearning to be alone. She'd even turned off the lights. After Barry and Paula she'd had enough company for the day. 'Yeah, sorry. I got back late.'

Sonia thrust a copy of William Blake's poetry into her hands. She placed it on the top shelf, to the left of Cicero.

'Did he ask about me?'

'No. He asked about your dad though.'

Eve wasn't sure if that was good or bad. Probably the latter the way her luck was going. Her eyes strayed again towards those invisible words of Henry's enclosed within the starched white envelope: *He claimed it was an ongoing investigation*. She still hadn't told Sonia that Shepherd was the same cop who'd been making inquiries about her in London. It was all just too weird – and too worrying.

'What did you tell him?'

'What do you think?' Sonia said, grinning. 'Fuck all.' She paused to lift her cigarette to her lips before passing her a paperback copy of *A Bend in the River*.

Eve glanced uncertainly at the cover: V.S. Naipaul. She slid him in after Lawrence and before Virginia Woolf. Then she looked back at Sonia again. 'I still don't get it. Who is this guy? Why's he so interested?'

Sonia's mouth puckered into disgust. 'He's the filth, love. He doesn't need a reason.'

But Eve wasn't convinced. In her experience, every cop, good or bad, had a reason for what he did. Not always a good one, or a moral one, but a reason nonetheless. So what was Eddie Shepherd's?

They were quiet for a while as she continued to line up the books: Henry James, Simenon, Oscar Wilde. Her fingers groped along the shelves, nudging, separating, creating spaces. Why she was even doing this was a mystery to her. It didn't matter where they went. Her father wasn't here to see them, or to read them, any more. It was just some crazy way of holding on to him, of continuing to cling to some precarious sense of order.

When they were done, when every last book had been returned to its rightful place, she stared back down at the letter again. She had no choice: she had to ring Henry. She had to hear from his lips exactly what Shepherd had said. Something bad, something nasty, was snapping at her heels – and she was going to go mad if she didn't find out what it was.

She checked her watch. It was almost four o'clock, Friday afternoon. Henry would still be there; he never rushed home for the weekend. But how was she going to get through to him? All lines went through the main switchboard and she had no doubt that Richard would have given instructions for Henry's calls to be carefully monitored. In fact he probably had her picture taped to the wall with a reward sign on it. Even if she managed to bluff her way past the practised ears of the SS receptionist, she still had the new secretary to deal with; Dickie's secret army would be on red alert and the last thing she wanted was to cause Henry more grief.

She had to find a means of contacting him that wouldn't arouse suspicion, and the only way to do that was to bring in reinforcements. Sadly, those were thin on the ground, although there was one person who might be willing to help. She picked up the envelope and held it against her chin.

'Sonia, could you do me a favour?'

Eve hadn't needed to go into detail. No sooner had she begun to explain than Sonia, presuming this was to do with some doomed love affair, had swiftly interrupted. 'Married, is he?'

'It's kind of complicated.'

'It always is, love,' she'd sighed. 'And none of them are worth the effort.'

But she'd agreed to help her out. They stood shoulder-to-shoulder as the phone rang at the other end.

'Baxter & Baxter,' a cool female voice announced.

'Henry Baxter, please.'

'May I ask who's calling?'

'Mrs Lennox.'

There was a short pause. 'Mrs Lennox?'

Eve could almost feel suspicion leaking down the line. She held her breath and prayed that the witch wasn't going to embark on a lengthy cross-examination. She couldn't possibly know the names of all Henry's clients.

'He's expecting my call,' Sonia insisted sternly. There was an edge of authority to her voice that Eve hadn't heard before.

It seemed to have the desired effect.

'Just one moment,' she said. 'I'll put you through.'

But not straight through. The line went on hold while Vivaldi graced the airwaves. They glanced at each other, both raising their eyebrows. Just as Eve was starting to wonder if the receptionist was already conveying to Richard her pathetic attempt to circumvent Baxter security, the music abruptly cut out.

'Mr Baxter's office,' a smaller and much less confident voice declared.

'Henry Baxter,' Sonia requested yet again.

'I'm afraid Mr Baxter's just gone in to a meeting,' the girl said, in a tone so sorrowful that she might have been relaying his recent death. 'Could I take a message?'

Eve quickly shook her head. If it was one of Richard's tedious meetings, Henry could be stuck in it for hours.

'No, I'm afraid it's rather urgent. Tell him it's Mrs Lennox.' Sonia paused and then repeated emphatically, '*Lennox.*'

The girl hesitated. 'I'm not sure if—'

'He's expecting my call.'

'Oh, but . . .' the girl dithered again.

Sonia, sensing weakness, put her foot down. 'It *is* after four o'clock, isn't it? *After* four o'clock was when Mr Baxter specifically asked me to call.'

Henry's new secretary went quiet. Then, as if her limited repertoire of excuses had been exhausted, she gave a small fragile sigh. 'All right. I'll try him for you.'

Eve hoped that he'd guess who it was from the name. Terry Lennox was a character from *The Long Goodbye*, and Henry, like her father, knew his Raymond Chandler inside out.

There was another short delay, another burst of Vivaldi, before she heard the connecting click. 'Henry Baxter.'

With a smile of relief she took the phone from Sonia and held it tight against her ear. 'Henry, it's me.'

'Mrs Lennox,' he said politely. 'How nice to hear from you. How may I help?'

Eve got the message. 'I take it Richard's with you?'

'Indeed,' he replied briskly. 'I can see how that might make things difficult.'

Instantly she lowered her voice. 'Look, I have to talk to you about your letter. It's important. Can you ring me back later?'

'Yes, indeed. I think we are probably looking at about *six* thousand.'

'Six is fine,' she said. 'Thanks.'

'Very well.'

They said the customary goodbyes and hung up.

'Mrs Lennox?' Richard asked interrogatively, as soon as he'd replaced the receiver.

Henry nodded. Aware that he was still under his son's hypocritical surveillance, he kept his tone casual. 'You remember old Lennox, don't you? Nice chap, used to run the bookshop on King Street. Passed away a couple of months ago. A stroke, I believe, or was it . . .' He scratched his head as if trying to recall. 'You know, now I come to think of it, it may have been . . .'

But Richard's eyes were already starting to glaze over. He had no interest in his father's fusty clients, dead or alive. 'Yes, well, shall we get on? I'm sure we'd all like to leave before the weekend's over.'

As Henry dutifully resumed his seat, there was nothing in his manner to suggest that the phone call was anything but a routine inquiry from a grieving widow. Had anyone taken the trouble to look closely, however, they would have noticed a small smile tugging at the corners of his mouth.

As soon as Sonia had left, Eve pulled on her raincoat and grabbed her purse. She felt jumpy and anxious, frustrated by her brief conversation with Henry. With another two hours to wait for his return call, she'd go stir crazy if she stayed in the flat.

Out on the street, the air smelled of damp, of frying fish and exhaust fumes. She turned left and then left again, striding quickly up the alley towards the supermarket. She didn't care much for this bleak passageway but it was broad daylight and a few other women, laden with bulging carrier bags, were struggling back in the opposite direction.

As she walked, she thought about Henry. She thought about his amber eyes and the way he always listened to her, intent, his head tilted slightly to one side. No one, not even her father, had listened the way he had. Perhaps she shouldn't have called him. Hadn't she done enough damage? His wife and son already thought he was an adulterer. Not that she gave a damn what Dickie thought – he'd spent the last decade cheating on his own wife – but Celia was a different matter altogether. It had never been Eve's intention to cause *her* any grief.

But she had to know what Shepherd had said.

One last phone call. Surely that couldn't do any harm?

In a couple of minutes she emerged into the busy car

park and crossed the forecourt towards the low brick building. She passed through the automatic sliding doors. Inside, it was teeming with shoppers. She frowned, remembering too late that Friday afternoon wasn't the smartest time in the world to buy groceries. Still, what did it matter? She was better off standing in a queue than pacing the floor of the flat. At least she was doing something useful.

Negotiating a path through the crowded aisles, she picked up apples, oranges, onions and mushrooms and dropped them into her basket. Milk and tea bags followed. She added pasta, tinned tomatoes and a couple of chicken breasts. Then she ran out of inspiration. What else? She should have made a list. Her culinary skills, as Patrick had never jokingly failed to remind her, left a lot to be desired. They had lived off sandwiches and takeaways for the two years they'd been together. A domestic goddess she was not. Then again, his frequent inability to find his way home hardly made him the perfect husband either.

Eve found her lips sliding into a smile. Why was she thinking of Patrick? It was years since she'd last seen him. They'd had some good times – some *very* good times – but they were in the past.

She wandered down the next aisle, following a young fraught-looking woman with two toddlers and a baby. Perhaps, if things had been different, she and Patrick might have made a go of it, had some kids of their own. She glanced down tenderly towards the two little blond boys in front of her. Appropriately, they chose that moment to screw their tiny faces into deep red rage and to scream as loudly as the devil.

Any sentimental notions about the idylls of family life were instantly extinguished.

Eve headed for the wine.

She checked her watch as she left the building – ten

past five. Only another fifty minutes to go. The rain had started to fall again. She scowled at the sky, pulled the hood up on her coat, hefted the two carrier bags into a more comfortable position, and crossed the car park.

This time she didn't think twice about using the alley.

She was about a third of the way in, her head bowed towards the ground, when she heard the footsteps approaching from behind. She half-turned, more curious than concerned, to glance over her shoulder and then . . .

He was on her before she knew it. Her face was up against the wall, her forehead scraping the stone. There was only blind panic. She couldn't breathe. She felt the air rushing from her lungs, her legs giving way. She opened her mouth to scream, and a hand closed firmly over her jaw. A body was crushing her, heavy and violent. She struggled but her left arm was twisted behind her back, pulled up so tight that she thought she might pass out. From somewhere distant came the sound of breaking glass.

Rape was what she dreaded most as hot breath invaded her neck. She could hear the grunt in the back of his throat, the purpose as he shifted his weight against hers. *Please God*, she silently begged. There was a vile smell; sweat, stale beer, tobacco. It's still daylight, she thought pointlessly, while a tiny voice kept repeating, *No, no*.

Her heart thundered in her chest, a beat so explosive she was sure the world must hear it. But no one came. She was alone. All she could see was the old chipped brick of the wall, the crumbling mortar and the line of dark hair that ran along the rim of his thick clammy hand. Bile rose from her stomach. She fought to keep it down. She found herself thinking of Patrick again, of her father, a slow-motion reel of images that ran weirdly in tandem with the sharp bitter fear.

She made another futile attempt to free herself, to bite

94

against his flesh, but he pressed against her harder. 'Bitch!' he swore softly. His stinking palm clamped more forcefully against her lips. He jolted her head back, just far enough to let her know how easily he could break her neck.

Eve stopped resisting. She closed her eyes and prayed again.

And then, just as she was sure that what would follow was inevitable, a vicious voice whispered in her ear: 'Don't mess us about, Evie. Joe wants it back. You understand? He wants it fucking back.'

He twisted her arm another brutal inch. 'You understand?'

Hot pain scorched from her elbow to her shoulder. This was not the time to get into a discussion. She grunted her acknowledgement into the palm of his hand.

'Don't let us down,' he said.

He let go so abruptly that her knees buckled and she fell towards the ground. He was considerate enough to provide a final push to help her on her way. As she sprawled in the dirt, she heard his steady tread retreating down the alley.

Fury battled against relief. Slowly moving her head, Eve shook the dust from her eyes and tried to get a look at him. The light was poor and all she could see was a broad silhouette, a thickset goon strolling away without a care in the world.

She glanced in the other direction. For a moment she was sure she saw a tall thin man standing at the other end, just standing there and watching. *Thanks, mate*, she murmured resentfully. But when she blinked her eyes again he was gone. Perhaps he had only been a figment of her imagination.

Eve felt groggy, sick, as she cautiously pulled herself to her feet, using the wall as leverage. It took her a while to get upright again. Her heart was still pounding, the fear still coursing through her veins. She rubbed at her arm. It hurt like hell. She couldn't remember releasing the bags but they were both lying at her feet, one of them split, the shattered contents of a wine bottle staining the surrounding litter red.

'Are you all right, love?' a voice behind her asked.

She jumped, the adrenalin kicking in again. But it was only an elderly lady, a frail woman dragging her shopping trolley behind her. Eve managed to dredge up a smile. 'I'm okay. I just tripped over.'

Her rheumy eyes screwed up in concern. 'Are you sure?'

Eve did need help, needed it badly, but she shook her head. The kind of assistance she required had little to do with a heap of spilled shopping. 'No, I'm okay,' she repeated, dropping quickly back on to her hands and knees. She started to frantically gather up the groceries, throwing them into the remaining bag.

The woman lingered, solemnly staring at her, before she slowly trundled off down the alley.

'Thank you,' Eve called out belatedly, when she was a few yards away. The old lady didn't look back. Perhaps she was deaf or more likely just glad to get away. The smell of red wine was pungent.

Stumbling towards the flat, half of her head remained in a daze. The other half maintained a scary clarity. She had thought she was going to be raped, killed . . . her mouth dried at the memory. But instead it had been a threat, a warning, a piece of less-than-friendly advice to return something that she didn't even have.

Or did she?

There was only one thing she could think of – there must be something in those boxes of Cavelli's. Something that someone desperately wanted, something that . . .

Damn him!

Eve pushed through the glass entrance and hurried up the stairs. She ran along the corridor. After unlocking the door, she rushed inside, slammed it shut and shot across the three solid bolts. Then she leaned against it, her legs starting to shake again. The carrier bag slipped out of her fingers. For a while she stood there, trembling, waiting for her breath to steady.

Joe wants it back.

Who was Joe? She didn't know any Joe!

She raised a hand and swept her hair off her face. It felt damp, disgusting. It smelled of *him*. Her whole body stank of him, rank, disgusting. Nausea rose from her stomach, making her want to gag. Placing her hands against the frame, she took a moment to steady herself, to take a series of long deep breaths before she thrust herself forward towards the kitchen. She found the brandy, poured herself a stiff one and knocked it back in one fast gulp.

Slumping down into a chair, Eve refilled her glass and glanced at her watch: it seemed like hours had passed but it wasn't even half past five. Her left arm still ached, a dull persistent throb.

She'd just been assaulted. What was she doing? Anyone sensible, with nothing to hide, would be straight on to the cops. But that wasn't her. If she rang, there'd be questions, awkward questions, and they'd eventually lead back to Martin Cavelli. And if she told them about how they'd met, about their deal, then it would all be finished . . . and Terry might be finished too.

Eve rubbed at her arm. She couldn't take that chance.

She stood up, still holding the glass, then put it down beside the phone, went through to the bathroom and turned on the shower. Quickly, she stripped off her clothes and stepped under the hot water. For a long while she scrubbed and lathered, trying to clean off her attacker's smell, the sense of his touch, to purge her flesh and hair of any vile residue. Finally, when the only scent was of shampoo and soap, she grabbed a towel and wrapped it around herself. After a further three minutes of steady tooth brushing, she began to feel almost human again.

She picked up her watch from the side of the basin. Ten to six. Eve looked in the mirror; her face and shoulders were a uniform shade of shrimp pink. The only remaining physical evidence lay in the light graze on her forehead and the ache in her arm.

Clean enough, she decided, although just for good measure she washed her hands again.

Walking through to her father's bedroom, she stared at the boxes. One large, one small, they were stacked beside the wardrobe. She should open them. All she needed was a sharp knife. But still she hesitated. What if she found something she didn't want to find? Not to mention that the minute she cut through the tape, her deal with Cavelli would be well and truly severed.

She took a step back.

No, she had to talk to him first. Maybe she should call the prison and leave a message . . . but no, that wasn't a good idea either. Even if he did ring back she could hardly start asking him *those* sorts of questions. A percentage of conversations were routinely recorded by the prison authorities and he wouldn't be too happy if she put him on the spot. And anyway, who was to say that *her* line wasn't being tapped? After the break-in, the letter, after what had just happened, anything and everything seemed possible.

She frowned. Maybe paranoia was setting in. But the connection had to be Cavelli. There was no other explanation. None of this crazy stuff had been going on before she met him. She had to see him on a visit, to speak face to face.

The phone rang, cutting sharply across her thoughts. She turned back to the living room, hurried across to the table, and picked up the receiver.

'Eve?'

It was Henry. She was so glad to hear his voice that she exhaled an audible sigh of relief. She breathed in again, trying to keep her own voice natural and steady. 'Hey, how are you? Sorry about earlier. I hope it didn't cause any problems.'

'Don't worry. Richard had other things on his mind. He was too busy trying to force me into premature retirement.' He gave a small mirthless laugh. 'If he has his way, I'll be pensioned off, evicted from the office and exiled to Spain by Christmas.'

'There are worse fates,' she said.

He paused. 'What's wrong?'

She had meant to stay calm, composed, but it all came out in a tumbling rush. 'You know what's wrong. The letter. *Your* letter. All this *investigation* stuff. I don't understand what's going on. Why were the police at your office? What did this Shepherd guy want? Do you know what he wanted?'

'I told you in the letter,' he replied gently. 'He just turned up. I presumed it was down to Richard – you know what he's like – that he'd rung them, made some kind of a complaint but . . .'

'But?'

'Well, now I'm not so certain. Richard was more than happy to talk but I don't think that he called them in. I don't think that was Shepherd's reason for coming here. To be honest, I'm not even sure if Shepherd himself actually knew what he was after.'

'What do you mean?'

'Just that. He wasn't specific. He wouldn't tell me what he wanted – but he *was* asking about you and me, digging, suggesting that we were . . .'

Eve winced down the phone. 'What's that got to do with the cops?'

'I asked the same question.'

She reached for the brandy and took a gulp. 'Even if it was true, it's not a criminal offence. How can it have anything to do with an ongoing investigation?'

'God knows. But it's like I told you, he wasn't forthcoming.'

'I don't get it. He's a local cop. He's from round here. Why would he travel all the way down to London from Norwich to make some inquiries about whether we might be more than good friends? It doesn't make sense.'

'It doesn't,' he agreed.

She had hoped he might say something reassuring like *It's probably nothing* or *I wouldn't worry too much* but Henry wasn't one for offering false comforts.

'First there was the police, then the break-in, and now . . .' She stopped abruptly, staring into her glass. She hadn't meant to mention the break-in, never mind what had happened in the alley.

He sounded alarmed. 'What break-in? What's been going on?'

She didn't reply.

'Eve?'

And then it occurred to her, a quick and disturbing thought. The goon had called her *Evie*. He had. She was sure he had. *Don't mess us about, Evie.* She shuddered, feeling his damp filthy hand against her mouth again. Who else called her that? Not her friends. Not even Henry. Only her father, Terry, Patrick, and . . . Martin Cavelli.

She hugged the receiver closer to her ear. 'Henry,' she whispered, 'I think I'm in trouble.'

*   *   *

Ivor Patterson wondered if he was getting too old for the job. It was a young man's game, standing around in the cold and the rain, waiting for the rheumatism to creep into your bones. And for what? For bloody peanuts was what. He turned up the collar of his coat and headed for the café across the road.

He was becoming a regular, always choosing a table by the window where he could keep an eye on the door to the flats. Ordering a coffee he settled down on the torn red vinyl bench. She had gone inside a while ago and he doubted if she'd be going out again tonight.

Not after what had happened.

He hadn't followed her to the supermarket. The passage was too narrow, too confined, for him to get close; most people glanced over their shoulders when they heard footsteps behind. Four times before he'd waited until she'd passed out of sight, before dashing in behind, catching her up, and trailing her across the car park to the store. Today, he'd decided that it wasn't worth the effort just to watch her buy a pint of milk.

He'd been waiting in the car, reading a paper with the window open. The street was more or less deserted. In the previous minutes only a handful of shoppers had emerged from the passage and a trio of shifty-looking kids.

It was the sound of breaking glass that alerted him. He'd moved quickly, hauling his arse across to the entrance of the alley, in time to catch the end of the incident. He'd watched her sinking to the ground, hands outstretched to break her fall. He had seen the heavy man retreating.

Ivor had hesitated, waiting to see if she got up again, assessing the damage before committing himself. She had slowly turned her head in his direction, maybe spotted him, but it was doubtful that she got a clear view.

He was only in her line of vision for a few seconds before he moved out of sight.

Did he feel guilty? Not really. It was only his duty to watch her, not protect her. He didn't get paid for playing the hero. And anyway, she didn't seem so much hurt as shaken up. By the time he had realized what was going on, it was too late to intervene, to make a difference. And it was hardly worth blowing his cover so he could help her pick the shopping up.

Ivor sipped his coffee. There were dull jobs and there were *very* dull jobs; this one, on the whole, had fallen into the latter category. Although having said that, there were worse people to tail than tall leggy redheads with their curves in all the right places.

He reached into his pocket and pulled out a small black book. A divorce case he'd presumed, when he'd started the surveillance, although the office hadn't been specific. Probably a husband looking for evidence of adultery. Perhaps it was the spouse she was going to visit at the jail; he'd followed her there twice.

By now he knew all the residents of Herbert Court, not just by sight but by name as well. He had searched through the mail, dumped into the rusting post boxes in the foyer, and taken note of all the details. There were only six flats. The ground floor was occupied by oldies, a Mr and Mrs Thorne and a Mrs Leonard, the first floor by a mousy pair called the Taylors and a single middle-aged man, Jeremy Smith, with a penchant for blonde brassy tarts who he frequently brought home. The top floor, and the only one he was really interested in, housed Sonia Marshall and Eve Weston.

Ivor flipped back through the pages. Today was Friday. Until the break-in on Wednesday, until the cops had arrived, there hadn't been much to report. Apart from her trips to HMP Hillgrove, Ms Weston had kept herself to herself: a few brief walks into town, some window shopping, nothing of interest. If she *was* playing away then she was being bloody discreet . . . unless the person she was cheating with happened to be a glamorous brunette with a very flashy sports car.

He shifted in his seat, trying not to focus too hard on that uplifting scenario . . .

Something less appealing was nagging at his thoughts. He sank his face into his coffee again. On her second journey to the jail he hadn't gone the full distance; as soon as he'd realized where she was headed he'd turned around and come straight back. No point wasting petrol. Finances were tight. He had debts, bills to pay – and he could add what he hadn't spent to his expense account.

Which was how he'd come to see what he'd seen – a stranger entering and later leaving Herbert Court, the man who must have broken in. *The same man, he'd swear, who'd assaulted her today.* The very same man he had captured with five consecutive shots on his digital camera. This time he hadn't got a look at his face but it hadn't been necessary. Even from a distance, he was distinctive: tall but heavily built, laden with blubber, his walk splay-legged.

He chewed on the edge of a ragged fingernail. Maybe there was more than one person interested in Eve Weston. If her spouse had arranged for her to be followed, he'd have to be a fool to have her publicly threatened too; he'd know there was a witness watching from the wings. So it was possible this had nothing to do with divorce at all. Perhaps Eve Weston was being pursued for other reasons.

Was she hiding out, on the run, involved in something dodgy? Either way, for a good-looking woman she was keeping a remarkably low profile. Her social life was worse than his. The office had been vague, too vague now he came to think of it, his only instruction to record her movements and the people she met. It could be worth a little extra digging. If he played his cards right, there could be a bonus to be had, a way to make some easy cash on the side.

All information had its price.

It was knocking on seven. He looked up towards the second-floor windows where a thin gleam of light was visible. It was doubtful she'd be going out again. Anyway, his relief would be turning up soon, that lazy bastard Charlie May who'd buy his supper from the Chinese takeaway, smoke twenty fags, and then fall asleep before the last of the drunks had even staggered home. If his own reports contained an element of fabrication, they were nothing compared to May's; he should be up for the Nobel prize for fucking fiction.

Ivor had a choice. When Charlie arrived he could either go home and put his feet up or start touring some of the less desirable pubs. It shouldn't take him long to find her assailant; with two visits in three days, he was most likely local, a thick-brained and familiar heavy hired to do the dirty work. A few greased palms and he'd have his name before last orders were called.

But was it worth the bother?

A quiet evening in front of the TV with a few beers and a curry was calling out to him. He was tired, filled with that kind of dull fatigue that comes from doing nothing much. Was there any point in wasting the rest of the evening? For all his suspicions, this could easily be a dead end, a mundane case of jealousy, of revenge, of payback from an angry and disappointed husband.

A night in or out?

Ivor scratched his head, finished his coffee, stood up and walked out of the café. Standing on the street, he stared up at a darkening pink-striped sky and smiled.

Chapter Seven

Eve picked up the phone again. Henry's final words of advice were right: she had to face this head on or not at all. And 'not at all' meant packing her bags and running for the hills, an option that was hardly open to her while Terry was still in jail.

And why should she run? She had nothing to hide from . . . apart from her past.

Reluctantly, she dialled the mobile number and waited. While the phone rang, she nervously flipped the card between her fingers. One ring, two, three, four . . .

'Jack Raynor,' he eventually answered.

She hesitated.

'Hello?'

'It's Eve. Eve Weston.'

'Hi,' he said. 'How are you?'

'Fine, thanks.' She tried to sound fine. 'I was wondering if we could meet. There's something—'

'Sure,' he said. 'Are you free now?' He didn't wait for a reply but promptly added, 'Do you know The Drifting Swan, down by the river? I can be there in half an hour.'

Eve hadn't expected an instant appointment. She'd been thinking more along the lines of Monday, a few days' grace while she worked out her approach. She was tempted to try and postpone it but then changed her mind. That would only be cowardice. Better to bite the bullet and get it over and done with. 'Okay. I'll see you there.'

After ordering a cab, she went to the bathroom and brushed her teeth again. She cupped her hand over her mouth and sniffed, hoping her breath didn't still smell of brandy. Turning up stinking of alcohol would hardly create a favourable impression.

While she flicked through the wardrobe she wondered just what kind of an impression she was intending to make. *One of innocence*, she thought wryly, instantly dismissing any article of clothing that had even a hint of vamp about it. In the end she settled on a pair of black jeans and a simple stripy jumper, casual but not too coy. She didn't want to overplay it.

By the time she'd applied a discreet amount of make-up and pulled on a jacket, the cab had arrived.

Ten minutes later she was standing on the gravel forecourt.

Eve knew this place. She'd been here a few times with her father. Part pub, part restaurant, it served good but rather expensive food, and had a large conservatory at the rear where customers could sit and admire the river without the inconvenience of the cold and damp.

She took a moment to get her thoughts in order and then walked swiftly through the door.

Raynor was already waiting at the bar. He smiled as she came in and raised a hand.

She wasn't sure what caused that tiny jolt deep inside. It was hardly as if she'd forgotten what he looked like: with his high cheekbones and striking blue eyes, he was way too handsome for that. Perhaps the response was more to do with fear than attraction.

'Inspector,' she said.

'Jack,' he insisted. 'Please, call me Jack. It's good to see you again. Let me get you a drink.'

'Thanks. A dry white wine, please.'

He passed the request on to the barman.

While they waited, he turned and asked, 'So, have you managed to get it sorted?'

'Sorted?' she echoed faintly. What had happened this afternoon came back to haunt her, followed by an unwelcome image of Cavelli's two heavily taped and infinitely suspicious boxes. She felt a flurry of panic. How did he know about them, how did—

'The flat,' he said, filling the silence that her hesitation left. 'It was rather a mess when I left. It must have taken some clearing up.'

The flat. He was only talking about the flat. She nodded with relief. 'Oh, yes. Just about.'

'Got a new lock?'

Eve nodded again, thinking of Barry's two-ton fortification. 'You don't have to worry about that. I think the place is pretty secure now.'

'Good,' he said.

Her drink arrived. She tried not to grab at it.

'Shall we go through?' he said, gesturing towards the back.

She got a vague whiff of aftershave, a subtle but expensive aroma, as she walked beside him. He was taller than her, by a good four inches. Which made him about six foot two. The same height as Patrick. There was something about his mouth as well, that slightly lopsided smile. He was wearing a dark grey suit, nicely tailored, and a crisp white shirt unbuttoned at the neck. No tie. He had nice hands. She always noticed hands. His were fine and slender, long fingers with short clean nails. Not manicured, thank God. She couldn't stand men who spent *too* much time on personal grooming.

It was busy, a typical Friday night, but the waitress showed them to a prize table overlooking the water and produced a couple of menus before leaving.

'Are we going to eat?' she asked, surprised.

'Why not?' He lifted his eyebrows. 'Please don't tell me you're one of those fanatics who never lets a lettuce leaf pass their lips after six o'clock.'

She laughed. 'And what if I am?'

'Then I hope you'll take pity and break the rules – just this once. I'm in serious danger of starvation, no breakfast and no lunch, and I don't much care for eating alone. Please say you'll join me. You'll be doing me a favour.'

Eve glanced mock-solemnly down at the menu. The food on offer was mainly Thai and it all looked good. After her earlier nerves, hunger was kicking in. She took a sip of wine before raising her eyes to meet his again. 'Well, if it's for purely humanitarian reasons . . .'

His mouth curled into a smile. 'You're a kind and generous woman, Ms Weston.'

She didn't contradict him. This was starting to feel more like a date than a fateful appointment with destiny. Surely she couldn't be in too much trouble if Raynor was prepared to wine and dine her. Unless he was just lulling her into a false sense of security . . .

The waitress returned and they ordered a selection of dishes – ginger prawns, fish with tamarind sauce, spicy chicken, spring rolls, rice . . . Eve couldn't recall the last meal she'd had that hadn't been pasta or pizza. Probably weeks ago – her last lunch in London with Henry. And thinking of Henry served as a useful reminder of what she was actually supposed to be doing here.

She took a deep breath. 'You haven't asked why I wanted to talk to you.'

'Ah, yes. That. Well, I kind of assumed it was about the break-in, about how much progress we've made as regards your uninvited visitor.' He paused, his lips sliding into a grimace. 'I'm sorry, but there's not a great deal to report. We don't have much to go on.'

'You could have told me that over the phone.'

'You said you wanted to meet.'

Eve kept her tone light as her grey eyes widened. 'Meet, yes, but I didn't expect to be wined and dined as well. Do you invite all your victims of crime to dinner?'

He put his elbows on the table and leaned forward a fraction. 'Actually it's a new police initiative, still in its early days. It works on the premise that if we're too stupid to solve a crime we can at least offer the solace of a decent meal to our disappointed public.'

'The Police Initiative for Gluttony,' she quipped. 'Nice acronym.'

He laughed. 'If I didn't know better, I might suspect a hint of scepticism.'

Eve noted the seductive contours of his mouth. She also noticed that he had that kind of skin that wasn't quite olive but close to it, a shade of pale honey that would never suffer, unlike hers, from the horrors of winter pallor.

When the food arrived, twenty minutes later, she realized that neither of them had made the slightest attempt to readdress the original question of why she'd called. Her excuse was simple: she didn't want to face the music before she had to. But what was his? Was he deliberately avoiding the issue or treating this as a purely social encounter? If the latter was true, she wasn't quite sure how she felt about it. Jack Raynor was amusing, good-looking – no, more than that, almost dangerously attractive – but he was also, first and foremost, a cop.

And the Westons and the Law had a less than happy history.

The steaming dishes descended on the table, accompanied by a glorious smell of herbs and spices. She sat back, placed her napkin politely in her lap, and tried to recall her table manners.

It seemed a shame to spoil the moment with her nagging anxieties. Perhaps, for the duration of the meal, she could consign them to the back of her mind. It was a while since she'd been treated to a candlelit dinner, even longer since she'd actually fancied the man she was sharing it with. But then again it was hard to appreciate even the most harmonious of flavours when the world might be about to come crashing down around you . . .

The words spilled out before she could contain them. 'So, is it also part of this new initiative to treat your suspects to a final supper?'

He stared at her. 'Suspects?'

To give him his due, he looked suitably bewildered. Not that that necessarily meant much. Cops came in all shapes and sizes, and with varying degrees of intelligence, but they all had the same unwavering ability to lie through their teeth.

'Isn't that what I am?' She put down her fork.

He shook his head. 'I don't understand.'

'I don't understand either,' she said, glancing regretfully at the dishes in front of her. 'I don't understand why a local officer has been making inquiries about me in London.'

'Has he?'

She sighed. 'A sergeant called Shepherd. I presume you know him.'

'Eddie? Sure. What's it about?'

'I was hoping *you* might be able to answer that. It's why I wanted to talk. He visited my ex-employer, Henry Baxter, told him it was part of an ongoing investigation.'

'That could cover a multitude of sins.'

Which was exactly what Eve didn't want to hear. She had hoped to keep *her* multitudinous sins firmly in the past. 'For instance?'

He frowned. 'Hard to say. What do you feel most guilty about?'

'I don't feel guilty about . . .' she began, before she

110

noticed the smile creeping on to those sensual lips again. She forced herself to smile back. He clearly wasn't taking this too seriously. Perhaps she should lighten up too. 'Ah, so this is how you squeeze out all those reluctant confessions.'

'Just think of me as a priest,' he said. 'Nothing you tell me will go further than the Chief Constable.'

'Thanks. That puts my mind at rest.' Eve picked up her fork again and speared a tiny cube of spicy chicken. She drew it towards her mouth and paused. 'So are you saying that you don't have a clue as to why I'm being investigated?'

'I doubt if you are. Not in any serious sense of the word.'

She lowered the morsel back on to the plate. 'What about in a frivolous sense of the word?'

'That's possible,' he agreed. 'Is your road tax up to date?'

Eve gave him a long cool look.

'Sorry,' he said. 'I'm sure it's nothing serious. How could it be?'

But that was a place she didn't want to go. She racked her brains for anyone who might have a recent grudge against her. Over the past seven months, since meeting Henry, her life had been relatively spotless. There was Richard of course. Maybe it was down to him. Although Henry didn't seem to think so – and if there was one person's judgement she could rely on, it was his. And before that . . . well, there *was* that guy she'd met in Bloomsbury – Donal was it, or Donald? They'd only been together a few days. And okay, so it hadn't been the nicest thing, to load up on the duty frees (courtesy of his very generous credit card) and then desert him in the airport lounge. But then it wasn't very loving for him to go cheating on his wife either. If he *had* made a complaint, he'd have a whole lot of explaining to do.

'How could it?' Raynor asked again.

Eve gazed into his piercing blue eyes. 'I'm just concerned. Wouldn't you be?'

He shook his head. 'No. Not unless I'd been doing something I shouldn't.'

'I haven't,' she insisted. To soften the impact of what she was about to ask next, she quickly smiled. 'And no offence, Inspector, but since when has doing nothing stopped the police from jumping to conclusions?'

In a perfect shrug, Raynor lifted those beautifully tailored shoulders of his again. 'Not me,' he said. 'I'm not that kind of copper.'

He took another mouthful of food. Their exchange clearly wasn't affecting his appetite. Even as they were talking, he continued to graze the dishes, tidily filling his stomach. She watched him closely. He chewed with his mouth shut, another tick in the box of those endless criteria that women demand of prospective partners. As soon as that thought crossed her mind, she flinched. What was she thinking? This man wasn't boyfriend material. He wasn't even *friend* material.

She placed her elbows on the table. 'Your sergeant came to see my neighbour yesterday. He was asking about the break-in.'

That, it seemed, was news to Raynor. He stopped eating. 'Did he?' It was followed by a short deliberative pause. 'Well, that's purely routine. And by the way, he's not *my* sergeant, he's just *a* sergeant. Gorgeous as he is, we're not permanently attached at the hip. If it makes you feel any better, I'll check out the London situation when I'm back in the office.'

'Why should you do me any favours?' she asked.

'You think I've got an ulterior motive?'

'Have you?'

'Yes,' he said, staring directly back. 'I have.' His

mouth curled into that wondrous smile again. 'I'd like you to enjoy your meal and stop worrying.'

Which was easier said than done. However, Eve nodded and pretended to relax. She nibbled at the food in front of her. She still couldn't make sense of Shepherd's visit to Henry but it was best, surely, to stop going on about it. If Raynor was lying to her, the smartest response was to play it cool. She had nothing to feel guilty about. Well . . .

For a while everything ran smoothly. Jack Raynor was charming company, the kind of man who talked but who had the good grace to listen too. The conversation flowed, along with the wine. And perhaps her suspicions about him, about his motives, created an additional frisson of interest. She always liked a challenge.

They had almost cleared their plates when her resolve to stay cool came under renewed pressure.

He peered at her across the table. 'Please don't take this the wrong way but what on earth happened to your face?'

She raised a hand to almost touch the graze above her right eye. Before leaving she'd covered it with a fine layer of make-up but her attempts at concealment must be wearing off. 'What, this?' she replied, dismissively, as if it were perfectly normal for any woman to sport the occasional bruise on her forehead. 'It's nothing. Just got a bit careless when I was clearing up – had a brief and unfulfilling argument with one of the kitchen cupboards.'

Even as she was explaining, Eve inwardly winced. *Kitchen cupboards?* Couldn't she have come up with something more original than that? She sounded like one of those desperate housewives trying to cover for a violent husband. But, hell, she could hardly be expected to think on her feet after the kind of day she'd had.

Raynor's brow scrunched into a frown. 'Looks like quite a bump from where I'm sitting.'

This time she actually touched her forehead. It was true there was a swelling there, a definite lump. There was a stinging too as her fingers pressed tentatively down. She was suddenly reminded of the afternoon, of the brute in the alley, of his sweaty palm pressing hard against her mouth. Quickly, she tried to blank it from her mind.

'There's no need to look so worried. What's the matter – you think someone's been bashing me around?'

He held her gaze for a few long seconds. Then he grinned. 'Hey, it's not you I'm worried about. I'm more concerned about what state that cupboard might be in.'

She forced a laugh. 'If it makes you feel any better, you could always invite it out to dinner.'

It was after eleven when Eve got home. Throwing her jacket over the back of a chair, she wandered over to the window and looked down on the street. The cab was just moving off. Raynor must have asked the driver to wait until he'd seen the lights go on in the flat. Old-fashioned courtesy or for a more disturbing reason? Perhaps he knew more than he was letting on. Perhaps he knew she was in danger.

Should she have told him about the assault this afternoon?

With a sigh, she went to the kitchen and switched on the kettle. She poured a hefty spoonful of instant coffee into a mug. It might leave her with insomnia but she had so many thoughts waltzing round her brain she couldn't even think about sleep.

No, she decided, as she carelessly added the boiling water, she'd been right to keep quiet. She couldn't trust him. He might be charm personified but he must be perfectly aware of Shepherd's trip to London – and its purpose. It was nonsense to pretend he wasn't. And way too much of a coincidence that the very same sergeant had turned up on Sonia's doorstep.

Eve took the mug to the table, sat down and lit a cigarette. She tried to recall exactly what he'd said about the 'investigation', about how he wouldn't be worried if it was him: *Not unless I'd been doing something I shouldn't*. She frowned down into the coffee. Or *seeing* someone she shouldn't? What did she really know about Martin Cavelli? Very little. Only what Paula had told her. And who was to say that *she* was telling the truth?

She found herself pondering on those boxes again. This was all getting too complicated. Not to mention dangerous. That bastard in the alley had meant business today. Perhaps she should bring her arrangement with Cavelli to an end, return his property, pay him and sever the connection. And then . . . and then what? Find someone else to take care of Terry? How could she do that? Take an ad out in *Prisoners' Weekly* perhaps: 'Wanted – strong unscrupulous con for visits, friendly chats and protection. Good sense of humour essential.'

Eve attempted a smile. It was late and she was too tired and too stressed to make any sensible decisions. She swallowed what remained of the coffee and stubbed out her cigarette. A long hot bath might help before turning in.

She was barely halfway across the room when the phone started ringing. Its shrill demand cut sharply through the stillness of the room. She jumped and then glanced at her watch. It was late. Who'd be calling at this time? Henry, maybe . . .

She hurried to the table and picked up the receiver. 'Hello?'

There was no response.

'Hello?' she said again. She waited hopefully for his voice.

It took a moment before the silence at the other end sank in. Except it wasn't silence, not complete silence. As she listened more carefully, the sound gradually became more audible – it was the coarse even rhythm of a man's heavy breathing . . .

God, this was all she needed!

She slammed down the phone.

A few seconds later it rang again. *Leave it*, every sensible neuron in her brain demanded. *Let it ring*. But instinctively her hand reached out and picked it up. Before she had the chance to speak, let alone deliver a well-deserved curse or two, a malevolent voice stopped her dead.

'Don't hang up on me, Evie. I don't like it.'

Closing her eyes, she shuddered. *Evie*. There it was again, that rarely used version of her name. So this wasn't just some sad random wanker in search of a thrill. She suddenly wished it was. 'Leave me alone.'

'You know I can't do that.'

Her hand began to shake. She pressed the receiver hard against her ear. 'Who are you? What do you want?'

'You know what I want. Don't play games. Don't even think about playing games.'

Was it the same man from the alley? She wasn't sure. The voice was muffled as if he might have a scarf or handkerchief over his mouth. 'Look, I don't—'

There was a harsh laugh. 'Joe's not a forgiving man . . . or a patient one. So no fucking excuses, okay? Just hand it over.'

'If you'd tell me what—'

But already the line had gone dead.

For a few seconds she stood listening to the bland relentless tone before putting down the receiver. Quickly she picked it up again and dialled 1471. The number was withheld.

'Damn you!' she whispered.

But it didn't make anything better. She was still standing in her dead father's flat, still scared, still shivering, still trying to understand what the hell was going on . . .

Chapter Eight

Cavelli stopped eating and stared up at Isaac. 'What?'

'It's true, man, straight up. Seems he crossed the Rowans big time. Seems they're mad as fuck about it.'

'Who says?'

Isaac's eyes grew wider. '*They* say it, man. The word's out. Trust me. You don't need it in no fucking writing.'

'Where are they – on the Island?'

'It don't matter where they are. They got family. They got friends. You hear what I'm saying?'

Cavelli heard him loud and clear. Parkhurst might be miles away, even separated from the mainland by a sizeable stretch of water, but distance was no object when it came to the tiny matter of revenge. He thought about it for a moment. Then he shrugged. 'Thanks for telling me.'

'What you going to do, man?'

'Finish my breakfast.' He picked up his fork again but Isaac continued to stand over him, shuffling from foot to foot. 'Unless there was something else you wanted?'

He looked hurt. 'I don't want to see you getting in no bother. I don't want to be picking no tool out of your back.'

'I'm not in bother.'

'What you mean, you not in no bother? You're

looking out for him, that Terry Weston. You're in their way.'

'I'll sort it.'

As if that was entirely the wrong response, Isaac frowned and scratched his head. 'Leave him be. He's nothing to you. What you watching over him for?' Although he already knew the answer. Martin was seeing that red-headed bitch sister of his, the one with the tits and the legs. 'She's just using you, man.'

Cavelli's chin jerked up. His voice was cold. 'What did you say?'

Isaac quickly withdrew a step, raising both his palms. 'Nothing, man. I don't mean nothing. None of my business, right?'

'Right. So just fuck off and let me eat.'

He didn't need telling twice. Three fast strides and he was out of the room. All he left behind was the faint scent of marijuana and the echo of a sigh.

Cavelli glared after the thin skinny figure. They'd shared the same cell for over a year and on the whole, except for those times when Isaac couldn't keep his opinions to himself, they got along okay. Mutual respect was what made their joint tenancy work. Isaac respected his reputation – a reputation that kept him safe and protected on the wing – and in return, he respected Isaac's ability to procure everything from extra bog rolls to a decent bottle of Scotch.

No longer hungry, Cavelli pushed his tray aside. He had to think this Rowan business through. He placed his elbows on the table and swore softly into his hands. If it was true about Terry then he had a major problem. No one liked a grass. No one liked to be connected to a grass.

He stood up and paced, back and forth, from one end of the cell to the other.

If he wasn't careful a ton of grief could be headed in

his direction. That was the last thing he needed. Another twelve months or so and there was every chance he'd be out of here. That's if he stayed away from trouble. And Terry Weston, it appeared, had trouble stamped all over him.

But it was early days, too soon to make any final decisions. A thin smile flickered on to his lips. With some imagination and a word in the right ear he might still be able to twist this turn of events to his advantage.

It was time for another little chat with Evie.

A stream of pale lemon sunlight filtered through the window, the first indication that spring might actually be on its way. She leaned against the sill and felt the faint but reassuring warmth against her face. Her mouth opened and stretched into a yawn.

Sleep hadn't come easily. For hours she had tossed and turned, her mind refusing to relinquish the voice on the phone, the threats, the feel of that brute's hand pressed hard against her mouth . . . Three times she had risen from her bed, sure that she had heard a noise, a sinister scratching at the front door. She had crept out and stood there listening. But there had been no one. Silence. There had only been silence.

Trembling, she had slipped back under the sheets.

Even when sleep had finally claimed her, it had done nothing to alleviate her exhaustion. Her dreams had been full of darkness and anxiety, claustrophobic nightmares that still drifted ominously at the edge of her consciousness. All too frightening. All too weird. Jack Raynor had been in there somewhere, watching, waiting. She tried to claw back the memory, to haul it into focus. Had he been there to help or . . .

No, it was futile. The harder she tried, the less she could recall.

Eve took a sip of coffee and gazed down on the street. She tried to shake the mist from her head. She had to contact Cavelli. She had to find out what was going on. But it was Saturday morning and there was something else she had to do first, something she'd been putting off for weeks.

She had to go and see Terry's mother.

Eve groaned aloud at the prospect. She was under no illusions as to what kind of welcome she was likely to receive. Their relationship could hardly be described as amicable. In fact it could hardly be described as a relationship at all. It was over three years since she'd last set eyes on her erstwhile stepmother; Lesley hadn't turned up for Terry's court case or their father's funeral.

Had it been left to Eve, she wouldn't have gone within a mile, but it wasn't her choice. It was Terry who wanted to see her again.

Of course she had tried the simple option, tried ringing her. But on those rare occasions when she didn't get the answer machine, Lesley always had an excuse as to why she couldn't visit.

'I'm sorry but we're away next week.'

Eve rang back.

'I'm sorry but Tara's got a temperature.'

She rang back again.

'I'm sorry but we've got people staying.'

By now Eve understood that these brief conversations were beyond pointless. Since leaving her father, Lesley had not just moved on but was aiming to sever *every* connection with the Weston family. After a few false starts, and a couple more divorces, she had finally managed to bag the husband of her dreams. Alexander Weston, along with his daughter, had been consigned to the bin. Eve wasn't grieving too hard over that. However, with two new children in tow, it seemed that she had effectively managed to dump Terry too.

121

She scowled at the thought. Surely she must have *some* feelings for him? He was her son, her firstborn, and it wasn't as if she even lived that far away – at the most it would only take an hour to drive down to Hillgrove. Still, recalling Lesley's priorities, perhaps her absence wasn't that surprising. Any free hour she possessed would probably be filled with having her hair done, her nails manicured, or searching the internet for the latest Gucci bag.

Eve checked her watch. It was almost nine. She should go before she changed her mind. A promise was a promise. She didn't hold out much hope but at least she could look Terry in the eye and tell him that she'd tried.

She stared down at her clothes: jeans and a navy blue sweater. Should she get changed? Perhaps it was too casual, perhaps . . . No, that would only give her another reason for delay. *Don't think about it. Just do it.* Quickly she grabbed her leather jacket, handbag and keys. She opened the door and pulled it firmly shut behind.

She only paused again when she was out on the street. Instinctively her gaze darted left and right, absorbing the people strolling by, the empty doorways, the passing cars. She was searching for the man from the alley. Other than a rough idea of his height and weight, she had no real idea of what he looked like. She couldn't describe a single feature of his face – but still she looked. If he was out here, if he was close, she was sure that she would know it.

For a moment she hovered by the entrance.

She waited. Nothing happened.

Wrapping her fingers securely round her keys, she started walking. Her car was parked fifty yards away, adjacent to the chip shop. The one advantage of owning a wreck was that no one ever thought about nicking it. She'd had the same shabby black Honda for the past five years. Dented, scratched and bruised, it wasn't the prettiest vehicle she had ever owned but it was certainly the most crime-proof.

It was only when she got in and locked the door that she realized she'd been holding her breath. She released it in one fast and grateful exhalation.

As she was driving out of the city she thought about what she would say to Lesley. Surely one visit to see Terry wasn't too much to ask? But Eve knew she'd have some persuading to do, even some grovelling, just to get her to consider it.

She wound down the window as the traffic ground to a halt. The sudden appearance of the sun had brought the day trippers out, apparently all with the same intention of heading towards the coast. She glanced in her mirror; there was already a long queue behind her.

Still, she wasn't in a hurry. It gave her extra time to come up with a brilliant strategy.

She racked her brains but nothing rose to the surface. They had never got on, never would. Not that that was very surprising. Few thirteen-year-old girls would celebrate their father getting hitched to a flighty twenty-one-year-old – even, or perhaps especially, one who was carrying his baby. And no young bride longs to share house space with a jealous adolescent witch. They had battled for Alexander Weston's affections with all the subtlety of a pair of feral cats; if they could have scratched each other's eyes out, they would.

She tapped her fingers against the wheel and sighed, hoping that this meeting wasn't going to descend into one of their old familiar rows. It was up to her to make sure it didn't, to bite her tongue, to at least *attempt* to act grown up.

She had to stay focused. She had to think of Terry.

Eve smiled. God, how she'd resented him when he was born. No, more than resented – she had loathed him with a vengeance. He hadn't even had the grace to be ugly. Just to rub her nose in it, he'd emerged into the world the perfect image of angelic fair-haired sweetness, a gurgling rosy cherub with a smile for everyone. But he hadn't won *her* over. He might have been heavenly, small and defenceless, but she hadn't been charmed. At the time there was no getting over the fact that if it wasn't for him and his upstart mother she would still have her father's full attention.

The lights switched to green and the traffic shifted again. As Eve eased the car forward she shook her head. It was hard to imagine just how much bitterness she had felt. Although she had never wished Terry any terminal harm, she had exerted a great deal of effort into imagining ways of mislaying him: leaving his pram in the park when she took him for a walk, accidentally leaving the door open as he learned to crawl, taking an ad out in the paper to secretly put him up for adoption . . .

It was ironic really. Once she'd been obsessed with losing him, now she was preoccupied by keeping him safe. She knew precisely when it had changed: as she was nudging fifteen, when he was almost two, at the exact point she'd realized Lesley didn't actually have much interest in him. That had been enough to turn the tide. Out of pure contrariness, perhaps even out of spite, she had finally chosen to pay her half-brother some attention.

Was that shameful?

Perhaps it was. But it didn't alter the fact that she had ended up doting on the little brat.

Fifteen minutes later Eve was on the main road, beginning to hit a respectable speed, when her phone started ringing. She picked it up. 'Hello.'

'Hi.'

Damn! It was Jack Raynor. 'Hang on a sec.' Had it been anyone else she would have carried on talking but, as if his profession provided him with an unerring

124

instinct for law-breaking, she pulled off the road and drew up into a rough track by a field.

'Sorry,' she said, once she was stationary. 'I'm in the car. How are you?'

'Pretty good, thanks. You heading anywhere nice?'

She hesitated. Over the years, she had got in the habit of evading the truth. There was no reason why she shouldn't tell him that she was going to see Terry's mother . . . but she didn't. 'Just up to the coast. I'm meeting a friend.'

'Lucky you,' he said. 'I'm stuck in the office for the next eight hours.'

'I'll try not to gloat.'

His soft laugh echoed down the line. 'I can sense you're already losing that battle. I just wanted to say how much I enjoyed last night. Thanks for keeping me company.'

'Thank *you* for dinner.'

Then it was his turn to hesitate. 'Er . . . I was wondering if you'd like to do it again sometime? During the week maybe?'

She grinned and looked out of the window. 'Are you asking me on a date, Inspector?'

He paused. 'Before I respond to that question, I'm afraid I'll need to know if your answer's likely to be yes or no.'

'Spoken like a true man of courage.'

Raynor laughed again. 'Shall I take that as a yes?'

He had one of those sensuous voices, melodious but with just the right hint of gravel. Perhaps, in the circumstances, it wouldn't do any harm to keep him close – but she didn't want him thinking she was a pushover. A girl had her reputation to consider. 'I'll let you know. Give me a call on Monday.'

'I'll do that,' he said.

There was a short silence before they both hung up.

Eve put down the phone and gazed out across the field. The bright yellow crop swayed a little in the breeze. Above it the sky was a pure cobalt blue. It was the kind of scene a child might have painted, so innocent, so pure and simplistic that it seemed to verge on the imaginary.

She sighed. The view might be enchanting but there was nothing innocent about the thoughts that were racing through her head. If she agreed to meet him again would that be a wise move or a dumb one? From a purely practical point of view it had its advantages – potential enemies, as her father had always insisted, were best kept within punching distance – but she could sense a complication looming. Jack Raynor was attractive. *Very* attractive. He was smart, witty and dangerously seductive. And he was also a cop.

Not a great combination.

Still, that was no excuse for turning him down. In her life she may have been guilty of a number of crimes but failing to rise to a challenge had never been one of them.

She switched on the indicator and tried to edge back out on to the main road. The traffic was solid and it took a few minutes before a gap appeared. Taking advantage of the opportunity, she put her foot down and accelerated out. She glanced in the rear-view mirror. It was then that she noticed it – another car, twenty yards back, suddenly drawing away from the verge, skidding out with the minimum of care. The driver either had a death wish or . . .

She squinted into the mirror.

Was he following her? No, it was just coincidence. But that didn't explain the weird prickling sensation on the back of her neck. She tried to peer around the vehicles between them. The car was dark blue, old, a Ford. The driver was male but that was all she could establish.

By the time she reached the Cromer road, he was still

behind. She deliberately slowed, letting the two cars between them overtake. But then, just as she was hoping to get a good look, he slowed down too. The gap between them was instantly filled. A white van skipped smartly into the space and her view was blocked.

Okay, there was only one thing for it. A supermarket was looming to her left. Without warning, without indicating, she waited until the last possible moment before veering sharply into the entrance. She left in her wake a gust of black exhaust and the audible sound of Mr White Van's disapproval. But at least it proved her point. Seconds later the manoeuvre was repeated by an old blue Ford. Damn! What was she going to do now?

While she thought about it, she embarked on a slow cruise round the car park. It was Saturday morning and the place was jam-packed. She tried not to stare too hard or too often in her mirror. Although he was keeping his distance, she could see him clearly now, a thin middle-aged sandy-haired man. She frowned. There was something vaguely familiar about him but she couldn't put her finger on it.

A cop maybe? But surely Raynor wouldn't have rung if she was being tailed. It was his phone call, forcing her to stop, that had alerted her in the first place. Eve was almost tempted to stop the car, to get out and confront him – only after what had happened yesterday it hardly seemed the wisest move. It was all very well facing your demons but it was probably best to know just what kind of demons they were first.

Instead she began to gradually edge towards the exit, briefly glancing to her left and right as if searching for a space. Unless they were going to play cat and mouse for the rest of the day, she had to find a way to lose him.

Oddly, she didn't feel afraid. At least not the sort of cold frantic fear she had felt in the alley. Perhaps it was to do with being in the car, with being protected, or maybe it was the old adrenalin kicking in. Getting out of tight corners had been a speciality of her father's. She'd been trained by a master.

An opportunity for escape arose a moment later. Forced to keep a reasonable distance, her shadow found himself impeded by an elderly couple with a trolley. As they meandered, oblivious, across his path, Eve promptly put her foot down and hit the exit with as much speed as she dared.

Recklessly setting back the cause for all female drivers, she rejoined the main road to a chorus of angry horns and screeching brakes. Curses echoed through the mild spring air. She tried not to take it to heart. A girl had to do what a girl had to do. Disapproval she could live with, uninvited company she couldn't.

As soon as she'd cleared the town she turned off, winding randomly along a series of thin country roads. Over the next fifteen minutes she completed a scenic tour of all the local villages and hamlets. Had she been less distracted she might have taken some pleasure from the scenery, the houses, even from the distant churches that appeared with almost alarming frequency. Her father had loved old churches. She smiled. He had dragged her along more chilly naves than she cared to remember.

When Eve was certain she had lost her pursuer – she was certainly lost herself – she found a place to pull up and reached over to the glove compartment for the map.

She opened it on her knee, sat back, and lit a cigarette. She felt a small warm glow of satisfaction. So she hadn't entirely lost the art of avoidance! Unless he had a tracking device attached to the underside of her car, he would never find her here. He'd continue driving along the main road until he realized she was gone.

But her sense of satisfaction was short-lived. What was she thinking? She might have temporarily shaken him off but he knew where she'd be tonight. Her problem had only been postponed, not cancelled. Suddenly she didn't feel quite so smug.

She was still in trouble, big trouble.

But she could only deal with one crisis at a time. With a sigh she bent her head over the map and traced out the best route to Blakeney.

It was approaching ten thirty by the time she arrived. As she crawled through the narrow congested streets, past the pretty brick and flint cottages, she found herself relieved that she hadn't spotted the man here. Unless she'd been prepared to plough down fifty innocent pedestrians, she wouldn't have stood a chance of evading him.

Pausing briefly by the front, she glanced out across the marshes. The briny smell of the sea wafted through the open window. A few kids were already sitting on the quay, their short legs dangling over the edge. Surrounded by all the paraphernalia of childhood, plastic buckets, fishing nets, discarded jumpers, they seemed suspended in a world of their own. Eve felt a sudden pang of envy. What she wouldn't give to change places for an hour or two . . .

Reluctantly, she glanced back down at her map.

She followed the road for another half-mile before negotiating her way through a series of much quieter side streets. The house, when she eventually found it, came as a shock. Sliding into the long smooth drive, Eve caught her breath. She'd expected something decent but nothing quite this grand. The building looked old, Georgian, very white, very large, and stunningly beautiful. A house to drool over, a house that must have cost a fortune . . .

Lesley had clearly used her charms to full advantage.

Passing under an arch of scarlet rhododendrons, Eve drew up and parked beside a brand-new Mercedes. She could almost hear its growl of disapproval. There was probably a servants' car park round the back.

She got out and looked around. Had her arrival been noted? She sensed that it had – although it wasn't possible, unless she acquired the ability to look at twelve windows simultaneously, to even tell if the curtains were twitching.

She went to the door and rang the bell.

There was no reply.

She pressed it again. The fancy car, she was sure, belonged to a woman. No heterosexual man would ever willingly drive a pink Mercedes. Which meant, as Lesley never walked any further than the bathroom, that she couldn't be too far away. All it would take was a little persistence . . .

She leaned on the bell again.

After a further few seconds Lesley swung open the door and glared at her. 'What are you doing here?'

Eve forced herself to smile. 'Hi! How are you?'

'What are you doing here?' she asked again.

'Look, it's about Terry. I thought—'

'I don't care what you thought,' she snapped. 'I'm busy. I'm sorry but I don't have time for this.'

'Please. Just a minute, just—'

'I've told you, I'm busy.'

As she went to slam the door Eve smartly inserted her foot in the gap. It was the kind of move she'd seen a thousand times on television but those guys were never wearing flimsy sandals. Like a ton of lead, the door crunched against her naked toes. With a cry, she fell to her knees. Red-hot pain travelled first-class return to her brain and back.

Lesley, perhaps more worried about what the neighbours might think than out of any real concern, crouched down beside her. 'God, sorry, I didn't mean to . . .'

Doubled up on the doorstep, Eve clutched at her foot and groaned.

'Are you okay?'

She wasn't okay. How could she be? Her left arm was still aching from yesterday's attack and now she had a battered right foot to match. Not to mention the lump on her forehead. Suddenly it seemed like everyone was intent on causing her damage. Perhaps she should just lie down on a railway track and save them all the bother.

'It's not broken, is it?'

Christ, she hoped not. She released her grip and gazed down. There was some blood, a thin red trickle from a broken nail, and the skin was a nasty shade of mauve, but she could still wriggle her toes. 'I don't think so.'

Lesley put a hand around her waist and helped her up. 'You'd better come inside.'

'Thanks.'

They didn't hold on to each other for any longer than was strictly necessary. As soon as the threshold was crossed they separated.

As Lesley strolled ahead, Eve limped slowly behind. This wasn't exactly the meeting she'd envisaged but, disregarding the pain, there were certain advantages. At least she'd managed to get inside – and to inadvertently gain the moral high ground. It was more difficult for anyone to refuse a favour when they'd almost lopped off your toes.

The room she was led to was all cream sofas and pale rugs, the kind of furnishings one really shouldn't bleed over. She glanced down at her throbbing foot again.

'Take a seat,' Lesley said. 'I'll get something for that.'

Eve lowered herself gingerly on to the edge of a soft plump chair. She gazed around. Impressive! She could have fitted the whole of her current living space into this room alone. At the far end a tall pair of doors led out into a palm-filled conservatory. Beyond it she could see a long stretch of perfectly manicured lawn.

Perhaps there was something to be said for marrying money after all.

Lesley reappeared a few minutes later with a pot of tea and two china cups and saucers on a tray. She saw Eve's surprised expression and smiled. It was a small tight smile. 'I thought we may as well be civilized about this.'

Eve grinned back. Perhaps she was worried about a writ. A claim of assault wouldn't go down too well at the local golf club.

Lesley passed her a bottle of antiseptic and a small wad of cotton wool. As if her unwelcome guest was an accident waiting to happen, she said, 'You can use the bathroom if you like.'

'That's okay. I'll be careful.' She dabbed tentatively at her foot, emitting a series of tiny exaggerated gasps. The pain was starting to subside but it never did any harm to play to your strengths. She was aware of Lesley's anxious glances but couldn't tell what she was more worried about – the possible damage to her reputation or to her rug.

The tea was poured and a cup placed solicitously by her side.

'Thanks,' Eve said. She stared down at the damp and slightly bloodied ball of cotton wool, unsure as to the etiquette of its disposal. Dropping it on to the table hardly seemed polite. She might currently have the advantage but there was no point pushing her luck. 'Er . . . is there a bin?'

Lesley winced before picking the offending object up with the tips of her fingers and carrying it over to the open fireplace.

Eve settled back in the chair. As the downy cushions consumed her she was far from convinced that she'd ever be able to get up again. It was time to move on to the tricky subject of Terry but first she threw in a little flattery. 'You have a beautiful house.'

'Yes, it's got four reception rooms *and* a pool.'

It was said with such queenly affectation that Eve had to stifle a laugh. She tried, rather unsuccessfully, to turn it into a cough.

Lesley glared at her.

'I'm sorry,' she said. 'I didn't mean . . . Look, I haven't come here to cause you any trouble.'

'You're a Weston,' Lesley snapped back.

As if trouble was their middle name.

Eve let the implication slide. And anyway there was an element of truth in it. She could have reminded her that she'd been a Weston once herself but from there it would only be one short step towards the fatal quicksand of old resentments.

Perhaps Lesley had the same idea. She flapped a hand and forced an apologetic smile on to her pink Cupid's bow mouth. 'I was sorry to hear about your father.'

Was she? Eve doubted it. And certainly not sorry enough to come to the funeral. Or to even send a card. But now wasn't the time to go into that. She nodded. She might have managed a thank you if the words hadn't stuck in her throat.

There was a brief uncomfortable silence.

As if on cue the phone rang and Lesley leapt up to answer it. 'Vince, darling.' She cradled the receiver against her pearl-studded ear and glanced over her shoulder. 'No, no, don't worry. It's fine. I'm not doing anything important.'

Eve's brows shifted up a fraction. Good thing she wasn't the sensitive sort. While Lesley walked over to the window and murmured sweet nothings to husband number four, or was it five? – there had been so many she'd

133

lost count – she sipped at her tea and grabbed the opportunity for some surreptitious scrutiny.

How old was she now? About forty-three, she estimated, but wearing it well. Small and slim, she had barely a line on her face. It was uncanny how similar she was to Terry: same build, same silky golden hair, even the same angelic butter-wouldn't-melt-in-her-mouth expression. They both looked as fragile as porcelain dolls. Only the eyes were different. Lesley's were a soft hazel whereas Terry, like herself, had inherited the Weston shade of grey.

All in all, she didn't appear that different to when they'd first met over twenty years ago. Of course, back then, Lesley hadn't been quite the lady she aspired to be now. It was Eve's father who had helped smooth out those rough Cockney edges, who had paid for elocution lessons and classes in deportment. It was her father who had taught her how to behave in polite society.

And back in those days the sly ambitious Lesley had been far from averse to a spot of trouble . . .

Eve knew what they'd done, how the two of them had generated an easy source of income. It was the oldest trick in the book. Although it wouldn't work so well now, adultery being virtually compulsory for anyone in the public eye, twenty years ago there were still plenty of men who preferred to keep their indiscretions private. Easy pickings for an angelic-looking girl with a small bank account and a big smile. A bit of research, an accidental meeting, and next thing the mark was lying stark naked in a hotel room. All it took from there was a distraught 'husband' bursting violently through the doors and it wasn't long before the wallet came out.

Everyone had their price.

She sighed. It had been a cheap trashy kind of con but Lesley had played it to perfection.

'Love you too, darling,' she whispered into the phone.

Eve watched as she came back across the room and replaced the receiver. She was dressed in a pale pink dress to match her car. Or maybe, with the exorbitant cost of designer clothes, it was the other way round.

'Sorry about that,' she murmured. Then, as if she didn't intend to be sitting for long, she perched down on the very edge of her chair. 'Look, Eve, I know what you want, why you've come here, but the answer's no. I told Terry, any more trouble and that was it. I've got Tara and Zak to think of now.'

Eve nodded, trying to look sympathetic. 'He's let you down, I realize that. He's let himself down. He made a big mistake and he knows it. But with everything that's happened . . . with Dad dying and . . . Couldn't you just go and visit him once? That's all he's asking.'

Lesley shook her head. 'I've told you.'

But he's your son, she wanted to protest. Instead she persisted with the more practical approach. 'Hillgrove's only down the road. You could be there and back in a few hours.'

'I'm sorry.'

'One afternoon. Even if it's only for half an hour.'

Lesley didn't reply. Instead she looked down at her watch, a deliberate gesture intended to convey that time was running out.

Eve's patience was starting to run out too. 'Why not? Come on, what harm can it do? Just one short visit. He only wants to see you, to tell you how sorry he is.'

As if the concept of Terry's repentance was beyond ridiculous, she gave a small scornful laugh. 'The only thing he's sorry about is getting caught.'

'That's not fair,' Eve retorted, springing to his defence. Although, deep down, she knew there was an element of truth in it. He always had been a handful – forever in one kind of bother or another – but then he'd hardly had the perfect upbringing. In various ways, they had all let him down. After Lesley and her father had split up, the six-year-old Terry had been passed between them like some unwanted parcel; he may as well have had 'return to sender' tattooed on his forehead.

Lesley glanced at her watch again. 'I'm afraid I really have to—'

'Is it because of Vince?' Eve interrupted, desperately trying to defer her dismissal. She had the feeling that if he hadn't rung she might have made more progress. 'Would he rather you didn't see Terry?'

'It's nothing to do with Vince. It's *my* decision not his.'

Eve sensed she'd hit a sore spot. Perhaps he didn't want his wife mixing with the riff-raff in prison – even if one of the riff-raff was her own flesh and blood. 'I mean, surely he couldn't object to you seeing your own son.'

'You don't understand. You have no idea how much . . .' Lesley stopped abruptly and stared down at the carpet.

Eve mentally attempted to finish the sentence: *How much it would affect his social standing? How much it would affect his opinion of his wife?* In the end, she just came straight out and asked: 'What don't I understand?'

'It doesn't matter.'

'Of course it matters.'

But as if she'd already revealed too much, Lesley declined to elaborate. Instead, she stood up and primly smoothed down her dress. 'Well, it's been nice to see you again.'

Their conversation, apparently, was over.

Eve dragged herself up, carefully testing her foot before she put her full weight on it. It still hurt but so long as she didn't indulge in any sudden braking she should be able to drive home. She limped slowly out into the passage where Lesley, who'd been walking beside her, suddenly rushed forward to open the door.

She had the vague sensation of being 'escorted off the premises'.

Eve passed obediently into the courtyard and then turned to look at her. She took a deep breath. There was nothing else for it. When all else failed, there was only the final resort – emotional blackmail. Lesley had never been the doting mother but surely there must be a few tiny threads of maternal instinct lurking somewhere in her DNA.

'*Please*,' she pleaded. 'At least say you'll think about it. You can ring me any time. He needs you. You're his mother, his family.'

She thought she saw a vague flicker of uncertainty in those wide suspicious eyes but if Lesley hesitated it was only for a second.

'Goodbye, Eve.'

She was still standing there when the door closed firmly in her face. It was only a slightly more cautious slam than the one that had originally greeted her.

Chapter Nine

If it hadn't been for Eve Weston's reckless driving, Ivor Patterson wouldn't have been at a loose end. And if he hadn't been at a loose end he might never have followed up the lead he'd got the night before. As it was, he had nothing better to do. She had managed to give him the slip and unless he was prepared to waste the rest of the day searching for a needle in a haystack he may as well do something productive.

Naturally, he wasn't going to tell the office that he'd lost her. Wherever she'd been going, she'd be back – hopefully before he changed shifts with Charlie May. As far as his notes were concerned, she hadn't stepped out of the flat. Who was to say otherwise?

It was bad news, though, that she'd sussed him. He was growing careless. Now she'd be watching out, making his job twice as hard. And there was no saying how she might react if she spotted him again – maybe even call the cops. What he was doing wasn't illegal but it would mean the end to any chance of an earner on the side.

No, if he was going to follow through it had to be today. He had to move quickly if he was going to make this shakedown work. Be a shame to let the opportunity slip through his fingers.

He drove back into Norwich and headed towards the

pub where he expected to find the man who had attacked her. For the price of a few drinks, it hadn't taken him long to put a name to the face or to find out his regular haunts. The name had surprised him at first. Perhaps he'd got the situation all wrong? But the more he thought about it, the more convinced he became that he hadn't.

Ivor had his instincts – and he knew what he'd seen.

A cosy little chat was what was called for next, with a few visual props to help aid concentration. A nice clear set of prints in a plain brown envelope. Not the sort of snaps that his burglar cum assailant would want turning up at the local cop shop.

What were they worth? Now that was a hard one to figure. Other than that they proved he'd been at the flats, right time, right place, there was nothing specifically incriminating about them. But he'd have a record, was bound to, and that would be reason enough for the Old Bill to give him a tug. And if there was one thing Ivor was sure of, it was that this thug was way down the food chain, a lackey being paid by someone else – and *that* someone else, hopefully, wouldn't want the cops sniffing around.

It wasn't the first time he had offered to lose the evidence but there was always an added risk when you didn't know exactly who you were dealing with. Probably best to stray on the side of caution.

A moderate amount, he decided, nothing too greedy.

DS Shepherd glanced up over the rim of his polystyrene cup. 'I don't see the problem, guv.'

Raynor slammed down an armful of files on his desk. 'Does anyone ever listen to a word I say? I told you. I told you to stay away from her.'

'I didn't go near her.'

'And how exactly is going round to Herbert Street and cross-examining her neighbour, *staying away*?'

Shepherd frowned. 'It was hardly a cross-examination.' He shoved a couple of aspirins in his mouth and took a sip of black coffee, a cure-all for his post-Friday-night hangover. Christ, with his head thumping like a jackhammer the last thing he needed was Raynor screaming in his ear. 'And as it happens, I had a reason.'

'It had better be a bloody good one.'

'It is, guv. I think it was Marshall, Peter Marshall, her ex, that did the break-in. Used to live there, didn't he? Just his style too. Hears about Weston snuffing it, knows the place is empty and decides to try his luck.'

Raynor didn't look impressed. 'You've got no proof.'

'Let me bring him in. I bet his alibi's as leaky as the bloody *Titanic*.'

'It's a waste of time.'

Shepherd gulped down the rest of his coffee. 'Just give me ten minutes with him and I'll—'

Raynor could imagine what he'd do. 'No, I don't want him brought in.'

'What?'

'You heard.'

'Why the fuck not?'

Jack Raynor leaned over his desk and lowered his voice. 'Because I fucking say so, Sergeant. Is that good enough for you?'

It wasn't good enough – not even approaching it. Shepherd narrowed his eyes. A bit of pressure, a bit of gentle persuasion, and he could have Marshall banged to rights, get the idle beggar off the streets for a few months. And that, as he understood it, was his fucking job.

'Sergeant?'

He tried not to snarl. 'Yes, guv.'

His status re-established, Raynor sat down beside him and sighed. 'Look, okay, I see where you're coming from but there's more to this case than some opportunistic break-in. I mean, what are you actually planning on charging him with – breaking and entering and causing a mess? You've got no proof and it's not worth the paper-work. It's not as if anything was even taken.'

'So far as we know.'

'So far as we know,' he acknowledged. 'But if we bring Marshall in now, they're going to get spooked. Every other door is going to close double quick.'

Eddie wasn't convinced there were any other doors. As far as he was concerned this was a straightforward case, open and shut, no complications. Still, with a head-ache like the one he'd got, it wasn't worth arguing the toss. 'Cavelli?' he said wearily.

'Trust me, there's more to this.'

Eddie shrugged. The inspector, he was sure, was talk-ing through his over-educated arse; whatever was going on between Eve Weston and Martin Cavelli had nothing to do with Herbert Street. But what the hell! Give him enough rope and he'd eventually hang himself. 'Fine. If that's what you think.'

Raynor got up from the chair. 'So we're agreed. We leave Peter Marshall alone?'

He nodded. 'Whatever you say, guv.'

It was almost one o'clock by the time Eve arrived home. She parked the car and limped across the road. It hadn't been the most productive of mornings. Apart from another injury to add to her collection, she'd come away with very little. What was she going to tell Terry: that his mother didn't want to see him or that she was *think-ing* about it? She wasn't sure which was worse – dashing his hopes or giving him false ones.

In the foyer, she paused to check the mailbox. There were three flyers for the local pizza place, a generous invitation to take out a crippling loan, and a letter sent by first-class post. She quickly tore it open. It was a visiting order from Cavelli. Well, that saved her the bother of chasing him up; it seemed he wanted to see her as urgently as she wanted to see him.

Eve had just turned towards the stairs when old Mrs Leonard emerged from the flat to her left. She was a tiny bird-like woman with bright dark eyes, wrinkles as deep as a walnut, and a long grey ponytail. In her usual eccentric style, she was dressed in a pair of violet dungarees and a skinny yellow polo neck.

'Hello, dear,' she chirped. 'Lovely day!'

Lovely hadn't been quite her experience to date but Eve managed to paint a smile on her face. 'Beautiful,' she agreed.

'And how are you?'

'Fine, thanks.'

'And how's that delightful father of yours?'

Eve felt her heart sink. On two previous occasions she had gently explained that her father, sadly, had 'passed away' but the information clearly hadn't registered. Unwilling to go through the traumatic process yet again, she found herself murmuring, 'Oh, just the same.'

Her neighbour's beady eyes gazed quizzically up.

Eve quickly veered back to the less emotive subject of the weather. 'It's really quite warm out there, like spring. It's good to see the sun again. Are you going for a walk?'

Mrs Leonard nodded. As she bobbed her head a pair of dangling silver earrings made a soft tinkling sound like wind chimes. 'I'm slipping out before they come back, dear. They're watching the house, you know.'

Eve knew better than to inquire. Sometimes it was espionage, other times a minor revolution. Last week she'd been insistent that secret messages were being relayed into her kitchen. The source, if she remembered rightly, had been that hotbed of subversion, *Just a Minute* on Radio 4. She smiled. 'Well, I won't keep you. Enjoy yourself.'

Eve tucked the mail into her bag before starting her slow ascent of the stairs. She sighed into the silence. As her father would have put it, Dorothy Leonard was a few pence short of a sixpence – but maybe, all things considered, that wasn't so bad. A world where the BBC was intent on infiltration, and the dead, apparently, remained immortal was surely more alluring than any dreary day-to-day existence on Herbert Street.

Her foot had become a dull heavy throb – perhaps driving back hadn't been quite such a good idea after all – and she clung on to the banister, half stumbling, half dragging herself up the two flights.

She was barely through the door when the phone started ringing. Answer it or not?

Not, she decided.

If it was her heavy breather, she could do without the aggravation. And if it was anyone else they could leave a message or try her mobile.

Eve went through to the bathroom, poured some hot water into a bowl and added a capful of antiseptic. Back in the living room, she slumped down on the sofa, carefully eased off her sandal and with a wince lowered the foot into the water. It looked even more swollen than when she'd left Blakeney.

Sitting back, she tried to concentrate on what she should do next. At the top of her list was confronting Cavelli – she needed some answers and fast – but the lines for booking would be closed by now. She could ring on Monday but still wouldn't be able to get a visit until the Wednesday. If her foot didn't improve over the next few days, she'd be catching the bus out to Hillgrove, in fact two buses and a cab. She frowned at the prospect. Without a car that place was hell to get to.

The phone started to ring again but Eve continued to ignore it. The way her life was going it was hardly likely to be good news. Was the man who had tailed her in the car the same person who had made the threatening call? She didn't think so. And she was certain he wasn't the brute who'd attacked her in the alley: that man had been bigger, wider, more solid than today's pursuer. Perhaps they were working together. Or perhaps not. And if they weren't, that meant there were at least two people out there, three if she included the mystery 'Joe', who had an unhealthy and frightening interest in her.

And then, of course, there was Jack Raynor. God alone knew where he lay in the scheme of things.

She took her foot out of the water, peered down, and tried to flex her toes. It was painful but possible. If she rested up, she might be able to drive again by midweek. In the meantime, the best thing to do would be to sit tight. She'd be safe enough here. Glancing over her shoulder, she checked to make sure she'd shot the bolts across. At least no one was coming through *that* door in a hurry.

As Eve stretched out on the sofa, a wave of tiredness swept over her. She yawned. Last night's lack of sleep was catching up. She would just close her eyes for a minute . . .

It was nudging five o'clock when she was woken by a soft pervasive noise. For a moment, disoriented, she couldn't think what it was. Shifting on to her side, she carefully opened her eyes; they felt sore and gritty. She squinted into the afternoon light. Perhaps she'd been dreaming.

Then the sound came again, louder this time, a series of impatient knocks on the door.

Eve shot upright, her heart beginning to pump. Who was that?

With both hands gripping the edge of the sofa, she held her breath. She had to keep quiet. Whatever she did, she mustn't answer it. It could be *him* again, the man from the alley. Could he get in? Was he strong enough to break it down? Maybe he wasn't alone. What if . . .

The knocks came again, one two three, one two three, in fast succession.

Instinctively, she leapt up, forgetting about her foot. As a jarring pain shot the length of her leg she let out a cry. It must have been loud enough to permeate the thickness of the door because there was a sudden pause on the other side.

Then a faint rasp as if a throat was being cleared.

Then an anxious voice: 'Eve? Eve, are you in there?'

She *knew* that voice.

Stumbling across the room, she quickly drew back the bolts and pulled the door open. A familiar figure was standing on the other side. She was so relieved she could have thrown her arms around him, but as he had never been one for overt displays of emotion, she hugged him with her eyes instead. 'Henry! What are you doing here?'

'Sorry. I did try to ring before I left.'

So that was who it had been.

She stared at him, taking a moment to absorb his presence, his quiet reassuring solidity. He was dressed in his usual pinstriped suit, white shirt and tie.

Perhaps mistaking her open-mouthed silence for disapproval at his unannounced arrival, he gave a sheepish smile. 'I was worried after yesterday, after we talked. I thought . . . but look, if it's a bad time I can always—'

'No!' she insisted. 'No, of course it isn't.' She reached out and lightly touched his hand. 'Come on in. It's good to see you. It really is.'

As she shut the door and locked it securely behind them, she felt his inquiring eyes on her.

'Are you worried I might make a run for it?'

'Yeah,' she laughed, 'my guests are always doing that. Must be something to do with the company.' She ushered him forward. 'Take a seat. How are you? How are things at the office? I bet you're in need of a coffee. You can't always get one on the train. Not that you can call that stuff coffee, in my experience it's usually more like—'

'Eve?'

She heard the mild remonstration in his voice and stopped. She knew she was rambling. He hadn't come all this way to bring her up to date on office gossip or to hear her opinions on the palatability of railway refreshments. 'I know. I'm sorry. Just give me a minute. I'll make a drink and then we'll talk.'

He nodded and sat down.

Eve walked towards the kitchen.

She hadn't taken more than a few limping steps before Henry leapt up again. His voice was tight and angry. 'Did *he* do that to you?'

With the surprise of his arrival, Eve had stopped thinking about her foot. Now, on being reminded, she suddenly felt the pain again. She gazed down at the bruised and swollen toes. 'No, it wasn't him, he didn't . . .'

God, there was just so much to explain. Henry knew about the break-in, about the incident in the alley, but not about the other man who had tailed her today, or the threatening calls, or the less than brilliant welcome she'd received on the doorstep of her former stepmother. Where to begin? It was going to be a long story. 'I'll tell you. I promise. I'll tell you everything. But I need a strong coffee first.'

Henry followed her into the kitchen. 'I'll make it,' he said sternly. 'You sit down.'

146

She did as she was told. It felt odd watching him glide around the kitchen, filling the kettle, organizing the cups. She watched the tidy efficient movements of his hands. She felt almost as she had as a child, when she'd been sick, when her father had fussed around her making hot tomato soup. Protected. Cared for. Except her father wasn't here any more and . . .

'Are you all right?'

'Sure.'

'Do you have any whisky?'

'There's some brandy in the cupboard.'

He found the bottle and poured a measure into each of the mugs. He gave the contents a stir before passing hers across the table.

She took a sip and shivered. It was a good kind of shiver, the sort you got from a warm flow of relief rather than a bad encounter down a lonely alley. 'Thanks,' she murmured. Henry could have been pressing her for answers but he wasn't. And she was grateful for it. She wanted to talk about what had happened – but not just yet.

They took the drinks into the living room and settled on the sofa. Henry promptly stood up again and disappeared back into the kitchen.

'What are you looking for?'

'Nothing.' He stuck his head in the fridge and pulled out the ice tray. Flicking the cubes out, he neatly wrapped them in a corner of a tea towel. 'Here,' he said, sitting down beside her, 'let me put this round your foot. It might help bring the swelling down.'

She felt the cold hit her toes and flinched.

'Sorry,' he murmured.

'It's okay.' Then she sat back and asked softly, 'Henry, where are you supposed to be?'

He looked at her and frowned.

'You know what I mean. Where does Celia think you

are?' Eve was sure she wouldn't have given him permission to come and play doctors and nurses.

'In Cambridge,' he said. 'At my brother's.'

'I didn't know you had a brother.' For some reason she had always thought of him as an only child. She paused but he didn't elaborate. 'What if she rings you there?'

'She won't. They don't get on. And anyhow, she'd view it as undignified. It would look like she was checking up on me.'

Eve raised her eyebrows. 'And how is it at home?' She couldn't imagine it had been easy for him after Richard's spiteful 'revelations'. At the thought of his son, of what he'd done, a pink angry flush appeared on her cheeks. That no-good louse had a lot to answer for.

He hesitated before answering. 'Well, a touch on the chilly side. But not too bad, all things considered.'

She instantly felt guilty. It was the sneaking around that had caused all the grief in the first place. And now here they were, doing it all over again. If Celia found out . . . 'I shouldn't have called you.'

'Of course you should. You don't need to deal with this on your own.'

On her own. Was that what she was? It had a lonely kind of sound to it. She shifted forward, put her elbows on her knees and shook her head in frustration. 'But that's the trouble, Henry. I'm not even sure what I'm supposed to be dealing *with*.'

He leaned forward too, took off his glasses and wiped them with a spotlessly clean white handkerchief. 'I think you'd better tell me everything.'

It had taken over half an hour for the full story to be told. Henry had listened carefully, only interrupting when he felt the need to clarify a point. Now, while he wandered around the room, he meticulously went over the facts again before filing them away in an orderly fashion.

Eve was curled up on the sofa. She looked pale and tired.

He stopped by the desk and picked up a family photograph: Eve with her father and brother. There was no glass in the frame; it must have got shattered in the break-in. He stared long and hard at Alexander Weston. So this was the man she had told him so much about. Even from the picture, he could see how he might have the capacity to charm. It was a handsome face, friendly, and most interesting of all, deceptively honest. It was the kind of face you would instinctively trust. He had the curious impression that even the photographer had been beguiled.

Henry felt a faint pang. He could not admire Weston – he'd been a cheat and a con artist – but there was something about him he envied. He had led an existence free from the suffocating restraints of society. How tame his own life had been in comparison, a single straight line without troughs or peaks – rather, he thought wryly, as if he was the one who was already dead and buried.

He frowned as he continued to stare at the picture. What motivated people like Weston to act as they did? He'd read about it somewhere. Some kind of superiority complex, allegedly, allied with a lack of conscience. The furrows in his brow grew deeper. What did it matter what he'd read? Perhaps that was the crux of the matter, that where her father had *acted*, albeit immorally, he in turn had consistently stood back, a spectator on the sidelines, a quiet grey man with his head in a book.

He was Henry Baxter, nice, steady, reliable Henry. If he had one outstanding skill it was his ability to merge effortlessly into the background. He was sixty-two years old and had never quite found the courage to step outside his tiny world – a world, now he came to consider it, which was as devoid of colour, as bleakly stark, as any prison cell. And like a forgotten prisoner, he had almost lost the capacity to imagine any kind of escape.

At least until he'd met Eve.

Henry glanced over his shoulder.

She raised her head and smiled.

Things happened when he was with her. Not always good things, granted, but things that shook him up and made him think. Wherever she went, she attracted attention. And it wasn't just because of how she looked. It was something more, something intrinsic to her nature.

Henry wasn't in love but he was intrigued. He had never met anyone like her before. She fascinated him. Her life, right from its beginning, had been the diametric opposite of his. With nothing laid out, nothing predestined, she had constantly drifted from place to place, never rooted, always open to endless possibilities. Was she like her father? He couldn't say. She was certainly a rule breaker, and perhaps more than capable of deceit, but he had never doubted that their friendship was genuine.

He laid the photograph back on the desk and turned to look at her again. 'So you think this is all connected to Martin Cavelli?'

She raised her slim shoulders and shrugged. 'It has to be. Doesn't it? In one way or another.'

'What do you know about him?'

'Only what I've told you, what Paula told me.'

That didn't add up to much. He was still astounded by what she'd done, amazed that she'd approached a total stranger to take care of her brother. There was one almighty gap between taking a judicious risk and leaping headlong into an abyss. 'I still don't understand why you asked him.'

She raised her hands in frustration. 'What else could I do? At least this way I know that Terry's safe.'

But at what cost? Henry thought. It seemed she had traded his safety for hers. Yet the facts, when he added them up, didn't quite make a whole. He couldn't see why this Cavelli character should put her in such obvious danger. He must have guessed, if he was passing on anything valuable, that it wouldn't take long for his enemies to catch up with her. On the other hand, he *had* arranged for the door to be reinforced. Which suggested that he knew she would need protection.

'Can I see the boxes?'

'Sure.'

Eve went to stand up but he waved her back down again. 'It's all right,' he said. 'You should keep the weight off that foot. Just tell me where they are.'

She directed him towards a door to the left. 'They're in the bottom of the wardrobe. But Henry, you won't open them, will you? I want to wait until I've seen Cavelli again, at least hear what he has to say. Then, maybe . . .'

He nodded. 'I won't. I promise.'

He went into her father's bedroom and glanced around. It was a man's room all right, bare, without any of the prettification or comforts that women insist upon. The walls were a dull, rather murky shade of green. There was a lamp and a few books on a table beside his bed. Henry idly picked one up, and flicked through the pages. It was one of his favourites, *The Long Goodbye*, by Raymond Chandler.

He suddenly remembered Eve's call to the office, how she had used the name Lennox to get through to him. He smiled. But the smile soon faded. He hadn't even asked her about how she was coping. Living here, surrounded by all these reminders, couldn't be easy. He felt a tiny spurt of resentment towards the brother he had never met. If it wasn't for Terry she'd be safely back in London by now.

151

'Have you found them?' she called out.

Henry quickly put down the book and opened the wardrobe. 'I've got them.' Kneeling down, he pulled the two cardboard boxes towards him and laid them on the worn carpet. He could see how hard it would be to surreptitiously break them open. They were sealed with yards and yards of dark red tape. It was an unusual colour, a deep shade of magenta. Which would make it hard to replace. And which was probably the reason it had been used in the first place.

Starting with the larger box, he pressed around its edges. It felt solid, like books. But who knew what might be hidden inside. Drugs perhaps? He knew that was Eve's suspicion. Heroin or cocaine. Something that was important enough, valuable enough, to warrant a break-in, an assault, threats . . .

He turned his attention to the smaller, lighter box. It was only half full and as he shook it he could hear the contents moving around, a brisk rustle that sounded like papers. He gently shook it again.

Then an idea suddenly came to him.

Bundling the boxes back into the wardrobe, he rushed into the living room. 'What did he say – the man in the alley? What did he say *exactly*?'

Eve glanced up at him in surprise. She took a moment to consider before repeating carefully: 'Joe wants it back. You understand? He wants it . . . fucking back.'

He noticed the way she paused before murmuring the expletive, as if considering whether to spare his sensitive ears. That, however, wasn't the word he was interested in. 'You're sure,' he asked. 'You're sure he said "it" and not "them"?'

She nodded. She wasn't about to forget that demand in a hurry. 'It. He definitely said "it".'

Henry leaned against the desk and folded his arms across his chest. 'So, singular rather than plural. Surely if it was drugs he would have said "them", he wants *them* back. Wouldn't that be natural?'

It hadn't occurred to Eve before. 'I suppose so.' Her eyes brightened a fraction. The thought of a haul of narcotics stashed in the flat hadn't been appealing. Although that still didn't solve the problem of what she *was* supposedly hiding.

'Also,' Henry continued, 'it must be relatively small. Why else would your burglar have had to turn the place upside down?'

'Unless it was a blind, a cover. Just to make it seem like a casual break-in.'

'But why bother? If it's something illegal – and judging from recent events, we can probably presume that it is – you wouldn't be calling the police. You wouldn't want the attention.'

'Except I didn't call them,' Eve replied. 'Sonia did. They might have guessed that someone else would notice the broken door and report it. Perhaps they were covering their tracks. If it looked routine, maybe even the work of kids, the cops wouldn't delve too deeply.'

Henry, who had thought he was making progress, felt momentarily deflated. She had a point. But he swiftly rallied. There was something nagging at the back of his mind. In his usual methodical way, he ran through the options, stopping to speak only as another idea grew in clarity. 'Actually, there's nothing to directly link the break-in with the subsequent attack – or the phone threats.'

Eve tried, not that successfully, to keep the incredulity out of her voice. 'What? You're suggesting it's just a coincidence?'

'No, not at all.' He was speaking more rapidly now, trying to articulate his idea before he lost the thread. 'But maybe we're coming at this from the wrong direction. I mean, what happened the next day?'

As if he were slightly mad, she lifted her brows, but had the good grace to humour him. 'Well, Cavelli rang. I was supposed to go to London and pick up the boxes but I told him I couldn't, that the flat had been broken into, that I had to clear up the mess. He wasn't best pleased – I mean about the boxes rather than the flat. And then, about an hour or so later Barry arrived, he's the guy who fixed the door, and then later, around mid-day, Paula turned up. After that—'

Henry raised a hand to stop her. 'Right. So in fact the break-in gave Cavelli the perfect excuse to provide you with a spot of first-class security. At least for the flat.'

'And for his precious boxes.' She sank her chin thoughtfully into her hands and stared at the carpet. 'And I wouldn't be likely to object, would I? God, you could be right. You know, at the time it did cross my mind that he could be responsible but not for that reason. I thought he might be sending me a message, a warning, one of those "you stick to your side of the bargain and I'll stick to mine" kind of deals. You know what men like him are like.'

Henry, whose experience of 'men like him' was confined to the pages of novels, uttered a vague grunt of agreement. Unlike Eve, he had never had the pleasure of meeting any hardened criminals or studying their habits. Another example, had he needed it, of the vast gulf between the two of them.

She looked up. 'And then, after everything that happened, I just presumed it couldn't be him, that it had to be to do with the others, the goon in the alley, this Joe person.'

'It still might,' he said. 'I'm not sure.' Frustrated, he rapped his knuckles against the surface of the desk. 'But unless they're a complete bunch of amateurs, why would they make such a mistake? All they had to do was to wait another twenty-four hours and they could have taken the boxes off you in the street. Or even stolen them from the car when Paula was first up here.'

'Just bad timing?' she suggested. 'They might have thought they'd already been delivered.'

'So what *could* be inside?' he murmured, as much to himself as to her. 'What could be so important that—'

'I'm not opening them,' she insisted. 'I can't. He could ring up tomorrow and ask for them back. He could send someone round, someone who'll know if they've been tampered with. I can't take that chance.'

But Henry was still pulling on a vital loose thread. 'Maybe this has nothing to do with the boxes. Maybe they're only an excuse, a red herring, something to distract you from what he really wants to protect.'

Eve shook her head. 'You're losing me.'

'Well, how could Cavelli take that risk? I mean, that you *wouldn't* open them, especially if you came under pressure. It's a natural reaction, isn't it? The first thing you'd do. And if there is anything illegal, anything valuable inside, how could he trust you not to pass it over to the police – or to anyone else?'

She stared up at him, wide-eyed. For a while she didn't answer.

He waited.

'Because,' she said eventually.

Her reply was simple but telling. She didn't need to explain, to go into detail. He immediately knew what she meant: she'd do anything for Terry, anything to protect him . . . even if that meant keeping sealed boxes sealed, blatantly breaking the law, and making undesirable deals with the devil.

Just like her father, she had no rules.

Henry frowned. No, that wasn't fair or true. She did have rules, just a kind he'd never come across before. She lived by a different set of regulations, a set of laws that bore no relation to his.

155

Eve's face, bleakly serious, gradually softened. Her mouth broke into a grin. 'So you're saying we should think *outside* the box?'

She was the only woman he knew who after being assaulted, threatened, followed by some stranger, and reduced to a limp by her former stepmother, could still come up with a comment like that. But for all her bravado he knew that she was scared. All the smiles in the world couldn't hide that.

'Perhaps.'

'Tell me more,' she demanded.

'I could be way off the mark.'

'Tell me!'

Henry shrugged. 'I was just wondering if . . . if it was possible that someone, Paula, Barry, anyone who was around that morning, might have taken the opportunity to hide something else here. You were still clearing up. You might not . . .'

'Have noticed?'

'Is that possible?'

She opened her lips as if to say no but then clearly had second thoughts. 'I don't know. I made them both drinks. I was in the kitchen for a while.'

'But you can see from there. Did you look back?'

She screwed up her eyes as she tried to recall. 'No, it couldn't have been Paula. She followed me. She was standing talking by the kitchen door.'

'She wasn't ever out of your sight?'

'Not really. For a few seconds maybe but that was all. But as for Barry, well, I went to make a brew and left him measuring up the door. He'd have had a few minutes.'

'And he's a more likely candidate than Paula,' Henry mused. 'I mean, originally you were supposed to be going to London, not her coming here. Do you know anything about the man?'

Eve sighed. 'Only that Martin Cavelli sent him, so

156

I doubt if he spends too much time in church.' She took the ice pack off her foot and stood up. She looked around. 'You think he might have hidden something in here?'

Henry's gaze followed hers. There weren't any obvious places. This space was almost as small and as stark as the bedroom. There was the desk, the bookshelves, the rest of the cheap shabby furniture. Nowhere that instantly drew his attention. But then they wouldn't be looking for anywhere like that. It would help if they knew exactly what 'it' was.

His confidence was beginning to ebb. 'I could be wrong.'

But that didn't stop Eve from embarking on an examination of the room. She slowly limped the length and breadth, running her hands over and under all the surfaces. After a moment, Henry joined her. Together they investigated every nook and cranny. And that didn't take a lifetime. It was hardly a room with much potential.

Eve looked up at the shelves. 'There's nothing there. I'd have noticed. I put all the books back with Sonia.' She opened and closed the drawers of the desk.

'Leave it,' Henry muttered, admitting defeat. 'It was a mad idea.'

'Hey, don't say that. At least you've had an idea. It's more than I have.' Then she delved into one of the drawers again. 'Although, what I do have is something that could be useful for you.' She began to root through the contents. 'I'm sure . . .'

'What is it?'

Frowning, she pulled out the drawer and emptied a heap of magazines and papers on to the top of the desk. She scattered them. 'It's gone. His phone – it's missing. It was here.'

'Was it there after the break-in?'

'I don't know. I . . . no, I don't remember seeing it. But

157

it was such a shock. I wasn't thinking straight.' She tried to recall. 'I don't think so.'

'So your burglar didn't go away empty-handed after all.'

'Apparently not.' She looked down, her fingers continuing to flick aimlessly, pointlessly, through the papers. There was a tremor in her voice. 'I bought him that phone, Henry. A few years ago. I bought it for his birthday.' She paused, tears springing to her eyes. 'You could have used it. I wouldn't have minded you using it.'

He touched her shoulder. 'I'm sorry.'

As if to free herself from the burden of his sympathy, Eve quickly shrugged him off. 'I'm okay.' She walked across the room and sat down, leaning forward to put her chin in her hands. For the next few minutes she stared silently down at the floor.

Henry let her be. He sensed her grief and understood it. She had barely had time to take breath, to even begin to come to terms with the death of her father, before being thrown headlong into this new unholy mess.

When she spoke again her voice, although not completely steady, was more angry than regretful. 'So perhaps it didn't have anything to do with Cavelli. Perhaps it *was* coincidence. Just some low-life who broke in looking for cash, for something to sell. Do you think?'

Henry didn't. There was more to this, far more. It didn't go anywhere towards explaining all the later events. There had to be a connection. But now wasn't the time to go into it. He decided to keep this particular theory to himself. As his recent brainwave had so disastrously proved, he was hardly Sherlock Holmes. 'Yes, it's possible.'

Eve overturned a cushion and slid her fingers down the side of the sofa. She came up with a handful of dust and a one pound coin. She smiled. 'Looks like dinner's on me. Come on, I've had enough of this place. I need some air. Let's go and get something to eat.'

'What about . . .?' He glanced at her foot.

'Oh, it's fine. I can make it down the street.' Then, as if to make amends for earlier, to apologize for recoiling from his touch, she stood up and gently slipped her arm through his. 'That's if you don't mind helping me along a little.'

Which was how Charlie May snapped the picture of them, leaning in close, as intimate as lovers, as they left the building.

Chapter Ten

Joe Silk wasn't happy. Three hours it had taken them to get here, to get to this muddy field of shit in the middle of nowhere. He had a charity gala to attend. It had cost him four hundred quid for a pair of tickets and at this rate he wouldn't make it back before the after-dinner speeches.

'He's here,' the driver said.

Silk adjusted the mirror. The filthy bastard was waiting, leaning up against a fence. 'Tell him to get in the car. And tell him to wipe his fucking feet first.'

Chase got out and beckoned him over. After some futile scraping, the back door opened and he crawled in. The smell was immediate, sour and disgusting, stale beer and fags combined with the unmistakable stench of fear.

Joe wound down the window. 'This had better be good.'

'I told you,' he muttered. 'I'd not have rung you else, would I? She's on to us. Got a bloody private dick on my tail. They know I was at the flat. They can prove it.' He rummaged in his pockets and came up with a grubby brown envelope. He opened it and passed forward three clear photographs. 'Copies, they're only copies. He's got the real ones. Wants two grand for them.'

Joe took the pictures with the tips of his white-gloved hands and stared down at the images: one print of his stinking passenger entering the flats, two of him leaving, all with an accurate recording of the date and time. He wondered which son-of-a-bitch had invented the camera. He'd like to meet him. He'd like to tear his fucking throat out.

'So what do they prove? That you went round to see the missus, that she wasn't there, that you waited around for a while and came back out again.' He shrugged. 'It's circumstantial, nothing more.'

'Enough for the pigs to give me a pull.'

'So what? You stick to your story, they can't prove otherwise.'

He shifted in his seat and started to rock, his palms rubbing anxiously along his thighs. 'They won't believe it, they won't. They'll have me back inside, they'll—'

Joe turned and silenced him with a look. He might have known Peter Marshall would screw up. And now he was sliding into panic. He was a liability. They should have got rid of him right at the start.

'Okay,' he said calmly. 'Tell this bloke – what's his name?'

'Patterson, Ivor Patterson.'

'Okay. Tell him you need a week to get the cash together.'

Marshall's round sweaty face relaxed. His mouth broke into a grin of relief. 'So you're going to pay him off?'

'A week,' he repeated. 'You make the arrangements. We'll be in touch.' He paused. 'Now get the fuck out of my car before I have to get it fumigated.'

He didn't need asking twice. Scrambling clumsily back into the mud, he started to walk away.

161

Joe stretched his arm out of the window. 'Haven't you forgotten something?'

Marshall looked furtively over his shoulder and pretended not to understand. But only for a second. There were some people you could take liberties with; Joe Silk wasn't one of them. He dug deep into his pockets again and produced the slim silver phone. He scurried back and placed it in his hand. 'It's been wiped. I was going to get rid of it.'

'I'll save you the trouble.'

'I was just—'

But the window was already rising, ascending with the kind of smooth easy closure that only money could buy. He didn't hang around. Lowering his head, he walked as quickly as he could towards the light and safety of the road.

The two men watched him retreat.

'You really going to pay?' Chase asked.

'You ever know a time when they didn't come back for more?'

'No.'

'Well then.'

He nodded. 'I'll sort it.'

'Both of them. Patterson *and* Marshall.' He lit a cigarette, exhaling the smoke softly into the dusk. 'And no more mistakes. We need to bury this once and for all.'

'And what about her?'

Joe peered through the windscreen. Evie. Little Evie. It had been a long time. Over twenty years. She couldn't have been more than ten or eleven when he last saw her, still in those early stages of adolescence, all long gangly legs and awkward smiles. Little Evie with her flaming red hair. He could still see her standing by the pool, wide eyes raised to the sky, the perfect picture of innocence.

He should have realized. He should have seen what

was coming. Any daughter of Alexander Weston was born to make trouble.

Fucking secrets. You could ignore them, drown them, bury them as deep as a coffin – but they always found a way to rise back to the surface.

He shook his head. 'We'll deal with her later.'

Chapter Eleven

As she drove, Eve gave more attention to the rear-view mirror than to the road ahead. Was she being tailed again? She glared at every car behind her, scrutinizing the drivers, wondering if this might be the one. It didn't have to be a man. They might have switched over to a woman. In fact there was a woman behind her right now, a tweedy innocuous fifty-something female – just the type she might not suspect.

She indicated and pulled into a lay-by.

The car swept on past.

Eve sat back and stared after the disappearing vehicle. She leaned over the wheel and sighed. What was she doing? This was the third time she'd stopped. If she went on like this she wouldn't get to Hillgrove before visiting was over. She took a moment to catch her breath before carefully pulling back out.

She tried to concentrate but her head was full of shadows. All her old fears were returning. From Sunday until Tuesday, she had sat tight, holed up inside the flat. Better safe than sorry. She winced as the phrase came into her head. She was supposed to be a fiery redhead. Since when had she become such a pale imitation?

She snarled. Since a man had pushed his groin into her back and placed his filthy hand over her mouth. But she mustn't think about that. After today, after she'd talked to Cavelli, it could all be sorted.

Half an hour later she was driving up the long winding path to the Visitors' Centre. She booked in and went to buy a coffee. Despite the slowness of her journey, there was still another ten minutes to wait before visits began. Time to get her thoughts in order. She had to be prepared. Calm and collected was the way ahead: no rows, no arguments. She had to make sure that their deal wasn't jeopardized. She took her drink to an empty table and sat down. She'd barely taken a sip when she was interrupted by a sharp female voice.

'You ignoring me then or what?'

Amber was standing beside her with her hand on her hip. She was dressed in her usual minimalist fashion, a tiny skirt, crop top, her skinny legs clad in fishnets.

'Sorry,' Eve said. 'I didn't realize . . .'

Amber laughed, taking the seat beside her. 'You looked miles away, that's why. In a right old daze. I haven't seen you for a while. Thought you and your bloke might have had a row or something.'

'He's not . . .' Eve began, but couldn't really be bothered to explain. It would only lead to more questions and she could do without those at the moment. 'No, I've just been coming on different days.' She paused. And how's . . .?' Suddenly her mind went blank. For the life of her, she couldn't remember his name.

'Dan,' Amber reminded her. 'Just the same old, same old. He never changes. Still complaining – can't stand the screws, can't stand the cons, can't stand bloody anything! I've told him, you think it's hard in here, try surviving out in the real world on your own. Rent, bills, food. There's no end to it.' She raised her baby blue eyes to the ceiling. 'They don't have a clue, do they?'

Eve gave a vague murmur of acknowledgement.

'I guess they get a bit preoccupied with their own situation. A bit, you know, selfish.'

Amber, apparently unimpressed by this remarkable insight into the psyche of the male prisoner, smartly changed the subject. 'What have you been up to then?'

'Oh, this and that. Work mostly.' The truth was so bizarre, so extraordinary, that even if she'd chosen to tell it – and of course she wasn't going to – it wouldn't have been believed. 'I've just been doing some temping,' she added, giving a touch of veracity to her story. 'Office stuff. Pretty dull but it doesn't pay too badly. What about you?'

Fortunately Amber's recitation of her trials and tribulations, consisting mainly of her mother's disapproval of her choice in boyfriends, filled the rest of the time until visits were called.

They collected their numbers and traipsed along the familiar path to the main building.

'You look nice,' Amber said.

Eve glanced down at what she was wearing. 'Thanks.' She would have worn a skirt but they never worked with flatties and no one, not even Cavelli, was going to force her bruised toes into a pair of high heels today. But, preferring to keep on his right side, she had made the effort: a clingy black jersey top that flattered her curves and a pair of silky hip-hugging trousers. As her father had always said, there was nothing wrong with using the cards you'd been dealt.

'I wish I was tall,' Amber sighed. 'I mean, it makes you look kind of classy, like a model.'

Eve smiled. 'Does it?' There was nothing like a compliment to rev your confidence back into gear. And she currently needed all the confidence she could get. She lifted her shoulders and strode on a few paces before remembering that one compliment deserved another. 'But men prefer smaller girls,' she said. 'They always have. More petite girls like you. It makes them feel protective.'

Amber beamed. 'Do you think?'

'Of course.'

'Still,' she said, as if offering the greatest of consolations, 'you must feel small beside your bloke.'

Eve's stomach took a dive.

They went through the usual routine, in and out of the holding area, across the courtyard and up the stairs. She had just got used to feeling calm when she came here and now her nerves were fizzing again, a thousand Catherine wheels revolving in her guts. *Her bloke*, as Amber had so inaccurately described him, would be waiting for her.

What if it all went horribly wrong?

No, it wouldn't. It couldn't.

But her optimism wasn't boosted as she cleared the search procedure and walked into the room. She saw his eyes, those menacing slate-blue eyes, rise darkly to meet her own. He looked about as happy as a man on the way to the gallows.

Forcing a smile, she made her way over and sat down beside him. 'How are you?'

He didn't smile back. 'I think we need to talk.'

Eve couldn't argue with that. 'I guess,' she said. In a way it was a relief, cutting straight to the chase. At least they weren't going to spend ages dancing around the subject. This way she didn't have to start explaining everything. Or to start laying blame either. The sooner they could put this behind them the better. She leaned forward and smiled again.

'Look, I know you didn't mean for any of this to happen but . . . well, we might have a deal but you have to agree that it never included the rest of this stuff. And I'm not asking any questions. Believe me, I don't want to know. I'm not interested. All I am asking is that whoever this Joe is, that you sort it out. Just get him off my back.'

He stared at her. 'What?'

'I don't know what he wants and I really hope that I don't have it. But if I do, then it has to stop. Surely you can see that? I can't spend the rest of my life a prisoner in my own home.' As soon as she said it, she flinched. Bearing in mind his circumstances, it was hardly the most diplomatic turn of phrase. 'I mean, I don't want to be afraid to go out. I don't want to be scared to answer my own phone. We've got a deal, okay, I understand that, but you never mentioned anything about—'

He shifted forward and raised his hand. 'Hey, slow down, slow down. What the hell are you talking about?'

Eve frowned. 'About being followed, about the threats . . .'

'What threats?'

She glared at him. 'You know what I mean.'

'News to me,' he said. 'What's the matter? You been having trouble?'

It was the grin on his face that raised her hackles. She was sorely tempted to call him a liar but that was hardly going to smooth the road towards conciliation. Yet despite her best efforts, she couldn't quite keep the sarcasm out of her tone. 'So don't tell me, you don't know anyone called Joe either?'

'As it happens,' he said, 'I do. Joe Callaghan. But he's seventy-eight and living in Skipton. Is he the one who's been hassling you?' The grin grew wider. 'He always did have a weakness for redheads.'

She sat back in her chair and scowled. 'I'm glad you think it's a joke.'

'I don't know what it is,' he said. 'I don't have a fucking clue.'

But she wasn't prepared to just roll over. Cavelli, she was certain, knew more than he was letting on. 'So if this has nothing to do with you, why did you go to so much trouble over the door?'

He shrugged. 'Can't a man do a favour for a *friend*?' He stressed the word as if it amused him. 'You sounded worried. I thought you might appreciate some extra protection. It's tough for you ladies out there on your own.'

She narrowed her eyes. God, there were some things she could take but being patronized by a six foot four smirking gorilla wasn't one of them. 'Extra protection for your boxes, more like.'

'That too,' he agreed. 'I admit it. No one wants to see their personal belongings trashed.'

'What, as opposed to their friends?'

With a leer, he slowly looked her up and down. 'You don't look too trashed to me.'

Eve took a deep breath. *Don't rise to it.* Stay calm and collected. Remember? The worst thing she could do was to lose her cool. She had to think of Terry. Cavelli might be a cheap lecherous bastard but at least the bruises had faded from her brother's face.

But that didn't solve the problem of where to go next. It was like banging her head against a brick wall; all she was achieving was one almighty headache. It was pointless even trying to get the truth out of him. But she still made one final attempt, laying it out in black and white. 'So you don't know this Joe? You don't know who he is? You don't know why his goons have been threatening me or asking for *it* back?'

'Like I said, I've never heard of him.' He folded his wide muscled arms across his chest. 'Maybe you need to look a little closer to home.'

She frowned. 'Meaning?'

'Maybe someone from your own past.'

'Don't be ridiculous,' she snapped, losing patience. 'Stop playing games. I'm only here because you sent a

169

visiting order. That's why you wanted to see me, isn't it, because of what's been happening?'

'Fuck no,' he said.

She stared at him.

'I think you'll need a drink first. Mine's a tea.'

Eve was glad to get away, even if it was only as far as the kiosk. What did he mean? Her stomach was turning somersaults again. She glanced across the room and saw Amber leaning in close to Dan, holding hands, whispering sweet nothings. If only life were so simple . . .

She carried the two plastic cups back to the table. 'So what's this about?'

'What do you think? Terry of course.'

'What about him?' She could feel her heart start to quicken. 'Has something happened? Is he okay?' Her hand jerked and some of the tea spilled out across the table.

Cavelli leaned forward and mopped at it with a tissue. 'He's fine. For the moment. But I need to know if it's true.'

Now it was her turn to look bemused. 'Is what true?'

He scrunched up the damp tissue in his fist. 'Is Terry a grass?'

Eve's mouth fell open. She stared at him aghast. 'Terry?' She shook her head. 'Christ, of course not. Why are you asking that?'

'Because there's a rumour going round.'

'There can't be. I don't understand.'

Her voice must have risen, panic invading its tone, because Cavelli drew a finger to his lips. 'Keep it down,' he said, glancing over his shoulder at the screws. 'I'm not saying I believe it, I'm just telling you how it is.'

Eve's face, at first hot, now turned cold and clammy. She knew what happened to grasses in prison. She shivered. 'It isn't true. It isn't. Where's it coming from?'

'I take it you've heard of the Rowan brothers.'

She nodded. 'The Broadlands robbery. It's what Terry got sent down for, handling the stolen property. He—' She stopped abruptly. 'So it's them? But why would they? It doesn't make any sense. Terry's serving a sentence too.'

'Twelve months,' he said. 'Six if he keeps out of trouble. It hardly compares to fifteen years.'

'But it was only handling,' she repeated.

Cavelli gave her one of his dark looks. 'Was it? You see, the rumour is that Terry was on the job too. Only strangely most of the evidence against him went missing. You can see how that might appear from their point of view.'

Eve's head was reeling. 'But he wasn't on the job,' she insisted.

'Are you sure?'

'Yes!'

'So why would the Rowans make up a story like that?'

'I don't know,' she said, briefly covering her face with her hands. 'It's crazy.' She couldn't think straight. And to make matters worse, a tiny seed of doubt was growing in the back of her mind. She couldn't actually put her hand on her heart and swear that Terry hadn't been more involved. What if he had? Over the past few years he'd been getting into deeper and deeper trouble. The only thing she was sure of was that he couldn't be a grass.

'Eve?' He was still waiting for an explanation.

'Perhaps they're after some kind of legal appeal, something to muddy the waters.'

Cavelli shrugged. 'It's possible. But that doesn't explain why they want to hurt him.'

His words hit like a violent punch to the stomach. 'Hurt him?' she croaked.

'Men like the Rowans can get very bitter and resentful.'

Eve was starting to feel sick. This was turning into a

nightmare. 'He's not a grass,' she said. 'You don't know Terry. He's not. He'd never do anything like that.'

There were a few awkward seconds of silence.

'You must see how difficult this makes it for me.' He shifted in his seat and sighed. 'With these rumours going round, these accusations, I really can't afford to—'

'There's no need to spell it out.' It was a devastating blow but there was nothing she could do about it. She'd have to make other arrangements, go to the Governor, get Terry moved into solitary. It wasn't the best solution – going down the block would be like admitting his guilt – but at least he'd be safe there. 'You're pulling the plug, right? You can't protect him any more.'

But then he surprised her. 'I didn't say that. If you're giving me your word that he's not a grass then I'm prepared to accept it.'

Her eyes lit up. 'You are?'

'Sure,' he said. Then he paused, a grimace curling down the corners of his mouth. 'It's just that it makes it so much harder. You understand? A bit of bullying on the wing I can sort, no problem, but something like this . . . Well, it could get much nastier.' He sighed again. 'And that means a lot of time and effort, not to mention extra muscle. And that means . . .'

She got his drift; it was floating over loud and clear: *Cavelli's price had just gone up.* 'How much do you want?'

He frowned. 'Oh, don't be like that. Surely one good turn deserves another.'

'How much?' she repeated stonily.

'It's not money. Have I ever asked for money?' That smug expression had appeared again. 'But there is one little favour you could do for me.'

Eve shuddered. She was still recovering from the last favour she'd done. 'How do I even know you're telling the truth about these rumours? What if you're making it all up?'

'Fine,' he said, sitting back. 'Let's wait and see.'

She wished she had the nerve to call his bluff but she didn't. If anything happened to Terry she'd never forgive herself. But it was hard to give in graciously. 'Don't tell me,' she said, 'you've got a few more boxes you need putting into storage?'

'No.'

She waited but he didn't continue. 'So?'

'So there's no point if you're not interested.'

Eve gripped her hands together in her lap. Now wasn't the time to get into a battle of wills. She had to put her own feelings aside. She had to beg, plead, even get down on her bended knees if that was what it took. 'Look, I'm sorry. I *am* interested. Of course I am. Just tell me what you want.'

That familiar smirk appeared on his face again. 'And you'll do it?'

They were back to square one, to the first time they'd met. And just like then, he had the upper hand. He was still holding all the cards. She took a deep breath. 'Anything.'

As if savouring the moment, his tongue flicked out and slid along his lips. His heavy brows lifted. 'Are you sure?'

'I'm sure.' She forced a smile.

He paused, giving her another of his long scrutinizing looks. 'This is serious, Evie.'

On hearing that version of her name again, she instinctively flinched. For one dark second she was back in the alley. *Don't mess us about, Evie.* And she suddenly realized that she still hadn't got any answers, still didn't know why she'd been threatened. Yet here she was, preparing to jump in even deeper. It was madness. But what choice did she have?

'I am serious,' she said. 'I swear. I promise.'

But still he made her sweat. Frowning, he gazed sullenly around the room as if trying to make up his mind as to whether she could be trusted.

'Tell me what you want,' she urged.

'It isn't much. I . . .' As if to layer on the agony, he hesitated again. 'I just want you to find someone for me.'

'Find someone?'

He shrugged. 'But if you don't think you can do it . . .'

'Who?' she asked quickly. 'Just give me their name.'

'All right,' he finally said. 'It's Jimmy Reece. R, double e. Also known as James Reece. He'll be in London somewhere. Turn over a sordid rock or two and he should crawl out. Soho's as good a place as any to start.'

Eve tried not to look as disheartened as she felt. So now she had to go poking around the red-light district searching for some sleazeball. 'Why do you want to find him?'

It was a question she instantly regretted.

Cavelli's eyes darkened. 'That's my business,' he said. 'Terry's yours. Are you up for it or not?'

Like she had a choice. She nodded earnestly. 'But I'll need a few more details. I mean, like how old is he, what does he look like, what does he do?'

'Do your homework,' he snapped back, 'and you'll soon find out.' Then, as if regretting the outburst, he added in a more moderate tone: 'He's about forty, a lush, a junkie, used to be a so-called actor. And be discreet, okay? Don't *ever* mention my name. All I want to know is where he is, who he's with, and what he's doing now.'

'Okay,' she said. This wasn't sounding good but Cavelli had her in a corner. 'That's fine. I'll find him.' Inwardly, she tried to justify it to herself. After all, she wouldn't be doing anything that a private eye couldn't.

The only difference was that her bill came in the form of protection for Terry.

A look of satisfaction appeared on his face. 'Good,' he said. 'I'll be waiting to hear from you.'

As she rose to leave, he gestured her back down. 'Oh, and there's one more thing. You should start writing to me.'

'Writing?'

'Yeah,' he said, 'letters. You know the type of thing, bits of paper that go in envelopes. One or two a week should do. Write and tell me how much you miss me, how much you're looking forward to seeing me again. The usual stuff. I'm sure if you dig deep enough you can find some suitably heart-warming phrases.'

Confusion swept over Eve, along with a sensation that bordered on repulsion. Then anger swept into her eyes. How dare he! She glared at him. Okay, so she was hardly an innocent – she was more than prepared to use her charms to get what she wanted – but that still didn't mean she was his for the taking. Far from it. What did his perverted mind imagine, that she was part of this deal too, that she came with the package, that—

'Oh, for Christ's sake,' he said, observing her expression. 'What do you think I am? I'm not *that* fucking desperate.' He laughed. Then he leaned forward, keeping his voice low. 'It's a means to an end, sweetheart, nothing more. I thought you'd realize that. It's an easy way for me to get hold of an extra visiting order. If anything urgent comes up then just say that you have to see me, that we have to talk, some crap like that. Put it in writing and make it emotional.' He glanced around, wary as always of anyone who might be listening. 'Woman trouble – this place is full of it. Threaten to leave me and they'll be handing out VOs like sweeties. But first it needs to be established that we have some kind of a relationship. All the letters get read by the screws so try and make it convincing, huh?'

Eve's initial rush of relief was rapidly replaced by a seething resentment. He had led her on deliberately, she was sure he had. He had done it just to wind her up, to have a laugh at her expense, to keep control. Well, not to worry, she wasn't going to walk away without getting the last word. But first things first. Although she didn't relish the prospect of a regular correspondence she could see that it had its advantages. Accordingly, she nodded. 'Sweet nothings it is then.'

He grinned. 'And it would help, when you visit, if you tried to look a little more affectionate and a little less like you hated my guts.'

Now he was really pushing his luck.

But she nodded again. 'Okay. I get it.'

As they both rose to their feet, she placed a hand on his arm. He looked down at her. She looked up. If she had a moment's hesitation – a man with eyes this cold really shouldn't be crossed – she rapidly dismissed it. Rising on to her toes, she tentatively leaned forward as if to kiss him. She waited until the last possible moment, until his mouth was moving towards hers, before smartly averting her face. With her cheek against his, she softly whispered in his ear: 'That's the thing about relationships, don't you find? There's always such a thin line between love and hate.'

Ivor Patterson was feeling pretty smug when he rang the office and made his excuses. He spluttered dramatically down the line. He wasn't too well, a bad dose of the flu. Yes, it did seem to be doing the rounds. No, he wasn't sure when he'd be back. They'd have to find some cover. Naturally, he'd forward his report; he'd send it through straight away. He replaced the receiver and laughed out loud. There was no point standing round street corners when he already had 2K in the bag.

The shakedown couldn't have gone better. The photographs had provided the *coup de grâce*. The expression on Peter Marshall's face had been priceless, a wondrous combination of astonishment and fear. Maybe he should have asked for more. But no, a couple of grand would do fine. A holiday was what he'd spend it on, somewhere hot and relaxing, maybe the USA. He'd always fancied Florida.

The call had come a few hours ago. A week, just seven days, was all he had to wait. In the meantime he'd grab a beer, put his feet up and relax . . .

Louise shifted forward a fraction as Richard Baxter leaned over her shoulder. She could feel his warm breath on her neck. 'Keeping busy?' he asked.

'Oh, yes,' she murmured.

He hovered for a moment before sliding around and perching casually on the edge of the desk. He smiled. 'Lord, it's dreary down here, isn't it? Positively dismal. Must be like working in a mine.'

Unwilling to give offence, she produced a small smile too. 'It's not so bad.'

'Well, don't worry,' he said. 'I'm sure we can find room back upstairs before *too* long. This is hardly the place for a girl like you.'

Louise felt a faint flush suffusing her face. So far as she could recall, this was the most he had ever said to her in the past two years; she had been so far outside his orbit that she may as well have been living on a different planet. Now he was suddenly gazing into her eyes with what could only be described as rapt attention. She might have been flattered if she hadn't been a realist. She knew she was pretty but only in a quiet rather undefined kind of way. She could never compare to the more startling beauty that stalked the upper floors. Richard Baxter was after something . . . but it certainly wasn't her body.

He lightly cleared his throat before continuing. 'You know, my father's not been very well recently. He's been working too hard and . . . Well, he's not as young as he was and I'm concerned that things have been getting on top of him. The trouble is that sometimes, in these situations, people have a tendency to take advantage.'

The stain darkened on her cheeks. 'I hope you're not suggesting—'

'Good Lord, no!' he exclaimed. He reached forward to touch her on the arm, allowing his hand to linger. 'I know I can trust *you*, Louise. That's why I'm telling you all this. I know I can rely on your absolute discretion.' Slowly, as if with the greatest of reluctance, he removed his fingers. He sighed. 'Unfortunately your predecessor wasn't of the same calibre. I don't want to go into detail but suffice to say she had neither your integrity nor your principles. And it's worrying, *very* worrying, that she might attempt to approach my father again. So I was thinking, if you could maybe keep an eye on the situation, let me know if she calls or writes . . . for his own sake naturally.'

The light dawned. *He wanted to recruit her as his personal spy!*

Mistaking her silence for a shy combination of acceptance and awe, he bestowed another of his well-practised smiles. He gently patted her arm again. 'I knew you'd understand.' Then, as if an unspoken agreement had been signed and sealed, he snaked upright, smoothed the invisible creases in his trousers and headed for the door.

As it closed behind him, Louise sat back and raised her eyes to the ceiling. It was hard to imagine that, like all the other girls, she'd once had an almighty crush on him. Now she was seeing him for precisely what he was: underneath that sleek exterior was nothing but pure slime.

Originally she'd been disappointed to be posted to the subterranean depths of the building. It had felt like a backward step, an embarrassing demotion, but to her surprise she had found that it had certain advantages. Henry Baxter was kind, polite and respectful. Apart from his pedantic attention to detail, he was otherwise undemanding; there were no added obligations, no errands, no items of dry cleaning to pick up, no constant demands for coffee or tedious sandwich runs.

She had soon adjusted to her new environment.

Even the clients were more agreeable. Elderly gentlemen for the most, they treated her with a quiet old-fashioned courtesy. Compared to the glitzy world of the upper floors, their attentions were sedate and curiously old-fashioned but she didn't miss the occasional glimpses of the rich and famous or their arrogant dismissive glances. She didn't miss the gossip of the other secretaries either. With her less-than-rampant love life and her conservative taste in clothes, she had never really fitted in.

Upstairs, she had been invisible. Here, she felt valued.

And if Richard Baxter thought she was going to give all this up for a fleeting touch of his smarmy hand he had another think coming.

Eve huddled behind the wheel and lit a cigarette. She had to calm her nerves before she started back. The visit had been nothing but bad news. She had walked in with one problem and come out with another. What were the odds? She had to talk to Terry. She had to see him soon.

179

Opening the window, she glowered at the red brick building ahead. Cavelli was probably back on the wing by now, quietly gloating over his latest triumph. He had her exactly where he wanted. Damn! This whole Jimmy Reece business stank. If she did find him, who-ever he was, what would it mean? What did Cavelli intend to do? She shut her eyes tight. She didn't want to go there.

The less she knew the better.

Gradually, the other visitors pulled away until the car park was almost deserted. Alerted by the guttural sound of a motor in distress, she glanced across to see a bright red Mini with its bonnet up, a swirling gust of thick grey smoke, and one very unhappy woman. Eve groaned. If waving your arms and swearing blind was the way to fix an engine then Amber would shortly be putting every local mechanic out of business.

She wanted to get home but couldn't just drive away and leave her stranded. Reluctantly, she got out of the car and walked across the forecourt. 'Are you okay?'

It was a question, like so many she'd volunteered this afternoon, which barely seemed worth the effort of asking. Together, they stared down at the steaming mass of hot twisted metal.

'What's the matter with it?' Amber asked.

Eve peered inside and sighed. 'God knows. But it looks pretty terminal. You'd better ring your breakdown people.'

She stared at her. 'Huh?'

'You know, the AA, whoever you're with.'

'Er . . .'

Eve felt another crisis looming. She wasn't sure if she could deal with it. 'Oh, please tell me you're kidding.'

Amber's lower lip trembled and her face started to crumple. 'How am I going to get home?' she wailed. 'What am I going to do?'

Putting an arm around her shoulder, Eve tried to offer some comfort. 'Don't worry. We'll sort it out.' But clearly the only way it was going to be sorted was if *she* did something about it. 'You wait here. I'll see if I can find someone.'

She went back into the Visitors' Centre and asked if they had a directory she could borrow. As she flicked through the pages she considered ringing the garage her father had used but then had second thoughts. There was probably an outstanding bill and she couldn't afford to be landed with it.

'That your car?' the young screw asked, glancing out of the window.

She followed his gaze. Amber was still glaring down at the engine as if the sheer force of her personality might will it back to life.

She shook her head. 'No, I'm just helping out.'

'She a friend of yours then?'

Hearing a hint of incredulity, Eve looked up. 'Why?'

He shrugged. 'No reason.'

But his brown eyes, shifting sideways, suggested something different.

'Is there—'

'Here,' he said, scribbling down a number on a scrap of paper. 'Try this place. They're reliable and not too pricey. I've used them before. Might take them a while to get here though.'

'Thanks.'

She got out her phone and dialled. Within a couple of minutes and after some minor persuasion – she was getting used to the fine art of begging – she was able to make the necessary arrangements.

'You were right,' she said as she hung up. 'It'll be a couple of hours. Do we have to stay here or can we just leave the car? I'm pretty sure it's going to be a tow-job.'

As if a tow-job was the kind of service the lads got down the local brothel, he sniggered. Then, seeing her expression, he quickly straightened his face. 'Leave it with me. I'll make sure security knows.'

'Thanks,' she said again. 'Thanks for all your help.' She was tempted to pursue their earlier exchange but decided against it. You could never tell with screws, some were the wind-up merchants from hell and others were as thick as a 50-tog duvet. And even if he was neither, she was pretty sure that he had said as much as he was going to. She did, however, take the time to read the name tag on his shirt and to make a mental note of it: David Hammond. You could never tell. It might come in useful one day.

As Eve turned and walked towards the door she could feel his eyes on her. Perhaps he was admiring her remarkable self-restraint. She glanced back. No, he was just staring at her arse.

They were starting to hit the rush hour traffic. Eve could have dropped Amber off at the station but it had seemed pretty pointless her travelling all the way back to Essex only to turn around and come straight back tomorrow. But she was still fretting over her decision to invite her to stay overnight. Herbert Street was hardly a safe haven. What if something happened while she was there? What if the man from the alley was waiting and . . .

That was one anxiety but she had plenty more. She was still pondering on what the screw had said, or rather what he'd implied, about her helping Amber out. Or had he? Maybe that was just her paranoia working overtime.

But even that wasn't especially important. There were far more serious worries circling her mind. While Amber chattered on, Eve nodded her head and murmured the obligatory 'listening' sounds as she tried to prioritize all her other fears. Terry was right at the top of the list. Perhaps he *had* been more involved in the Broadlands job. As Cavelli had said, why would the Rowans lie about it? But then he could hardly be trusted himself. If there was a Nobel prize for smart double-dealing manipulation he'd be picking up a generous cheque before the year was out. She scowled through the windscreen. Although if he *was* lying, he must realize that she'd eventually find out.

And then there was Lesley. As she thought of her, Eve's foot began to ache again. Did Lesley know the truth? Perhaps that was why she'd been so uptight, so stubborn, so unwilling to give Terry any more chances. Eve hadn't been around when he'd been arrested. All she knew was what her father had told her. And that was nothing much. Only that he was in trouble again.

She pulled up at the lights, tapping her fingers restively against the wheel. On top of all that were the threats, this crazy Joe business. She was still no closer to knowing who *he* was – or what he wanted.

'So have you two been together long?'

'What?'

'You and your fella,' Amber said. 'Is it serious?'

It was serious all right, but not in the way she thought. 'No, Martin's not my . . . We're just good friends. I've known him for years.'

'Oh,' she murmured.

Then Eve suddenly remembered. She'd been stressing over so many other things, she'd almost forgotten about her new 'arrangement' with Cavelli. Weren't they supposed to be an item? Damn! Perhaps she ought to suggest that their friendship was moving on, that . . .

But then, surprisingly, Amber started to laugh. As if in relief, she raised a hand to her chest and made a small fluttery motion with her fingers. 'Thank God for that!'

'What is it?' Eve gazed at her, puzzled.

'It's just that last week . . .' She took a moment to recover her composure. 'Well, he had this other girl on a visit. A blonde piece, not classy or nothing. Had a mouth on her too. You know the type. All over him she was. And you've been so nice to me, I didn't know whether to say. I mean, it's not really my business and I didn't want to cause you grief.'

Eve grinned. She could see how it might have created a dilemma. And it explained why Cavelli might be rather short on visiting orders. Well, she couldn't change her story now without causing major embarrassment. And anyway, it didn't really matter. Just so long as the screws believed it . . .

'Lots of blokes are at it,' she continued. 'They see different girls on different days. I'd fucking kill my Dan if he did that to me. I thought she might, you know, be his bit on the side. That's why I was asking, if it was serious like.'

The lights changed to green and the traffic began to move again. Eve edged the car forward. 'Of course *I* could have been the bit on the side.'

She shook her head. 'No, you're not the type.'

'What, too dull?'

'No!' she insisted. 'Because you're way too smart to put up with any crap like that.'

Smart? Considering her current circumstances, Eve didn't think that was the most apt description but she accepted the comment with a smile. She wondered vaguely who the mystery girl might be. Not Paula, that was for sure. Anyway, it was no concern of hers. Who Cavelli chose to see was entirely his own business.

'Just out of interest,' she asked, 'if we *had* been an item, would you have told me?'

Amber frowned before lifting her shoulders in a tiny indecisive shrug. 'I dunno. It's rank seeing someone being messed about, especially someone you like, but . . . well, if you spill it's always going to cause big trouble. Don't you reckon? That kind of trouble always comes back one way or another. And not just on you but on your man too. You know what I mean? It's like being a grass or something.'

Eve shuddered at the words. 'Yeah, I guess.'

'Although it's hard,' Amber muttered. 'I mean, you don't want to get caught in the middle but then *I'd* really want to know if Dan was cheating, doing the dirty. And if someone else found out and they didn't tell me, then I'd feel . . .'

Eve sensed that they'd hit a sore point. Dan, she suspected, might have a rather bad track record in the field of fidelity. 'I'm sure he wouldn't.'

Amber didn't look convinced. As if she might be about to cry, her eyes had assumed a liquid quality. 'You can't—'

'If it helps,' she said quickly, hoping to divert from any emotional outbursts, 'I spend a fair amount of time at Hillgrove and I've never seen him with anyone else. Did I tell you that my brother Terry is in there too?'

This surprising piece of information proved a big enough distraction to keep the tears at bay. 'God, so you have to visit both of them?'

Eve laughed. 'Well, it's not obligatory. But as I only live down the road it's not too great a hardship. Anyway, all I'm saying is that I don't think you have to worry. I've never seen your Dan on a visit with anyone else. I'm sure he's not messing you around.' What she didn't mention was that she wouldn't have recognized the whinging Dan if he'd been placed in a line-up of two at the local nick. Today, at the kiosk, was the first time she'd actually looked at him but she'd been so preoccupied that her memory of his features was a complete blank.

Amber's mouth curled into a smile. 'Really?'

'Absolutely.' Mentally, Eve crossed her fingers, hoping that the lie wouldn't come back to haunt her. And not just for her own sake. For all her mindless chatter, she liked Amber. At least she said what she thought – and that made a refreshing change.

By now they were approaching Herbert Street. Although another crisis had been temporarily averted, Eve was instantly on red alert again. They were almost home and she was starting to get anxious. What if someone was waiting? There was safety in numbers but she didn't want to put her guest in danger. It was hardly the most hospitable of moves, inviting someone to stay only to have them attacked by some violent, filthy, foul-mouthed hood.

She drove slowly around the corner and pulled up at an empty space outside the café. She looked in her mirror. Nothing suspicious. She looked around. Usually she was back earlier but with all the problems over the car it was almost six o'clock and the street for once was reasonably busy, too busy she hoped for anyone to take the risk of another attack. The commuters were on their way to the station and the kids, out of school, were strutting their stuff and trying to look cool as they loitered outside the chippy.

No, there were too many potential witnesses.

She got out of the car. Out of the corner of her eye, she thought she saw a movement. But then she was starting to see shadows everywhere. She had to pull herself together. She forced herself not to look over her shoulder again.

They were approaching the door to the flats when his voice cut through the air.

'Eve!'

She turned to see Jack Raynor walking towards her. Her heart sank. God, this was the last thing she needed!

'I was just passing,' he said.

She raised her brows. No one just passed along Herbert Street. Not unless they lived in the vicinity, were after a fish and chip supper . . . or were searching for a whore. And Jack, armed with a perfect bouquet of soft cream roses, didn't seem to fit into any of those categories.

'I wanted to say thanks for the other evening, for keeping me company.'

'My,' Amber murmured admiringly. And she wasn't just looking at the flowers. Her eyes made a blatant scan of his body, from his pretty blue eyes to the tips of his toes. She gave a soft appreciative sigh.

Eve skipped the introductions and quickly thrust the keys into her hand. 'It's on the top floor,' she said. 'Number five. I'll catch you up.'

She hoped Amber was too young and inexperienced to sniff out a cop. If not, and this ever got back to Cavelli, she'd have a hell of a lot of explaining to do.

Chapter Twelve

Cavelli stopped by the open cell door. 'Can we talk?'

Bryant, who was sitting reading a newspaper, slowly raised his head. His two lackeys, a pair of brainless bruisers, put their hard faces on and sneered.

'Busy,' one of them said.

'Fuck off!' the other contributed.

'Five minutes,' Cavelli said, ignoring them both. He addressed the boss directly, looking straight into his eyes.

Bryant thought about it for a long second but eventually nodded.

Cavelli stepped forward. 'In private,' he added.

One of the morons opened his mouth but was silenced with a glance. Their master flapped a hand. 'Wait outside.'

Obediently, they got to their feet. As they swaggered through the door they took the opportunity to practise their glaring technique. One of them gave a low threatening growl. Cavelli grinned back. He'd known tough men in his time and these two didn't even come close.

He turned to Bryant. 'Don't you ever tire of the intellectual conversation?'

A smile quivered on his lips. 'Whatever you want, make it quick. I haven't got all day.' He gestured towards a chair.

George Bryant didn't exactly run the wing – Hillgrove was a low security prison and cons weren't usually around long enough to establish a truly effective power base – but for the moment he had more influence than most. An intelligent man, approaching fifty, he was in the final years of a long murder sentence. He had seen it all and done worse.

Cavelli sat down. 'It's about Terry Weston. You know what's going down?'

'You tell me.'

'The Rowans are claiming he's a grass.'

Bryant nodded. 'That's what I've heard.'

'Well, I've heard different.' Cavelli splayed his palms across his wide thighs and leaned forward. 'I've heard the Rowans are full of shit.'

Another smile, this one slyer than the last, made a fleeting appearance. 'Ah, so that's why you're protecting him. How very gallant. You're defending the young man's *honour*.'

Cavelli stared at him, his anger stirring. He knew what he was implying. Had anyone else come close to the suggestion he'd have been tempted to teach them some manners but this wasn't the time to take offence. He needed him on side. But for all that, he couldn't just let it pass. The retort slid out before he could think better of it. 'You trying to say something?'

Bryant gave a low laugh. He knew Cavelli's reputation; strike first and talk later. And his size always gave him an advantage. Any inclination towards disagreement was vastly reduced in the presence of six foot four of solid muscle. 'Lighten up. You think I'd say it if I believed it?'

'You're hardly the shy type.'

Bryant laughed again, a quiet mirthless sound. 'I heard

you had a temper.' Sitting back, he placed his hands sedately in his lap. For a while he gazed silently at his uninvited visitor. He was still a mystery. When Cavelli had first arrived, over a year ago, Bryant had expected trouble. Any man built like that, with a short fuse and a violent history, was bound to be bad news but the challenge he'd expected had never materialized. Surprisingly, Cavelli had kept himself to himself. Until now they had never gone beyond the occasional nod in the corridor. 'So what's your interest?'

'I've got my reasons.'

'And what have those reasons to do with me?'

'People listen to you. You can put them straight.'

Bryant shrugged. 'I could but why should I? It's no business of mine. Why should I give a fuck?'

Cavelli stared at him again. 'Because whatever else he might be, Terry Weston isn't a grass. You have my word on it. The Rowans have got it wrong. You think I'd defend a fucking grass? If these rumours aren't stopped soon, they're going to grow. They're going to grow and eventually they're going to fucking explode.'

'And?'

'And you've got a nice quiet life here, Mr Bryant. Nice and quiet. Nice and orderly. No mess. No questions. But if this crap with Terry continues, that's all going to change. If he gets hurt again, there are going to be repercussions. And then no more happy days. And after it's over, however it pans out, the screws are going to slam the lid; this wing's going to be shut down as tight as a fucking coffin.'

He frowned. 'Are you threatening me?'

'I'm just telling you how it is.'

Bryant sat back and thought about it. There was some sense to what he was saying. A feud on the wing wouldn't be good for business. Eventually he came to a decision. 'I'll see what I can do. I can't promise anything.'

Cavelli stood up.

Bryant waved him away. The interview was over.

Through the glass in the office door Louise saw Henry Baxter bent over a mobile phone, his brow furrowed, his fingers pressing various buttons as he valiantly battled with the complexities of modern technology. As she knocked and walked in, he quickly slid it under a sheaf of papers. He looked as guilty as a schoolboy hiding a dirty magazine.

She placed the letters on the desk. 'If you could sign these for me.'

He nodded. 'Thank you.'

'New phone?' she asked casually.

As if she possessed previously undisclosed psychic powers, Henry's mouth dropped open.

She gestured towards the manual lying in front of him. 'It all seems a bit complicated at first, doesn't it? But it's okay once it's set up. And they're handy, you know, if you break down in the car or anything. Saves having to find a phone box.'

'Yes,' he mumbled. 'That's why I wanted it, in case of a breakdown or . . .'

Louise fought back a smile. Poor Henry was not a good liar, particularly in the realm of personal affairs. Perhaps the relationship with Eve Weston was still going on. Perhaps Richard had cause for concern after all. But so what if he did? They were *his* concerns and not hers. She reached out a hand. 'Here, let me help.'

'No, really, it's . . .'

'I don't mind. It won't take a minute.'

And with her palm still patiently outstretched, he had

no choice but to burrow under the papers and reluctantly pass it over.

Louise sat down and examined the tiny silver phone. 'We need to set up an address book,' she said. 'That way you don't have to dial the number every time you make a call.' She went into the relevant part of the menu. 'Who would you like to start with?'

A faint look of panic crossed his face. 'Er . . .'

She didn't approve of extramarital affairs – if that's what was going on – but she still felt a pang of sympathy. Deceit clearly didn't come naturally to him. And anyway, it wasn't her place to make judgements; she had been on the receiving end of too many arbitrary opinions herself. 'Well, how about the office?' she suggested. 'That could be useful if you're going to be late in or you're delayed in a meeting.'

Henry nodded. He was beginning to wish he'd never bought the darned thing. He watched, uncomfortable but resigned, as she tapped in the digits.

'And home?' she said next.

Again he went along with the suggestion, carefully reciting the information. They added in numbers for Richard, the AA (which he found on a card in his wallet), a few important clients and a couple of old friends.

'Anyone else?'

He hesitated. Maybe he could put Eve's details in himself . . . but then again, maybe not. And it would be useful to have them there. He had memorized her land line but not her mobile; he was still carrying *that* around on a scrap of paper. For a moment he couldn't decide but then, remembering her face, recalling the fear in her eyes, he put his doubts aside. 'There is one more.'

Louise heard the uneasiness in his voice, the faint rustle as he went through his pockets, but she didn't embarrass him by looking up. 'Fire away.' When she'd successfully inserted the number, she asked, 'And a name?'

Again, that hesitation. 'Er . . .'

She waited.

He shifted in his chair. 'Alex,' he said eventually. It was the first male name that came into his head and yet strangely, using her father's name made it feel a little less like a lie.

'Alex,' she repeated. She pressed a couple of buttons. 'There. All done!'

'Thank you.' He reached out to retrieve the offending object, glad that the ordeal was finally over. 'That was very kind of you.'

But she didn't immediately relinquish it. 'All you need now,' she insisted, 'is one quick lesson in how to use it.'

Henry's heart sank. What had he been thinking? He should never have let her help. He should never have let her even touch the phone. One ordeal might be over but the worst was yet to come. He knew what the secretaries were like: gossips, every one of them. By this time tomorrow it would be all around the building, how Mr Baxter senior had suddenly leapt from the Dark Ages into the twenty-first century, buying a piece of equipment he had no idea how to use, needing a slip of a girl to give him instructions. It would only be a matter of time before Richard heard about it and then . . . God, he didn't even want to think about what would happen then. The conclusions Richard would jump to were obvious. He'd realize he was seeing Eve again and . . . Well, there was no alternative. He'd have to get in there first. He'd have to tell Celia about the new phone, tell her tonight before . . .

'It's all right,' Louise said softly, 'your secret's safe with me.'

Henry flinched. As if all his private fears had been publicly exposed, he stared at her in dismay. 'I'm sorry?'

'I mean, don't worry. There's loads of stuff I'm not so good at.' She gave him a shy smile. 'I won't say a word if you promise to keep quiet about my spelling.'

Unsure of how to respond, he dropped his gaze to the phone.

She smiled again. 'Come on. I'll run through the menu with you.'

Eve had dropped a grateful Amber off at the garage; by now she should be safely on her way back to Essex. Once she'd got rid of Jack Raynor, the evening had gone all right. No threatening phone calls at least. That had been a relief. She'd made pasta and they'd shared a bottle of wine. Of course she'd had to endure the interrogation first.

'Is he your fella?'

'No. Just a friend.'

'A friend who brings you roses,' she said slyly. 'I wish I had friends like that.'

'He's a florist,' she lied, saying the first thing that came into her head. 'It's no big deal. He gets them for free.'

'He's pretty fit, though. Don't you think?'

Well, that couldn't be denied. He was way too good-looking to be a cop – she was sure Amber hadn't sussed him – or a boyfriend either come to that, the kind of guy that other girls would always be giving the eye. She'd had enough of that with Patrick.

Eve stood by the window and gazed down on the street. Automatically, she scanned the faces passing by. She should go out and do some shopping, her supplies were getting low. Except she wouldn't need anything for this evening. She'd agreed to have dinner with Jack. Just once more. She wasn't going to make a habit of it. Once she'd found out about Sergeant Shepherd, about why he'd gone to see Henry, that would be the end of it. She couldn't take the risk of being spotted by a screw; there were plenty who liked to stir things up and consorting with the local constabulary wouldn't go down well with Cavelli.

She sat down and lit a cigarette. There were plans to make, the foremost being a trip to London this weekend. She'd need to find somewhere to stay, a cheap hotel perhaps or a friend's sofa. But first she had to do some digging on Jimmy Reece. She had to find out who she was looking for. The internet would be the logical place to start and that would mean a trip down to the library.

With a sigh, she stubbed out the half-smoked cigarette and went in search of a notepad and pen. As she rooted through her father's desk, she felt the dark familiar sadness expanding in her chest. For a moment she paused, her fingers poised above his papers. She had the peculiar sensation that if she turned she would find him still sitting in his favourite chair, his grey eyes watching her, his mouth curling gently into a smile.

She swallowed hard. She should have spent more time with him. She should have been here when . . .

No, she couldn't start thinking about that. Now wasn't the time. She had to hold herself together, to keep her mind on the present. There were things to do. Suddenly eager to be out of the flat, she grabbed the items she needed and threw them in her bag.

Still distracted, she slid back the heavy bolts, swung open the door and instantly stopped dead – there was someone right in front of her, a figure with its arm raised, a fist about to— Her mind went blank. Gasping in alarm, her heart pumping, she blindly staggered back a step.

Then the person laughed. 'Sorry, love.'

Eve took a long frightened second to recognize her. God, it was only Sonia!

'What's the matter? You're as white as a sheet.'

She shook her head, willing her frantic pulse to slow. 'Nothing,' she eventually mumbled. 'You just gave me a fright.'

'Look at you. You're shaking like a leaf.' Sonia reached out to touch her lightly on the arm. 'What's the matter? You've been a bag of nerves ever since the break-in. Is that what it is, love? Are you still worried about that?'

'No.' Eve's breath was uneven, rising from her lungs in short sharp bursts. She shrugged. 'I don't know. Maybe.'

'Come on,' Sonia said, edging forward. 'You sit down and relax and I'll make us a nice cup of tea.'

'No,' Eve protested. 'I can't. Sorry. Thanks, but I've got to go.' If she sat down now she might never get up again. She had to get on. The last thing she needed was the third degree from Sonia – or her sympathy. She was feeling so exposed, so stupidly vulnerable, that one more word of kindness and she might be tempted to break down and tell her everything. 'I'm okay, really I am.'

But Sonia wasn't taking no for an answer. 'You can't go out in this state. Shopping, is it? Well, it can wait. They'll still be open in half an hour.'

'The library, actually.'

Sonia peered at the rows of books on the shelves and snorted. 'Huh? You not got enough to read?'

Eve unexpectedly found a smile on her lips. She could imagine her saying exactly the same thing to her father, could almost hear him laughing. 'No, I need a computer. I need to check out something on the internet.'

'Oh,' Sonia said. 'Well, you don't need the library for that. You can use our Darren's. He keeps his spare round here. He likes to play his games on it when he stays over. It's nothing fancy but it works.'

Darren was her oldest grandchild, a skinny twelve-year-old with attitude. Eve wasn't sure if she wanted to leave a trail of evidence of what she'd been looking at on his computer – or have Sonia leaning over her shoulder while she was doing it – but couldn't think of any good reason to refuse. 'I don't know. I'm not sure . . .'

But, as if the matter had been decided, Sonia had already turned away and was opening her door.

Eve locked her own and reluctantly followed her inside.

'It's in the spare room,' she called out. 'You go ahead while I get a brew on.'

The second bedroom was the same size as the one Eve slept in, but due to the presence of a pair of bunks and a cot it felt considerably smaller. The walls, painted a startling shade of red, were covered with posters and pictures and the floor was a clutter of discarded toys. Yet despite the chronic untidiness, it had an upbeat cheerful air to it. Eve could almost feel her spirits lifting as she fought her way through to the small table, sat down and turned on the machine. Perhaps this wasn't such a bad idea after all. Even if she had gone to the library, there was no guarantee of any privacy and at least here she could take her time.

The computer flickered into life and went through the usual motions. She made the connection to the web. She typed in his name, Jimmy Reece, and the results came up. Thousands of them. Bingo! How easy was that? It was only as she began to scroll through the list that she began to spot the problem. The Jimmy Reece she was reading about was an American racing driver who had died back in 1959. This couldn't be the man she was searching for.

She peered at the screen.

Sonia came in and put a mug down on the table. 'How's it going?'

'Yes, not bad. Thanks for the tea.'

'Need a hand?' Without waiting for a reply, she pulled up a chair and sat down.

Eve knew there was no polite way to get rid of her without rousing her curiosity so instead she said casually, 'No, I'm fine. I just promised to look up something for a friend. It's not important.' She stared at the screen some more. A minute passed. Then, as Sonia clearly wasn't going to leave, she thought, *What the hell!* She needed all the help she could get and it was hardly indiscreet to mention the name – especially as the chances of Cavelli finding out were virtually nil. 'I don't suppose you've heard of someone called Jimmy Reece, have you? Not this one,' she said, glancing at the results on show, 'another one, more recent, some kind of actor maybe.'

'Oh,' she said, 'you mean that rich gangster guy?'

'Gangster?' Eve repeated tentatively. Her stomach shifted a fraction. That didn't sound promising.

But then Sonia added, 'You know, that guy who was in all those gangster films a few years back. Was that his name?' She nodded. 'Yeah, I think so. You know the one I mean, dark hair, one of those accents, posh bloke, some kind of lord or something.'

'Could be,' Eve replied with a barely disguised sigh of relief. Tracking down a real-life gangster had never figured high on her list of priorities. She'd known plenty of bad boys in her time but they were in a different league, hustlers like Patrick, cardsharps and grifters, small-time players with an eye to the main chance. She knew her way around *that* world. She'd been raised in it.

'Something happened,' Sonia continued. 'It was in the papers. Don't you remember? Some weird stuff, a fight. He got beaten up. There was a court case, I think.'

Eve shook her head. She didn't read the papers much these days and had been reading them even less several years ago. What had she been doing then? Best not to think about it. After the split with Patrick she'd gone off the rails for a while. Well, more than a while. It was nudging on nine years since they'd split and it wasn't until she'd gone to work for Henry that she'd felt her life was finally getting back on track.

She returned to the search engine and typed in the name again, carefully adding *actor* and *court case*.

This time she got a completely different set of results.

The one at the top of the list read *Vicious attack on actor*. She clicked on the heading and waited.

'That's him,' Sonia said, as a thumbnail photograph appeared. She poked a finger towards the screen.

They both leaned forward to scan the text. It didn't make for easy reading. Jimmy Reece had been attacked in his home in Notting Hill, brutally punched and kicked and left for dead. As Eve read the words, she could feel her spirits slowly sinking. She knew what was coming next. She was waiting to see another name, a name she would recognize, and it didn't take too long for it to appear: yes, there it was in black and white – *Martin Cavelli* had been charged with the assault.

'Shit,' she murmured.

Sonia gave her a look. 'What's going on?'

'Nothing,' she said. Her heart had started to thump but she couldn't keep her eyes off the screen. According to the report, Cavelli had gone to the house, a row had broken out and . . . the details weren't pretty: six cracked ribs, a ruptured spleen, a broken arm, and serious facial injuries. Jimmy Reece had spent weeks in hospital.

She clicked on a couple of later entries, articles covering the court case. The altercation had been over Cavelli's ex-wife. Nadine had left him for Reece and when he dumped her . . . Well, Eve knew the rest, knew what she had done. So what Paula had told her was true.

She read on. The prosecution claimed that the assault was a premeditated act born of jealousy, of rage, and vengeance. The defence claimed Cavelli had gone to the house purely with the intention of retrieving some of Nadine's possessions. It was only when Reece had goaded him about her death that the meeting had turned sour and a fight had ensued. Whatever the truth, there was no disputing the damage Cavelli had inflicted. Although cleared of attempted murder he'd been found guilty of GBH and sentenced to eight years.

She made a fast mental calculation. With good behaviour, he'd only serve two thirds which meant that in a year or so he'd be up for parole. So was he preparing for a second bite of the cherry? She couldn't think of any other explanation as to why he would want to know his whereabouts. And once Reece was found and Cavelli was free, he would hardly be planning to go round and shake his hand. If she gave him the information he wanted, and he went on to finish the job, would that make her an accessory to murder? She shivered. Was he intending to kill him? It only took a glance from those cold blue eyes to realize what he was capable of. Inside Cavelli was a dark brooding anger.

'Eve?'

She tried to ignore the interruption. She had to concentrate, to think this through. Perhaps she could spin it out for a few months, string him along, pretend that she was still looking but that she couldn't find him. Would he believe that? She doubted it somehow. Unless Reece was actually in hiding, she should eventually be able to track him down.

'Tell me what's going on.'

She frowned. 'I can't. I mean, nothing. I don't know. It's just something that I'm checking for—'

'Oh, don't give me that crap,' Sonia snapped. 'I know trouble when I see it. Is this to do with your Terry?'

'What makes you say that?' Eve retorted too quickly.

Sonia placed her hand gently on Eve's arm. 'Look,

love, whatever it is, I'll understand. It's me, Sonia.' She gave a low laugh. 'You think I'll be shocked? Believe me, there's not much I haven't seen or heard before.'

'No,' Eve began, 'really, you don't need to worry. It's . . .' But already her resolve was starting to weaken. What the hell had she got herself involved in? Other than Henry, she had no one to talk to, and he hadn't called for several days. Maybe he'd finally seen sense. Maybe he would never call again.

'You think your dad would want to see you like this?'

Perhaps it was the mention of her father that finally pushed her towards making the decision. Or maybe she just couldn't bear the thought of facing this alone. Either way, she needed someone to share her worries with. And she could trust Sonia, couldn't she? She'd been her father's friend, a good friend, always there for him.

'So?' Sonia persisted.

And it only took a few more minutes for the truth to trickle out.

Eve didn't go into detail. She provided the edited version, about how she'd gone to visit Terry and the state he was in, about how she'd accidentally bumped into Cavelli, about the idea she'd had, the deal they'd made, and where that deal had recently led her – finding Jimmy Reece. All the rest, the attack in the alley, the phone calls and threats, she kept to herself. She still wasn't sure if they were connected and there was no point muddying the waters.

When she was finished Sonia gave her a long hard look. For a moment Eve thought she'd made a mistake, that she should never have confided in her. Her face was tight and drawn, faintly angry, the way people tend to look when you've told them something that they really didn't want to hear. Sharing your worries was one thing but inflicting major burdens was an entirely different matter. She glanced down at the carpet. 'Sorry, I shouldn't have . . .'

'And you've been coping with this on your own?'

She looked up again and nodded. Sonia was making a vague attempt at a smile. Eve could see now that she wasn't stressed about the information, only about the fact that she hadn't been told.

'Christ, I'm only across the hall. Why didn't you talk to me?' Then, before Eve had a chance to respond, she briskly continued: 'Right, well, we're going to have to make plans. When are we going to London – tomorrow, is it? Afternoon or evening? What time? I'll have to ring Val, sort out arrangements for the kids. Are we going to get the train or drive down?'

Eve stared at her. '*We?*' she repeated.

'Well, you're not going on your own. That would just be stupid.'

It might be stupid but she didn't want to drag Sonia any further into this mess. This was her problem and no one else's. Just because she had shared it didn't mean she was willing to share the repercussions too. 'To be honest,' she lied, 'I don't know if I'm going at all.'

'Of course you are. What choice do you have?'

No choice. She was right. But she wasn't about to admit it. 'I could just say I couldn't find him.'

'Risky. If he finds out you're lying . . .'

'How would he?'

'Perhaps Jimmy Reece isn't that hard to find.'

'So why does Cavelli need me?'

Sonia picked up her mug and took a sip of tea. 'Perhaps it's a test, something to prove that you're on side.'

Eve scowled but yes, that made a kind of sense. Something to prove that she was being straight, cooperating, doing what he wanted. 'Do you think?'

'He's still inside for at least another twelve months, so

you don't have to worry about anything you tell him. By the time he gets out, it'll all be history.'

That thought had crossed Eve's mind too. A lot could change in a year. Reece could move, change addresses, disappear. Which begged the question of why Cavelli wanted the information *now*. Unless . . . 'What if he's intending to get someone else to do the job, a professional, someone who'll do it while he's still locked up? That would put him in the clear. They couldn't prove that he had anything to do with it.'

She didn't have to explain what the 'job' was. Sonia knew exactly what she was talking about. But she didn't seem too bothered. 'He could,' she agreed. 'But from what you've said he strikes me as the kind of man who'd rather do his dirty work himself.'

And she was right, absolutely right. If Cavelli was still intent on revenge – and Eve was sure that he was – then he'd never get anyone else to commit the final act. He'd want to be there, to exact his own personal retribution. And she suddenly saw another way out. If that was the case, then she could warn Reece after she'd found him, send him an anonymous letter or make a phone call, let him know that he was in danger. Terry should be out in five months and all she had to do in the meantime was to keep Cavelli happy.

'Okay,' she said, 'but you don't need to come with me.'

Sonia snorted. 'You think I'm going to let you traipse round Soho on your own?'

An hour later Eve was pacing her living room. She had her phone in her hand and was still searching for somewhere they could stay. Cheap hotels in London were hard to come by. Perhaps she'd be better off asking a friend – but she couldn't think of anyone who wouldn't ask too many awkward questions. On her own, she might have managed, but how was she going to explain Sonia's presence?

And how was she going to find the man she was searching for?

Although there was *one* person who might be able to help. She stopped, flipped open her address book and stared down at his phone number. No, she couldn't.

She went to the kitchen and gazed longingly at a bottle of red wine. She could do with a glass to steady her nerves but she was meeting Jack Raynor in a few hours. She had to keep her wits about her. Instead she filled a glass with water.

She took a gulp. What next? Should she? If there was one person who might know where Jimmy Reece was, it was Patrick. He knew the seedier parts of London like the back of his hand. She dialled the first three digits. Quickly, she put the phone down.

She took another sip of water and lit a cigarette. Why was she even worrying? The chances of him still being in the flat were slight. It had been years. It was probably only a stranger who would reply, someone who would sound bemused, and say, 'Who?'

She dialled the whole number but hung up as it began to ring. What if she was wrong? What if he *was* still living there?

Eve took a deep breath before she picked up the phone again. It rang at least five times before it was finally answered.

'Hello?'

She recognized his voice. What was she doing? *Hang up!* Her teeth clamped together. Of all the idiotic ideas she'd ever had . . .

'Hello,' he said again.

'Patrick?'

'Yes.' There was a short pause. Then a laugh. 'Hey, gorgeous, how are you doing?'

There was no going back now. 'Okay,' she replied, trying to lift her game and to sound upbeat. 'Pretty good. How are you?'

There was a short silence. 'It's been a while,' he said.

'I was ringing because . . .' She cleared her throat. 'Er, I'm trying to trace someone and was hoping you might be able to point me in the right direction.'

'And here was me thinking that you just had to hear my voice again.'

'Sure,' she quipped back, 'I've only managed to hold out for nine years. I guess my willpower must be weakening.'

'Don't beat yourself up about it. I've heard I'm irresistible.'

Her mouth widened into a smile. He always had been the modest type. 'Really? Are you sure that wasn't *irresponsible*? They sound kind of similar.'

He laughed. 'So, who are you looking for, someone we know?'

'Not exactly. A guy called Jimmy Reece, used to be an actor. Does it ring any bells?'

'The guy who got his face smashed in, right?'

As if she needed a reminder. 'Yeah?' she said, pausing, pretending she wasn't too sure. 'That could be him. I'm only asking for a friend, someone who's lost touch and wants to look him up.'

'Right,' he repeated softly.

And with that single word, she knew he didn't believe her. But then she never had been able to lie to Patrick. Come to that, she hadn't been too convincing with Sonia either. Perhaps she was losing the knack. She sighed down the line. 'I need to find him.'

This time it was Patrick who paused. 'He isn't worth it, Evie.'

She frowned at the wall, taking a moment to translate what he was saying. 'Oh God,' she replied, 'I'm not . . . we're not . . . Honestly, I've never met him before in my life.'

There was silence from the other end.

'Oh, come on,' she insisted. 'You know me better than that. It's not my style. Since when have I gone chasing after any man?'

'So what's the deal?'

'There's no deal. I've told you. But it *is* kind of delicate. I can't go into it. Just trust me, okay? All I need to know is where I can find him. I've heard that he's a bit of a low-life, that he hangs out in Soho, likes a drink, likes—'

'So you instantly thought of me,' he interrupted.

She winced. 'No, I didn't mean . . .'

'It's okay,' he laughed. 'Chill out! I wasn't being serious. As it happens, I might be able to help. I've seen him around. There are a few bars and clubs he tends to turn up in.'

'Great.' She opened her notebook and waited. A few seconds ticked by. 'I've got a pen,' she prompted.

'Are you still in London?'

She tapped the biro impatiently against the side of the table. She wanted to get on with it but knew what he was like; the more she pushed the less likely he was to give her the information she needed. 'Off and on. But I'm coming back down tomorrow. I've been in Norwich for a while.'

'Are you staying with your dad? How is he?'

Eve felt the shock of his questions like two rapid thumps to her abdomen. She leaned over the table as if she'd been winded. He didn't know. Of course he didn't. Why should he? She closed her eyes, trying to find the right words. How many times had she said them? More than she cared to remember. But it was so much harder with Patrick. While they'd been together, he'd been close to her father, as close as a son. There was no easy way to tell him.

'Evie?'

She forced herself to speak. Her voice was barely more than a whisper. 'He's dead, Patrick. He died over a month ago.'

She heard his sharp intake of breath. 'Shit no. Christ, I'm sorry.'

'He was ill,' she said quickly. 'He had cancer.' She couldn't bear to tell him the rest, the terrible details of his lonely walk into the river. She still hadn't come to terms with that herself.

'You should have called me,' he said.

A rush of guilt ran through her. Perhaps she should. It wasn't as if he'd been hard to find. All it would have taken was a phone call. But a divorce is a divorce. Their lives had drifted apart. But perhaps he'd still had the right to know. His friendship with her father had only been severed by circumstance. 'I'm sorry.'

'No, I didn't mean . . . I just wish . . .'

'I know,' she said. She was drawing close to tears, trying to hold herself together. She felt like she was walking a trembling tightrope, poised somewhere between two impossible points of despair; whichever way she looked, forward or back, there was only grief.

'Are you okay?'

She wasn't. 'Yes, I'm fine.'

'Like fuck,' he said.

And there wasn't much she could reply to that.

'Evie?'

'Yeah, I'm okay.' She tried to keep her voice steady. She took another deep breath. If she didn't move on quickly, she would never move on at all. The past was a place that she couldn't afford to visit. 'So, what about these clubs Jimmy Reece goes to?'

'Frith Street,' he said. 'There's a pub on the corner called—'

'I know it,' she said. As if she could ever forget. It was where they used to meet. She could still recall the dim interior, the horseshoe bar, the wooden benches and the dark scarred tables. 'Does he go there?'

'No,' he said. 'I don't think so.'

'So why—'

'I'll meet you there tomorrow evening. What shall we say, about seven? Or is that too early?'

She scowled. 'What?'

'We need to talk.'

'No we don't,' she insisted. 'All you need to tell me is where I can find Jimmy Reece.'

'And I will,' he said. 'I promise. Do we have a deal?'

She groaned. Not another deal. She was getting sick to death of them. 'Do I have a choice?'

'No.'

'Okay, I'll see you tomorrow.'

Chapter Thirteen

'Keep an eye on her,' Joe Silk said. 'I want to know where she goes, everyone she meets.'

The man nodded. He picked up the photograph from the desk, stared at it a while, and then flipped it over to read the details on the back. He spent a long time studying the address.

'Norwich,' Joe snapped impatiently. 'Head north and turn right. Try not to get lost. And take Micky with you. She shouldn't be able to give you both the slip.'

'Right now?' he asked.

Joe glanced at his watch. 'No, five fucking minutes ago.' He hissed as the man quickly left the room. What was the matter with people these days? They had to be told everything twice and even then they couldn't find their way to the bottom of the street. He lit a cigarette and leaned back in his chair. Maybe retirement wasn't such a bad idea after all. Once he'd got this business sorted out, he'd give it some serious consideration.

Chase made a grunting sound, uncrossed his long legs and stood up. 'Drink?' He didn't wait for a reply before walking over to the cabinet and pouring him a large one.

Joe looked at his back, at his tight hunched shoulders. 'What's on your mind?'

Chase shrugged. Then he turned and walked slowly

back. He put the glass on the desk. 'I don't get it. Why don't we just pick her up, have a quiet word. If she has it, she'll tell me soon enough.'

Impulsive. That was the only fault with Chase. Always act now and think about it later. It had never been any different. And yes, his powers of persuasion were certainly legendary but a dead Evie Weston could be even more dangerous than a living one. At least at the moment.

'There's plenty of time for that. First, we need to find out who she's working with. Anyone could have it by now. She must have passed it on.' He took a delicate sip of his drink. An expensive Irish whiskey should be savoured not gulped. 'Fucking Marshall,' he murmured. 'He couldn't find a five-pound note in a fucking bank. If it was ever in the flat, it'll be long gone by now.'

'What about the kid?'

'No, the little bastard doesn't know what day of the week it is. Weston might have been a lot of things but he wasn't a fool. The only person he'd have trusted with it was *her*.' Evie was the smart one, the one with the brains. And that was the major worry. What the hell was she playing at? If she was intending to stick to her father's side of the bargain, then she'd have contacted him by now; she'd have returned the property. A deal was a deal. The fact that she hadn't, that she was refusing to cooperate, that she was messing about instead with some dodgy private eye, made the situation crystal clear. His hand tightened around the glass. It didn't take a genius to work out her intentions. A couple of grand to test the waters and then . . .

'The kid's still a problem,' Chase insisted. 'It needs sorting.'

Joe took a deep drag on his cigarette, inhaled, and blew the smoke out in a sweet straight line. 'Rumour has it that the Rowans aren't too happy about Terry's lenient sentence. Someone must have been whispering in their ear. Rumour has it that he might have got a touch too friendly with the cops.' He lifted his face and gazed up at the ceiling. He wasn't sure how long it would take, a couple of weeks, maybe a month, but no matter what the time scale, the rot was starting to set in. Terry Weston's days, God bless his soul, were numbered.

'But she's going to freak out, as soon as she hears she's going to—'

Joe shook his head. 'It won't come to that. We'll have dealt with her by then.' He paused. '*You'll* have dealt with her by then.'

Chase's sullen mouth curled into a smile. The fine art of persuasion, the painful separation of fact from fiction, was where his true talent lay. He could make anyone talk – and quickly. But he'd take it slow with Evie. She was worth the effort, worth the wait. Her confessions shouldn't be rushed. 'She's mine?'

'Sure.' Joe nodded. 'She's yours – when the time comes.' It was a shame – she'd been a sweet kid – but what could he do? The ties had been severed. And she was the one who'd cut them. There was no room for sentiment; it was fucking sentiment that had created this bloody mess in the first place. He should have sorted it there and then but he'd known Alex Weston for over thirty years. Shit, he'd liked the guy, had even trusted him. Except, of course, when it came to poker. No one could trust Weston in the presence of a pack of cards.

After it had happened, they had got together and talked. Christ, how they'd talked. But a pact had eventually been made, hands had been shaken, the deal had been sealed. Not the best of deals, he had to admit, but a reasonable compromise. With everyone having so much to lose, it had felt safe enough.

Until Weston had broken his word.

Joe took another sip of whiskey. He could just about

find it in his heart to understand why he'd done what he'd done. A father had obligations. He had feelings, loyalties. If he'd been in his shoes, he might have done the same. But it didn't change anything. From the moment Alex Weston had chosen to hold them all to ransom he'd sealed his own death warrant. And he'd known it. That was why he had jumped before he was pushed.

If Evie had been sensible, if she'd stuck to his side of the bargain, they might have worked this out in a civilized fashion.

But that was never going to happen now.

Isaac glanced at the photograph in Cavelli's hand. Every time he took that picture out and stared at it, his head got screwed. Women. Fuck. All they ever caused was grief. And that Nadine with her big brown eyes was the worst. Okay, don't speak ill of the dead and all that, but if it hadn't been for her inability to keep her legs closed, the poor sod wouldn't even be in here.

He didn't let his gaze linger. Cavelli was touchy about the bitch; one wrong look and he was liable to go into one. Thin-skinned, that's what he was, about *her* at least. Still defending her honour after everything she'd done, still shifting the blame as if the tart had been dragged kicking and screaming into some other bastard's bed. No good. That's what she'd been. He was well rid.

But Isaac had the sense to keep his mouth shut. When Cavelli was in one of his brooding moods, it was best to leave well alone. And he would have walked straight out again, without a word, if Cavelli hadn't spoken first.

'You heard anything?'

Isaac stopped by the door. 'What, man?'

'About Weston.'

He shrugged. There was another scumbag loser

Cavelli was intent on defending. Would he never learn? 'I heard you went to see Bryant.'

'You got a problem with that?'

There you go, touchy as fuck. Just itching for a row. Well, he'd fallen into that trap too many times before, and learned his lesson good and proper. He wasn't going there again. 'No problem, man. Why should there be?'

'You tell me.'

Now wasn't the moment to mention that Bryant never did nothing for nothing. Or that he was as sly as Eden's fucking snake. No point stating the obvious. Along the line, next week, next month, there'd be a price to pay. 'I'm cool,' he said.

But Cavelli wasn't going to let it go. His voice was softly vicious. 'Because you can always get a shift if you don't like it, fuck off to another wing, find someone else to aggravate – that's if there's any mug left willing to tolerate your filthy habits.'

Isaac lifted his skinny shoulders again. When you were as small as he was, you couldn't afford to be confrontational. Bodies his size didn't bounce too well and bones broke easy. You had to find other ways of dealing with tricky situations, smart ways that didn't involve your head being painfully disconnected from your spinal cord. Not that he was too worried on *that* score. He knew this wasn't personal. Cavelli was only venting his frustration. He leaned against the door and groaned. 'Shit, man, you know there ain't no one else could put up with me.'

Cavelli's face stayed hard for a few more seconds before his bitter mouth slowly cracked into a smile. 'Yeah. That's fucking true.'

With a jerk and a rumble the train pulled out and Eve settled back in her seat. In another two hours they'd be

213

in London. In another three she'd be seeing Patrick again. She wished he could have just given her the information she wanted instead of insisting on a meet. She wasn't in the mood for playing happy reunions.

Perhaps she should have driven down. The decision to take the train had been a last-minute one and she was starting to question it. Since when had anyone made a quick getaway on the British rail system? She stared at the glass in the window, frowning at her own reflection. Relying on public transport was a big mistake. But then again, since when had anyone been able to find a parking space near Soho? At least this way she didn't have to worry about meters or wheel clamps.

Beside her, Sonia rustled through a glossy magazine and sipped at the coffee she had bought in the station. Eve had passed on the caffeine; she still had a faint headache from the night before. She had drunk too much. Not enough to make a fool of herself but enough to let her guard down. That was the thing about Jack Raynor: he had the ability to slip effortlessly through your best defences. One minute you were casually chatting and the next you were giving him half your life story.

The bistro where they'd met had been off the Prince of Wales Road, not one she'd ever visited before but she had found it easily enough. It was one of those dim shadowy places where the modern thrills of electricity were sacrificed to the more dubious charms of 'atmosphere'. Still, there were advantages to candlelight. Hopefully, it had disguised the suspicion in her eyes.

But what about *his* eyes, too sweetly blue for any man. What had *she* seen in *them*? No, she didn't want to think about that.

It had taken a while to bring the conversation round to DS Shepherd and his visit to London. She could hardly launch straight into it. But once they'd polished off the first few glasses of wine, she had delicately broached the subject.

And he had brushed it aside as swiftly as if it were a minor misunderstanding. 'Hey, you're not still worried about that, are you? I told you it was nothing.'

'As I recall, you told me you'd look into it.'

'There's nothing to look into.'

She smiled. 'Any particular sort of nothing?'

Then, when he saw that she wasn't going to let it drop, he put his elbows on the table and grinned at her. He hesitated for a second. 'Well, okay, I probably shouldn't be telling you this but if it helps put your mind at rest . . .' He paused again. 'You're not the type of girl who shoots the messenger are you?'

Now that was hardly the kind of question to put even the most virtuous of minds at rest. Everyone has a few guilty secrets and hers stirred miserably in her guts while she gazed at him, still smiling. 'That depends on the messenger – and how slow he is in passing on the news.'

Raynor laughed, raising both his hands in a gesture of surrender. 'Okay, okay.' But he still kept her on tenterhooks while he picked up his glass and took another sip of wine.

She waited, holding her breath.

When he spoke again, she could sense his reluctance. 'It was nothing. It was only down to a phone call. I'm sorry, Eve, but we had to follow it up. There was an anonymous call suggesting that there may have been . . . and I'm quoting here, *a misappropriation of funds from your ex-employers' bank account.*'

'What!' she exclaimed. It came out louder than she intended and a few curious faces turned to stare from the adjacent tables. She leaned forward and lowered her voice. 'What?'

He shook his head, his hand reaching out to fold around her wrist. 'Hey, I know it's not true.'

She quickly pulled away. 'Are you talking about Richard Baxter?' Why was she even asking? Of course it was him. Who else could it be? Henry was wrong. There was no limit to his son's capacity for vengeance. 'It was him, wasn't it?'

'It was anonymous,' he repeated.

'So why did you bother to follow it up? You must get hundreds of crank calls. What made this one so special? All you had to do was ring Baxter & Baxter and check, you didn't need to actually go there.' Even as the words spilled out, she wondered if she was sounding too frantic, too defensive, as if she was protesting too much. Like someone who was guilty. Except for once in her life she wasn't. Maybe that was the problem. She was used to declaring her innocence – lying was easy – but telling the truth was a new and faintly disturbing experience. And then another thought occurred to her. 'Why were you dealing with it anyway? What had it got to do with you? Surely it was down to the London cops?'

As the questions slipped relentlessly from her mouth, Raynor folded his arms and gazed down at the table.

Warning bells were starting to go off in her head. 'There was more to it, wasn't there? There must have been.'

He glanced up again. In a gesture that could have sprung from either irritation or embarrassment, he raked his fingers through his hair. The candlelight flickering on his face made it hard to read his expression. For a moment, undecided, he sat in silence and then, as if she had finally worn him down, he expelled a small defeated sigh. 'Okay, there was something else. I don't suppose it matters now. At the time of the call, there were still a lot of goods missing from the Broadlands robbery and, with your connection to Terry, it was suggested that you might be able to . . .'

'What – help with your inquiries?' Eve gave a snort. She could hardly believe it! Richard had really excelled himself. If it wasn't so tragic, it might almost be funny. 'Are you kidding? Is that what he told you? God, I hadn't even seen Terry for six months.'

'It wasn't taken that seriously, I promise, but we have to follow up on every lead we get. We have to go through the motions. As it happens, we've recovered most of the haul now.'

'Good,' she said. But after an initial burst of relief – it could have been worse – Eve suddenly grew serious again. A malignant voice was whispering in her ear. *Joe wants it back. He wants it fucking back.* 'It was jewellery, wasn't it?'

'Gold and silver mainly, and a load of designer watches.'

'Pretty valuable then?'

'Valuable enough to shoot a security guard. He was lucky, if you can call it that. At least he can still walk.'

Eve felt a clenching inside her, a cold fist squeezing her heart. She had been aware of the shooting but it was the first time she had thought of it in direct relation to Terry. If Cavelli was telling the truth, if he had been on the job, then . . . Christ, what had happened to her kid brother? Handling stolen property was one thing, armed robbery quite another. She scowled into her glass. How the hell, *why* the hell, had he linked up with the Rowans? And that in turn begged a further question – was it possible that all this Joe business was connected? It might account for all the recent madness. If Terry *had* been more deeply involved, he could (theoretically) have passed something on before he'd been arrested, something Joe wanted, something precious, something worth the effort of prolonged intimidation. But what?

217

'Are you all right?' Jack asked.

There was only one way to find out the answers she needed. She had to squeeze out more information. Glancing up, she quickly laughed. 'Sure. I'm fine. I was just savouring the sensation of being under police suspicion. If some of the goods are missing, couldn't I still be in the frame?' She widened her cool grey eyes and looked at him.

He smiled back, showing two rows of perfect white teeth. 'Sorry to disappoint but you're completely in the clear. We think the missing goods were sold on quickly and they were only the cheaper items, the stuff that was easy to shift.'

Well, that was *that* theory down the drain. She couldn't say she was sorry. If Terry had been responsible for all her grief, she wasn't quite sure how she'd have dealt with it. Although it didn't entirely rule out the Joe connection. Perhaps he was one of those gangster parasites, a few hundred rungs up the ladder, a user muscling in on someone else's act – a cheap percentage-taker on a promise. If he hadn't known that the majority of the goods had already been recovered, he could have been searching for a lead to their whereabouts. And his burglar might have been hoping to find a clue in the flat. That would even explain the theft of the phone. If they thought it was hers, then . . . Well, it was all vaguely plausible but it didn't quite ring true. There was something more scarily personal about what had been happening recently.

Picking up the bottle of wine, Jack refilled her glass. 'Look, I'm sorry. I hope you're not too mad at me. I should have explained earlier but, to be honest, I was hoping I wouldn't need to. The investigation's over and done with and—'

She shrugged. 'There's no need to apologize. You were only doing your job, right?'

He pulled a face, his mouth turning down at the corners. 'Oh, don't say that. Please. You make me sound like one of those self-justifying members of the Gestapo.'

Eve tried to see beyond his smiling blue eyes. Was he genuine? She thought she was a reasonable judge of human character – she'd been raised in the art of deception – but she had got it wrong before. There was a certain type of man who always managed to sneak beneath her radar. She had the divorce papers to prove it.

'I don't think that,' she said. 'Although if you'd like to salve your conscience, there is one last thing you could explain. Why didn't you just come and talk to me? I don't understand why you were creeping around behind my back.'

'We weren't creeping around,' he insisted, looking genuinely offended. 'We didn't know you were in Norwich then. We didn't know *where* you were. You left London and disappeared without a trace.'

She could see how that might seem a touch suspicious. 'I just needed to get away.'

There was a short silence.

'No hard feelings?' he asked.

'Why should there be?'

He leaned forward, his hand roaming dangerously close to hers again. 'And no immediate plans to shoot the messenger?'

She smiled. 'Oh, don't worry about that. It's not you who's in the firing line.'

The Shepherd business had created a temporary awkwardness but it had passed. By the time they were on to the second bottle of wine they had put it behind them. She couldn't recall exactly what they'd been eating, something Mexican and spicy. All washed down with too much wine.

And it hadn't been long before a few life experiences had started to trickle out. She had told him about Patrick, about their short and stormy marriage. Was there such a thing as love at first sight? She'd been certain of it when she first met Patrick Fielding. There had been a spark, an instant understanding between them. But no, it hadn't been real; true love was something different, something lasting, an emotion that grew and deepened. What they had shared was more of a passion, one of those sudden bursts of flame, a brief conflagration that roared and scorched before quickly burning itself out.

Her father had liked him. Patrick was just the kind of son he longed to have had, witty and charming, always good company. (She omitted to mention the other attributes they had in common, like their limitless ability to mislead and cheat and con. Some things were better left unsaid.) Poor Terry, with his lack of concentration and careless ways, had been a constant disappointment.

She had wondered, as she sat in front of him, if Raynor had any idea of her past. He could hardly believe she was whiter than white with a parent like Alexander Weston. And of course she wasn't. From early childhood, she'd been inculcated with the 'knowledge' that the gullible rich were there to be exploited. Not *stolen* from – her father abhorred that word – but simply persuaded, through greed or guilt or fear of the consequences, to part with a small proportion of their income. And through the years she had done her fair share of persuasion. She'd been good at it. She'd inherited his natural talent.

Done. She thought about that past tense. Did it mean she was finished with that way of life, that she'd moved on, changed? She'd certainly been clean for the past seven months. But that was more down to circumstances than to anything more profound. There had hardly been a revelation on the road to Damascus. Maybe it was just a case of growing older, of growing weary of it all . . .

Before she might let slip something that she shouldn't, Eve had smartly turned the subject around. 'Enough about me.'

Jack Raynor, it transpired, was divorced too. His ex-wife, Clare, was a barrister working out of Lincoln's Inn. They'd met at university and been married for over ten years before she dumped him for another man. No kids, no other complications. He claimed that was why he had left London three years ago, to make a fresh start, to make a new life somewhere else. Whether it was the truth or not . . .

Well, what *was* the truth? Especially when the wine was flowing freely. Bitterness had a nasty habit of rising to the surface in the presence of alcohol but he showed no signs of it. The conversation moved on to lighter themes and she found herself laughing, enjoying herself, for the first time since her father had died. They talked and talked. And then, as the evening wore on, as the alcohol hit a different spot, she began to feel guilty. And then she felt guilty about feeling guilty. Her father had always lived in the present, never in the past. He wouldn't have wanted her to wallow in grief. But then he'd hardly have been overjoyed at the sight of her consorting with a seductive, blond-haired, blue-eyed cop, either.

'How about meeting up again over the weekend?' he asked.

She picked up her glass, took a sip and gazed at him over the rim. She felt a frown forming on her brow and raised a hand to disguise it. Okay, she liked him, was undeniably attracted, but she couldn't afford to get any closer. Her life was already too complicated. 'Sorry. I'm in London for a couple of days. I've promised to catch up with some friends.' There she went – lying again. Although the story contained an essence of truth. And she could hardly explain the real purpose of her visit.

'Oh, right,' he said.

She saw the disappointment in his face, the way he quickly glanced away. It wasn't the kind of expression that was easy to fake. So perhaps he *was* really interested, but so what? It was time to cut and run. Then, ridiculously, she found herself saying, 'But next week would be good – if you're free.'

His mouth broke into a smile. 'I'd like that,' he said.

God, what was she doing? This was supposed to be the last supper. She'd already got the information she wanted. Thank you and goodbye. Why on earth was she agreeing to see him again?

The answer was sitting right in front of her. Love at first sight might be a fantasy but lust was another matter altogether . . .

Her mobile was going off. Eve scrabbled in her bag, pulled it out and examined the number. Unrecognized. She had a moment's hesitation, worried that her heavy-breather might have tracked her down, before she finally decided to answer it.

'Hello.'

'Eve?'

She sighed her relief down the line. 'Henry.'

'How are you?' he said.

'I'm fine.'

'I've been trying to call. Where are you?'

She heard the anxiety in his voice. She could have made up some story but she didn't want to lie to him. 'Something's come up. I'm on my way to London.' And from telling him that, it was only a short step to agreeing to meet him at Frith Street. It was the easiest option;

surrounded by all the other passengers, she couldn't go into detail and she knew he wouldn't rest until she told him exactly what was happening.

Eve slipped the phone back into her bag.

'So your *friend's* joining us,' Sonia said, not even attempting to pretend that she hadn't been listening. She laid a sly emphasis on the word as if it was a euphemism that they both understood.

'He *is* just a friend,' Eve insisted. 'I used to work for him.' She didn't know why she was bothering – it didn't matter what Sonia thought – but she felt obliged to at least try and protect Henry's reputation. These days, it seemed, she exerted more effort into denying relationships than in actually forming them. Jack Raynor sprang uninvited into her mind again; he lingered for a few delightful seconds before she rapidly dismissed him. 'It's only for a quick drink. He's been concerned about Terry and everything.'

'So he knows?'

Eve glanced at the man and woman sitting opposite, both with their heads in newspapers. But that didn't mean they weren't eavesdropping. 'Some of it,' she murmured, hoping Sonia wouldn't pursue the subject.

Thankfully she didn't. Instead she simply raised her dark eyebrows, gave her a searching look and returned her attention to the magazine.

It was only as they were approaching London that Eve began to get a serious case of the jitters, to worry that she might be being followed again (she peered around the carriage but saw nothing suspicious), to worry about finding Jimmy Reece, or, perhaps even worse, *not* finding him, to fret about seeing Patrick, to stress about compromising Henry, and last but not least to question the fairness of involving Sonia in this whole mad venture. Perhaps her neighbour had only insisted on coming out of some misplaced sense of obligation to her father.

Although she was glad of the company, it was hardly fair on Sonia, especially when she wasn't in possession of all the facts. Should she tell her about the attack, about being followed?

Eve decided she would. As soon as they got off the train and could talk with some degree of privacy. She'd tell her everything. She definitely would. And then, two stops later, she changed her mind again. Was there any point in stressing her out unnecessarily? She hadn't even heard from Joe Friendly in the last few days. Maybe he'd realized he'd got the wrong person and moved on. She might never hear from him again.

Or was she just fooling herself?

She was still mentally arguing the point as the train cruised gently into Liverpool Street. Eve stared out of the window. Grey, grimy and . . . God, so infinitely glorious! She couldn't resist a smile. She wasn't looking forward to the evening ahead but there were certain consolations.

If nothing else, she was back on home ground.

Chapter Fourteen

They descended into the underground and took the first available tube along the Central line to Tottenham Court Road. Standing up, sardine-squashed between the weary commuters, they were assaulted by the intermingling odours of stale tobacco, sweat, garlic, and the sickly scent of perfume. Eve tried not to breathe too deeply.

A briefcase jolted for the second time against her thigh, its hard edge hitting precisely the same spot. She winced. By this time tomorrow, she'd have a bruise the shade of violets. Another bruise. Shifting a fraction, she glared at her assailant but the portly middle-aged businessman, oblivious to the lethal weapon he was carrying, stared blankly down the length of the carriage.

'Nearly there,' she said, as much for her own benefit as Sonia's. She was starting to feel a creeping claustrophobia, a sense of oppression from the bodies pressing in around her. Dark thoughts invaded her mind: Cavelli's obsession with Jimmy Reece, the danger Terry might be in, the death of her father. She closed her eyes. That persistent question, the one that wouldn't leave her alone, caught the rhythm of the rocking train and fell into a loop: *What are you doing? What are you doing?*

When the train finally drew to a halt and the doors swished open, Eve urgently elbowed her way through the crowd. She had to get out, break free. Sonia, accustomed to the rather more polite ways of Norwich society, followed in her wake, mumbling, 'Excuse me. Ta. Excuse me.'

They half-fell on to the platform, took a moment to orientate themselves, and then made their way to the escalator. Eve, still preoccupied, frowned as it carried them upwards. Behind her, Sonia embarked on a low but heartfelt monologue about the gross perversities of tube travel. 'Like a cattle truck . . . right on my foot he was . . . the stink . . . Can't think how they do it every day. Not natural, is it?'

Eve nodded as the words flowed over and around her, only partially heard, only partially recognized. Her heart was beating faster than it should. Like a drowning woman, she felt the urge to rush, to scramble towards the surface, but forced herself to stand perfectly still. Now wasn't the time to panic.

Once outside, she gradually regained her calm. Away from the stuffy confines of the underground the air had a different quality, the cool sharpness of dusk overlain by petrol fumes. There was something else too, something she couldn't quite put her finger on. Perhaps it was just the familiar smell of the city.

From the station it was only a short walk to Frith Street. After a while, Eve stepped up the pace, eager to get on with whatever lay ahead.

'Hang on,' Sonia complained, tottering behind on her high heels. 'Where's the bloody fire?'

'Sorry.' Stopping, Eve waited for her to catch up, taking a moment to look around, to take in the surrounding restaurants and bars. Already they were starting to fill up, to bustle with their Friday night clientele. In a few hours they'd be packed solid, filled to bursting, buzzing with that volatile combination of relief and anticipation – relief that the working week was over, anticipation of the two free days to come. She sighed. There was nothing like the atmosphere of a West End Friday night. Strange that she'd almost forgotten it.

It was twenty to seven when they arrived at the pub. They were early but Henry was already there, seated at a table with the evening paper. As if a sixth sense had alerted him, he raised his head as she approached and got smartly to his feet. His mouth broke into a smile. It faded a little as he realized she wasn't alone. Usually, he'd have leaned forward, placed a hand on her shoulder and given her a kiss on the cheek, but this evening, constrained by the unexpected presence of a stranger, he seemed at a loss as to how to greet her.

To cover the awkwardness, she quickly made the introductions. 'Henry, this is Sonia, a friend of mine. Sonia, this is Henry.'

They shook hands.

'Nice to meet you,' Henry said.

'Likewise,' she replied.

There was a brief silence, an uncomfortable pause, while the two of them stared at each other. Eve was aware of their mutual scrutiny. Glancing from one pair of eyes to another, she could almost read what they were thinking. Henry, without looking down, was still absorbing the cheap shortness of her skirt, her black stockings and high heels. Who *was* this woman? Sonia, on the other hand, was blatantly examining his smart but rather tired grey suit and the lines on his face. What could this ageing man offer Eve?

He was the first to recover his composure. Gesturing towards the chairs, he said, 'Please, sit down. Let me get you both a drink. What would you like?'

'Gin and tonic,' Sonia said. 'Ta.'

Eve asked for an orange juice. She could have done with a real drink, a large one, but the night might be a long one. She couldn't afford to take the easy option.

There was too much at stake. She had to try and stay sober.

Sonia, who had clearly decided that Henry was some kind of eccentric sugar daddy, examined his back as he stood at the bar. She tilted her head. 'He's a bit older than I imagined.'

Eve raised her eyes to the ceiling. 'Not *that* old.'

'But nice enough. You could do worse. At least he's got manners.'

They were still sitting round the same table over an hour and two drinks later. The conversation was starting to wane. She'd updated Henry on the latest events, trying to keep it low key, acting like it was no big deal to go searching for some dubious guy in the back streets of Soho. He wasn't convinced – she could see it in the way his mouth drooped down at the corners – but he kept his opinions to himself. Had they been alone, it would have been different, but the presence of Sonia created a useful barrier against a more probing and intense interrogation.

It was only when Sonia excused herself and went to the Ladies that he sighed and leaned forward. 'Are you sure you're doing the right thing?'

She shrugged. 'What *is* the right thing?'

'You don't know anything about this Jimmy Reece, Eve. He could be involved in all manner of stuff. He could be dangerous. He could be—'

'He could,' she said. 'But from what I've heard, I doubt it.'

'And what about Cavelli?'

She frowned. 'What about him?'

'How dangerous is he?'

Eve shrugged her shoulders again. She couldn't answer with any honesty. *Very* was the word that sprang

228

to mind but she couldn't bring herself to say it. 'He's got his own agenda,' she murmured. 'That's his business, not mine.'

'And you're happy with that?'

She lifted the glass to her lips and drank down the last of her juice. 'What do *you* think?'

'So why are you doing it?'

'You know why. A deal's a deal. He's taking care of Terry and I'm . . .' She gazed down into her empty glass. 'I'm sticking to my side of the bargain.'

Henry laid his hands on the table, his fingers restively touching and intertwining before breaking free again. 'But what kind of bargain is it?' he asked. 'What about the rest, the man who's been following you?'

'That's over,' she said, with more confidence than she felt. 'I'm sure it is. There's been nothing for days, no phone calls, no threats. It must have been some kind of mistake. They got the wrong person and now—'

Before she could finish, Sonia came back. She slid into her seat and gazed at them both. 'Sorry. I'm not disturbing anything, am I?'

'No,' they declared simultaneously.

Eve glanced over her shoulder towards the door. Patrick, unsurprisingly, was late. For all his fancy watches, he had never been able to get anywhere on time. It was almost eight o'clock. What would she do if he didn't turn up? She wasn't looking forward to seeing him but was dreading even more the prospect of haphazardly roaming the local bars, searching for a man she might not even recognize. All she had to go on was the tiny photograph she'd printed off the internet.

'Shall we go?' Sonia said. 'I'm starving.'

Eve looked up at the clock. She hadn't mentioned that there was going to be a fourth member to their party which, all things considered, was probably a wise move. Why she had ever imagined that Patrick would keep to any arrangements they had made was a mystery. He was probably still hustling in some dim seedy pool room on the other side of London.

'Yeah, let's make a move.' She stood up and put on her coat. There was no point waiting around any longer. He had her number; if he ever managed to make it to Soho, he could give her a ring.

Pushing their way through the crowd, Eve tried not to feel too resentful. It wasn't as if he had ever been the reliable sort. And she knew she could easily pick up her phone and give *him* a call but she was too stubborn and too proud to go chasing after him.

They were only feet from the door when it swung open and there he was – Patrick Fielding in all his sexy, blue-jeaned, smiling glory. Dramatic entrances were always his speciality.

'Evie!' he said, rushing forward and wrapping his arms tightly around her. 'Great to see you again!'

'You're late,' she snapped into his shoulder.

'Late for what?' he murmured seductively in her ear.

She felt his warm breath against her neck. Struggling free, she took a step back and gave him a cool look. 'I believe you said seven.'

'Oh, I'm sorry.' He grinned. 'Have I missed something important?'

It came as no surprise to find he still had the same flippant wisecracking attitude. She was sure he'd been born with it. And just to make matters worse, that pretty face of his had hardly changed at all, just a few faint lines around the eyes, which, if anything, made him appear even more attractive.

Eve tried to keep her tone light, to pretend – although it was a pointless exercise – that he hadn't got under her skin. 'Well, you'll never know now, will you?'

'Hey, we've got plenty of time to catch up. Our mutual friend won't be coming out to play before ten. That's if

230

he's sobered up by then.' He turned and bestowed the glorious pleasure of his smile on her two companions. 'I don't think we've been introduced.' He stretched out his hand. 'Patrick Fielding, devoted ex-husband. Delighted to meet you.'

Sonia didn't waste a second in grabbing his hand. As if an angel from heaven had miraculously descended, she squeezed his slender fingers and gazed up at him with awestruck wonder. 'Sonia Marshall,' she eventually managed to murmur.

While this touching exchange was taking place, Henry shot Eve a confused and questioning glance. His expression said it all. What on earth was going on? Having only just come to terms with the unexpected presence of her garishly made-up neighbour – a woman who looked, and even Eve couldn't pretend otherwise, rather less than respectable – he now had to deal with the sudden appearance of her long-divorced husband. His handshake, although not overtly unfriendly, was of a hesitant and cursory nature.

She should have warned him, Eve thought. He wasn't the kind of man who dealt too well with surprises.

'So, quite a posse,' Patrick said, his amused eyes sweeping over the three of them. 'Shall we go somewhere quiet? I think we need to talk.'

As they made their way slowly towards Greek Street, their progress impeded by the Friday night throng, he managed to skilfully manoeuvre her away from the other two. Linking his arm through hers, he slid them smoothly through a gap in the crowd. 'You look wonderful, Evie. You haven't changed a bit.'

'And you can still lie for Britain.'

'I mean it,' he said. 'You still look as great as the day I first met you.'

231

She paused a moment before she burst out laughing. 'You bastard! I was flat on my back and lying in the gutter.'

'You were doing a runner from The Ivy.'

'Not a runner,' she corrected. 'I was making a hasty but discreet exit from a slightly compromising situation.'

'Ah, yes, very discreet. And the way you slid off that pavement was the epitome of grace. If I recall rightly, you were being followed by an irate banker's wife with nothing but murder on her mind.'

'Yes, well,' she grinned. 'Not one of my finest moments.'

'It had its consolations.'

'For you, perhaps,' she said.

He shook his head in mock astonishment. 'There's gratitude for you. I saved your skin, babe!'

'You reckon? What's that saying – out of the frying pan and into the fire?'

'I don't recall you complaining at the time.'

As she laughed again, their bodies instinctively drew together. 'Well, you know me. Never one to cause a fuss.' And slowly, as her laughter dissolved, she leaned against him, her shoulder fitting neatly under his. Just like old times. The past was like superglue; no matter how hard you fought, it always held fast. And their past was stickier than most.

He sighed. 'I wish you'd told me, Evie, about your dad. He was . . . I could have been there for you.'

She shook her head. 'It all happened so quickly.'

'We should have stayed in touch.'

'Should we?' Perhaps he was right. You couldn't just throw away history. It was always there, always a part of you.

He pulled her closer, placing his chin on the crown of her head. 'You could have called me.'

'Maybe.'

For a while, like an island in a stream, they stood as one while the world flowed unnoticed around them. As if the past nine years hadn't happened, as if they'd never been apart, she clung on to his familiarity. She had loved her father. Patrick had loved her father. The three of them would always be connected.

Then, as if waking from a dream, she blinked and moved hurriedly away. What was she doing? Barely ten minutes had passed and Patrick had already lulled her into a false sense of security. She couldn't afford to let herself slide into that comfortable, distant, nostalgic place, a place, she knew, that wasn't even real.

Eve smoothed out the invisible creases in her coat. 'Where are the others?' she asked briskly.

He gave her a long hard look before he turned and glanced down the street. 'Not far behind.' Then he grinned. 'So, what's the deal with Darby and Joan – did you get a discount from Bodyguards Inc?'

They were sitting in a restaurant where the food was cheap and cheerful and the service a disgrace. Still, that suited her just fine. She didn't need some over-attentive waiter hovering obsequiously round the table while she tried to explain to Patrick the reasons for the manhunt.

She provided him with the basic version of events, the same one she had given Sonia: Terry was in prison, in trouble, and he needed help. Someone inside was willing to give it but only at a price; that price was finding Jimmy Reece.

She kept it simple, hoping that Henry wouldn't decide on any impromptu contributions about the break-in, the threats or her mystery stalker; the less Patrick knew about all that, the better. 'All I need are the whereabouts of some bars or clubs where he's likely to show.' She

233

smiled as if it was no great shakes. 'Nothing else. That's it.'

But simple wouldn't wash with Patrick. First he had to know the details of why Terry was in jail and then, when she told him, the identity of his 'protector'.

'That doesn't matter,' she said.

He raised his brows. 'It matters to me. If I'm going to help, I want to know who I'm doing it for.'

'You're doing it for *me*,' she insisted. 'And for Terry.'

But he wouldn't budge. 'Not good enough.' He leaned back and folded his arms across his chest. 'I want a name. It's not too much to ask, is it?'

She glared at him, unwilling to give in. She knew him too well; he was playing games, calling her bluff, hoping she'd be unnerved enough to throw her cards on the table. But, as their eyes remained locked, her resolution gradually wavered. Perhaps she was only being obstinate for the sake of it. And, being purely practical, if she didn't tell him soon, they could be there all night.

'Okay, but you have to keep it to yourself. He's called Martin Cavelli.'

She waited for a reaction, some sign of recognition, but his face remained blank. If he had read about the trial, he had long ago forgotten the name of the man in the dock.

Naturally, he asked the obvious question. 'So what's his interest in Reece?'

She shrugged. 'I didn't ask.'

Sonia shifted unhappily beside her. 'Don't you think—'

Eve threw her a warning glance but it was too late. Patrick had already picked up on the fact that there was more to be told. Before he could squeeze it out of his latest acolyte, she decided to come clean. 'Well, probably nothing good,' she admitted. 'I believe Jimmy Reece ran off with his wife.'

Henry, who was unaware of this particular detail, dropped his fork in alarm. It clattered noisily on to his plate. 'What?'

Seeing his reaction, she decided to skip the postscript; if he found out the whole story, the truth about what Cavelli was actually serving time for, he might try and call a halt to the search. 'I know, I know,' she said. 'But it sounds worse than it is. Honestly. I mean, even if we manage to track Reece down, he can't *do* anything with the information, can he? He's inside and he's not coming out for at least another year.' She paused. Henry looked distinctly unimpressed. Then, recalling her own fears about Cavelli's lust for vengeance, she hastily added, 'And he's not the type to get someone else to do his dirty work.'

Henry scowled, the lines on his forehead sinking into deeper ridges. 'You don't think so? Well, correct me if I'm wrong, but it would appear that he's already doing *exactly* that.' He expelled a short frustrated breath and turned towards Patrick as if in this wilderness of madness he might find another voice of reason. 'Wouldn't you agree?'

But Patrick, as unfazed by this revelation as he was by all the other absurdities of his life, only raised his glass to his lips and laughed. 'Perhaps he just wants to send him a thank-you card.'

It was after nine when they made their next move. Henry had been quiet for the preceding ten minutes, uttering only a few words. Despite her protestations, he'd insisted on picking up the bill. Apart from herself, no one else had offered to contribute. As they climbed the stairs she hung back and took his arm. 'Hold on a sec.' She waited until Patrick and Sonia had reached the exit and the door had slammed shut behind them. A gust of chill evening air blew down from the street. 'I just wanted to say thanks. Thanks for dinner and everything. And I'm sorry . . . sorry that I didn't tell you about . . .'

'I'm sure you had your reasons.' The tone of his voice was flat, expressionless.

The stairway was badly lit. She could only see half his face, the rest was in shadow. She tightened her grip on his arm and peered at him through the gloom. 'Haven't I got you in enough trouble?' Then, with a long sigh, she admitted: 'Yes, I should have told you. The only reason I didn't was because it was easier, because I didn't want to hear what I knew you'd say. Right at this time I just can't afford to listen to reason. The moment you learned about Cavelli's connection to Reece, I knew you'd try and talk me out of trying to find him – and I don't want to be persuaded. I *need* to do this, Henry. I don't expect you to condone it. I don't even expect you to try and understand. I know it isn't smart, isn't even sane maybe, but . . .'

As her voice began to break, she bit down on her lip.

She waited. A thin brittle silence hung between them. When he didn't reply, she cleared her throat and said: 'Look, why don't you call me in the morning? I'll let you know how it goes.'

Again, there was no response.

'Or I could call you.'

'There's no need,' he said.

So Henry was finally calling it quits. She was disappointed, dismayed even, but she wasn't surprised. And she certainly didn't blame him. There was a limit to the amount of grief anyone could bring into someone else's life. 'Okay,' she murmured, trying to keep her voice steady. 'That's fine. That's okay. I understand.'

But as her hand slipped from his arm, he reached out to retrieve it. 'What I'm saying is that there's no need to call because I'm coming with you.'

She lifted her head. 'What?' Out of pure relief, she laughed. So he wasn't deserting her. 'Thank you,' she said, squeezing his hand. But then, recalling that he still didn't have all the facts, her mouth twisted back into anxiety. 'Trouble is, there's more. There's something else.'

He waited, his eyebrows raised.

'Er . . . a couple of things really.' She hesitated but then, realizing there was no way to present the facts as any less bleak than they actually were, she swallowed hard and blurted them out. 'Reece dumped Nadine – she was Cavelli's wife – and then she . . . she took an overdose . . . and later, well, that's why Cavelli's in jail, because of what he did to him.'

As if all his worst fears had been confirmed, Henry gave a long deep sigh. 'God, Eve, have you really thought—'

'I know,' she said. 'You don't need to spell it out. I know how it sounds. But once Terry's out, I can warn Jimmy Reece, let him know that Cavelli's still on his trail. I'm sure he's safe while he's inside.'

'And if you're wrong?'

'I'll have to take that chance.' She paused. 'Look, it's okay. I'll understand if you want to change your mind.'

'Did I say that? I don't agree with what you're doing. How could I? I think it's wrong. I think you're being used. And I don't believe you've thought it through or even considered the consequences – but that's as may be. It doesn't mean that I'm going to walk away.'

But by now Eve was beginning to have second thoughts herself. She shouldn't be dragging him around the seedier parts of Soho. 'Maybe it's better if you do. Well, for tonight at least. It's getting late and some of the bars we may be visiting . . .'

'You think they may be too racy for me?'

Eve smiled and shook her head. 'It's too risky. What if someone sees you, sees *us*, if Celia finds out . . .'

'I'll take that chance.'

'But you don't have to. I appreciate it, I really do, but I'm not on my own. I've got Patrick and Sonia with me.'

As if that provided even greater cause for concern, he made a small growling noise in the back of his throat.

The door swung open again. Patrick peered down the stairwell. 'Are you two coming?'

'No,' she said.

'Yes,' Henry said.

She frowned at him.

'Just for an hour or two. Where's the harm in that?'

Micky Porter swirled his whisky, making the ice cubes chink against each other. Through the fug of cigarette smoke he watched as she walked back from the bar. Not bad. He let his gaze slide the length of her body, lingering for a second on her breasts and hips. He wouldn't mind a piece of that himself.

He had no idea why Joe wanted her followed but, shit, he wasn't complaining. There were worse jobs than pursuing a bit of skirt round Soho. Mind, he could have done without the earlier fiasco. They had barely arrived at the address in Norwich when she'd emerged from the flats with the old bint, got in a cab, and headed straight for the station. On the forecourt he'd left Frank Gruber in the motor while he checked out their destination. Of course it had to be fucking London! What were the odds?

He laughed into his glass. Sod's law. That's what it was. They could have saved themselves the journey. Still, with Gruber taking the car back to the city and him on the train, he'd enjoyed a temporary break from his driver's scintillating company. That man was so morose he could make a bloody angel weep.

The crowds had made it easy to trail her, first to the pub and then the restaurant. By then the party had increased by two. He'd used his phone to take some pictures. He hadn't followed them into the Greek joint; from the street he couldn't tell how busy it was and a man could stand out if he was eating alone. No point drawing attention to himself. Instead he'd gone to a pizza place across the road, found a spot by the window and waited. They'd emerged over an hour later. By the time Gruber had caught up, they were well into a tour of the local bars.

'So what do you reckon? They searching for someone or just out for a good time?'

Gruber shrugged and grunted into his beer.

Micky lit a cigarette and returned his attention to the group. The four of them were seated at a table about ten feet away. They were a bizarre combination, like odd pieces of a jigsaw that didn't fit together. Without staring, he took another look at Eve; cool, classy, expensive. You'd never get a cheap date out of *her*. Still, and he smirked at the thought, she'd probably be worth it. The older woman, however, had a definite air of coarseness. A tart. He'd stake his life on it. What was their connection? Related, maybe? They'd come out of the flats together but he couldn't see much of a family resemblance. He shifted his gaze to the tall good-looking blond guy in his thirties. Shark eyes. Smooth and confident, smart, always ready to oblige. Micky knew his type; he could spot a hustler when he saw one. Friendly with the Weston girl but were they a couple? Hard to tell. Perhaps the three of them were planning a shakedown on the old geezer.

Except he didn't look worth the effort.

He didn't look very happy to be here either. There was

something tight and wary about him, not nervous exactly, more . . . bemused. As if he'd walked in off the street expecting a tea dance and inexplicably found himself in a brothel. Not that this place was quite that. Although if sleaze was what they were after, they were certainly getting their fair share.

He flicked the ash off his cigarette on to the floor. An accountant, that's what the guy looked like, not one of those flash City types but the quieter, greyer, old-fashioned sort. And accountants, no matter how dry and dusty, could always be useful.

Micky wondered what Joe Silk's interest was in the redhead. He opened his mouth, intending to ask Gruber, but then closed it again. Why waste his breath? If the man ever had any opinions, he rarely chose to share them. It made for dull company on a long night but perhaps he shouldn't be too critical. For all his shortcomings, there was no one he'd rather have beside him in a tight spot; what Gruber lacked in conversational skills, he made up for in solid unyielding muscle.

He turned to him and smiled. 'All right, mate?'

Gruber nodded.

Micky went back to thinking about Joe. Something had rattled the boss recently, something that he wasn't sharing. Well, except with that fucking psycho of course. He'd been holed up in his office with Chase for the past few weeks, plotting, planning, doing his nut at the slightest provocation. Yeah, something serious was going down, no doubt about it.

He shifted in his seat and scowled. Even after all these years Keeler Chase still gave him the creeps. A queer for sure. He'd never seen him with a woman. Not that he had anything against queers, so long as they kept their eyes off his cock, but this one – and he wasn't ashamed to admit it – scared the shit out of him. He could slit a man's throat with a smile on his face. Violence was more

240

than second nature to Chase; it *was* his fucking nature. Inflicting pain brought him pleasure. A sadist, that's what he was. And he and Joe were close. Too close, some people said, although personally he'd never believed the rumours. Joe was as straight as they came. Had a wife and kids, didn't he? Not that that stopped some blokes from . . . but no, he wasn't the type. He'd noticed the way he looked at the women in the clubs, heard the way he talked to them.

Micky knocked back the last of his drink. Whatever was going on, Eve Weston had a part in it. He wouldn't be here otherwise. Joe never used him for the scrappy shit. If he wanted him to follow her then he wanted to make sure that it was a job done properly. Had she stepped on his toes, tried to do him over? That would take one very brave or very stupid woman. Or was his interest more personal than professional? Perhaps the sexy Ms Weston had made a different kind of impact.

He'd never known the boss play away from home but then there was a first time for everything. She was a looker, no doubt about it, not in the first flush of youth perhaps but there was a lot to be said for experience: those knowing wide grey eyes, that sultry mouth, the way she walked across a room . . . it was enough to turn any man's head.

But no, tempting as the idea was, he couldn't quite swallow it. This wasn't about infatuation or some muddled mid-life crisis. Whatever was bugging Joe had nothing to do with her neat little arse. Business was what came first with him, always had and always would.

So what the fuck was going on?

He glanced at her again. Where did she figure in all this? He didn't like being kept in the dark. It made him anxious, jumpy. He quickly looked away in case she caught him watching. Women had a sixth sense for when they were being scrutinized. Instead he transferred his attention to a group of girls at the bar, three blondes and a brunette, rating their availability with one part of his brain while he continued to think about Joe Silk with the rest.

He had only seen him like this once before, a couple of years ago. He'd never found out what that was about either. A short holiday, a trip abroad, and he'd come back acting like the devil was on his heels. Spooked, that was the only way to describe it. And with a temper short enough to shame his psycho sidekick. One wrong word, one wrong look, and there'd been no accounting for his reaction. Micky had been smart enough to keep his mouth shut but there were others – well, the ones who were still alive to tell the tale – who wouldn't forget those days in a hurry. He'd wondered then if Joe was losing his grip, getting too old for the game, but the crisis had passed and everything had returned to normal.

The blonde on the left looked at him for the second time. He grinned back at her. Nice smile, nice tits. Yeah, she'd be up for it. Perhaps he should go to the bar and introduce himself. No point wasting a God-sent opportunity.

He was halfway to his feet when Gruber nudged him in the ribs.

'What?'

He gestured towards the table they were supposed to be watching.

The party had got to its feet and was making its way towards the door.

They were on the move again.

Chapter Fifteen

They had been sitting in the dim smoky gloom for over twenty minutes. It had gone midnight and Eve was starting to despair of ever finding Jimmy Reece, starting to wonder too if Patrick was leading them all on a wild-goose chase. She wouldn't put it past him. There were occasions when his sense of humour left a lot to be desired.

Soho had plenty of excellent bars, some cool, some quirky, but they hadn't had the pleasure of setting foot in many of them. Reece's taste, if Patrick was to be believed, lay with the more downmarket establishments, and boy they'd visited enough of those this evening to write the definitive tourists' guide to sleaze. Still, there was *one* small mercy: the waitresses weren't topless here. Over the last few hours she'd seen enough naked breasts to last her a lifetime.

In comparison, this bar was verging on the respectable. She couldn't exactly call it classy – it hadn't seen a lick of paint or breathed a can of air freshener in the last decade – but it was less overtly disreputable. Even so, there was something oppressive about the place. This was maybe down to the walls, painted a too heavy shade of red (reminding her momentarily of the tape around Cavelli's boxes), or just the thin pinkish light that barely penetrated the darkness. The circular tables, marble-topped, were arranged either side of a wide central aisle and securely bolted to the floor. But at least the music, a soft rhythmic jazz, was at a volume where you could hear yourself speak.

She glanced at Patrick. He was busy enchanting Sonia, gazing into her admiring eyes while he unleashed the full force of the Fielding charm. She realized, with a wry smile, that he had probably learned more about Sonia's life in the last few hours than she had managed to acquire in the entire time that she'd known her. That was his skill, getting people to talk while he listened, routinely harvesting every tiny piece of information that came his way.

He caught her looking and grinned. 'Everything okay, babe?'

She nodded. 'Fine.'

Eve took another generous sip of her cocktail – so much for her resolution to stay sober – and turned her attention towards Henry. He had a vague bewildered expression on his face as if he had slipped so far out of his comfort zone that he was struggling to recall what normality was. Or perhaps she was just being overprotective. At sixty-two, he had probably forgotten more than she had ever seen.

'It's getting late,' she reminded him. 'You don't have to stay. If you want to get off then—'

An explosion of laughter drowned out the end of her sentence. Next to them another foursome, two young men and their girlfriends, were drunkenly falling all over each other. A glass slipped off their table and smashed on the floor. After a brief silence, a second of surprise, they burst out laughing again.

Henry gave her a faint smile.

'Perhaps we should call it a night,' she said.

And he might have agreed if Patrick hadn't suddenly

leaned forward. He kept his voice low. 'I thought you wanted to find Jimmy Reece.'

'I did.' She shrugged, reaching for her coat. 'I do. But we can always try again.'

'We don't need to.'

It took her a moment to realize what he was saying. And when she did, she wasn't best pleased. 'Is he here? Where is he?' She quickly scanned the room but couldn't spot the face she was searching for. Frustrated she looked back at him. 'Where is he?'

'The same place he's been since we came in.' He gestured with a tilt of his head. 'Don't look now but . . . up near the bar, the small table to the right, the guy with the blonde.'

'Why didn't you tell me?' she hissed.

His mouth slid into its silky hustler smile. 'Because you might have stared.'

'I never stare,' she retorted. 'When do I ever stare?' She deliberately waited before she slid her gaze cautiously towards the bar. Despite the photograph, it was doubtful she'd have recognized him. He looked ordinary, slim, in his early forties, with dark straight hair that flopped a little over his forehead. His eyes, although she couldn't see them clearly, were probably dark too. From a distance there was nothing much to distinguish him from any other man in the room. He was dressed in a suit that was expensive but crumpled. And he was drunk, *very* drunk if the expression on his companion's face was anything to go by; she looked about as happy as a gold-digger who had just struck dirt.

'Are you sure?' Eve said.

'Yeah, that's him.'

Reece was lighting a cigarette for the blonde, touching her arm, whispering in her ear. The girl sat back and laughed, one of those false brittle laughs that floated through the air. Almost immediately her mouth closed again and tightened in a thin straight line.

'So what's the plan?' Patrick said.

Eve frowned. She hadn't got quite as far as a plan. Finding him had seemed a mission in itself and, now that they had, she wasn't sure what to do next.

'What do you need to know?' he prompted.

'Where he lives, what he's doing, who he's doing it with . . .' As she recited the list, she began to feel progressively more uneasy. What had Jimmy Reece ever done to her? And okay, she'd never been Miss Perfect but conning some gullible bloke out of a few quid was an entirely different proposition to what Cavelli might have in store for this particular victim.

Henry shifted beside her. 'Perhaps we should give it some thought.'

Patrick's lip curled a fraction. 'What's there to think about?'

'The consequences?'

The consequences. The way he said it made them sound like a death sentence. A shiver ran through her. And perhaps he wasn't far wrong. She could be making the biggest mistake of her life. What if—

'Oh come on, we're here now,' Patrick snapped impatiently. 'Let's just do what we came to do and think about that later. We might not get another chance.' He looked towards Sonia hoping to garner some support. 'What do you reckon?'

'Well,' she replied, hesitantly, glancing at each of them in turn. Clearly torn between her unwillingness to upset Eve, her desire to please Patrick and her complete indifference to Henry, she eventually came down on the side of compromise. 'Well, I suppose, it's like you said yesterday, love. You don't *have* to pass on the information but at least this way, if we talk to him, you get to keep your options open.'

Eve nodded. She had a point. 'Henry?'

But before Henry could make his contribution, the blonde girl suddenly stood up, grabbed her jacket and flounced past them towards the exit. A mixture of anger and sullen disappointment was etched across her face. In her wake she left a breeze of expensive scent. For a second it looked as though Reece was going to follow her. He rose unsteadily to his feet and peered between the tables.

'Shit,' Patrick murmured.

But then, as if the effort was too much for him, or he couldn't quite recall why he had got up in the first place, his forehead scrunched into a frown and he sat heavily back down.

A small sigh of relief slipped from three pairs of lips.

Patrick used the opportunity to press home his argument. 'Evie, make a decision and make it now. If we don't do this tonight, it could take you weeks to find him again. He doesn't always come here. If you change your mind, do you really want to be touring the bars of Soho for ever and a day?'

Put like that, she knew she had to make a choice. And fast. If Reece had left with the girl and jumped in a cab she could have lost her best, perhaps her *only* opportunity, to stick to her side of the deal. What she mustn't forget, what she had to concentrate on, was that Terry needed her. She had to do this for him. 'Okay,' she agreed. 'Let's go for it.'

'Right,' Patrick said firmly. Before Henry had time to plant any more doubts in her mind, he quickly summoned a waitress. 'Whatever the gentleman by the bar is drinking,' he said, pointing him out. 'And make it a double. With our compliments.'

Eve waited until the woman was walking away. 'You've got an idea?'

He shrugged. 'Not really. Let's just play it by ear, see how chatty he is.'

They waited.

At first Reece, confused, tried to push the glass away. He glared at the waitress. They could see him shaking his head. He hadn't ordered it. He wasn't paying for it. It took her a while to explain that the drink was a gift. She turned and indicated towards their table.

Reece narrowed his eyes and squinted at them.

Patrick gave him a friendly wave.

Eventually he got to his feet again and this time managed to stumble the five long yards to their table. As if he was standing on the deck of a moving boat, he swayed a little as he stood in front of them. 'Most kind,' he said, patting the side of the glass with the palm of his hand.

'Good to see you again,' Patrick said. 'Grab a seat. How are you?'

He frowned but slumped down obediently beside him. 'Sorry, old chap, but . . . hope this doesn't sound too ungrateful and all but . . . do I know you?' Although he was clearly sloshed, his cut-glass accent held only the hint of a slur.

'Patrick O'Connell,' he said. 'We met on the set of *The Fall of Charlie Payne*.' Then he laughed. 'But I guess that *was* a few years back.'

'Ah,' he said, as if the light had dawned. 'So you're . . . an actor . . .?'

'God, no. Production, that's more my line. I worked alongside Bill Morton on the movie. You remember Bill, don't you? Great guy. What a character. I was his right-hand man for longer than . . . But look, sorry, what am I thinking? Let me introduce you to everyone: this is my lovely wife Evie and our good friends Henry and Sonia.'

Eve shot him a sharp suspicious glance. What was with the lovely wife stuff? And so much for playing it by ear; unless Patrick had become an overnight expert on small-budget gangster films, he'd been doing his research on Jimmy Reece. And that was a worry. Was he really trying to help or was he working to a more personal agenda? He was hardly renowned for his acts of self-lessness. But there wasn't time to think about that now. Their mark had leaned across the table to take her hand.

'Wonderful to meet you,' he drawled.

She smiled sweetly back. 'Hi. Nice to meet you too.'

He paused, his brown bleary pupils expanding a fraction as his gaze slowly focused on her face. 'My pleasure entirely.'

It took a few seconds to gently extricate her fingers. He seemed determined to hold on to them. And even when she broke free he continued to look into her eyes. She forced herself to keep on smiling. Once this whole clichéd scene would have come to her as naturally as breathing but tonight she felt self-conscious, awkward, almost embarrassed. Perhaps it was because Henry was there. She wished he wasn't. She wished she'd persuaded him to go home hours ago. Sliding back into the old seductive routine wasn't quite so easy when the one person she respected, whose friendship she valued above everyone else's, was sitting right next to her.

Thankfully, remembering his manners, Reece turned back towards the others.

It gave her the chance to scrutinize him. It was only up close that you could see the damage Cavelli had inflicted, the broken nose, the twisted mouth, the deep brutal scars that ran from his left cheek to his chin. So this was the man who had seduced his wife. This was the man he despised, who he'd hated so much he had beaten to a pulp. This was the man he was serving time for. She tried not to stare – although it was difficult not to. Reece had probably been quite handsome once but now his whole face was aslant, distinctly asymmetric, as though one side had been smashed into a hundred pieces and cleverly, although not altogether accurately, put back together again. What Cavelli had done could never be repaired.

She reached for her drink and finished it in one fast gulp.

Her glass was empty and so was Jimmy Reece's.

'You want another?' Patrick asked him. 'In fact, look, why don't we get a bottle of champagne? Let's celebrate. It's not every day you run into old friends. What do you say – will you stay and have another drink with us?'

He took about as much persuasion as any drunk with a raging thirst.

Patrick caught the attention of a waitress again. He ordered the champagne but then, rummaging in his pocket, only came up with a tenner. He glanced towards Henry. 'Er . . . I don't suppose you could . . .'

As he reached for his wallet, Eve put her hand on his arm. 'It's okay, I'll get it.' She drew out her purse and threw her credit card on to the tray. It was bad enough that Henry had to witness this whole deception; she didn't expect him to pay for the privilege too. She should never have dragged him into this. He'd been more than decent to her and if it all turned out as she feared then . . .

The bottle of champagne was swiftly delivered. Patrick poured the drinks, passed them around, and then made a toast. 'To old friends!' he announced.

'And to new ones,' Jimmy added, his eyes deliberately seeking out Eve's, his right leg roaming dangerously close to hers under the table.

As his knee made contact for the second time she tried not to flinch, to pull away too quickly. It was too late now to change her mind. The game had begun. There was no going back.

'To new friends,' she repeated sweetly.

They all raised their glasses and smiled.

Micky had found a table in the darkest part of the bar, a corner where they could sit without being seen too clearly. He got out his phone and made a call. It was his third of the night. 'Boss? Yeah, it's me. We're in Pearl's. They've linked up with someone. Yeah. And guess who? It's our old mate Jimmy Reece.'

He listened for a moment, nodding, before snapping shut the mobile and returning it to his pocket. He couldn't tell if Joe had been surprised by the news or not; he always kept his cards close to his chest. Just stick with the girl was his only instruction. And Micky was no closer to understanding why.

He glanced over at the party again. It had seemed to him that the meeting hadn't been prearranged, more accidental, a chance encounter, but he could be wrong. Maybe they'd just wanted it to look like that. Something was cooking but whether Jimmy was the victim or a player wasn't clear yet. Originally, he'd thought the old guy might be the mark but now he wasn't so sure. But if it was Jimmy instead, if they had some kind of scam planned, they'd be sorely disappointed. Since his movie career had hit the skids, he didn't have a pot to piss in. Reece might have a title but he didn't have the inheritance to go with it. He owed a fortune and he owed most of it to Joe.

'What's going on here?' he asked Gruber.

He took a while to deliberate, the cogs turning slowly. 'Reece needs some dough,' he said eventually.

'He always needs some dough. But do they look like a bunch of fucking money-lenders to you?'

'Who says he's borrowing? Maybe he's trading. Maybe he's got something they want.'

Micky looked at him, surprised. Gruber might not say much but all that time in the boxing ring clearly hadn't mashed his brains completely. He could be on to something. But what could Reece possibly have that Eve Weston wanted? And what did it have to do with Joe Silk?

He stared at the group, wondering if it was safe to move closer, to try and listen in on their conversation, but decided against it. No unnecessary risks. No mistakes. Not with the mood the boss was in.

He studied the blond guy, the hustler, again. His first thought had been that he was her boyfriend – there was an intimacy between the two of them, a closeness. But Jimmy Reece was all over her like a rash. If she was his girl he'd have punched the bastard's fucking lights out. So why was he just sitting there and taking it?

They had to be working some kind of con.

As Eve walked back from the Ladies, she glanced around and saw the two men sitting in the corner. She felt a nervous flicker of recognition. The light wasn't good but she could have sworn she'd seen them before, earlier in the evening, in one of the other bars. They were both big guys, solid, distinctive – the type it was smarter to never pick a fight with.

Was it possible that she'd got her shadow back? Could the older one be the man from the alley? She peered through the dimness. Her heart skipped a couple of beats. Christ, she hoped not. She let her gaze linger for a couple of seconds longer but neither of them looked up or paid her any attention. Perhaps she was overreacting. After all, it was Friday night. Lots of people moved from

252

bar to bar. It was inevitable that a few familiar faces would crop up.

But as she took her seat, she automatically glanced over her shoulder again. Now the younger guy, the one with the square jaw and close-cropped hair, was leaning across to chat to a giggly brunette at the next table. She relaxed. No, they were just a couple of blokes out on the pull, two mates out for a good time.

Which was a long way adrift from the type of time she was having. The attentions of Jimmy Reece were beginning to wear thin. What had Nadine ever seen in him? But then she'd married Cavelli. There was no accounting for taste. However, she had caught an occasional glimpse of what some women might find attractive: a lazy arrogant charm, a public schoolboy confidence, the sporadic emergence of a sharp but cruel wit. It didn't do anything for Eve but then she'd had too much experience of rich, spoiled boys to ever be beguiled by them.

Hopefully, they could leave soon. She'd had enough and Reece was too drunk to get anything more out of him. All he was interested in now was the fastest route up her thigh. As his hand slid under the table again, she swiftly shifted away.

Sonia, coming to her rescue, picked up the bottle and refreshed his glass. 'That Charlie . . . er, whatsit film,' she said, 'I just loved that. It's one of my favourites. Brilliant. You're such a great actor, really great.'

And while Jimmy lit another cigarette and basked in the glory, Eve looked down at her watch. Twenty past one. She shot a glance at Patrick, a conspiratorial glance from the old days. *Get me out of here* was what it was supposed to convey but he simply grinned back, picked up his glass, and joined in the conversation.

'Yeah, you should make more movies.'

While the rest of them talked, she made a rapid review of the information they'd managed to acquire so far.

They hadn't done too badly. Not only had they established that Reece had moved from Notting Hill to Chelsea and found out his address, they'd also learned that he was married, trying to revive his acting career, and desperate for anyone who could help him back on to the silver screen. Fame was what he missed – and what he craved.

Most of this, surprisingly, had been down to Henry. He had spent the first half-hour in virtual silence but, as if woken from a trance, had abruptly come awake and embarked on a cross-examination so subtle and skilful that the Old Bailey would have been proud of him. It had happened shortly after Patrick had asked about the girl Jimmy had been with earlier.

'I couldn't help noticing but . . . I hope you don't mind me asking . . . was that your wife?'

He had laughed into his champagne. 'Hell, no. She may be somebody's wife but she certainly isn't mine.'

It might have been that ugly dismissive comment, his general arrogance, or his increasingly blatant advances towards her which had finally spurred Henry into action. Or maybe he had just wanted to get the whole damn thing over and done with as quickly as possible. Whatever the reason, he'd done an excellent job, prising one small piece of information after another from Jimmy's drunk and careless mouth.

She could imagine what Reece saw when he looked at Henry: someone old, dull, grey, non-threatening. And Henry knew it too. And had used it to his full advantage. She smiled. He'd done her proud!

And Patrick, although she was loath to admit it, had been smart too in introducing her as his wife. Jimmy Reece clearly liked to take what he perceived as belonging to other people. For him, that was the challenge, the kick, the thrill. He wasn't interested in anything available. He was a thief of the lowest kind, the sort who stole only for the hell of it, for the power, the control, for the hurt he could inflict – before he carelessly threw it all away. Had Nadine imagined it was some great romance? What a fool! But then as soon as Eve thought it, she was sorry. When it came to love, everyone made mistakes, and if anyone had paid the price for following their heart, it was that poor girl.

Frowning, she looked down at her watch again. 'It's getting late,' she said.

'Ah, you're not going,' Jimmy objected. He wrapped his hand possessively around her wrist. 'Don't go. I know this club, just down the road. You should come. You really should. It's delightful. You'd love it, it's—'

'I wish we could,' she said, 'I really do. But we've got an early start in the morning.'

'A *very* early start,' Patrick added, finally coming to her rescue. 'We're supposed to be on set at six.' He stood up. 'But look, keep in touch. It's been great to see you again. Perhaps we can meet up for dinner.' He took a small white business card from his pocket and passed it across the table.

Jimmy, releasing his hold on her wrist, stared at it for a while. Then he took a pen from his pocket and scrawled a number on the back. He passed it deliberately, almost provocatively, back to Eve. 'I always lose cards,' he said. 'It's probably better if *you* hold on to it.'

She smiled and slipped it into her bag. 'We'll be in touch.'

As they made their way out of the bar, Eve glanced back. She looked first at Jimmy, his face stuck firmly in his glass, and then at the corner where the two guys had been sitting. The space was empty now. Good. Thank God. She'd been right; there was nothing to worry about.

Out on the street, they gave the first cab they came across to Henry. Eve insisted that he took it. There were three of them, safety in numbers and all that, and he had a wife to go home to – Lord knows what he'd tell Celia. Working late at the office would hardly cut it. She put her hand on his arm as he climbed in. 'Thanks.'

'I'll give you a ring,' he said.

'We'll talk tomorrow. Take care.' She would have kissed him on the cheek if the others hadn't been there. Instead, she gently squeezed his arm and retreated.

'Smart guy,' Patrick said, as the taxi disappeared round the corner. 'That was quite a performance. Very smooth. If I didn't know better, I might almost think he was a pro.'

'He is,' she said softly, 'but not in the way you think.'

Patrick opened his mouth as if to respond but thought better of it, paused, and said instead: 'So where are you staying? Have you got a hotel booked? You won't get a train back at this time of night.'

'We'll head towards Liverpool Street, find something there.'

'It'll be expensive. Look, why don't you stay at the flat? I think we can just about squeeze in – and there's no point wasting cash on a bed you're only going to sleep in for a few hours.'

Eve was about to refuse but then changed her mind. It had been a long evening; Sonia was yawning and she was tired too. And he was right about the money; she shouldn't be throwing cash away needlessly. 'Okay,' she agreed, rather grudgingly. 'Thanks. If you're sure.'

They flagged down another cab a few minutes later.

And if Eve had glanced over her shoulder one last time she would have seen the dark estate pulling carefully out from the kerb behind them.

Chapter Sixteen

She stared out of the window, gazing at the night lights of the city. Patrick and Sonia, their voices low, were talking about Jimmy Reece, a conversation which in turn led to Terry, and which eventually led on to the subject of her father.

It was inevitable that in her flimsy construction of secrets and lies a few nails would eventually fly loose. She just hadn't expected them to come adrift in a black cab on the Kingsland Road. It was Sonia who let it slip, first about the break-in, and then about the manner of her father's death. Too much champagne had loosened her tongue. Although neither was exactly a secret, Eve had privately been hoping Patrick wouldn't find out.

Why? She wasn't sure why. Because it wasn't any of his business? She breathed a heavy sigh against the glass. Or perhaps because she just didn't have the answers to the questions she knew he would ask.

The burglary, of course, didn't faze him too much – living in London, it was almost an occupational hazard – and there was no reason for him to connect it to her current business with Cavelli. But her father's suicide was another matter altogether.

He sounded shocked, stunned. 'Evie?'

And she knew he was hurt, pained not just by its dreadfulness but also by the fact she hadn't told him.

Cancer, she had said. She hadn't mentioned anything about his lonely midnight walk into the river.

'What?' she said, huddling closer to the door, pretending that she hadn't been listening. And perhaps there was something in her tone of voice, something he recalled from years past, that made him decide not to pursue the matter.

At least for now.

And she was grateful. Although she knew it was only an agony postponed and not cancelled.

Sonia, aware that she'd inadvertently put her foot in it, did her best to make amends. For the next few minutes, acting as if nothing had happened, she made enough idle small talk to fill what might have become an uneasy silence. By the time the cab drew up beside the old Victorian terrace, a faint sense of normality had returned.

Patrick, despite his alleged shortage of cash, miraculously produced a twenty-pound note and passed it over to the driver. Eve had intended to pay half but instantly changed her mind. A few hours ago, he'd only had a tenner. What was that all about? She didn't need to ask. Once a hustler, always a hustler. But as he'd been so generously wined and dined, courtesy of Henry and herself, she saw no reason at all why he shouldn't make a small contribution to the evening's expenses.

She made her way along the short drive towards the basement flat they'd once inhabited together. As she descended the flight of six stone steps, it was like slipping back into the past. Even the lamp above the door gave off the same thin slightly flickering light.

'How come you never moved?'

He rummaged in his pockets for his keys. 'I could never do that,' he said. 'What if you'd wanted to come back and couldn't find me?'

She snorted.

'You know your problem?' he said, grinning. 'You've got no sense of—'

'Don't say it,' she interrupted, raising a hand. 'I don't respond well to criticism. Just unlock the door and get the coffee on.'

But for all her attempts at flippancy, she couldn't deny that it felt odd, disconcerting, to be here again, to step inside the narrow hallway, to walk slowly through into the living room. She turned on the light and looked up. Even the same long crack was on the ceiling, an ominous zigzag that ran precariously from one corner to another. The back windows, like the ones at the front, were protected with strong iron bars. Everything was familiar. She knew the whole place inside out, not just this room but the others too – the bedroom barely big enough to hold a double bed, the tiny kitchen, the bathroom with its chipped blue tiles.

'As you can see,' he said, walking in behind her, 'in deference to your memory, I've kept everything exactly as it was.'

'Very touching,' she replied. 'I'm sure Miss Havisham would be proud. But I hope that doesn't extend to a lack of milk in the fridge.'

It was only after Sonia had gone to bed that he raised the subject of her father again. She was sitting in the easy chair. He was sitting on the sofa with his boots up on the coffee table.

'I can't believe he did that.'

She buried her face in her mug and sighed. 'Do we have to—'

'Not Alex,' he insisted, as if she hadn't spoken. 'He wasn't the type. I don't get it. I don't understand.'

'He was sick,' she said.

'But why that? Why would he do *that*?'

'You know why. He was ill, tired, maybe he . . . maybe he just couldn't face what was coming.'

Patrick shook his head. 'No, he never ran away from anything.'

She glared at him, suddenly angry. 'He wasn't running away. How can you call it that? He made a decision, a choice, and until you're placed in the same position, until you're facing a bloody death sentence, you shouldn't be so fast to pass judgement.'

He stared at her before getting to his feet. Walking over to the cabinet, he kept his back turned as he took out a bottle of brandy and poured two stiff measures. Then he slowly looked over his shoulder. 'I'm sorry,' he said. 'I didn't mean—'

She raised her eyes. 'I know. Forget it. I'm sorry too. I shouldn't have snapped. It's just hard to deal with.'

He placed the two glasses on the table and sat back down. 'So how's Terry coping with it all?'

She picked up the brandy and took a gulp. 'I'm not sure if he is.'

'You see, that's what I don't get. Not so much why he did it, but why he would do it while Terry was still inside. I know they had their ups and downs but . . .'

She felt her stomach sink. That was *it*. That was what didn't make sense to her either. And it was why she'd never wanted to have this conversation with Patrick in the first place. He had a nasty habit of cutting straight to the chase. He knew her too well. He knew them *all* too well. There was every chance her father could, probably would, have survived the length of Terry's sentence. So why had he chosen to take the path he had? 'Maybe the cancer was more advanced than he said. You know what he was like, never one for hospitals. He couldn't stand the places.'

As if this might be a feasible explanation, he nodded.

'God, Evie. It must have been devastating. Did he . . .' He hesitated. 'Did he leave a letter or anything?'

She frowned as his question hit yet another emotional sore point. 'No. Most suicides don't, apparently. Perhaps he didn't plan it.' But even as the suggestion spilled from her mouth she knew the notion was ridiculous. Planning was her father's middle name. 'I mean, perhaps he didn't plan it for that particular night, he just went for a walk and . . .' Her explanation petered out. She'd run through it a thousand times in her head, churning through the possibilities, but saying it out loud just made her realize how wrong it all sounded.

'Maybe,' he said. 'Or maybe, when it came to it, he just couldn't find the words.'

There was a short silence. Eve could feel the tears pricking her eyes. It was still tormenting her: how he could have left, how he could have done that, without so much as a farewell note. If this carried on she'd be crying on Patrick's shoulder before the night was out. And that wasn't such a good idea. Kicking off her shoes, she curled her legs under her, stared down at her feet and quickly changed the subject. 'So how did you know all that stuff about Jimmy Reece – about his films, about that Bill Morton guy?'

It wasn't the most skilful diversionary tactic but he let it pass.

'I go to the movies,' he said.

'Right,' she replied. 'Don't we all. But since when did you become such an expert?'

His mouth broke into a smile. 'Be prepared. Isn't that what they say? Okay, so I might have done a bit of research. I thought I was being helpful. Whatever happened to old-fashioned gratitude?'

She shrugged. 'Hey, I am grateful, but I didn't ask you to come with us. *You* were the one who insisted on doing that.' She took another sip of her drink and gazed around. Her eyes were searching, although she would never admit it, for any signs of a new female influence – the presence of silk cushions or a vase of flowers or any of those other accessories that so many women use to establish their territory. But there was nothing. Other than a couple of new prints on the wall, the room was unchanged. Even the damp patch by the back door was still there.

'I live on my own,' he said.

She glanced quickly back at him. 'Did I ask?'

'You didn't need to.' He laughed, lifting his arms and placing his hands behind his head.

It was such a familiar gesture that she felt a brief pang of . . . of what? She struggled to identify it, worried for a moment that it might be regret, but then gradually relaxed as she accepted it was only a sense of sadness, a faint nostalgia for what had been lost and could never be recovered. She sighed into her brandy.

'How about you?' he said.

She looked up at him.

'Are you and Henry . . .'

'No, God, of course not. He's just a friend.' She noticed his brows shoot up and added, '*Please*. Not *that* kind of a friend. Henry's a good man, someone I can talk to.'

Patrick lowered his arms and then raised a hand again to sweep his fingers through his hair. 'That's nice,' he said.

She heard the edge to his tone; although not blatantly sarcastic, it wasn't far off. She had a sudden almost perverse impulse to ask if he had been faithful to her when they were married. The question rose in her throat but she smartly swallowed it down. What was she trying to do – rake up old ghosts, pick a fight? She already knew she'd resent any answer he gave: 'Yes', because it would be a lie; 'No', because it would dredge up all the old hurt and betrayal. Some agonies, like old scars, were best left alone. And anyhow, they had both lived a life so full of falsehoods, of such easy casual deceit, that perhaps neither was capable of any real kind of truth.

She studied his face, still so ridiculously beautiful, his soft blue eyes and wide seductive mouth. It was a face she had once loved to distraction. He didn't look back. He was staring at the ceiling. There was something in his expression, something . . . and then it came to her, a touch too late, that her comment about Henry – *someone I can talk to* – might have been less than diplomatic. He had interpreted it, possibly, as a subtle dig, a reminder of what she hadn't revealed, of what she hadn't felt able to confide. Bother. She hadn't meant it like that. She hadn't meant to suggest . . . She'd only been trying to keep things simple, uncomplicated, but of course there was no such thing when it came to emotions.

Should she apologize? No, that would only make it worse.

Instead, searching for another way to make amends, she reached for her bag, took out the small white card, and examined it. 'Patrick O'Connell,' she said, reading off the name on the front. She laughed. 'I can't believe you're still using that one.'

He dropped his gaze to her again and smiled. 'Now, what's wrong with that?' he said, deliberately emphasizing his lilting Dublin brogue. 'What objection can you possibly be taking to such a decent, solid, Irish name?'

She grinned back. Apart from his phone number, there was nothing else on the card. 'You're slipping. What's the matter, didn't you have time to print up the film producer version?'

He flapped a hand, sliding back into his more natural accent. 'Hell, no. That would just be showing off. These days I go for the more economical approach. Less is more. A successful man doesn't need to brag about his achievements.'

She flipped the card between her fingers, turning it over to see the number Jimmy Reece had scrawled across the back.

'Pass it over,' Patrick said, reaching out his hand.

She gave it to him. He laid it down on the table and copied out the number on the corner of a magazine.

'What are you doing that for?'

'Better safe than sorry,' he said. 'What if you lose it and want to get in touch with him again? It's always good to have a back-up.'

The thought of *having* to get in touch with Jimmy Reece again made her stomach turn over. She could still feel the dirty crawl of his fingers on her skin. Rubbing her hand along her thigh, she made a futile attempt to wipe it away. 'Do you think I will?'

'Who knows,' he said, passing the card back to her.

She placed it carefully in the inside pocket of her bag. 'And you're not keeping his number for any other reason?'

'What do you mean?'

She hesitated, assailed by another wave of guilt. After her earlier transgression she was reluctant to reoffend, to compound her mistakes, but then again she knew how Patrick worked. Once he'd discovered a door, he could never resist walking through it. And if he got involved in this particular mess, it might do more than just muddy the waters – it could be positively dangerous. 'You know what I mean.' She forced herself to look directly into his eyes. 'If you've got any intention of . . . well, pursuing any ends of your own, then I'd rather you didn't. At least not for the moment.'

'As if,' he said, smiling broadly.

'Promise?'

'I swear,' he said, crossing his fingers religiously across his chest. 'On my honour.'

Did she believe him? Not entirely. But it was the best she was going to get unless she told him the whole damn story. And she was way too tired, not to mention unwilling, to go down that road. But perhaps she could ask his advice on another issue.

'Patrick, do you think I'm doing the right thing? I mean this whole Cavelli business. I don't know if I should tell him about what we found out. What if it all goes wrong? What if I'm putting Reece's life in danger?'

'I wouldn't worry about that,' he said. 'On tonight's evidence, I'd say the world would be a better place without him.'

'Thanks. That's very helpful.'

'Look,' he said, leaning forward to lift a pack of cigarettes off the table. He placed one in his mouth, lit it, and passed it over to her. 'It strikes me you're stuck between a rock and a hard place. There's no point getting stressed. You'll just drive yourself crazy. If Cavelli wants to find Reece, then he'll find a way of doing it – with or without your assistance.'

'But if I tell him, I'll still be partly responsible.'

'For what?' he said. 'He's not *that* hard to find. We did it in a night, a few hours. It's not as though he's on some witness protection programme. And anyway . . .' He stopped to light his own cigarette.

'Anyway?'

Patrick exhaled a long thin stream of smoke. 'I doubt if his address is what he's actually after.'

'What?'

'Oh, come on,' he said, as if she was being ludicrously slow on the uptake. 'Cavelli didn't send you to find out where he lives. He could have got that, or paid someone else to get it, from the electoral register. It's the *details* he's after. He wants to know what mental state he's in, if

265

he's suffering, if he's in pain, if he's paying the price for what he did.'

Her mouth slowly opened as she stared back at him. Yes, he was right. Why hadn't she realized that? 'So what am I going to tell him?' she murmured.

'Exactly what he wants to hear.' He took a drag on his cigarette and expelled a couple of perfect smoke rings. 'That he's a broken man, destroyed, on the scrap heap. That he's going nowhere and doing it fast. That he's filled with remorse over what happened to Nadine. Just lay it on thick and make it sound convincing.'

'And if he already knows otherwise?'

'He doesn't know anything,' he said, 'at least not for certain, or he wouldn't be asking you to find out.'

At the mention of her name, Eve found herself wondering if Nadine had left a letter, a few well-chosen words, or if like her father she had just . . . and then, out of the blue, she suddenly recalled the scrap of paper she had found in his desk. She caught her breath. What if she'd been wrong and it *did* mean something? Soho – isn't that what she'd thought when she read it? W1 was how the sequence started. Some numbers in the middle, a few letters at the end. What were they? She racked her brains but nothing fell out. And then, with an inner groan of dismay, she remembered something else – the note was in the pocket of her old faded jeans, the jeans she had already put through the machine, washed and dried and put away. Damn! How could she have been so stupid?

'Evie?'

She jerked up her head. 'Sorry. I was . . . Yeah, you're right. I'm sure you're right.' But she couldn't stop thinking about what she'd done. The image of her jeans whirling round in a drum of soapy water was already beginning to haunt her. Why in God's name hadn't she made a copy?

'Are you okay?'

She tried to chase it out of her mind. There was nothing she could do until tomorrow and even then . . . 'Yeah, I'm just a bit tired.'

Patrick narrowed his eyes and looked at her. 'It wasn't all bad, was it?'

She frowned back, not understanding.

'I mean us, you and me. We had some good times, didn't we?'

'Of course,' she said. She stubbed out her cigarette and finished off her brandy. 'And I'm sure if I made an effort, if I really tried hard enough, I could probably remember some of them.'

He shook his head, smiling. 'You always were fucking impossible. Do you—'

But before he could embark on some drunken trip down memory lane, she quickly got to her feet. 'Hey, thanks for the coffee and everything but I'm shattered. I'm going to turn in.'

'Are you going to kip down with Sonia?'

'That was the intention.'

'What if she snores?'

'What if she does?'

He grinned. 'Well, I wouldn't want you to lose any beauty sleep. And this is a very comfortable sofa. It might be a squeeze but there's definitely room for two.'

She hesitated, looking down at him. And she couldn't claim she wasn't tempted – for old times' sake, for the comfort, for a few glorious hours of forgetfulness. There was no one to betray, no one she'd be cheating on. So why was she suddenly thinking about Jack Raynor, about the way he had kissed her not so many hours ago? It wasn't as if she was ever going to fall for that love at first sight nonsense again.

'Thanks. It's a very generous offer but . . .'

Chapter Seventeen

Keeler Chase pulled up the lapels of his coat, cocked his head to one side, and listened. All he could hear was the patter of rain on the water and some thin drifting music. He was waiting for the sound of footsteps.

There was light from the windows of the pub behind him but it slid only as far as the upper slope of green lawn, fading well before it reached the bank. Here the darkness was profound. Even the river was invisible, its presence marked only by a rippling reflection when the clouds briefly parted to reveal the glory of a full silver moon. When this occurred he stepped softly back into the shadow of the willows.

It was already after ten but his face showed no signs of impatience. His victim was late but there was no hurry. He would arrive soon enough and the wait was part of the pleasure. It was during these quiet moments that he had time to savour the anticipation. He dragged the soles of his shoes experimentally along the ground; the grass beneath his feet was sodden. It was the kind of place, he considered, where people might slip, where accidents could easily happen.

Chase had been involved with accidents from as early as he could recall. His childhood toys had lost their arms and legs, his friends had crushed their tiny fingers, and the pet dog, a docile brown Labrador, had mysteriously drowned in the garden pond. And then, on his twelfth birthday – a day fraught with disappointment at not receiving the sleek ivory-handled fishing knife he had begged for – even his parents had succumbed. He shuddered to think of it, of the flames leaping, of his mother screaming, 'Keeler! Keeler!' How could he ever forget those cries? They would never cease to haunt him; it wasn't as if his heart was made of stone. If the smoke hadn't got to her, if her protests hadn't been silenced by that choking grey fog, he might finally have capitulated and unlocked the door.

Lucky. That was how his own escape from the raging blaze was described by the neighbours, the cops, the social workers, who in a collective swarm of sympathy had appeared out of nowhere and settled all around him. He hadn't been so sure. With over twenty dollars of birthday money burnt to a crisp, there hadn't seemed much cause for celebration. Still, if the experience hadn't entirely curbed his impetuosity it had at least taught him the importance of some basic forward planning.

Chase raised his eyes to the sky and sniffed the damp night air. No, he couldn't grumble. On the whole he *had* been lucky. Perhaps his greatest good fortune, other than to have found his way across the Atlantic and into the employ of an ambitious up-and-coming thief called Joe Silk, was to have the kind of face people never remembered. It had served him well through the years. Other vainer men might have been dissatisfied, even dismayed, by such a bland inheritance but for him it was a gift beyond gold. How often had he been picked out in an identity parade? He didn't need to think about it. His lips curled into a smile. Never! Even his body was nondescript, of average height and build. He had no distinguishing features. He was so ordinary, so mundanely grey, that he rarely received as much as a second glance. In broad daylight he could walk down a busy street and openly stab a man to death without anyone being able to accurately describe him thirty seconds later.

He was still pondering on this remarkable, surely God-given attribute, when he heard the clumsy stumbling of someone descending the slope, shortly followed by a thick spew of curses. His nose wrinkled in disgust. He could smell the stink from fifty yards away. As the clouds shifted to reveal an outline, he watched the big man stagger down, his belly so full of beer that if he'd even wanted to stop the weight of his gut would have continued to propel him forward.

Peter Marshall might have been less willing to agree to the meet if his judgement hadn't been impaired by eight pints of bitter and an almost empty wallet. As it was, the call had come at a propitious moment. Joe Silk might mean trouble but he also meant money. Had he been even slightly more sober he might have questioned the smartness of agreeing to meet in a place so dark he could barely see his feet but he wasn't; he was drunk, very drunk, and the opportunity of making a few quid was beyond irresistible.

He came face to face with Chase as he drew to an unsteady halt. Although logical thinking was a distant memory he wasn't entirely beyond caution. He looked around. 'Where's the boss?'

'He couldn't make it.'

'Yeah?'

Chase looked at him, his smile innocuous. 'He sends his apologies. A prior engagement. He asked me to come instead. He's got another job for you.'

Marshall thought about it for the entire two seconds that it took to get the question out. 'How much?'

'Don't worry about that. He'll make it worth your while.' Chase went to the edge of the bank. 'There's a boat moored along the way. To the left.' He gestured him forward. 'There. Can you see it?'

Marshall had no reason, other than the meagre brains he was born with, to ignore the invitation. He took a few steps, leaned out over the deep water, screwed up his eyes and peered through the darkness.

Chase found a sigh escaping from his lips. It was all so easy, too easy. And where was the thrill in that? Stupidity might be useful but it was also to be pitied. Not pitied enough, however, for him to have any second thoughts about what he was going to do next.

Marshall was a far bigger man but with his massive gut he was already ill balanced. All it took was one hard push to the base of his spine to send him hurtling into the river. The subsequent splash, in direct proportion to the amount of blubber that had just been deposited, sounded grotesquely loud in the stillness of the night.

Chase glanced towards the pub but there was no sign of anyone having heard. He turned his attention back to the drowning creature. Apart from one stifled cry as he had hit the icy water, no further utterance had come from him. The shock, or perhaps simply the energetic battle to prevent his body sinking, had rendered his vocal cords silent.

For this Chase was grateful. It offended his sensibilities when people made such a song and dance about it all. What was the point – the screaming, the pleading, the pathetic crying – when they knew that what was coming was inevitable? It was better, surely, to accept one's fate with dignity.

He watched intently as his victim thrashed around. For a fully clothed drunk Marshall wasn't doing so badly. And as he clawed frantically at the edges of the bank, his flabby white hands grasping for a hold that might yet save his life, Chase allowed him a tiny glimmer of hope before placing his foot firmly on his shoulder and pushing him back down.

For all his confidence in the blandness of his features

271

what Keeler Chase didn't realize was that his eyes, normally a pale washed-out shade of blue, became extraordinary when he was roused. Then they flashed with a colour and intensity that might almost be called passion. The reason he didn't know was that no one had ever told him and the reason they had never told him was that, by the time they had acknowledged that intense, almost climactic brilliance, they were usually more preoccupied with the essential business of staying alive.

Marshall came up twice more before the fight eventually went out of him. He sank beneath the surface leaving only a feeble trail of bubbles.

Chase stood and waited for a moment. Then, when he was sure the job was done, he turned on his heel and walked smartly up the slope.

Chapter Eighteen

DS Eddie Shepherd stamped his feet and blew warm breath into his hands. It was Monday morning, barely daylight, and the air was chill as winter. Still, he wasn't half as cold as the corpse that was lying on the ground behind him.

He turned to take another look, peering between the bustling white figures of the SOCO team. The victim was on his side, curled around a heap of stinking bin bags. At first glance it was possible to imagine that he was merely asleep or, at the very worst, collapsed in a state of drunkenness; it was only on a closer examination that you noticed the thick coagulation of blood at the base of his neck. He had a faint look of surprise on his face, as if in the second just before he died he had realized that . . .

Eddie reached for his fags but reluctantly returned them to his pocket as the silver Peugeot drew up at the kerb.

'What have we got?' Raynor asked, striding over to join him.

'Male, mid-forties.' He gestured over his shoulder. 'Been dead a few hours, four or five. Hit from behind with some kind of cosh – more than once. They're getting ready to move him now.'

Raynor took a long hard look at the body. And then,

as if the sight of a man with his skull caved in offended his aesthetic sensibilities, he sniffed and wrinkled his nose. 'A mugging?'

'Could be.' He shrugged. 'No house or car keys and his wallet's missing but we found his driving licence. Ivor Patterson. And this.' He handed over a business card. On it, Patterson's name was printed in large type and underneath, in smaller letters, *Clark & Able, Private Investigators*.

'Get it checked out.'

'I'm on to it, guv.' Eddie could have added that he'd already been there for twenty minutes, freezing his bollocks off, while the inspector was having a shit and a shave and making sure his hair looked pretty – but he wisely kept his mouth shut.

Louise had already opened the thick brown envelope by the time she realized it was for Richard. She raised her eyes to the ceiling. Beautiful as the new office help was – a visual masterpiece with immaculate curves – she still hadn't quite grasped the simple difference between the two Baxters. She'd been delivering the wrong post for over a week.

Louise was about to shove the contents – the results of yet another surveillance job – back inside the envelope when a name on the cover letter caught her eye: *Eve Weston*. Frowning, she stared at it. Why was her predecessor being investigated? Even as she asked herself the question, she had a sneaking suspicion that she knew the answer: Richard was taking matters into his own hands.

Out of curiosity she read quickly through the report. Well, he seemed to have wasted his money. If he'd been hoping for some dirt there wasn't anything here. Eve's life currently appeared to consist of supermarket

shopping, prison visiting, and the occasional meal out –
hardly the pastimes of an evil seductress. She grinned,
imagining his disappointment. At the back lay a sheaf of
photographs: several snaps of Eve entering and leaving
the building alone, one of her with a stunning brunette,
a woman who looked Mediterranean in appearance, one
of a small fair girl in a miniskirt and fishnets, a couple of
shots of a tall good-looking blond guy – she lingered
over these for a moment, appreciating the finer points
of his keenly chiselled features – and then finally . . .
Louise almost dropped the picture in surprise. *It was
Henry!* There was no mistaking him. There, clear as
daylight, was a picture of Henry and Eve, arm in arm,
coming out of the door to the flats. She was gazing up
at him and . . . Oh God! How could he have been so
stupid, so careless!

She laid it face down on the desk while she scanned
through the report again. There was no mention of
Henry's name, only of an unknown male who was on the
premises for a period of about four hours. So he hadn't
stayed overnight – that was something – but there was
plenty that two willing partners could get up to in four
long hours on a Saturday afternoon. And she wouldn't
like to be in Henry's shoes if his wife ever found out
about it.

She could destroy the picture but what if Richard
noticed it was missing? Clark & Able were bound to
have copies. No, if she was going to get rid of the
photographic evidence she had to obliterate the written
evidence too. Could she Tippex it out and take a copy? It
wasn't ideal, it would leave a small gap, but with luck
that might just pass for a typing error. She'd have to take
the chance. If Richard was expecting the report, he
might realize it was missing, and send the lovely Denise
tottering downstairs to retrieve it.

Folding the photograph in two, she slipped it into her bag. And then quickly went to work with the Tippex . . .

Paul Clark, still dripping from the shower, took the call at eight forty-five from his secretary. She sounded flustered. The police were waiting in the office, he had to come in straight away – *Ivor Patterson was dead.*

'What?'

'Killed,' she murmured dramatically down the line.

'W-what? Shit, when?' He stuttered out the questions. 'How?'

But all she could tell him was that he'd been found in the Prince of Wales Road earlier that morning. 'They had to close off the entire street.' Her voice was filled more with awe than sorrow as though the extraordinary manner of his death, and its traffic-stopping consequences, had bestowed an element of glamour and respect he had never warranted in life.

Paul took a deep breath. Despite the gruesome news, he had the presence of mind to think about the repercussions; the last thing he needed was his files being ransacked by the local constabulary. It would hardly do a lot for client confidentiality or the reputation of the business. 'Okay, God, look, that's terrible, awful. I'll be right there. Twenty minutes max. Make them coffee, Jane, and . . . and I'd rather you didn't say anything about . . . well, anything relating to our cases. You know what I mean. These things can be sensitive. It's better if I talk to them myself. I'll fill them in on anything they need to know when I get there.'

He put the phone down and took a moment to pull himself together. His hands were shaking. He couldn't claim he was filled with an overwhelming sense of grief; he had never especially liked the man – or trusted him – but sudden death was always shocking. It also had a nasty habit of reminding you of your own mortality. One minute you were there and the next . . .

Throwing his damp towel across a chair, he went through to the bedroom and quickly got dressed. He was on his way out, the door half closed, when he had another thought. He could be caught up with the police for a while. Perhaps he'd better warn Richard. Ivor's murder couldn't have anything to do with the recent surveillance – he'd rung in sick and been off the job for the past week – but it was still the last case he'd been working on. If his death remained suspicious, and the police didn't have any other leads, their next port of call could be Baxter & Baxter.

It took him several minutes to get through. The receptionist, her response on some perpetual and infuriating loop, kept repeating that he was in a meeting.

'It's important,' he insisted. 'I need to talk to him straight away.'

'I'm sorry, but he's—'

Frustrated, he glanced down at his watch. Time was ticking by and he didn't want to keep the cops waiting any longer than he had to. He raised his voice a few decibels. 'Then get him out of the meeting, *now*. Tell him it's Paul Clark. Tell him it's urgent. Tell him it's more than urgent. I need to talk to him. Believe me, love, he'll thank you for it.'

She didn't reply. There was only a click before he found himself listening to some bloody string quartet. He spent another thirty seconds on hold. He paced the floor, softly cursing. Was she actually trying to connect him or just sitting back and filing her nails? He was about to hang up – he couldn't wait around any longer – when the extension was finally picked up.

'What's the panic?' Richard asked.

Relieved, Paul quickly passed on the news about Ivor Patterson.

'What?'

'He's dead,' he repeated for the second time. 'They found him this morning. He was attacked but I haven't got any details. I don't know any more than that. I'm on my way in to the office now. The police are waiting. I just thought I should warn you, let you know, in case . . .'

'In case of what?'

'In case the London cops come round to talk to you.'

Richard's voice took on an icy tone. 'And why on earth should they do that?'

'Because yours was the last job that he—'

'I don't see why you have to mention that.'

Paul's hand tightened around the receiver. Fuck, he hadn't expected this. 'So what are you suggesting?' he asked nervously. 'That I shouldn't tell them? You want me to lie about it?'

'Of course not,' Richard said slickly. 'I'd never consider standing in the way of any police inquiry. All I'm asking is that you think very carefully about what you *need* to say. Do you really think this has anything to do with Baxter & Baxter?'

'Of course not.'

'So what exactly is the point in dragging us into it?'

Paul opened his mouth but swiftly closed it again. Just telling the truth was what he'd had in mind but there was no denying that Richard had provided enough work over the past five years (and enough fat cheques), to guarantee a few second thoughts. The London branch especially had made a healthy profit from the jobs put their way. He couldn't afford to fall out with him. 'Well . . .'

'I thought we could rely on you,' Richard said.

'You can.'

'So can we also rely on your discretion? We really don't need this kind of publicity.'

Paul could have said that he didn't need it either. Who

the hell did? No one wanted to have an employee bludgeoned to death. No one wanted the cops crawling all over them either. He sighed. 'Okay. I'll try. I'll do what I can.'

'I'd appreciate it.'

Richard Baxter slammed down the phone and scowled. All he'd wanted were a few pictures, a discreet report on what Eve Weston was currently up to. Provided with the evidence – and it was bound to be damning – he could have finished her once and for all. It was what she deserved.

He'd been looking forward to the moment when he could watch her eyes widen into fear and disbelief. She'd have been sorry then that she'd ever crossed him. And thankful enough, once he'd ventured to suggest a compromise, to show her appreciation in the time-honoured way. He'd had a deeply erotic image of what she would do to prevent him from spilling the truth – but none of that was going to happen now. In fact, if Paul Clark didn't hold his nerve, he could be up to his neck in one embarrassing pile of shit.

How was he going to explain to the cops why he'd had her followed? Because he hoped to gather enough dirt to be able to shag her? He'd look like some sort of twisted stalker. And if *that* ever got into the public domain he'd be finished.

It was typical that the idiot employed to watch her had managed to get himself killed. The fool didn't deserve to be alive.

And as for that bitch – well, what could he say? – with luck, she'd rot in hell.

Eddie Shepherd blew his nose into a scrap of tissue. Was he coming down with flu? He felt like crap. And it was probably all down to standing around on freezing street corners in the early hours of the morning. That was the thing about corpses; they had a nasty habit of turning up not just in the most inconvenient places but at the most inconvenient times too. Being dragged out of bed before the sun had barely risen was a sure-fire invitation for any lurking virus to stroll straight over and kick you in the teeth.

He looked around for a bin but, failing to find one, thrust the sodden piece of tissue back into his pocket. Yeah, he was definitely coming down with something. That was all he needed. The lying, scheming twathead sitting in front of him wasn't doing much to improve his frame of mind either. He'd been listening to Paul Clark for over half an hour and still wasn't convinced that he'd heard a word of truth.

'So he'd been off sick for over a week?' he asked again.

'Yes.'

'And then decided to go on holiday?'

'Yes.'

'And you don't find that odd?'

Clark lifted his shoulders and shrugged. 'Why should I? He sounded convincing enough when he rang Jane. Everyone gets sick, especially at this time of year. And everyone needs a break.' He gave a thin smile. 'Come to mention it, you don't look so hot yourself.'

'I didn't mean then,' Eddie growled. 'I mean *now*. Don't you find it odd, looking back, that he chose to take time off so soon before he was killed?'

Clark frowned. 'What do you mean?'

'What do you think I mean?'

Clark's eyes gradually lost their confidence and took on that same expression he'd had when he walked in – cautious, uneasy, suspicious. Then he said, defensively: 'I'm sure it's completely unrelated to his work here. It was a mugging, wasn't it? He was just unlucky, wrong time, wrong place. He certainly wasn't working on a case that might have led to . . . well, anything like that. The last one he was dealing with was – God, it was weeks back, an insurance job, nothing serious. I've got the file if you want to look at it.'

He walked over to the cabinet, pulled open the door and retrieved a buff folder.

Eddie flicked through the pages inside but there was nothing to suggest any motive for revenge. In fact, the very opposite. His surveillance had only proved that the subject was still incapable of work, still walking on crutches. 'And there's been no other work since then?'

'No, I've already told you. He signed off sick and that was it.'

'But there's a gap, a couple of weeks, between this job and then.'

Paul Clark sighed. 'That's the nature of the business, Sergeant. Sometimes there's too much work, sometimes there's none.'

'So after his last job, before he got sick, he wasn't doing anything?'

'Nothing for *us*.'

'Are you sure?'

Clark paused but only for a fraction of a second. 'Of course I'm sure.'

'Could he have been working for someone else?'

He shook his head. 'I doubt it. I don't know. How could I?'

'Or doing a spot of freelancing?' Eddie found another tissue and blew his nose loudly. 'Maybe he found out something and decided to go it alone. It must happen from time to time.'

Clark stared back at him grimly. 'It's not the kind of behaviour we encourage, Sergeant. And if there'd been any hint of it, we'd have fired him straight away.'

'Well, no need to worry about that now.' Bored by the exchange, Eddie lumbered to his feet. He stopped by the door and turned. 'Oh yeah, if anything comes to mind, you know where we are. Don't be shy. Feel free to call us any time.'

Eve rolled the pen around her fingers and stared down at the sheet of paper. She was trying to write to Cavelli, to compose an all-encompassing letter that would not only fulfil her obligations as regards their imaginary 'relationship' but also give him all the information he might want to hear about Jimmy Reece. That way, she hoped, she wouldn't need to visit him in the near future. Unfortunately, she had only got as far as *My dearest Martin*. She'd been stuck on those three ungodly words for the past twenty minutes.

With a sigh, she stood up and poured herself another coffee. With everything else that was going on, constructing a love letter to a man you didn't even like was a bridge too far. What was she supposed to say? *I am missing you so much. It hurts so much to be apart. I wish we could* . . . No, she couldn't go there, she couldn't even bear the thought of it. Perhaps she'd wait until later, try again this evening when a few glasses of wine might temporarily release her from her inhibitions.

But that was just delaying the agony. And the longer she left it the more difficult it would become. She sat down again, lit a cigarette, and stared down at the sheet of paper. It couldn't be *that* hard. In the past, she'd spent more than enough time persuading men of her heartfelt affection, bestowing words that had slipped easily from her lying careless lips, but this all felt so much more complicated. It might still be a con but it was one of an entirely different nature. Back then she'd only had herself to worry about but now she was playing another game, one where she had far greater responsibilities. The stakes had been raised. She had Terry to think about.

She picked up her pen again.

My dearest Martin, It was lovely to see you again.

She stopped, striking a line through *lovely* and replacing it with *good*. She added, *How are you?* And then, with a frown, crossed that out too. Maybe she should stick with *lovely*. But what to say next? The intricacies of the perfect love letter were a mystery to her. She screwed her pathetic attempt into a ball and threw it in the bin.

She put her head in her hands and groaned. She would make some notes first, work out what to say about Jimmy Reece – luckily Patrick had given her a few ideas – and then go back and add the sweet nothings later. Quickly, she began to scribble, using Jimmy's initials but inventing a completely new name.

I ran into my old mate Jason Reynolds the other day. You remember him, don't you? He moved to Chelsea after all that trouble he had. He got married again but I don't think it's working out. He's in a bad way, back on the booze and in a real mess. He hasn't had any work for years and is certainly not his old self, rather a tormented soul if you know what I mean.

She stopped again. Was that enough? She wondered how closely the screws actually read the letters. Not very, she suspected. There must be hundreds arriving every day, all filled with mundane snippets of news from home. If she slipped the paragraph in, about halfway through, there was no reason why it should draw any unwelcome attention. But that meant she'd have to pad the letter out. What else could she say? What did other women find to talk about?

Eve wrote the word *job* down, followed by a large question mark. Maybe she could invent a new career for herself, a fascinating post in the City or, alternatively, a position of utter drudgery. All things considered, the latter was a safer bet. That way, if anyone was skimming through, they'd be less inclined to linger. She could bore them into submission before they reached the important part.

And then there was family of course. A couple of kids could easily fill half a page, the intricate details of what young Liam was doing last Tuesday and how his little sister was coping with nursery. Yeah, that could be good, and tedious enough, to lull any disinterested party into instant paralysis. She smiled, her pen hovering over the page. Suddenly, it didn't feel like such a trial. She might have been forced into the position of having to write this ridiculous letter to Cavelli but *he* would have to endure the equally dreadful task of reading it – and it would serve him right for putting her in this position in the first place!

Eve glanced at her watch. It was almost three o'clock, not exactly a respectable time to open a bottle of wine, but now that she'd got the gist of what she was going to write she couldn't see the harm. Having started the letter, she wanted to get it finished as soon as she could – and to do that she needed a little extra help . . .

She was on her second glass, with a reasonable rough draft of the letter laid out before her, when she was forced to stop and think again. It wasn't looking too bad, a wonderfully boring rendition of her imaginary life, but she hadn't touched yet on the trickier problem of their so-called 'relationship'. Well, it may have been part of the deal but she wasn't going to give him the satisfaction of anything too sincere. In fact, if she was going to play along, then surely it was only right that she introduced a realistic element of angst?

It was wonderful to see you on the visit. I would like to believe what you said about your feelings for me but you have let me down so often, I have to ask myself why I should trust you now. Although I'm sure your feelings are genuine, perhaps we should wait a while before committing ourselves to anything more permanent.

She sat back and stared at the words. Not bad. She laughed but her smile didn't last. For some reason she was thinking about Patrick again, about Friday night, about how she'd almost . . . Was there still something there between them? No, there wasn't, there couldn't be. It had all ended years ago. But for some reason, she couldn't stop thinking about his eyes, the way he looked at her, the way his mouth curled up at its corners – and more than that, how he knew, how he *always* knew when she was in trouble.

There was a sharp knock at the door. For the first time since the break-in, too preoccupied by other thoughts, she didn't jump but rose slowly to her feet. It was only as she pulled back the bolts that she felt a small jolt of trepidation but the person standing on the other side was the very image of respectability, a smartly dressed man in his fifties.

'Eve Weston?' he asked.

She nodded.

'Vincent Player,' he said shortly. 'I've got some things for you.'

Vince. Lesley's husband. She stared at him. What was *he* doing here? It was only as he glanced down, that she lowered her eyes too. There was a black bin bag lying at his feet. Compared to his crisp white shirt and nicely tailored dark grey suit, it seemed a touch incongruous.

'Terry's things,' he said. His voice matched his expression, uptight, unhappy, and less than pleased to be there.

She was hardly overjoyed either. So Lesley had made her decision – and her answer was beyond doubt. She could have done it with a phone call but had obviously decided to drive the message home. And poor old Vince was the reluctant messenger.

They both looked up, and then down at the bag again. Well, if he expected her to carry it inside, he had another think coming.

She stood aside. 'You'd better bring it in.'

With a scowl he picked it up and dumped it in the living room. 'I hope this is the end of the matter,' he said, rather pompously. 'Perhaps we can view this as a clean break. I'd rather you – and Terry – left us alone in the future.'

'The end of it?' she said.

'I think it's for the best – for everyone.'

Eve frowned. 'For God's sake, she's his mother. How can it possibly be for the best?'

He flinched, his fingers sweeping over his jacket sleeves as if searching for invisible specks of dirt. 'I'd rather you left my family in peace.'

She wondered what Lesley had told him about her visit. A somewhat distorted version she imagined. 'So this is—'

'Please don't try and get in touch again.' He nudged the bag with the toe of his foot. 'And if you could make sure that Terry understands . . .'

Eve placed a hand angrily on her hip. 'What? That his mother doesn't want to know him any more? Oh, I think he'll get *that* message, loud and clear. And don't worry, I'm sure he'll be fine about it. I mean, it's perfectly under-standable that you wouldn't want him around, wouldn't want the old offspring littering up your decent respect-able lives.' She gave him a full-on indignant glare. 'You must feel very proud of yourselves.'

He faltered, looking almost ashamed. But her com-ments might have held more sway if he hadn't chosen that moment to glance over her shoulder and to see the open bottle and the glass of wine sitting on the table. She saw his eyes focus on it. And, as if provided with irrefutable proof of her lack of moral fibre – she was obviously a lush to be on the booze at this time of day – any shame that he might have been harbouring instantly evaporated.

'Well, I won't keep you,' he said. 'I'm sure you must be busy.'

She would have liked to have had the last word, to provide one final stunning retort, but it was too late – he'd already turned on his well-polished heels and was heading down the stairs. Thirty seconds later the front door clicked shut.

'Have a nice day,' she murmured.

Slamming her own door, she retreated into the flat. How could Lesley have done this? How could she have decided to turn her back so finally on Terry? She picked up the black bin bag and shook her head. So this was the sum total of his possessions. It wasn't much to show for twenty-one years on this earth. But then again, travelling light had always been a Weston speciality.

Taking it through to her father's bedroom, she sat down on the floor and tore the knot open. Carefully, she took out his clothes, his T-shirts, jeans and trainers, and laid them tidily on the bed. She collected his CDs and put them in a pile. There were no books but then he had never been a great reader. She found his mobile, a slim silver pricey model, and was instantly reminded of her father. Was there someone out there using his phone now – someone who had bought it cheap in a pub, indifferent to the fact it had probably been stolen? She shuddered at the thought of someone else's hands around it.

Eve had almost emptied the bag when she came across the passport. Frowning, she flicked through the pages. Yes, it was Terry's. She ran her thumb across his photograph as if she could smooth out the tiny frown between his eyes. She hadn't even known he'd possessed a passport or that he'd ever been abroad. It had been acquired two years ago but there were no stamps inside. Still, that wasn't proof of anything; there were plenty of places he could have travelled to. Although he'd have told her – wouldn't he – if he'd been away? Maybe he'd never used it. She'd have to remember to ask when she saw him next.

Eve transferred all his things to an empty drawer. Now she was living with the property of three other people: her father, Terry and Martin Cavelli.

It was mid-afternoon when they dragged the second body from the river. Eddie Shepherd glared down at the sodden mess and groaned. Jesus Christ, two bodies in a day. But at least this one didn't look suspicious. Well, no more suspicious than Peter Marshall usually looked.

Eddie had recognized the bloated features almost immediately. It didn't take a genius to work out what had happened. A few hundred yards from the bank was the timbered frame of The King's Head, not one of Marshall's usual drinking haunts, but a pub all the same – and any place that sold alcohol was a draw for an old soak like him. He must have had a skinful, maybe stepped outside to clear his head and then wandered too close to the water's edge. The ground was soft, slippery, and for a man whose sense of balance would have been less than perfect . . .

The body might have floated downriver if it hadn't got caught in some mooring ropes. A nice surprise for the owner of the *Mary Anne* when he'd come out on deck half an hour ago and peered over the rail of his sparkling white motor launch. Still, that was Peter Marshall for you; no bloody consideration for anyone else.

Eddie turned his head and spat into the rippling grey water. It would have been cold in there, dark and deep; the chances of scrambling out, especially when you were three sheets to the wind, were pretty slim. And even if he'd shouted, no one would have heard. The pub was too far away and the owner of the boat hadn't returned until after midnight. On a warmer evening there might have been the chance of a passer-by but last night the rain had been falling steadily.

He lit a cigarette while he waited, yet again, for Raynor to arrive. His eyes felt tired, scratchy, and his head had a fog in it. And, even worse, he knew it wasn't over yet. He still had the onerous duty of breaking the news to Sonia Marshall. It shouldn't exactly break her heart – if what she'd told him the last time they'd met was true – but you could never tell how people, and particularly women, would react. Unpredictable, that's what they were. Of course, he didn't have to do it, he could always shift the responsibility on to someone else, but he knew that he wouldn't. However, he *would* take a female officer with him just in case it turned uncomfortably emotional.

Eddie glanced behind him, just in time to see Jack Raynor strolling down from the pub. He quickly threw his cigarette into the river. The last thing he needed was another lecture on the importance of 'appearances' or the state of his lungs.

He nodded. 'Guv.'

Raynor emitted one of his familiar world-weary sighs. 'Another one?'

They walked together towards the covered corpse laid out on the ground.

'Yeah, but an accident by the looks of it. Probably had one too many and fell into the water late last night, after closing time maybe. No suspicious injuries. No one saw or heard anything.'

He was still talking, about to tell him who it was, when Raynor knelt down and slowly pulled the cover back. He reeled back suddenly, his face growing pale.

'Jesus!'

Eddie tried not to grin. The body had only been in the water for about fifteen hours, barely time for the fishes to start nibbling. Compared to some he'd seen, it was positively pristine, but the inspector clearly didn't feel the same way. He stood up, took a few deep breaths, and lurched unsteadily towards the water's edge. He had the unmistakable appearance of a man who was about to throw up.

Well, everyone had their weaknesses and had it been anyone else, Eddie would have left them alone, given them some space, a chance to catch their breath, but this was an opportunity too good to miss. He had never seen anything affect Jack Raynor before. He was always so cool, so smoothly professional. Following him, he asked disingenuously, 'Are you all right, guv?'

'Fine,' he croaked, with a dismissive wave of his hand. 'I'm fine.'

'Are you sure?' That he was about as far from fine as it was possible to be was obvious from the violent tremor in his voice. Eddie stared up at his face. It was white as chalk. A fine film of sweat had invaded his forehead and his mouth was hanging open.

Eddie took a step back. It had been his intention to exploit the situation – Jack Raynor was hardly his favourite person – but now he was having second thoughts. Death was a part of the job and they all had to deal with it. But they all had their personal horrors too. It was enough, perhaps, to know his weakness without rubbing his nose in it.

'I'll tell them they can move the body.'

It occurred to him, as he walked away, that it hadn't been so long since Alex Weston had been pulled from the same stretch of water. He and Peter Marshall were two men who must have known each other, who had once lived not just in the same building but right across the hall from each other. And Eddie had suspected Marshall of breaking into Weston's flat. Now they were both dead, both drowned, and in almost the same place. But there had been nothing suspicious about Alex Weston's death either. On the contrary, it couldn't have been more straightforward; he had walked into the river with his bones full of cancer and his pockets full of stones.

Just a coincidence?

It had to be.

Except Eddie didn't like coincidence, never had and never would.

Chapter Nineteen

Eve was driving back from the south side of the city. It was almost seven but the roads were still busy. A car had just cut her up but she'd refrained from giving her usual response. Instead, she rapped her fingers against the wheel and cursed softly under her breath. She'd had a couple of glasses of wine and although she hoped she was still under the limit, she couldn't be entirely sure.

Best not to draw attention to herself.

The second knock on her door had come an hour after Vince had left. She'd opened it to find Sonia standing there.

'He's dead,' she said.

Eve had stared back at her, bewildered. Sonia's face was bleached white, her eyes wide, and for one crazy moment Eve had thought she was talking about her father, that she was suffering from some weird kind of delayed reaction. It was only as she shifted her gaze to acknowledge the two people standing behind her – a man and a woman, clearly a pair of cops although only the woman was in uniform – that she'd realized who Sonia was actually referring to.

'God, Peter?' she murmured.

'He's dead,' Sonia said again. 'He—'

The tall brown-haired woman moved forward. 'I'm sorry. I'm afraid there was an accident.'

Eve gently pulled Sonia inside. She raised a hand to stop the other two from following. 'It's okay. Thanks. I'll take it from here. I'll take care of her.'

Had she taken care of her? She had tried. She had put her arms around her, had given her the last of the brandy, but there were no suitable words to say, nothing to do that could change what had happened. And for all the hate Sonia had felt towards him – and Christ, that man had made her life a misery – there was no getting away from the fact that he would always be the father of her child.

Eve had just dropped Sonia off at her daughter Val's house. She was feeling strange herself, a bit disoriented. Perhaps it was the *way* Peter Marshall had died that she was finding so hard to come to terms with. The river, that bloody river. First it had claimed her father's life and now . . .

She started thinking about the note she had rescued from her jeans pocket. Miraculously, or perhaps simply because she had folded it into such a tiny square, the code had survived. It was pale, washed out, but still legible. This time she had tried to memorize the sequence – W1/267/32/BC/8PR – before refolding it and placing it safely in the toe of her winter boots.

But what did it mean?

Taking a left turn, she twisted round the quieter back streets. If W1 was Soho, then what could the rest refer to? Or maybe it wasn't Soho at all. She shook her head. There was every chance she'd never find out the answer. If it was some kind of cryptic clue, she hadn't got the brainpower to solve it.

And there was another question she was asking herself too. Why, oh why, had she agreed to meet Jack Raynor tonight? He'd called shortly after Vince had left and for some bizarre reason, although her head was busy saying no, her mouth had mutinied and uttered the word 'Yes' instead. Now she was regretting it.

She had tried to get in touch with him, to make her excuses, but his phone was turned off. She could have left a message but, as much as she didn't want to see him, she *did* want to talk to someone. And she was worried that if she went home, if she finished that bottle of wine, she might be tempted to ring Patrick. And that was a road she really shouldn't be walking down again.

She pulled into the small car park by the side of The Drifting Swan. They weren't due to meet until seven thirty. She glanced down at her watch. Another fifteen minutes to wait.

Eve had not intended to stay for long but it seemed Jack Raynor was in even more need of company than herself. If her day had been less than appealing, his had been positively dire. As he sat across the table from her, he looked tired and crumpled, not quite his usual sartorial self.

'I don't know how you do your job,' she said.

His mouth staggered towards a smile. 'What, nicking criminals? Oh, it's not so bad. There are worse ways to make a living.'

She lifted her eyebrows, wondering – and not for the first time – just how much he suspected about her own past. Did he trust her? Did she trust *him*? 'You know what I mean. Having to deal with . . .' She shrugged, picked up the bottle of wine, and emptied the last of it into his glass.

'Bodies?' he said, finishing her sentence. 'I'd like to claim you get used to it but you don't. You just find a way of coping.'

It struck Eve that his coping mechanism had developed something of a glitch. He looked like a man who had been to hell and back. But then two corpses in one day was probably enough to challenge anyone's self-possession.

'Did you know him?' she asked. 'Peter Marshall?'

As if the question was a complicated one, he hesitated for a moment. 'Not really.' Then he took another sip of his drink and added, 'Only vaguely. We've picked him up a few times in the past, just for petty stuff, nothing serious.' He paused again. 'And you?'

'No, we never met. He moved out a while back. Sonia's upset but I think it's more shock than anything else. From all accounts, he wasn't the nicest bloke in the world.' She pulled a face. 'Not that she'd have wanted—'

'It's okay,' he said. 'I know what you mean.'

She glanced at her watch. It was twenty to nine. There was no chance now of driving home; she'd have to leave the car and pick it up in the morning.

Jack noticed her looking. 'Sorry, do you want to get home? I get the feeling I might have been boring you for long enough. I'm not exactly great date material tonight.'

'Are you ever?' she said, grinning.

He laughed. 'Thanks.'

'It's a pleasure.' And she might have been joking but she wasn't lying. It *was* a pleasure to see that amazing smile again. For all her reservations, she was finding it increasingly hard to come to terms with her instinctive attraction to him. 'Anyway, I've not had the greatest day either and I haven't even begun to bore you with *my* trials and tribulations. I was just thinking that maybe we should order a few plates of food, try and soak up some of this wine.'

'Are you sure?'

'Unless *you're* looking for an excuse to escape?'

He widened his pretty blue eyes in mock astonishment. 'What, and miss out on the story of all your woes?'

'It would be a pity,' she agreed.

Neither of them had eaten much but at least there was something in their stomachs. And Jack, perhaps glad of the opportunity to stop thinking about his own problems, seemed to have rallied a little. She told him about Vince's visit in the afternoon, about how Lesley was determined to cut Terry out of her life.

'I know he's been in trouble, that he's hardly the perfect son, but—'

'Maybe there's more to it,' he suggested.

'What do you mean?'

'Just that there may be more to her decision than the fact he's serving a prison sentence.'

She stared at him, frowning. 'What are you saying?' Suddenly, she was recalling those comments Lesley had made when she'd gone to see her. *You don't understand. You have no idea . . .* 'Do you know something I don't?'

The tone of her voice must have startled him because he drew back and raised his hands defensively. 'Hey, no, not at all. I promise. I wasn't suggesting . . . Sure, he's been in trouble with the police before but never for anything too serious. All I meant was that every family has its own difficulties, that maybe it's a crisis that's been building up over time. From what you've told me, they were never that close.'

Eve expelled her breath in a low frustrated sigh. What was the matter with her, jumping down his throat like that? Too much wine, probably. 'Sorry,' she murmured. 'I didn't mean to snap. And you're right, the two of them have never had the best of relationships. I guess Terry going to jail was just the final straw.'

'I wouldn't worry too much. He'll be out in a few months. Perhaps they can start to build some bridges then.'

'It's a nice idea but I wouldn't count on it.'

'Was he close to your father?' he asked.

And she wished, really wished, that she could say yes, that the tragedy of his cancer might excuse, or at least begin to explain, how Terry had managed to get involved with a pair of vicious thugs like the Rowan brothers. But she didn't have the heart to lie about it. 'Not very.' She picked up her glass and took a sip of wine. 'Well, they had their ups and downs. The thing about my father . . .' She paused, her eyes slowly focusing on the glass ashtray sitting on the side of the table. The nicotine devil was whispering in her ear. 'Look, would you mind if I had a smoke? I know it's a vile habit and I'm really trying to knock it on the head but . . .'

'It's okay,' he said. 'It's fine. Go ahead.'

She quickly got the new pack out of her bag, ripped off the cellophane and placed a cigarette gratefully between her lips. As she took out her lighter, he reached across and took it from her fingers.

'Allow me.'

Their hands met briefly, a fleeting touch, as the flame ignited. 'Thanks.' She took a deep breath, a grateful inhalation, turned her head and blew the smoke out as far away from him as possible.

Instead of moving back, he lingered for a few seconds. She was overly aware of his proximity, of his face still only inches from hers. She felt his eyes searching but preferred not to meet them. Instead, she glanced around the bar, looking at the tables, at the couples surrounding them. And she found herself launched into the past again, if only to a short time ago, to that moment she was last in the prison visiting room with Cavelli. She had looked over at Amber and Dan and seen them leaning close together, talking, touching, kissing. She had seen their intimacy and envied it. She knew what it meant to be in love, to be oblivious to everything else, and . . .

'You were saying,' he prompted, 'about your father . . .'

She looked back at him. 'Yes. Sorry.' Dragging herself into the present, she shook her head and smiled. 'The thing about my father is that he was always good at the grand gestures, the big surprises, but not so great at the mundane day-to-day stuff. He wasn't the kind of dad who'd ever be standing at the school gates or offering to help with your homework. He struggled with the basics.'

'But *you* were close to him.'

'Yes, but that was different. I was more like him, we understood each other, but he and Terry . . .'

'They didn't get on?'

She took another drag on her cigarette. 'No. Sometimes. I don't know. It was more complicated for them, because of Lesley, because of all that other angry adult stuff. When I was growing up it was just the two of us, until I was thirteen, just me and him – but it was different for Terry. He was always in the middle of a war zone.' She picked up her glass. 'Not that there's ever a *good* divorce but theirs was definitely less than friendly.'

A waitress stopped by their table and gathered up the empty plates. 'Would you like anything else?'

Eve shook her head. 'No thanks.'

'Coffee?' Jack suggested. 'They do a great cappuccino here.'

'No,' she repeated. 'I'm fine.'

'Just the bill then,' he said.

*   *   *

298

By the time the taxi pulled up outside the flats, Eve still hadn't decided what she was going to do. Say goodbye? Invite him in? It wasn't late, barely ten, but they were both a little drunker than they should have been.

She turned to him. 'You're welcome to come in, have a coffee, so long as you don't think . . .'

'What? That it's an invitation to anything else?'

'It's been known.'

'A no-strings coffee would be great,' he said.

She had another moment of doubt as he paid off the cabbie. It wasn't so much to do with his integrity as hers. Jack Raynor was a very attractive man. He was a smart one too. A fatal combination.

As they climbed the stairs, she was aware of him following close behind, aware too of the echoing clatter of their shoes on the old stone steps. The dim forty-watt bulbs were on a timer that clicked off every fifteen seconds. She pressed her hand against the switch as they reached the first floor.

They were on the landing of the top floor when the light turned off again. She reached out, searching for the button. His hand stretched out too. As their fingers touched, they both started to laugh.

But as she turned, the laughter caught in her throat and a half-scream hurled its way from the pit of her stomach and out through her mouth. The breath rushed from her lungs and her heart began to race. She staggered forward a step, reeling. Jack grabbed her elbow.

'What the . . .?'

Emblazoned across the door in bright white paint were the words, *Last chance, Evie*. And, running the entire length, was a childlike illustration of the hangman's noose.

'Jesus!' he hissed. His grip tightened protectively around her arm.

Eve stared wide-eyed at the threat before the landing

was plunged into darkness again. As she scrabbled for her keys, she could feel her knees starting to buckle.

'Oh, for fuck's sake!' Jack was forced to let go of her. He reached quickly back and slammed his palm against the switch. 'Don't touch anything,' he insisted.

But it was too late. She'd already unlocked the door, stumbled inside and turned on the light. Before her legs betrayed her, she hurried across the room and sank down on the sofa.

'You shouldn't have—'

She lowered her head into her shaking hands and waved his objection away. *Damn it!* She'd thought it was over but it had just got worse.

He got out his phone and started dialling.

Eve looked up. 'What are you doing?'

'Calling it in,' he said.

'No!'

'What?'

'I said no. I don't want you to.' She saw his eyes narrow into confusion. Christ, this was all turning into a nightmare. She tried to shake her brain into some semblance of coherency. 'Please. I mean, what's the point? It'll just be a waste of everyone's time. They won't find anything, will they – they're hardly likely to have left any prints.'

'You don't know what they may have left.'

'No offence, but it'll be a waste of time. I'm sure it will. And I just don't need the aggravation, all the fuss and the questions and . . .' What she did need was a stiff drink but she'd given the last of the brandy to Sonia.

Jack looked bemused. 'But you can't let them get away with it.'

'They already have. Come on, be realistic. Are you telling me that you're likely to catch them?'

'Don't you even want to try?'

'I've said no, haven't I? Can't you just leave it?'

300

He sat down beside her. 'Eve, what's going on?'

She shook her head. Then she jumped to her feet again. There was still some wine in the fridge. That would have to do. She went through to the kitchen and brought the bottle back along with a couple of glasses. She placed them on the coffee table and then went and shut the door; if she couldn't see the words, perhaps she could pretend that they weren't actually there. 'Nothing,' she said again. 'It's probably just some prank. Kids. You know what they're like. That intercom's been broken for months. Anyone can just wander in off the street.'

'Yeah, right. Anyone who knows your name is Evie.'

Ignoring the comment, she carelessly splashed out the wine, pushed a glass towards him and took a large gulp from her own. 'Do you think it will come off?' she asked. 'Maybe with soapy water or white spirit or . . . I could paint over it, couldn't I? If I buy some white gloss in the morning, I might be able to—'

'Look,' he said, 'if you won't let me call it in, at least *talk* to me. Tell me what's been going on. And please don't say nothing again.' He reached out and took her hand. 'Trust me. I might be able to help.'

Now the shock was subsiding, it was being replaced by a faint sense of nausea. She struggled to clear her head, to come up with any sort of feasible explanation – at least anything she could tell Jack Raynor – as to why she might be the target of such an attack. God, they must have done it when she'd left to take Sonia to Val's – which meant they must have been watching the flats, hanging around outside, waiting for her to leave.

She hesitated. There was no point in claiming absolute ignorance – that was more likely to provoke suspicion than to detract from it – but she had to be careful about what she chose to divulge. 'Well, there have been a few phone calls recently but nothing too awful, just the usual heavy breathing kind of stuff. I didn't take much notice of them.'

'And there's no one you can think of – any enemies, people you've crossed, old boyfriends . . .'

'I'm not *that* bad a girlfriend,' she said, forcing a smile.

But he continued to frown at her. 'This is serious, Eve. Think about it. If not in the past then maybe someone you've met more recently.'

She immediately thought of Martin Cavelli – and as quickly put him out of her mind. No, she wasn't going there. She couldn't afford to jeopardize Terry's future. A few months, that's all he needed, and then he'd be free. If the cops started sniffing round, asking awkward questions, one thing would lead to another and – if what Cavelli had told her was true – they might discover he'd been doing more than handling stolen property. And if that was the case he wouldn't get further than the prison gates before they arrested him again.

'No,' she said firmly.

'Are you sure?'

She pretended to think about it. 'No, honestly, I can't think of anything.' She paused again, trying to decide how much more she should tell him. 'Well, I suppose there was the break-in but I don't see how that could be connected.'

'And nothing else?'

Suddenly, she felt an almost desperate urge to confide, to share her fears, to let it all come spilling out – but she held her tongue. It was only a knee-jerk reaction to that vile warning on the door. If she came clean and told him about the attack in the alley, about being followed, there'd be no going back. The cops would get involved and then . . .

He shook his head. 'I don't like this,' he said. 'I don't get it. I don't understand. No one has to put up with this kind of stuff. Why won't you let me call it in? We can help you. *I* can help you.'

'By doing what – dusting for prints, testing for DNA, putting a twenty-four-hour guard on my door?' She tried to sound blasé but her voice had a thin nervy edge. 'Whoever did it is long gone.'

'Do you really hate the police that much?'

Eve turned her face towards him, startled. 'I don't *hate* them,' she insisted. 'Of course I don't. I'm here with you, aren't I? It's just . . .'

'Just?'

She leaned back, releasing a prolonged and weary sigh into the room. 'God, you know who my father was. *What* he was. Let's not play pretend. I was hardly raised in the spirit of friendly cooperation with the boys in blue. And this, this . . . graffiti business, isn't anything that serious. I'm sure it's not. It's only a bit of nastiness. There's no point in wasting everyone's time. Perhaps you were right, what you said before. Perhaps it *is* someone with an old grudge but whoever it is, they'll soon grow tired of it.'

'And if they don't?'

She shuddered. That was a scenario she didn't want to think about. 'Well, if anything else happens, then I promise I'll report it. How about that? Does that sound like a reasonable compromise?'

'No,' he replied, his hand still grasping hers and squeezing it more tightly. 'But I get the distinct impression it's the best you're going to offer.'

Chapter Twenty

Half a bottle of whisky and a handful of aspirins hadn't done anything to help Eddie Shepherd sleep. He'd dozed briefly through the night but woken over and over with the same question rolling through his head. *What the fuck was going on?*

A series of ideas niggled at the back of his mind but he couldn't quite pin them down. Which was why, at the ungodly hour of seven thirty, he was already at the lab trying to squeeze some information out of the pathologist.

'Come on, Ken, give us a break. You must have something by now.'

'He drowned,' he replied shortly.

'I kind of got that idea when we dragged him out of the water.'

Kenneth Pugh gave him a despairing look. 'Just because you pull a man from the river doesn't necessarily mean he died there.'

'But this was one that did?'

'Yes, he was definitely alive when he went in.'

Eddie tried not to breathe too deeply. Even through his blocked nose, and despite the powerful disinfectant, he could still smell the stink of death. He hated this place and avoided it whenever he could.

'So it *was* an accident,' he mumbled.

'You sound disappointed.'

'Nothing unusual then – nothing at all?'

This time Pugh hesitated. 'Well . . . it might not be important but there *was* some bruising to the left shoulder. Hard to tell though exactly how it was inflicted.'

Eddie felt a flutter in the pit of his stomach. It could have been hunger – he hadn't eaten yet this morning – but he suspected it was one of those tiny breakthroughs that came along when you least expected it. 'Go on.'

'Now I wouldn't swear on oath but it could be consistent with a weight being placed against it.'

Eddie stared at him. 'A weight?'

'Like a foot.'

'You mean . . .?'

'Yes. Someone could have prevented him from getting out of the water.' Then, observing the light that must have come into Eddie's eyes, Pugh quickly added, 'But it could also have happened before he fell in or, if he was still alive, when he was pushed up against the side of the boat.'

'Is that likely?'

'It's not impossible.' He paused. 'Would you like to see?'

Eddie wouldn't like to see, not one little bit. 'I'd rather you just explained it to me.'

Pugh smiled at him thinly. His expression seemed to combine a mixture of pity and contempt. 'Here,' he said, laying his hand on Eddie's shoulder, in the shallow dip between the top of his arm and his neck. 'And here.' He moved his fingers a fraction to cover the curve of the shoulder itself.

'And nowhere else?'

'No,' he said, standing back.

'I don't get it. I mean, if he was thrashing about, hitting the boat, wouldn't you expect there to be other bruises?'

'Perhaps,' he agreed. 'But he could have got these before he even went in the river.'

'But they *were* fresh?'

'Oh yes, no doubt about that. They definitely occurred around the time of death.'

Eddie touched the outer edge of his own shoulder. 'Okay, I understand how this part could get damaged by the boat – it's exposed, right? But this part . . .' He moved his hand towards his neck. 'It's more awkward, harder to reach.'

'Exactly.'

He thought about it. 'So someone could have . . .' He had a mental image of Marshall reaching out towards the bank, drunk and scrabbling for a foothold, only to be pushed back, again and again, into the icy black water. It was a nasty thought and not one to linger over.

'All I'm saying is that it's a possibility. It's a theory, nothing more. There's no conclusive evidence.'

But Kenneth Pugh knew his stuff and Eddie was certain he wouldn't have even raised the subject if he didn't see the death as leaning towards the suspicious.

'Okay,' he said. 'Thanks.' He was at the door, about to leave, when another idea occurred to him. 'I don't suppose you remember Alex Weston, do you?'

Pugh looked back at him blankly.

'Another death by drowning. A month or so ago. Walked into the river with his pockets full of—'

'Ah,' he said, nodding. 'The suicide.'

'Nothing struck you as odd about that?'

He shook his head. 'No. Why should it? It was perfectly straightforward.' Then his mouth slowly crept into a smile again. 'Well, apart from the obvious literary allusions.'

Eddie tried not to sigh. He didn't have a clue what he was going on about. Why couldn't these people speak in fucking English? 'I'm sorry?'

'Virginia Woolf,' he said, patiently. 'She was—'

'Yeah, a writer. I've heard of her. I'm not completely stupid.'

As if this was news to him, Pugh's bushy eyebrows rocketed upwards. 'Indeed she was, Sergeant! Well done! And a very good writer too. I didn't realize you were quite such an expert. But as you are, you'll also be aware that she walked into a river with her pockets full of stones. In her case, she was suffering from severe depression. However, Mr Weston, if I remember rightly, was suffering from cancer.'

'Fascinating,' Eddie said.

'Quite,' Pugh agreed. 'But to answer your question – or rather the implication behind it – no, there was nothing suspicious about his death.' And then, as if to prove his remarkable powers of memory, he scratched his forehead, closed his eyes and slowly opened them again. 'Yes, there was a fair amount of alcohol in his bloodstream and a lot of painkillers. With the stones and all, he wasn't taking any chances. If there was one thing that could be said for Mr Weston, it was that he *intended* to die.'

'Right.' Eddie glanced down at his watch. He had things to do. Best to make his escape before Pugh went off on another of his tangents. He had once endured a twenty-minute discourse on the merits of Tolstoy and had no desire to repeat the experience. 'Well, thanks. I won't keep you.'

Paul Clark went into the computer and deleted all the entries relating to the surveillance of Eve Weston. He could feel his palms sweating. This was madness. Even as the files disappeared into the ether, he knew that they weren't gone forever; any computer geek could eventually dig them out from their resting place.

But there was no going back now. He'd just have to pray that this side of the police investigation came to nothing, that Ivor Patterson had been the victim of an arbitrary attack. And if he hadn't? God, he didn't want to think about that. The fat cop had asked a lot of awkward questions, given him the third degree. Well, he'd held his own, just about, but he didn't fancy going another round with the bastard.

He went to the filing cabinet and removed the hard copy. Flicking through the pages, he wondered if there was more to the Eve Weston case than Baxter had told him. A divorce job, that's what he'd said. So why all the fuss? Why the need for the cover-up? Unless Baxter's client was so high-profile, he couldn't afford even a whiff of scandal. What if Ivor *had* stumbled on something and . . .

No, he mustn't panic. A cool head was what was needed now. He had to stay calm. He carefully went through the report again. There wasn't much in it. Ms Weston either led a very quiet life or was deliberately keeping a low profile. She did, however, have a brother in jail, a brother she visited regularly. Was that anything to be concerned about?

But surely if Ivor had stumbled on something dodgy, Charlie May would have picked up on it too. Not necessarily. Charlie wasn't the sharpest knife in the drawer. Especially when he was working nights. Which reminded him – he'd better shift him out of town in case fat boy came sniffing round again.

It was only as he started trawling through the photographs that he felt his heart skip a beat. There was a series of shots of her emerging from a pub by the river. He recognized the man she was with. Raynor. Inspector Raynor. A small but violent jolt of fear, as fierce as an electric shock, jumped across his hands. The papers fluttered in his fingers. If Raynor had a personal involvement then . . .

'Shit,' he murmured under his breath. That might explain why Shepherd had given him such a hard time.

He leaned back against his desk. As he tried to get his head together, one good point found its way into his reasoning: surely, if the cops knew that she was the subject of Patterson's last case, that she was being officially watched by Clark & Able, they'd be crawling all over the office by now. And they weren't. So they *didn't* know. They couldn't. They were just whistling in the wind. Where was the evidence? There wasn't any. They'd simply found a business card in his pocket and were going through the motions.

Paul took a few deep breaths and tried to relax. He had to stop stressing. The chances of Ivor's death being connected to the business were slight. His wallet and his keys had been stolen. His car had been found burning on Mousehold Heath and hopefully, fingers crossed, his laptop had gone up in the blaze. It was a violent assault. He'd been attacked and robbed. It was vile, gross, but it had nothing to do with the company. There was still a chance the cops might find some written notes in his flat but so what? They couldn't prove that Patterson had been working for Clark & Able within the last couple of weeks. And nothing to prove that Clark & Able had ever heard of Eve Weston.

He stared around the empty office and nodded. What he'd done, and what he was about to do, didn't really matter. He didn't need to justify his actions; he was only trying to keep things simple. There was no point in confusing the situation.

And as for Richard Baxter's part in this whole lousy mess . . . Well, he was only doing what he always did – behaving like an arsehole while he covered his back.

Turning on the shredder, Paul waited for the green

light to come on. He only paused for a second before he slowly fed the papers into its jaws.

Eve opened the tin of paint and gave it a vigorous stir. As soon as Jack had left, she'd got up and dressed and then walked straight over to the hardware shop. They had tried to scrub the words off last night but without much success. The threat was still clearly legible and she worked quickly, slapping on the white gloss with strong firm strokes.

Perhaps he was right; she should have reported it.

But all she could do was follow her instincts – and her instincts had told her that it would only make matters worse. So what had she done? Rather than calling for a cop, she'd slept with one instead. A groan escaped from her lips. Of all the mad, stupid things . . .

She could only put it down to the shock. She hadn't been in her right mind. Shock could do terrible things to the psyche, make you forget all your good intentions, make you believe (if only for a night) that it was perfectly reasonable to share your bed with a smart, sympathetic, attractive man who you'd previously decided was completely out of bounds.

Trouble was, she couldn't even pretend that he'd taken advantage. On the contrary he'd behaved like a perfect gentleman – until she'd encouraged him to do otherwise. And if only for a while, he had chased away her demons and made her feel safe. No, more than safe. She had to be honest. It had been a passionate encounter, and a surprisingly intimate one, as if it wasn't the first time they'd slept together, as if their bodies were mysteriously in tune, as if they already understood the deepest pleasure they could bring to each other.

But that didn't mean anything.

And it certainly wasn't love.

She winced as the word came unbidden into her head. Where had that come from? She didn't *do* love any more, hadn't been near the place since Patrick. And she sure as hell wasn't going to fall for a man like Jack Raynor.

'I'll call you,' he'd said, sitting on the edge of the bed.

She had pretended to be half asleep. 'Mm.'

He'd paused, as if about to say something else, but in the end had only reached out a hand, gently moved a strand of hair from her face, and leaned over to kiss her.

She had waited until the front door clicked shut before fully opening her eyes. Relief was what she'd felt at first. At last! He'd gone. At least she wouldn't have to endure that awkward morning-after-the-night-before conversation. But as soon as the relief hit her, it had been replaced by a more disturbing emotion – a peculiar sense of emptiness. Under the sheets she had stretched out her own hand to feel the cooling space beside her.

Eve frowned. She dipped the brush in the paint again, loading up the bristles. She didn't want to think about him any more. She didn't want to think about his eyes or his smell or the way that he had touched her. It had been a mistake and it wouldn't, *couldn't*, happen again. The Law and the Westons didn't mix.

Attacking the door with renewed vigour, she only took a few minutes to obliterate the threat. *Last chance, Evie.* She quickly moved on, trying not to shiver as she painted out the sinister noose.

Eve heard him before she saw him – a series of slow heavy steps accompanied by a thick unpleasant wheezing. She leaned over the banisters but it was only as he reached the landing that she recognized his face. He was the officer from yesterday, one of the two that had come to break the news.

311

Great. She just couldn't get away from cops this morning.

'Are you looking for Sonia?' she asked.

He took a few seconds to catch his breath, his hand clamped tightly round the rail. He managed a nod but seemed to be having trouble in managing to speak.

To spare him the effort, she said, 'She's not here.'

He leaned over, coughing something green and nasty into a ragged piece of tissue. He stared down at it before thrusting it back into his pocket. 'Sergeant Shepherd,' he eventually managed to splutter. He took out his identity card and waved it briefly in front of her. 'Do you know where she is?'

As soon as she heard his name her immediate response was to deny knowing anything. She stared at him. Eddie Shepherd. Not just the cop who'd been round yesterday but the one who'd been to see Henry, and the one who'd been asking questions after the break-in. She remembered how Sonia had described him – *a piece of shit*. And Henry's opinion, although phrased a touch more politely, had been equally damning.

She shrugged and turned away. 'Sorry.'

And she would have left it at that, continued with her painting, if he hadn't started coughing again. Doubled over, he looked about as bad as a cop could look. His nose and cheeks had assumed a worrying shade of puce and the noise rattling from his chest was positively fearsome.

She put down her brush. 'Are you okay?' Taking him by the arm, she reluctantly helped him inside. 'You'd better sit down.'

It wasn't so much that she felt sorry for him as that he seemed in imminent danger of expiring . . . and a cop dropping dead on her doorstep was the last thing she needed.

By the time she'd parked him in a chair, boiled the

kettle and made the tea, he was looking almost human again.

'Ta,' he said, picking up the mug and taking a long noisy slurp. The sugar rush (he'd asked for three) seemed to consolidate his recovery. He glanced towards the door. 'Doing a spot of decorating?'

She followed his gaze, hoping that the first coat had been enough to disguise the delightful message that had been left for her. It was probably only her imagination but she was sure, as she stared at it, that she could still see the vague outline of the hangman's noose. 'Yeah. Just thought I'd spruce the place up a bit.'

'Planning on staying here, then?'

She couldn't imagine what business it was of his. Or even why he might be interested. 'I might,' she said. She sat down on the sofa and smiled nicely. 'So, is there a problem?'

'A problem?'

'Why you want to get in touch with Sonia.'

He shook his head. 'Just routine. A sudden death has a habit of providing more questions than answers.'

'Questions?' she repeated. 'I thought it was an accident. I thought he was drunk and fell into the river.'

He didn't deny it but didn't confirm it either. 'There are always questions, love.'

And there was something about the way he said it, about the way he lifted his sly copper eyes and stared at her, which set her nerves on edge. As if he wasn't just referring to Peter Marshall's death . . .

She glared silently back at him.

He took another slurp of his tea. 'So, do you know where I can find her?'

There was no point in lying and anyway, the sooner she got rid of him the better. 'I'm not sure. She's probably still with her daughter, with Val.' Eve could have given him the address but she didn't. Why should she? He could find it out for himself.

'Did you know him?' he asked.

She was reminded of asking Jack the same question last night. (And where was he now? Did he know his sergeant was here?) 'No. I never met him. He hasn't lived here in ages. Why?'

He didn't immediately reply. Instead he rummaged in his pockets. For a moment, Eve thought he was digging for another of his fetid tissues. Then he produced a small black and white photograph and passed it over to her. 'Have you ever seen this man before?'

As she took it from his fingers, she felt a faint uneasiness. 'Why?' she asked.

'Do you recognize him?'

She looked down at the picture. At first she shook her head. He was middle-aged with pale eyes and thinning hair. 'Sorry.' Then, as she was about to pass it back, a memory clicked in her brain – the man who had followed her to Blakeney. Could it be him? She had only seen him in her rear-view mirror but there was something about his features, a vague familiarity. 'Who is he?'

'He's called Ivor Patterson.'

Shepherd had seen her hesitation. It was too late for her to try and hide it now. 'I don't know the name,' she said, 'but I *may* have seen him around. I couldn't swear to it.' She examined the photo again. 'Perhaps.'

'Seen him where?' he asked.

'Just around, in the street.' She gave a casual shrug. 'But I could be wrong.' She wasn't about to share her suspicions. That was none of his business. 'What's this about?'

'We found his body yesterday.'

As Eve flinched, the photo slipped from her fingers and fell to the floor. Quickly, she bent over to retrieve it, lowering her face to hide her alarm. 'His body? You mean . . . Is he . . .?'

'Yeah,' he said. 'We're treating it as a murder inquiry.'

Murder! God. And if it *was* the same man who had followed her . . . 'Murder?' she repeated stupidly. Her heart had started to pump against her ribs, a frantic beat that took her breath away. She didn't want to look at Shepherd but forced herself to meet his eyes. She mustn't panic. It probably wasn't the same guy at all. 'That's awful.' Her mouth had gone dry and the words emerged as little more than a croak.

'So, if there's any information you could give us . . .'

Aware that she was still clutching the photograph, she hurriedly passed it back. 'I told you – he just looks vaguely familiar. That's all. I've never met him.'

'He was a private investigator.'

Eve swallowed hard. 'Was he?' Her body was growing cold, a chill that was spreading from her toes to her fingertips. She fought back a shiver. The odds had shifted; it now seemed more than likely that it *was* the same man. That's what private eyes did, wasn't it – follow people? And if he'd been following *her* and he was dead then . . .

Fear began to eat at her resolve. She didn't like Sergeant Shepherd but perhaps the time for discretion had passed. *Last chance, Evie.* That warning had suddenly acquired an even more ominous note. She opened her mouth but abruptly closed it again. No, she mustn't make any rash decisions. Once said, it could never be withdrawn. And if she was going to talk to anyone it should be Jack.

As if sensing that she might have something else to add, he sat back and waited.

The seconds ticked by. Eve could feel his expectation, thick and heavy, like a thunder cloud that had rolled in from the sea. A peculiar stillness filled the room. Even the rumble of the busy midday traffic faded into insignificance. As she struggled to straighten out her head, to get her thoughts in order, she tried to read his face. Did he suspect that she was lying? Did he *know*? He might. If the dead man had been employed to tail her then there had to be a record of it. In which case, Shepherd wasn't here to see Sonia at all. He was here on a completely different mission and—

But she couldn't afford to make those presumptions. The worst thing she could do was to jump to any hasty conclusions. *Stay calm. Think.* She glanced towards the window, towards that small expanse of silvery sky, before she looked back at him again.

Shepherd lifted his crafty eyes to return her gaze. But still he said nothing.

She felt obliged to fill the silence. Clearing her throat, she tried to keep her voice steady. 'I wish I could help but . . .' And then, as that sounded faintly hollow even to her own ears, she quickly searched for some other way to distract him. 'You think there's a connection to Peter Marshall?'

He shifted forward in the chair. 'Why should there be?'

She hadn't thought there was, not for a moment, until she saw that bright anticipatory light come into his eyes. And then her stomach twisted. *Damn!* Oh Christ! 'Because . . . because you're here to see Sonia and . . .' She stumbled over the words and stopped. She could almost feel her father turning in his grave. *Never say more than you need to, Evie. Keep it simple. Don't give them the chance to catch you out.*

There couldn't be a link between the two deaths. It wasn't possible. It didn't make any sense.

'We're just making general inquiries,' he said. 'Asking around.'

She nodded. 'I see.'

Like a lumbering elephant, he rose slowly to his feet. 'Well, thanks for the brew. If you remember any-thing—'

'Yes, I'll call you.' She stood up too, eager to be rid of him.

But, as if unwilling to leave, he halted again by the door. 'Oh, and I was sorry to hear about your father.'

'Thank you,' she said, although she doubted his sincerity.

'Yeah, very sad.' He turned and began to walk down the stairs. 'Very . . . Virginia Woolf.'

Frowning, she stared after him. What in heaven's name did that mean?

Chapter Twenty-One

Eve had picked up the phone over twenty times and almost dialled his number. But on each occasion she'd hesitated, her finger poised above the buttons, before she gently laid it back on the table again. The thought of telling Jack, of revealing *everything*, was too great a leap – and an irrevocable one. She had to be sure that she was doing the right thing.

One more day wouldn't make any difference.

True to his word, he had tried to call her. Guiltily, she had let it ring until it switched to answer mode. Later, in case he began to worry – he could hardly have forgotten about that warning painted on the door – she had sent through a brief text. *Am fine. Will call you tomorrow.*

Would she? At the moment she still had no idea.

She had anticipated a restless night, her mind churning over the death of Ivor Patterson. Why had he been following her? Why had he been killed? But oddly, as soon as her head touched the pillow, she had fallen into a deep and dreamless sleep, not waking again until the dawn light filtered between the narrow gap in the curtains. Anxiety, perhaps, had left her too exhausted to think.

And she was glad now, as she left the traffic on the busy bypass and headed towards Hillgrove, that she'd waited. First, she had to talk to Terry. Whether she'd manage to extract the truth was another matter altogether but she had to try. Either Cavelli was lying about his involvement in the robbery, or Terry was. She knew who she wanted it to be but suspected she'd be disappointed.

A few miles on, she veered into a winding country road. Wide flat fields stretched out on either side. It was the perfect place to put a prison. Any poor soul trying to escape by foot would have nowhere to go – and nowhere to hide.

Rounding another curve, she saw the sign for the jail and turned left up the long driveway. Already this place was becoming more familiar than she'd like. A few more journeys and she'd be able to get here with her eyes closed.

She pulled the car into a space by a bright red Mini. So Amber was here as well. Good. At least that meant she'd have someone to talk to for the next twenty minutes, someone to distract her from what she might or might not say to Terry. She hadn't decided yet whether she would tell him about the delivery from Vince.

Inside, the room was busier than usual and she joined the back of a short queue waiting to sign in. She glanced around but there was no sign of Amber. She must be in the Ladies, putting the finishing touches to her make-up.

The officer on duty was the same guy who had given her the number for the garage. David Hammond. He looked up as she slid the piece of paper under the grille and smiled.

'Hi. How are you doing?'

'Fine, thanks.'

His brown puppy-dog eyes focused rather too intensely on her face. 'You get the car fixed okay?'

She nodded. 'No problem.'

She tried to keep the exchange short but friendly. Fraternizing with the enemy didn't always go down well with the other women but then you didn't want to get on the wrong side of a screw either. It was a delicate balancing act.

Fortunately, there wasn't time for any further chit-chat. A couple more visitors had joined the queue behind her. He stamped her form and passed it over. His cheeks, she noticed, had turned an interesting shade of pink. She swept back her hair and offered him one of her more seductive smiles. 'Hey, thanks again.'

As if he'd just won the lottery, his jaw dropped open.

Eve was still grinning as she bought a cup of coffee and sat down at an empty table. It was good to know she hadn't lost all her charms since leaving London. A girl needed to feel desirable and a little reassurance never went amiss. But gradually, as she stirred the coffee, her smile began to falter. If she *had* needed any proof, the other night should have been enough to . . . And suddenly, as she recalled the feeling of his touch, of his skin against hers, a faint tremble made its way into her fingers. She quickly put down the spoon. It clattered into the saucer. God, what was she going to do about Jack Raynor?

Dump him! a voice inside her cried. *You know it was a mistake. The sooner you get rid of him the better.*

And she couldn't argue with that. Not only was he a cop – and that was bad enough – but her whole life was too complicated, too messy, to even think about moving things on. A relationship just wasn't on the cards. Except . . .

Except what? that strident voice demanded again. Don't start getting second thoughts, Evie. Be sensible. Be smart. Since when was one night of passion and a few sweet words enough to turn your head?

Never, she agreed. Except . . .

But it was a possible exception she didn't get the chance to explore. At that very second, the door to the

Ladies swung open and Amber, attired in a tiny scarlet dress, flounced out into the room.

Eve waved. 'Hi.'

'Hiya!' she said, tottering forward on her matching red stilettos. 'You here to see Terry?'

'Yeah. Look, I've just got a coffee. Do you want one?'

'Best not.' She raised a hand towards her newly painted lips; triple-glossed, they shone brightly in the artificial light. 'Guess what?'

Eve shook her head.

She lowered her voice to an excited whisper. '*She's* here.'

'Who?'

Amber sat down and nudged her elbow like a school-girl passing on a secret. 'You know, the one I was telling you about.' She gave a nod towards the far side of the room. 'That's *her*.'

Eve still didn't have a clue. Following her gaze, she saw a girl sitting by the window. She had long straight hair, dyed a harsh and unconvincing shade of blonde, and a wide sulky mouth. Every few seconds, she glanced with irritation at her watch as if the concept of being made to wait was not only alien but bordering on a personal insult.

'Martin's bit,' Amber finally explained. 'His . . . you know, the blonde cow, the one with the—'

'God!' Eve almost dropped her cup in surprise. She hadn't even considered that Cavelli might be out on a visit too. How awkward was this? Apart from the fact that she had absolutely no wish to see him, weren't they supposed to be pretending to be some kind of an item? That was why she'd written the letter, wasn't it, so . . .

Fortunately, Amber took her exclamation as an affirmation of her own bad opinion on the matter of his taste. As if she herself had just stepped out of the pages of *Vogue*, she wrinkled her nose and gave a contemptuous sniff. 'Yeah, hardly classy, is it?'

Eve made a vague but hopefully acceptable noise – she hadn't quite recovered her wits – while she turned again to scrutinize the girl. She was in her early twenties. Dressed in a low-cut lacy blouse, her ample and no doubt much-admired cleavage was on full view. Between her generous breasts lay a long gold chain with an oval medallion. She had numerous gold bracelets adorning her wrists as well as two thin chains around her ankle. Skintight three-quarter-length satin trousers and a pair of four-inch high heels completed the outfit.

Subtlety was not this woman's middle name.

Eve glanced down at her own casual attire – faded blue jeans, a simple navy jumper and trainers. She was hardly looking her best and couldn't even begin to compete in the glamour stakes. Not that she wanted to. She hadn't been expecting to see Cavelli today and didn't give a damn about what he thought of her. Except – and there was that word wriggling its way into her thoughts again – when push came to shove, she *was* relying on him to maintain some level of interest in their deal . . .

She took a comb from her bag and ran it quickly through her hair. 'Amber, could you spare me some of that lip gloss?'

Eve had managed to get across the room without looking at him once. Well, okay, that wasn't quite true. She had glanced at him briefly as she walked in – and seen that sly familiar smirk – but from that point onward she'd been careful to keep her gaze averted. If she was going to get through this visit the best thing, the *only* thing, she could do was to ignore him, to pretend he wasn't there.

Which wasn't too arduous a task. Terry had proved to

be a big enough distraction for the first hour. She'd expected him to be down, depressed, but he was the complete opposite – high as a kite and clearly on something more potent than the tea he was drinking. His eyes were dancing, his head on some other distant planet.

'Hey Evie, this is funny. Did I tell you about . . .'

And every other minute he was off on another tangent, relating some new story that had a vague beginning, a rambling middle, and always ended up in a mass of uncontrolled giggles.

'We need to talk,' she said softly.

He grinned at her. 'You mean *you* want to talk.'

'Seriously.'

'I am being serious,' he said, putting his face momentarily straight before he started laughing again. 'What? What's the problem?'

The problem was that there was slim chance of getting any sense out of him – but still she smiled and persevered. 'I need you to tell me something.'

'Sure.'

'The truth,' she said.

As if the truth was equivalent to requesting Einstein's Theory of Relativity, he stared blankly back at her. Then he lifted his skinny shoulders. 'Oh, okay. Go for it!'

She leaned forward, placing her hand on his arm and lowered her voice. 'About what happened,' she said. 'About the robbery.'

'Yeah?'

'I need to know, Terry. Please. Be straight with me. You were there, at the warehouse, weren't you? You were a part of it. You were there with the Rowans.'

She had caught him off guard. He only paused for a second, a fraction of a second, but it was enough. The look in his eyes was enough to tell her everything.

'Jesus,' she murmured.

'No—' he began, but then abruptly stopped again. 'I mean . . .'

So it *was* true. She felt her heart plummet. And before his fuddled brain could come up with anything even approximating a convincing lie, she pressed home the advantage. 'Why the hell didn't you tell me?'

Hearing the anger in her voice, he shifted uneasily in his seat and stared down at the floor. 'I'm sorry, okay. I'm sorry. I didn't know he had a shooter, Evie. I swear.'

But there was time enough for *that* conversation. There were other matters to sort out first. Now she'd got his attention, she couldn't afford to let it drift. 'You took something when you were there. What was it?'

'You know, the watches and stuff.'

'And the rest,' she persisted. 'What *didn't* the cops find when they picked you up?'

'What?'

'Something that's gone missing, something that a friend of the Rowans might want back?'

He raised his wide grey eyes and stared at her. They were filled with confusion. 'What?' he said again.

She saw his expression and faltered. 'So the Rowans aren't connected to anyone called Joe?'

'Who?' He shook his head. 'I dunno. Who? No. Why?'

She didn't think he was lying. No, he wasn't. He definitely wasn't. Although she felt some relief – at least her recent experiences were nothing to do with him – she felt a brief rush of dismay too. If you knew what you were facing, no matter how bad, you could usually find some way of dealing with it – but when you were left in the dark . . .

But she'd think about that later. For now she still had to establish if there was any truth in those other 'rumours' of Cavelli's. What if Terry *had* made a deal with the cops? She tried to keep her voice calm. 'So how come they only got you for handling?'

Terry's mouth, annoyingly, slid back into that familiar cocky grin. 'Didn't have the evidence, did they? Couldn't prove I was there.'

Revealing that the Rowans were claiming he was a grass would wipe the smile off his face – but was it wise? He might panic, do something stupid. 'And no other reason?'

'What do you mean?'

She couldn't bring herself to come straight out with it and ask. If it wasn't true – and she was *almost* certain that it wasn't – he'd never forgive her for even suggesting it. 'Nothing. Forget it. I'm just trying to make sense of it all.'

As if he guessed there was something more behind the question, his delicate forehead puckered into a frown. He tilted his head to one side. Fortunately his brain was too mashed for any logical thought and, try as he might, he couldn't figure it out. Producing a sorrowful smile, he fell back instead on the well-worn technique of empty excuses and plaintive apology.

'Ah, I'm sorry, Sis. I'm really sorry. I wanted to tell you. I meant to. It was just . . .'

She had heard it all before. While he embarked on yet another of his self-justifying rambles she automatically tuned out and glanced instead across the room towards Cavelli. Their eyes met, locked for a few vital seconds, and an understanding passed between them. She watched as he leaned over to whisper something in the ear of his visitor. The blonde immediately got to her feet and tottered off towards the refreshment counter.

Eve inwardly snarled. Blind obedience! That was probably what Cavelli liked in his women. But now wasn't the moment to be dissecting his possibly endless personality defects. She'd just got the opportunity she wanted. Quickly, she stood up. 'Hang on. I need a drink.'

She tried not to rush across the room but knew she couldn't afford to waste any time; the queue at the counter was short and she had to make sure that she had a few minutes of his undivided attention before Ms Cleavage came back on the scene. Weaving her way smoothly between the tables, aware of the screws and their constant scrutiny, she attempted to make the meeting look casual. 'Hey,' she said, stopping by his chair and smiling.

'Hello, darling,' he said. 'Nice to see you again.'

She saw his dark dirty eyes make their usual uninvited sweep of her body and felt every muscle in her body tighten. But she maintained the smile, the appearance of a friendly exchange, while she leaned forward and hissed, 'I thought you were supposed to be taking care of him.'

'I am.'

'So how come he's off his head?'

Cavelli shrugged. 'I'm not his keeper.'

She battled to keep her expression benign – and lost. The smile quickly dissolved as she glared at him. 'I thought we had a deal.'

He stared smugly back at her. 'He's still alive, isn't he?'

And there wasn't much she could say to that – at least not without losing her temper. She took a couple of deep breaths. Cavelli's sly, mocking expression was enough to expel any rational response. *Just walk away*, her sensible inner voice advised. *Don't make this any worse*. But that inner voice had been nagging her all day. She'd had enough of it. And she still wanted some answers. 'Why didn't you let me know you'd be out on a visit?'

'Why didn't you?'

'I thought we were supposed to be . . . well, pretending that—'

He leaned back and folded his arms. 'Oh, right . . . *that*. Yes. Thanks for your touching letter.'

And there was something about the way he said it, about the way he looked at her, that triggered a deep subconscious alarm. It bubbled slowly to the surface. Oh God, the letter! Was that the reason why he'd chosen to have a visit on the same day she was seeing Terry – a chance to get his revenge, a pathetic kickback for some of the things she'd written?

'I presumed you'd see the lighter side,' she said. 'It's not as if we're actually—'

'No man likes getting a knockback when he's inside.'

Jesus. Was he being serious?

He shook his head. 'You think it isn't bad enough being locked up without all that extra grief?'

What? Talk about turning things on their head. She'd come over to have a go at him and now he was accusing her of . . . of what? Surely he hadn't, *couldn't* have thought that there was anything between them, that they were . . . But the expression on his face was deadly serious. His dark eyes stared angrily into hers. 'Hardly a knockback,' she retorted. 'We agreed. It was . . . I was only . . .'

But even as she started to stutter out an explanation, his mouth was breaking into a grin.

Damn! He was just winding her up – and she'd fallen for it. What was the matter with her? Over the past few weeks she'd turned into a nervous wreck. Perhaps it was time to regain some lost ground. She glanced down at the plastic cup on the table. There were still a few inches of cold tea left in it. All she had to do was pick it up and . . .

It didn't take him long to grasp her intention. 'You do that, sweetheart, and they'll throw you out.'

'Could be worth it.'

As if daring her to go through with it, his grin grew even wider.

Which was like a red rag to a bull. Her hand instinctively reached forward but she managed to restrain herself. She couldn't create a scene. She was here to try and sort out her problems, not to create even more. And even though she was tempted, sorely tempted, she was prevented from doing anything irretrievably stupid by the return of the *Playboy* blonde.

'Ah, Kimberley, sweetheart,' he said. 'This is Evie.' He paused. 'Have you met? She's an old friend of mine.'

She didn't seem impressed. Pushing rudely past, she slammed the tray down on the table.

'Nice to meet you,' Eve said.

Kimberley turned and looked her up and down. Her eyes narrowed in that suspicious way that women's often do when they think there might be a hint of competition. 'Oh yeah?'

Courtesy clearly wasn't in this woman's repertoire. 'Excuse me?'

'Don't let me keep you. Shouldn't you be somewhere?'

Eve felt her hackles rise. She really wasn't in the mood for anyone, never mind some bleached blonde tart, telling her where she should be or what she should be doing. 'And that's your business because . . .?'

'We're busy,' she said, shifting a wad of gum from one side of her mouth to the other. 'Why don't you just piss off.'

Eve looked at Cavelli but he clearly wasn't going to intervene: he was enjoying himself too much – having two women fight for the pleasure of his company was probably a dream come true. Well, it was a dream she had no intention of prolonging.

She smiled sweetly at the girl. 'And here was me thinking it was just a rumour.'

'Huh?'

'That artificial blondes are even more stupid than the real thing.' Then, before Kimberley's tiny pea-sized brain could manage to send a message to that gaping scarlet mouth, Eve smartly turned and walked away.

'You see,' Amber murmured, as they waited for the doors to open and release them. 'I told you. I said she was a bitch.'

Cavelli's girl, a few yards in front, had turned to glare again. She'd been looking daggers ever since the visit had ended. Eve shrugged. She had more important things to worry about than some daft tart's insecurity. 'Don't worry about it. Ignore her.'

But Amber wasn't the type to let things rest. Out of some misguided sense of loyalty, or maybe because she simply fancied a scrap, she raised her voice and said, 'So what do you think *you're* staring at?'

Which gave Kimberley the perfect opportunity for some playground retaliation. She put a hand on her hip, and looked her up and down. 'Not a lot,' she replied.

Eve was close enough to feel Amber bristle. She was also aware of the faint frisson of excitement that ran through the other visitors. The doors had opened but instead of moving swiftly out as they usually did, they all stopped to listen. No matter how good or bad their day there was nothing like an old-fashioned cat fight to round off the experience. She saw the screw who was escorting them glance back over his shoulder. He was a fifty-something male with a weary expression – the kind of expression that had it been translated into words would have read, quite clearly, *Bloody women!*

'Come on,' he said curtly. 'Let's move it along.'

She didn't want the grief either. 'Leave it,' she insisted, taking hold of Amber's arm and heading for the exit. 'She's not worth the bother.'

A faint sigh of disappointment accompanied their departure.

And that might have been it if Kimberley hadn't decided otherwise.

They were almost at the car park when Eve was caught hard on the shoulder and sent reeling. 'Hey!' she protested, stumbling forward.

The blonde swung round defiantly. 'Oh, sorry. Did you say something?'

'God, what *is* your problem?'

'You cow!' Amber said, just to add fuel to the fire. 'You did that deliberately.'

'Piss off!' Kimberley said, glaring at her. 'Shut your gob. This has nothing to do with you.'

As Amber automatically opened her mouth, Eve quickly intervened. 'Don't,' she said, pushing her gently aside. She didn't want this turning into anything nastier than it already was. 'It's okay. I can deal with it. It's me she's got the issue with.'

A small crowd had started to gather again. A few of the women rooted in their handbags, pretending they were searching for fags or keys, but most just blatantly stood around waiting for it all to kick off.

'Too fucking true.' Kimberley took a step closer and pushed her face into Eve's. 'Let's get one thing clear, bitch. Martin's not interested.'

Now there were lots of things that wound Eve up – like having someone else's chewing gum breath in her face – but being accused of pursuing a man she would rather walk over red hot coals to avoid wasn't one them. She pulled away and gave a derisive snort. 'Are you kidding? You think I'm interested in *him*? Help yourself,' she said. 'He's all yours.'

But as if she'd just admitted to some sordid affair, Kimberley's eyes flashed into rage. 'Fuck you! Keep your filthy hands off him.'

'It'll be a pleasure.'

Up to now Eve hadn't taken the confrontation that seriously. This was just a girl with a big mouth and an even bigger inferiority complex. 'Well, if you've quite finished . . .' she said.

But as she went to walk away Kimberley launched herself forward again. 'You stay away from him,' she snarled.

It was the speed of the attack that caught Eve off guard. One moment she was standing there and the next . . . Astonishment quickly gave way to a searing pain as her head was yanked brutally to the side. A large clump of hair, wound around her assailant's fist, strained at its roots. As her knees began to buckle, she could feel the tears coming into her eyes. Somewhere in the back of her mind she knew her response was all wrong – she should be going with the pull, not fighting against it – but still she struggled instinctively to get free. Reaching out for the long blonde locks, she grabbed a reciprocal handful and wrenched it as hard as she could. Kimberley gave a satisfying yelp but didn't let go. Within a few seconds it had turned into an undignified scuffle, the two of them joined in a bizarre circular shuffle around the gravel forecourt, slapping and kicking, arms flailing, their breath emerging in short fast bursts interspersed with abuse.

'Bitch!'

'Maniac!'

Eve knew it was pathetic, ridiculous, but she couldn't let go. Kimberley had a wild expression on her face; she was out of control. Given the opportunity, she was crazy enough to scratch out her eyes. No sooner had Eve thought it, than she felt those sharp red talons rip viciously into the back of her hand. She cried out at the stinging pain and looked down to see three brutal stripes of blood. Damn her! Cursing the fact that she was only

331

wearing trainers, she drew back her foot and kicked as hard as she could against the bare skin of her opponent's shin, a resounding thump that produced a thoroughly gratifying howl. Kimberley doubled over and sank to the ground.

With her hair now free, Eve was able to step aside. But not fast or far enough. She had barely drawn breath before Kimberley snatched at her ankle, caught her off balance and sent her toppling. She crashed down on to the gravel, the tiny stones grazing her palms as she tried to break her fall. The next thing she knew, she was rolling across the forecourt with the mad witch spitting and clawing at her again.

For God's sake! This was insane! She'd only come to see Terry and . . .

The pale blue sky flashed in and out of her field of vision. One moment she was staring up at its vast expanse, the next she had her nose pressed hard against the gravel. She was distantly aware of Amber jumping up and down and squealing – although it was hard to tell if it was out of panic or encouragement. Her more immediate concern was with Kimberley's rage, a fury that showed no sign of abating. A frenzied rabid sound, guttural and barely human, escaped from the girl's throat as she lunged again and again, trying to bite, trying to punch, while they struggled in their angry embrace.

Eve fought back, managing to land a few well-aimed digs and slaps. She couldn't claim she was stronger – they were both around the same height and weight – but she was sure she was starting to fight smarter, to not do anything too rash, to not leave any unnecessary openings, to *think* about what she was doing. Emotion inevitably got in the way of technique. It was a well-known fact, wasn't it? So long as she protected herself, kept her cool, Kimberley would eventually begin to weaken and then . . .

Whether this theory would have proved to be accurate – or simply one of the last thoughts she had before waking up in a hospital bed – she never got the chance to discover. Another body suddenly forced its way between theirs, abruptly levering them apart.

'Christ! Fuck! What are you doing? Ladies, *please*!'

As she sprawled on her back, Eve gazed up to see David Hammond staring down at them. Oh great! A screw. So now the whole jail was going to know about it. She closed her eyes for a second before she rose slowly to her feet. Yet despite her mortification, she suddenly found herself wanting to laugh. With their torn clothes and bedraggled appearance, they looked about as far from 'ladies' as they possibly could – more like a pair of cheap tarts fighting over a client on a slow Saturday night.

'What's going on?' he asked officiously.

He glanced from Eve, who said nothing, to Kimberley.

She was still sitting on the ground, rubbing at her shin. 'It's none of your fucking business!'

'It *is* my business when you're doing it on prison grounds.'

'Yeah, right,' she said. 'Why don't you go fill in a complaint form?'

There was a faint ripple of laughter from the surrounding crowd. It ran like a soft wave, rising and falling, before they swiftly dispersed. It had all been good fun, a spectacle, but now an official was on the scene, they were quick to make themselves scarce. There was no point asking for trouble.

He turned towards Eve again. 'You want to tell me?'

'It was nothing,' she said, dusting herself down. 'Don't worry about it. A misunderstanding, that's all.'

She looked at Kimberley who had finally managed to haul herself upright. She was a mess, her sweaty face a disaster, her eyes ringed with dark shadows of mascara. Even her mouth was leaking lipstick. Eve probably didn't look a million dollars herself – all her muscles were aching and her hair was in rat's tails – but it was with some satisfaction that she weighed up the balance of the damage. All things considered, her casual jeans and jumper had been a godsend, not the height of glamour perhaps but more practical when it came to a scrap. Kimberley's lacy blouse was torn across the shoulder, her satin trousers stained and wrinkled. One of her high-heeled designer shoes was still lying a few yards away.

Eve smiled – but she couldn't afford to be too smug. She was sure she'd have her fair shares of bruises by the morning.

'Look,' Hammond said, 'I don't know what's going on but—'

Kimberley raised her eyes to the heavens as she brusquely shoved past him. 'Sorry, mate, I'd love to talk but things to do.' She threw Eve one last nasty glance as she hobbled a few feet, picked up her shoe, and got into her car. With a violent squeal of the brakes, she reversed a few yards out and then accelerated away.

Once the grey cloud of exhaust had cleared, Hammond glanced at her again. 'You sure you're okay?'

'I'm fine.'

'And you don't want to—'

'No,' she said. 'Although thanks for stepping in. What would I have done without you?'

His cheeks flushed pink and like some Arthurian knight his chest puffed out an inch or two. 'Oh, I don't know,' he said magnanimously, 'you seemed to be holding your own.'

'That's very sweet,' she said, 'but actually, I just meant thank you for stopping me from killing her.'

334

Chapter Twenty-Two

As Eve drove towards home she stared at the three long scratches on her hand and sighed. She was starting to wonder if she had one of those signs pinned to her back that read: *Kick me!* It seemed she barely got through a day now without someone having a go. Gingerly, she touched her scalp, feeling the sore point where her hair had been yanked by its roots.

She was beginning to understand what Paula had meant about Cavelli's taste in women. *You're not his usual type.* Wasn't that what she'd said? Well, thank God for small mercies. That was one category she was well out of. She might have the odd flaw in her character but Kimberley was positively deranged.

The sun was sinking, lying low on the horizon and shining straight into her eyes. Bugger, she'd have this for the next five miles or so. She flipped down the visor and squinted into the mirror. It had become a habit recently, this constant checking to see if anyone was on her tail, slowing down and speeding up, testing the drivers behind her. Except now of course, if the man who'd been following her was dead . . . But she didn't want to believe that. She didn't want to believe that her shadow had been Ivor Patterson, the man who'd been brutally attacked, the same man who was now nothing more than a cold corpse laid out in the morgue.

She shuddered, turning her thoughts back to the mad blonde who'd gone for her throat. Pondering on Kimberley was hardly comfortable but it was preferable to some of the other options whirling round her head. What on earth had possessed her to kick off like that? The woman was either psychopathically jealous – in which case she needed counselling – or someone had encouraged her to think that Eve Weston was a serious threat to her relationship. And that someone, now she came to think of it, could only be Cavelli.

But what would he have to gain from it? Well, a good laugh probably – and a chance to get back at her for what she'd written in the letter. He was the sort who always liked to be in charge, to have the last word. By winding Kimberley up, by telling her God knows what – that she was pursuing him? that she was an old girl-friend? – he could get her to do his dirty work while he stayed out of the picture. And Eve would never be able to prove that it had anything to do with him. Yeah, she wouldn't be surprised. It was just his style.

Unless there was something more sinister behind his actions.

She frowned as she considered another more worrying possibility. Perhaps Cavelli was the psychopath – a man who needed to manipulate, to control, to utterly possess the women in his life. Take Nadine for example: even after she'd left him, even after he'd married Paula, he hadn't been able to let go. There was something obsessive about it all. Even after her death, he was still acting as if she belonged to him. He'd gone round to see Jimmy Reece, confronted him and . . . She instantly tried to shake the image from her head. No, it didn't bear thinking about.

But there was no denying that Cavelli was dangerous. She had to face up to the fact that there had been no attacks, no threats, no shadows, until she'd met *him*.

Could that really be a coincidence? Maybe he got his kicks from frightening women. Maybe this was all some sick grotesque game, something to occupy his mind while he was banged up – a little friendly torment to make the time pass quicker.

It was possible but it didn't quite add up. For starters, it didn't even begin to account for Ivor Patterson's death. Or the whole Joe business. Or plenty of other things. She lit a cigarette and wound down the window. She sighed again, a long tired exhalation.

Eve was half a mile further down the road before a hollow laugh escaped from her lips. How had it come to this? Things must be bad if she was actually disappointed to work out that she *wasn't* being hounded by a six-foot-plus vicious thug with psychopathic tendencies and the eyes of a devil!

It was almost five by the time she drew up beside the fish and chip shop. The sky had darkened, turning from blue to filthy grey, and a few spots of rain were already coming down. She got out and locked the door. She'd made a decision as she drove slowly through the city traffic. So okay, there were lots of questions she didn't have the answers to but there was one she could sort out straight away: no more unnecessary mysteries – as soon as she got into the flat she was going to open those boxes.

She was walking fast, almost trotting, when she spotted the silver Peugeot parked up beside the flats. Jack Raynor got out and raised his hand. Damn! What was he doing here? Forcing a smile, she tried to keep the irritation from her voice.

'Hey, if I didn't know better I might think you were stalking me.'

He smiled back, his blue eyes searching hers. 'And

if I didn't know better, I might think you were avoiding me.'

'Sorry. I was going to call,' she lied. 'I've been kind of busy. I had a load of stuff to do this morning and then I had to go and see Terry.'

It was a lousy excuse of course and he knew it. He'd also been around long enough to recognize a brush-off when he heard one. 'Anyway,' he said, taking a step back, 'as long as you're okay. I only dropped by. I didn't mean to . . .'

And Eve was presented with the perfect opportunity to just let him walk away. He was making it easy for her. No awkward conversations, no recriminations. That was what she wanted, wasn't it? All she had to do was say goodbye, to stroll inside and it would be over. So why was she hesitating? What was it about Jack Raynor that made her doubt every inch of good sense she'd been born with?

And the very next second her mouth opened to say the exact opposite of what she'd intended. 'Well, seeing as you're here you may as well come in. I don't know about you but I'm desperate for a coffee.'

Joe was pacing the floor, back and forth, back and forth. His arms hung rigidly, his hands coiled into two tight fists. It was all getting on his nerves, the waiting around, the not knowing. Perhaps Keeler was right – they should just bring her in and beat the fucking truth out of her. But as soon as the thought crossed his mind, he dismissed it. It was a bad idea. Evie was smart. She'd have found a safe place to hide her father's little legacy. And she'd have made the necessary contingency plans for if she suddenly disappeared off the face of the earth – the kind of plans that would send him to jail for the next twenty years.

No, patience was what was needed here. No matter how much it galled him, he had to play the waiting game. With Patterson gone, she'd be starting to sweat, starting to realize just who she was up against. Eventually she'd have to show her hand, she'd have no choice, and then . . .

When the knock came at the door, he sat back down in his chair, took a moment to rearrange his features into cold indifference and shouted out, 'Come!'

Micky and Gruber entered the office, one either side of Jimmy Reece. They weren't exactly holding him up but providing a kind of buttress service. He was lightly swaying from left to right and Joe got the impression that if they suddenly moved he might accidentally tip over and end up on the shag pile.

'Hello, Jimmy,' he said.

Reece's eyes struggled briefly to focus. And then, as if surprised to find himself where he was, he glanced around the room and nodded. 'Oh, good evening, Mr Silk. How are you?'

It was barely five o'clock but he was already well on the way to oblivion. 'Sit him down,' Joe said to Micky, 'before he fucking falls down.'

He did as he was told, pulling out a chair with one hand whilst using the other to lean on his shoulder and to gently but efficiently depress him. Reece acceded without even a murmur. In fact, perhaps in the mistaken belief that this was a social occasion and Micky nothing more than an over-conscientious waiter, he even raised his face and smiled.

Joe gave a short dismissive nod in the direction of his two men. He waited until they'd left, until the door had clicked shut, before returning his attention to his guest. Then he sat back for a while and said nothing. Silence, as he had learned over the years, was always a useful tool, an unnerving precursor to what might be coming next.

And gradually, predictably, as the silence grew, Jimmy Reece began to squirm. He crossed his legs and uncrossed them. He stared at Joe, opened his mouth and then closed it again. He turned his head and glanced out of the window. As the minutes passed, the chill of impending sobriety began to creep into his bones.

'Mr Silk?' he asked. For the first time, a quiver of fear, of understanding had come into his voice. 'Is there a problem?'

'A problem?' Joe repeated. He rapped his knuckles softly against the desk. As he raised his eyes he narrowed them into a well-worn but convincing glare of intimidation. 'Now, just *how* much is it you owe me, son?'

Reece made an involuntary jump and shifted forward in his seat. 'But I thought . . . I mean, we've got an arrangement, haven't we? I pay you every—'

'And how often have you missed those payments? How many times have you let me down?' Joe shook his head and sighed. 'It doesn't look good, Jimmy. It doesn't look good at all. I've got a reputation to consider. You think I want to be the laughing stock of London – the fucking mug, the *moron*, the loser who lends money out but never gets it back? You're a man of the world. You can see the position I'm in. It's nothing personal, you understand, just a matter of principle.'

Reece's face, already white, was taking on a greenish tinge. A faint sheen of perspiration leaked from his forehead. 'I can sort it,' he pleaded urgently. 'I know I'm behind but just give me a few days. Please. Look, I'll talk to the old man. I'll get him to give me an advance. There isn't any need for—'

With a genuine appearance of regret, Joe slowly shook his head again. 'It isn't what I want, of course it isn't, but sometimes examples have to be made and—'

'Please,' Reece begged again. 'It doesn't have to be like

340

this. I'll make sure you get your money. Whatever you want, whatever you say.'

And Joe knew he had him right where he wanted – terrified and desperate. But he couldn't be seen to give in too easily. The offer of salvation had to come gradually, to be presented as a slim chance, a tiny window of opportunity. 'I'm sorry. It's too late, Jimmy. It's gone beyond the cash.'

He groaned and put his head in his hands. 'Jesus.'

Joe gave him a few more seconds to think about it, about the consequences, the pain, before throwing him a precious lifeline. 'However, I'm not an unreasonable man. You've let me down but . . .'

'Anything,' Reece said, lifting his head. His eyes widened into hopeful expectation. 'I swear. *Anything* you want.'

'Like the truth perhaps?' Joe leaned across the desk and stared menacingly at him. 'Like telling me what the fuck you were doing with Evie Weston?'

Reece looked genuinely bewildered. 'Who?'

'Don't piss me about, Jimmy. The redhead you met in Pearl's, the cutie you were playing footsie with under the table. Last Friday night. What's going on? What's the deal?'

But he still seemed to be struggling, his forehead crumpling into a frown as he tried to dredge up the night from his sodden brain. Joe wondered if he was bluffing, play-acting, but his abilities hadn't been that great even at the peak of his career. Shit! He'd been relying on Reece, certain he could shed some light on what that fucking bitch was up to.

He reached into a drawer, pulled out a photograph and slid it across the desk. 'Here. Let me jog your memory.'

Reece stared down at the picture and gradually his face began to clear. 'Yeah,' he said, shifting forward.

'Yeah, I remember her now.' He touched the edges of the photograph. As if delighted by his powers of recollection, his mouth broke into a smile.

'So why did you meet up with her, Jimmy?'

'I didn't,' he said. 'I mean, I did but not deliberately. *He* was the one who bought *me* a drink.' He prodded a face with his forefinger. 'It was him. Patrick something. Said we worked together once, years ago. I couldn't place him but . . .' He continued to peer down, to try and concentrate, to provide the information that was so clearly wanted. He licked his drying lips and gazed up pleadingly. 'Don't suppose you have a drink, Mr Silk?'

Joe got up and poured them both a large one. At this point gratitude would do more to loosen his tongue than any amount of threats.

Reece attacked it greedily, knocking back half the contents in one gulp. It seemed to clear his head. 'O'Connell,' he said triumphantly. 'That was it! Patrick O'Connell.'

'And what did he want, this Patrick O'Connell?'

'He wanted to buy me a drink . . . a few drinks.'

Joe could see how that would have been appealing. 'And?'

That frown appeared on his forehead again.

'What did you talk about?' he prompted.

Reece shrugged. 'I don't know. The usual. Nothing special. Films and stuff.'

'He didn't ask you for anything?'

'For what?'

'I don't know. You tell me. Did he offer you any kind of deal?'

'What kind of deal?'

Joe felt the beginnings of one of his dull pervasive headaches but he persevered. 'And the woman, the red-head – what did *she* talk about?'

'Oh, she wasn't doing much talking,' Reece said, with

a small but lascivious grin. 'I don't think she was too happy with that husband of hers. She was looking for something . . . well, a little more thrilling, if you get my gist.'

'And you'd never seen her before, you'd never met her?'

'No, I swear. Never. It was the first time, Mr Silk. I'd have remembered.'

Joe was sure that he would. Evie Weston – for various reasons – wasn't the kind of woman you'd forget in a hurry. 'Did you arrange to see her again?'

Reece shrugged again. 'Not exactly.'

Joe took another swig of his drink. Christ, this was like getting blood out of a stone. He was pretty sure now that Reece wasn't directly involved – he was too shit scared to lie to him, he didn't have the balls – but it still begged the question of what Evie had been up to that night. Just laying the foundations perhaps, taking it easy, taking it slow, gaining his confidence until . . . But he still couldn't work out the motivation. Was use was Jimmy Reece to her?

'Not exactly?' he repeated.

'He gave me their card. The film geezer, the husband. He said to give him a ring.'

Joe put out his hand.

Reece rooted in his pockets for a few seconds then got out his wallet and flicked through the contents. Then he scowled. 'Ah, God no. I didn't keep it. I wrote my number on the back and . . .' Sensing Joe's frustration he quickly looked up and apologized. 'Sorry, I'm really sorry. Only I'm always losing them, you see, so there didn't seem much point in holding on to it. Yeah, I wrote my number on the back and gave it to her.'

Joe shook his head again. A soft growl escaped from his throat. It seemed that even the fates were conspiring against him. Would she ring? Maybe she would, maybe she wouldn't, but he wasn't going to sit around waiting to find out.

'Sorry,' Reece murmured.

'Don't worry, son. Don't give it a second thought.' Joe paused, watching him relax a little, before delivering the denouement. 'Because as it happens, I *do* know a way that you can make it up to me.'

Joe waited until the room was empty, until his guest had been escorted from the premises, before he dropped his face down into his hands. By now his headache was starting to hammer. Jimmy Reece might have left but the problem remained and he couldn't stop going over and over it. He already knew who O'Connell was – Patrick Fielding, a chancer, a hustler who had once been married to Evie. But they'd been divorced for years. So what had brought them back together? Well, the answer to that was clear: Alexander Weston's enduring legacy.

He glanced around his office, at the plush furnishings, the excellent view across the Thames, at everything he'd worked so hard to achieve. Then he knocked back the rest of his whisky and slammed the glass down on his desk. What Evie had inherited could destroy him. She was taking him for a fool – and no one did that to Joe Silk. *Especially not a fucking woman*.

Chapter Twenty-Three

They were lounging on the sofa, side by side. Eve leaned her head against his shoulder, lifted the glass to her lips and took a few sips of the excellent claret. All the trials of the day had long since slipped into oblivion. Somehow, since arriving back home and inviting Jack Raynor in for a coffee, she had inadvertently managed to rip off all his clothes, enjoy the seductive pleasures of his body *and* take advantage of his comprehensive knowledge of the finest fast-delivery pizza services in town.

So much for good intentions. Still, she'd never been renowned for playing it safe.

The remains of their dinner, a few curling crusts, lay in a cardboard box on the low table in front of them. She reached out a leg to nudge it away but then changed her mind and instead ran her bare foot along the length of his shin. For the sake of propriety he had put on his trousers to answer the door and she, in turn, had appropriated his large cream shirt. It fell in soft milky folds around the top of her thighs.

'So, Inspector Raynor,' she murmured, 'would you like to explain how you just *happened* to have this bottle of wine in your briefcase? You don't think it was a little – well, presumptuous?'

'Not guilty,' he insisted. 'Cross my heart. I was expecting to be drinking it alone. Something to console myself with after you gave me one of those kind but slightly embarrassed looks and said: *It's not you, Jack, it's me. I think you're really nice but . . .*'

She laughed. 'Did you really think I was going to dump you?'

'You didn't ring.'

'It was only a day.'

'Ah,' he sighed, 'but such a *long* day.'

He bent to nuzzle the crown of her head. As his mouth touched the sore point on her scalp, the place where her hair had almost been yanked from its roots, she flinched and pulled away.

'What's the matter?'

She pulled a face. 'It's okay. I had to dry it in a hurry this morning. I must have had the heat turned too high.'

Then as she tentatively reached up to feel the damage for herself, he noticed the scratches on her left hand. He took hold of her fingers. 'Christ, what happened? You look like you've been fighting with a cat.'

'Do I?'

'You want to tell me about it?'

'There's nothing to tell, honestly.'

He stared down at the three red stripes while he anxiously stroked her fingers. 'What's wrong, Eve? What's going on?' There was a hurt edge to his tone. 'First the stuff on the door and now . . . I'm not that hard to talk to, am I?'

'No,' she said. 'Of course not.' The problem was the very opposite; he was way too easy to talk to. As if she'd known him for a lifetime, she was in constant danger of telling him everything, of blurting out the truth before she had time to consider the consequences. She wondered if it was because he reminded her of Patrick – except they weren't really similar at all. Okay, physically they bore some resemblance, that whole fair-haired,

346

blue-eyed thing, but that was only superficial. Their characters were completely different.

'No,' she said again. 'And this has nothing to do with what happened to the door. It was just an accident. I was careless. I wasn't looking where I was going and caught it on some nails that were sticking out and . . .'

But he wasn't convinced. 'Where?'

She inwardly groaned. That was the trouble with lies – they often led you into deeper water. But the truth hadn't even been an option. It would have led to other questions and these in turn would have inevitably led to Cavelli. And there was also the fact that she wasn't exactly proud of having rolled around the prison car park like a demented banshee.

'What does it matter?' She lifted her eyes and grinned. 'Or do you want to go and question them?'

'I might,' he said. 'It sounds like a clear case of GBH to me.'

She made a clicking noise with her tongue. 'Ah, so that's what this is all about. You're just after another arrest. Do you cops ever think of anything else?'

'Never. Our quest in life is to protect the innocent and punish the guilty.'

'So we can all sleep safely in our beds at night.'

'That's why I'm here,' he said, leaning over to kiss her. 'As the cliché goes, it's a tough job but someone's got to do it.'

She relaxed into his arms, relieved that the crisis appeared to have passed. And for the next few minutes, their mouths otherwise preoccupied, she had no need of any further lies. There was no need for any talk at all. Sinking against his naked chest, she breathed in the smell of him, his male musky scent and the faint aroma of his aftershave. She touched his bare skin. She ran a finger along the line of hair that swept briefly left and right, following the contours of his muscles, before it dropped south and disappeared beneath his belt. There was something erotic about that barrier. As his hands slid around her breasts, she felt the desire rise in her again, a heat that travelled the length of her body, growing and intensifying, settling like a fire between her thighs. She moved even closer. But as her own hand continued in its journey, as it brushed against his groin, he suddenly drew back.

'Eve, can I ask you something?'

She looked up at him.

'Is it because I'm a cop?'

'What?'

'Is that why you feel you can't talk to me?'

She frowned. God, and they said it was women who always wanted to analyse everything! Here he was, being presented with yet another opportunity to taste the glorious delights of her body and all he wanted to do was *talk*. 'You mean, as opposed to the fact that you might simply have a vile personality?'

He laughed. 'That apart.' Then he glanced down at the floor and looked up again. 'Sorry, but I'm worried. And I'm worried because I care about you. Is that such a bad thing?'

'No,' she said.

'So why do I get the feeling that you're holding out on me?'

Confronted with the truth, she instantly fell back on flippancy. 'I don't know. Perhaps you have a naturally suspicious mind.'

He shook his head. 'Are you ever serious about anything?'

She shrugged.

'So is this always going to be between us, the fact that I'm a copper and you're . . .'

'The daughter of a conman?'

He stared at her. 'I didn't mean that.' He quickly reached out and took hold of her hand again. 'Just that you were close to your father and . . . well, I don't suppose the local constabulary were ever on his Christmas card list.'

Eve curled her feet beneath her and pulled down his shirt to modestly cover her knees. The moment of passion, failing to fully ignite, had now cooled and passed them by. Still, she shouldn't complain; most men didn't know the meaning of conversation. 'Does it bother you, who he was?'

'Why should it?'

She shrugged again. 'I don't know – like father, like daughter?'

'I've never thought that, not for a minute.'

'But what if it was true,' she said. 'What if I *am* the same?'

He put his arm around her shoulder and pulled her closer. As if she was still joking with him, he laughed. 'I trust you.'

Did he? She wasn't really sure. Maybe he just liked flirting with danger. But then maybe she did too. Perhaps that was the attraction between them – the thrill of the forbidden.

'What was it like?' he continued. 'I mean growing up with a father who . . .' He paused. 'I'm sorry. Do you mind me asking? I don't mean it to sound like I'm interrogating you.'

'It's okay.' But she made a mental note to be careful, to not let her tongue run away with her. It was warm in the room and nestled in the crook of his arm she felt deceptively safe and secure. 'To be honest, I don't suppose it was that different to anyone else's childhood. He always kept that side of things away from me.'

It amazed her how easily she could lie, the words sliding from her lips as smooth as honey. But she could hardly tell him the truth – about how, when times were rough, when money was tight, they'd roam the West End together, him in a perfectly tailored suit, her in some pretty party dress, carefully picking out their marks. They'd cruise around the theatres and the fancy hotels. Her father could spot a man with money from a hundred paces. He'd provide the spiel – the story of having mislaid his wallet or having had it stolen and just needing enough money to get his young daughter home – while she stood beside him, the epitome of wide-eyed innocence. He would always thank them politely. He would always, meticulously, take down their names and addresses. It wasn't big money but it paid the rent.

She understood now how much it must have galled him. He must have seen it as a waste of his skills, as only a few theatrical steps up from begging. But he had done it for *her*, to keep her safe, to keep her fed and clothed, until the next big opportunity came along. And after a few weeks, when they might have run the risk of becoming too familiar, they had always taken off for a while and disappeared to pastures new. 'We moved around a bit,' she said, 'but then plenty of other kids do the same.'

'Didn't you want to settle down, have a regular home somewhere?'

'Sometimes,' she agreed. 'But then you don't really miss what you've never had.'

'How did you feel, finding out what he did for a living?'

She raised her face to look at him. 'Are you sure you're not cross-examining me?'

He grinned. 'Sorry. I'm just curious. I can't imagine what it was like to live that way. I had what you might call a conventional upbringing. Very dull, very ordinary.' He wound a lock of her long red hair around his fingers. 'So what about your mother – what happened to her?'

It was a long time since Eve had thought about her. 'She was called Helen. She went AWOL before I was two. Not, apparently, the type who was into playing happy families; she couldn't bear to be tied down. I can't even remember her.'

'And you haven't been tempted to try and track her down?'

She shook her head. 'Why should I? She wasn't interested then so I don't see why she should be now. It's all old history, water under the bridge etc. There's no point in raking it up.'

'Still, it must have been tough, and for your dad too bringing you up on his own.'

'He usually found someone to help him out. My father was a very charming man. Never short of company.'

'And you didn't mind – about his *company*?'

'God, no. Most of them spoiled me rotten. I'm surprised I've got any teeth left with the amount of sweets they used to bribe me with. And I never felt they were a threat – they came and went at regular intervals. Some of them I liked more than others but I never had time to get particularly attached.' She sighed into the warm curve of his shoulder. 'But then, unfortunately, he met Lesley.'

'Ah,' he said.

'Ah indeed. The one who *didn't* get away. Five foot three of pure blonde ambition. She was years younger than him but that didn't bother her. They met during one of his more lucrative periods and she decided she was definitely on to a good thing. An *accidental* pregnancy quickly followed and the rest, as they say, is history.' She lifted her head and frowned. 'God, am I sounding horribly bitter and twisted?'

'Yes,' he said, 'but carry on.'

She settled back against him. 'That's about it really. Terry was born, the marriage stumbled on for about five years, she took him for everything she could and then dumped him for a richer man.'

'Did she break his heart?'

She laughed. 'No, only his wallet.' But then she

wondered if that was true. Perhaps he *had* truly loved her because he had never been quite the same after. Somehow all his energy and spirit had drained away. There were no more smart ideas, no brilliant cons. He had started to gamble more and to lose more and had finally ended up in this tiny flat in the back streets of Norwich.

'What are you thinking about?'

'Nothing,' she said. 'So tell me about *your* family?'

'There's not much to tell. I've got a couple of sisters, one living in Sydney, the other still in Surrey. My dad's a banker – you know, the high-flying City type – and my mum's a housewife who lunches. They have a nice big house in the green belt, three cars, a conservatory, and a golden retriever.'

'Mr Posh,' she quipped.

'That's me. He wanted me to go into banking too but, Christ, just the very idea bored me to distraction.'

'No, I can't see it somehow. You don't strike me as a behind-a-desk kind of guy.'

He shifted slightly, his leg pressing against hers. 'Oh yeah? And what kind of guy *do* you see me as?'

It might just be her imagination but the temperature seemed to have risen a few degrees. In an exploratory foray, she slid her palm across his chest. 'Oh, more the action type, the sort who likes to get involved, to get things done. But most of all – without a shadow of a doubt – a man who loves to be in charge.'

He leaned over, his breath hot against her ear. 'I hope you're not calling me a control freak, Ms Weston.'

She kissed the side of his throat. 'No, just a professional. A man who takes pride in what he does best. Talking of which, haven't you got some poor unsuspecting victim you should be fixing with an icy stare right now? I wouldn't like to think that I'm distracting you from your work.'

'Hey, it's touching that you're so concerned.' His fingers roamed along the nape of her neck and down the first few inches of her spine. 'But the one great advantage of being an inspector is that you can occasionally delegate and leave the dirty work to your sergeant.'

'And I'm sure he's very good at it too,' she purred. 'Once he makes it up the stairs.' Her hand found its way on to his thigh again. She ran her fingers slowly, exploratively, from the curve of his knee towards his groin.

'Mm,' he murmured. 'Shepherd's not exactly in the best of condition.'

'He certainly didn't look too good yesterday.'

It was an innocuous comment but, as if he'd been slapped, Jack suddenly recoiled. He jerked his leg away and stared at her. 'He was here yesterday?'

The mood was instantly broken again. Eve tried not to groan. It seemed, after a promising start, that she was doomed to an evening of perpetual frustration. It never happened like this in romantic novels: by now his hungry lips should have been searching out hers, her breasts crushed against the hardness of his chest, her body ravished. But for the second time in an hour, her desires had been well and truly thwarted.

'Don't you two ever talk to each other?' she said.

'What did he want?'

She wished she'd never mentioned it. 'I don't know. He didn't say. He came to see Sonia but she's still staying at her daughter's. I presumed it was to do with what happened to Peter.'

'Jesus, that man can't leave anything alone.'

She looked at him, confused. 'What do you mean?'

'It doesn't matter.'

'So why are you getting so stressed about it?'

'I'm not,' he insisted. 'It's just that I was out of the office yesterday and didn't get a chance to talk to him.' He picked up his glass and took a few sips of wine.

'Look, I probably shouldn't be saying this, and I'm counting on you not to repeat it, but he can be a bit . . . less than sensitive at times. And he's had a few run-ins with Peter Marshall in the past. Sudden deaths are always a shock and I know she was separated from him but I was worried that he might have . . .'

'Put his size tens in it?'

He forced a smile. 'Something like that. And we get enough bad press as it is.'

'Well, if he did, he didn't do it here. And I wouldn't worry; Sonia's more than capable of taking care of herself.' She was about to add *I think they have some history* when she thought better of it. It was none of her business. 'Anyway, he looked like he was about to drop.'

'He always looks like that.'

Eve waited until he put down his glass before settling against his shoulder. Resigned to the fact that unbridled lust was temporarily off the agenda, she decided to embark on a few discreet inquiries of her own.

'So how's the investigation going?'

'There is no investigation,' he said. 'It was an accidental death. There'll be an inquest of course but there isn't any doubt that he drowned.'

'Not Peter Marshall,' she said. 'The other guy. Patterson, was it?'

'Oh *him*. No, that's nothing to do with us any more. It's in the capable hands of MIT.'

'Really?' Eve asked, confused. She opened her mouth to say, *Perhaps someone should tell that sergeant of yours*, but smartly closed it again. Whatever Shepherd's motives for showing her the photograph, Jack clearly knew nothing about it. 'So you're completely off the case?'

'Yeah, why?'

'No reason.' She ran a finger along the fine silky hair on his forearm. 'I was just curious.'

Chapter Twenty-Four

Henry Baxter couldn't put his finger on exactly what was bothering him. It was more an atmosphere than anything solid, a tension, a peculiar sense that the people around him were walking on eggshells.

Louise had come into the office twice, dropped off his typing, and then waited by his desk as if about to speak. On both occasions he had lifted his head and asked, 'Was there anything else?' But she had only paused, given him a vague smile and then scurried out again. He hoped she wasn't about to hand in her notice. Despite his early doubts, she had settled in quite well. At least she was reliable; she didn't spend the whole day filing her nails and didn't even seem to gossip. Then again, this dusty basement was hardly the most exciting place for a young girl to be interred. He shouldn't be selfish. Perhaps he should have a word, broach the subject with her . . .

But not right now. He wasn't in the mood for awkward conversations; there were too many other things on his mind. And top of the list was Richard. He was being unusually solicitous which meant he either wanted something or had already *done* something he knew his father would strongly disapprove of.

This morning he had turned up with a frothy cappuccino from the local Starbucks. 'Hey, how's it going?'

'To what do I owe the honour?' he had said drily.

Richard planted his elegant backside on the edge of his desk. 'Just thought I'd touch base, see how you are.'

'I'm quite well, thank you.'

'Good. Good, that's excellent. I wanted to check that everything's okay between us, you know, after all that rotten business with . . .'

Henry noticed how he couldn't actually bring himself to say her name. 'Eve Weston?'

'Yes, right.' His mouth shifted into a thin nervous smile. 'And so it's all fine down here?'

'What are you after, Richard?'

'Nothing,' he said too quickly, his eyes shifting slyly to the side. He attempted a laugh that didn't quite come off. 'Lord, it's a poor show if I can't pop down and see the old man once in a while without being accused of having ulterior motives.'

Henry was tempted to claim that he *always* had ulterior motives but, recalling what he had promised Celia, took a deep breath and exercised the last remaining morsels of his paternal restraint.

'No recriminations,' she had insisted. 'I don't want you taking this out on our son.' She had said it as if Richard was the innocent one, the victim, rather than the instigator of the current conflict in their marriage. 'Do you promise?'

'Yes, of course.'

So he'd held his tongue and as a result still didn't have a clue what he was up to. Had Richard been a nicer person he might have given him the benefit of the doubt, believed that he was trying to make amends, perhaps even showing some signs of remorse – but Richard wasn't nice. He didn't even come close. And he certainly wasn't sorry for telling Celia about Eve. No, whatever was going on, it had nothing to do with a guilty conscience.

Finally Richard had stood up. 'Well, so long as you're okay.' But then instead of leaving, he'd continued to hover, his gaze roaming over the papers on Henry's desk. 'I don't suppose . . . I mean, you haven't been having any problems with your mail recently, have you?'

'Not that I've noticed.'

'Good. Glad to hear it. Only I'm not too sure about that new receptionist. She's not exactly on the ball, is she? In fact she barely seems to know what day of the week it is.'

Henry couldn't resist the easy jibe. 'You employed her.'

'Yes, well,' he said, defensively. 'I'm sure it's only teething problems. She's bright enough. I'm sure she'll get the hang of it.'

'Eventually.'

But still he didn't leave. 'It's just that we got some of your mail the other day and you got some of ours.'

'That's hardly unusual.' Henry stared up at him. He couldn't figure out if this was his real reason for being here or simply an excuse for continuing the conversation. 'Are you missing something?'

'No. Absolutely not. Well, not as far as I know.'

'Because I'm sure Louise would have dealt with any post that was misdirected.'

'Yes, of course she would.'

There was a short silence.

Henry was the first to speak again. 'Well, thank you for the coffee.'

'It's a pleasure.'

On his way out, Richard stopped to have a few words with Louise. Henry had strained his ears but the adjoining door was closed and he could only catch the occasional murmur. Were they discussing the post that wasn't missing or something completely different? He would have liked to know – perhaps Richard was trying to lure her back upstairs – but couldn't bring himself to ask her. It would have felt like he was spying.

Henry glanced at his watch. It was approaching midday now and he was having problems concentrating. He had always thought of himself as a mild-mannered man, content with his lot, but recently had been growing increasingly restless. Some kind of delayed mid-life crisis perhaps. A few more years and he'd be forced into retirement. The idea filled him with gloom and despair.

Surely there was still time for a little adventure before he put on his slippers?

He reached down into his briefcase, took out the sheet of paper he'd been working on last night, laid it on his desk and smoothed it down with the back of his hand. Eve's troubles were preying on his mind. He had called her yesterday after she'd been to visit Terry.

'Can you talk?'

'Hold on a minute.'

'What's wrong?'

'I'm okay,' she'd claimed.

But he could hear from her voice that she wasn't. She sounded flustered, out of breath, as if she'd been running. 'What's happened?'

'I'm fine, really I am.' She had gone on to mention about a woman having picked a row with her at the prison, a misunderstanding to do with that Cavelli character, but then had instantly dismissed it. 'It was just one of those things. It's not important. What I really wanted to tell you is that he was right, Terry *was* more involved than I realized. He came clean. He was there at the robbery but it's not connected to the other stuff. I'm sure it's not.'

Henry knew most of the 'other stuff' but still sensed she wasn't telling him everything. It had taken another few minutes to squeeze out the information about the warning on the door. And when she'd finally told him he had drawn in his breath. 'God, you can't let this carry on. You have to—'

She had cut him off mid-sentence. 'What? Go to the cops? I don't think so. That's only going to make it worse.'

'How could it get worse?'

'Because that sergeant's already been sniffing around. You know, Shepherd, the one that came to see you, the one that was asking all the questions. He showed me a photo, a picture of a guy who was killed a few days ago. And, it's just that . . .' She hesitated.

Henry held his tongue, not interrupting, understanding that it was best to wait.

'He was a private detective,' she said eventually. 'Ivor Patterson. And I *think* I recognized him. I couldn't swear to it, I could be wrong, way off the mark, but he may have been the man who followed me to Blakeney.'

What kind of danger did that put Eve in? A wave of panic, of bile, had risen sourly from Henry's stomach to his throat – *a man who had followed her, a man who was now dead* – but he had quickly swallowed it down. He tried to keep his voice calm and reasonable. 'But surely that's even more reason to go to the police.'

'No,' she insisted. 'Because I don't know, I'm not sure he was the same man and even if he was, if he *is* related to everything else, then talking to the cops isn't going to help. It's a murder inquiry and if I step forward then I'm going to put myself bang in the middle of it all. The minute they think I might be connected they'll latch on to me and never let go. And apart from the fact that being dragged in and questioned for hours on end isn't my idea of a great time, they're going to want to know everything, all the finer details, and that's bound to lead back to Terry and I just can't afford to go there at the moment.'

He listened as she lit a cigarette and exhaled.

'I'm not saying never, I promise, but I need a few more days, some time to think about it.'

'Anything can happen in a few days.'

'I'll be careful.'

'You can't deal with this on your own.'

'I can deal with it in whatever way I like,' she snapped. And then she'd sighed and said: 'Sorry, I didn't mean to sound so . . . I'm sorry, I know you're only trying to help. It's just that I don't feel it's the right way forward. There are too many unknowns, too many blanks. I don't like Shepherd and I don't trust him.'

Henry couldn't argue with that. He hadn't been too keen on the man himself. But he was even less keen on Eve being exposed to unnecessary risk. 'I don't like to think of you alone in the flat. Isn't there anyone who could come and stay with you for a while?'

'Sonia's back tonight. She's only across the hall. I'll be okay. Honestly, don't worry.'

But of course he was going to worry. How could he not? He had promised to give her a call at the weekend. If he could think of a good enough excuse he might even get down for a day. In the meantime, all he had to offer was his brains and his logic. He carefully smoothed out the piece of paper again and stared down at it.

The initials AW, for Alexander Weston, lay at the top of the sheet. From there two lines descended to EW and TW, Eve and Terry. Under Eve he had listed Cavelli, Ivor Patterson, and an X for the man who had attacked her in the alley. There was also Paula (Cavelli's former wife – or was she still his wife?), Nadine, and Barry, the man who had fixed the door. As a final thought he had added Patrick, Sonia, and Peter Marshall, none of them particularly suspects but all connected to Eve. Under Terry's initials he had written The Rowans, and then Lesley and Vince Player. In the blank space between the two lists he had put Joe with a question mark and then directly underneath him, Shepherd.

So there it all was in black and white. And four of these people were already dead. Henry ran over the names again and thought about it. Was anyone missing? He raised his eyes to glance at Louise through the glass window in his door. It reminded him of Richard's visit this morning, which in turn reminded him of what he'd done to Eve. But his own son couldn't have anything to do with *this* business, could he? He might hate Eve but he'd already achieved what he'd set out to do – to banish her forever from the hallowed ground of Baxter & Baxter. Unless he'd somehow found out that he was still seeing her and . . . But no, Richard might be a lot of things, vindictive being just one of them, but even *he* wouldn't go this far. However, it couldn't be denied that he had been acting oddly and . . .

Reluctantly, Henry picked up his pen and added Richard's initials in tiny print and in brackets to the bottom of the list. He felt an instinctive urge to strike them out again – but didn't. No matter how uncomfortable it might make him feel, it wasn't entirely out of the bounds of possibility that in some minor way, hidden in the murky depths of this whole despicable mess, Richard might be playing a part.

Henry had given up smoking over thirty years ago but suddenly felt the urge to take a pack from his pocket, run a cigarette between his fingers, lift it slowly to his mouth and light it. He wondered what Philip Marlowe would do in the same circumstances. Probably exactly that, while he drank a pint of bourbon, put his feet up on the desk and tried to piece it all together. But then Marlowe hadn't been an old-fashioned solicitor and he hadn't had a wife called Celia.

She had come quietly into his study last night and

peered over his shoulder. 'Dinner's almost ready. What are you working on?'

It was fortunate that he'd only been using initials. 'Oh, nothing important. Bit of a tricky problem with a will. I'm working through the family tree.'

Since when had he learned to lie with such ease? The answer came back with surprising rapidity: since they had ceased to confide in each other, since she had taken Richard's side over his, since she had stopped trusting him.

Why couldn't she trust him?

Then again, had their situations been reversed – had she been taking secret walks with a charismatic good-looking man, leading a private life apart from him – would he have believed that it was completely innocent, that *nothing* was going on? The idea made him shudder, as if by simply thinking about it he might inadvertently make it happen.

He did feel bad about deceiving her, about still being in contact with Eve. Of course he did. Through all their years together, Celia had taken care of him, supported him, loved him. They were a partnership. He loved her too but didn't know what to say or how to behave to make things better. And he didn't want to have to tell more lies. By constantly apologizing he could only be admitting to a crime he wasn't guilty of – adultery had never been on the agenda – but the truth was something he could barely begin to explain.

And so they sat on either side of the dining table, making small talk, discussing his day, discussing hers, while this massive obstacle – like some almighty elephant they were both ignoring – remained firmly lodged between them.

The only way forward was to give Eve up. He would have to do it eventually. But not yet. It wasn't possible yet. He was too involved. He couldn't just walk away.

They were friends and to abandon her now, whatever the cost, would be the ultimate betrayal.

So what next? Henry picked up the piece of paper, folded it over and thrust it into his pocket. He needed to get out of the office. He needed some fresh air.

Micky had been following Patrick Fielding for most of the morning. Although the word *following* was somewhat of an exaggeration: at ten o'clock he'd watched him go and collect some groceries from the shop across the road and return to his flat where he'd remained for the next couple of hours.

He'd been about to give up hope – perhaps the bastard was going to spend the rest of the day indoors – when he'd finally appeared again, walked down the street and hopped on a bus to Islington. Micky had stuck on its tail until Fielding got off. Pulling up the car by the busy Upper Street bus stop, he watched him cross the road and enter one of the local fancy bars. He turned to stare at the man beside him. 'You ready?'

He didn't look ready. He looked grey, sick, like a man who was suffering from one almighty hangover. But then Jimmy Reece always looked like that before the clock struck one. A few stiff drinks and he'd be back to his own charming self.

'So what am I supposed to ask him?'

Micky sighed. 'We've been through it, haven't we? How many more times? You're not supposed to ask him fucking anything. Don't try and lead him, just let him talk. Let him ask you what he wants to ask. And don't take your jacket off.'

Reece immediately felt inside his jacket to the wires that were running under his shirt.

'And don't do that either,' he said. 'You want to draw attention to yourself?'

Reece frowned. 'What if he's already meeting someone? What am I supposed to do then?'

'Since when did you become so bloody shy? I'm sure you'll think of something. I'll park the car and come back. Make sure you keep him here, okay. If he's not already ordered, be friendly and offer to buy him lunch.' Micky reached into his pocket and took out three twenty-pound notes. 'And we're not a fucking charity,' he said, 'so don't even think about taking the piss. No champagne, stick to the house wine, and I want the change *and* a receipt.'

Jimmy nodded, the incentive of free booze brightening his eyes. He grabbed the cash, got out of the car, and then stood for a second on the kerb before walking straight across the street. A couple of cars screeched to a halt, their horns blaring. Micky closed his eyes. Jesus! Just how crazy was this guy? It was only when he opened them again that he was able to relax. By some miracle – perhaps with the help of the patron saint who looks after useless drunks – he had managed to make it safely across to the other side.

By the time Micky had dropped off the car and walked back, they were sitting outside together. If Fielding was meeting anyone else they hadn't turned up yet. A bottle of wine, unsurprisingly, had been opened and Jimmy's first glass was almost empty. Micky took a seat a few tables away and settled down with his paper. He deliberately avoided looking at Reece; the jerk was edgy enough already. A waitress came out and he ordered a sandwich and a coffee. Then he got on the phone and quickly passed the message on to Gruber. 'Go for it,' he said softly. 'We're all clear. You should have an hour or so.'

He leaned back in his chair and tried to eavesdrop on their conversation. He was close but not close enough to hear what they were saying. The sound of the traffic drowned out everything else. Typical, he thought, that they'd chosen to sit outside. Not only was it noisy but it was cold as well; although the sun was shining there was a chill wind whistling down the street.

He'd been planning on having a beer and then heading up West – until Jimmy Reece had appeared. Suddenly, there he was, strolling past with that slightly rolling gait of his, hands in his pockets, gazing idly around. For a second, as their eyes met, he thought his face hadn't registered but then Reece stopped, frowned, put out a couple of fingers like some gangster in a movie, grinned and said: 'Hey, it's Patrick, isn't it?'

'Jimmy!'

They'd gone through the usual rigmarole, exchanging pleasantries, smiles, handshakes etc.

'So how's it going?'

'Good, good.'

And from there it had only been one small step to agreeing to lunch. Why not? Okay, he'd felt a momentary pang of guilt, recalling what he'd promised Evie, about not getting in touch with Reece again, about not interfering, but it passed without having too much impact on his conscience. He hadn't planned this. It was just a chance meeting and perhaps, in addition to a free lunch – not an offer to be casually passed over – he could find out something useful.

'Do you mind explaining what you were doing there?' Raynor said. He sounded more resigned than annoyed as if Eddie Shepherd's visit to Herbert Street was further proof, if it was needed, of his inability to obey the simplest of orders.

Eddie assumed an expression of hurt innocence. 'I don't see the problem, guv. I only popped in to see

Sonia Marshall, check that she was okay – you know, some of that caring sharing policing that the Chief Constable's so keen on, and—'

'Bollocks!' he said. 'You were showing Eve Weston a photograph of Patterson. Why?'

Eddie wondered how he'd got to hear about that – unless he'd been round there himself recently. Perhaps he was conducting his own, more private inquiries, into the leggy redhead. 'Just a shot in the dark. I had it on me so I thought, why not?'

'Because it's not our case any more. It's nothing to do with us. And why should *she* know anything about it?'

'She recognized him,' Eddie said.

That stopped Raynor in his tracks. 'What?'

'Well, okay, not exactly *recognized* him but she thought he looked familiar, that she might have seen him around.'

'He was a private detective, tramping the streets. It's not a huge city. I'm sure thousands of people saw him around.'

'But odd, don't you reckon, that she maybe saw him around Herbert Street? He doesn't live near there and according to Paul Clark he wasn't working there either. So what are we looking at? Is it just a coincidence that these two guys who died on the same night and—'

'Marshall's death was an accident,' Raynor sighed. 'He got pissed, fell into the river and drowned.'

'Not necessarily.'

'What's that supposed to mean?'

Eddie picked up the pathology report and handed it to him. 'It means that yeah, he drowned all right but, according to our friend Pugh, he may have had some help.'

Raynor flicked quickly through the pages but didn't seem impressed. 'So there was some bruising on the shoulder? So what? It's not conclusive. Far from it.'

'It suggests that someone may have stopped him getting out.'

'Or that he did it before he fell in or that it happened while he was in the water, when he was struggling to reach the bank.' He dropped the report down on his desk. 'This doesn't prove a thing.'

Eddie didn't like his theories being dismissed out of hand. 'Oh, I dunno,' he said. 'It could prove that you were right about our flame-haired temptress. She does seem to be the common denominator in everything that's been happening recently. Perhaps she and Cavelli *are* involved in something big.' He didn't believe it for a minute – she was small-time, a grifter's daughter – but he watched with pleasure as Raynor's lips narrowed into a thin straight line.

'This has *nothing* to do with her,' he snapped.

Eddie heard the defensive anger in his voice and smirked. Yeah, he'd definitely hit the spot with that one. Now he was certain that the inspector's interest in the Weston bint was more than professional. And having put the knife in, he couldn't resist twisting it. 'Three deaths, all of them connected to Herbert Street. There has to be some connection. Or perhaps bad luck just follows her around.'

Raynor glowered at him. 'One suicide, one accident, and one murder that has little if anything to do with Herbert Street. What kind of dubious connection, exactly, is that?'

'You're probably right.' Eddie scratched at his nose, at the thin scab that was forming just below his left nostril. 'Only theorizing, guv, keeping the little grey cells ticking over.'

'Well, if you're looking for something useful to occupy your mind, how about dealing with these?' Raynor flung a pile of files at him. 'Four burglaries, in as many days, on the Richmond Estate. The Residents' Association are up in arms so if you're not *too* busy theorizing . . .'

'I'll get right on to it.'

Raynor picked up his jacket from the back of his chair and flipped it over his shoulder. 'I've got a meeting. We'll catch up later.'

Eddie waited until the door had swung closed before lifting his eyes to the ceiling. He'd been deliberately winding him up but it hadn't been a complete pile of bullshit. Pushing the files to one side, he leaned over and took out another from the top drawer of his desk. Opening it, he stared down at its contents: copies of the reports on Alexander Weston, on Peter Marshall, on Ivor Patterson. There *was* a connection, a thread, running between all the deaths. And it *was* Eve Weston. No matter which way you looked at it, no matter which way you turned it around, her name came up again and again.

Chapter Twenty-Five

Joe Silk shook his head and snapped off the tape. He was no nearer to the truth. That drunken shit Reece was a waste of space. What had he been listening to? Two hours of them filling their faces, swilling down the wine he'd paid for, while they talked about films, women and bloody football.

He poured himself another Scotch. 'Fuck all,' he said, looking up at Chase. 'What about the flat?'

'Likewise. Gruber turned the place inside out. There's no sign.'

Joe didn't get it; he'd just given Fielding the perfect opportunity to continue what he and Evie had started in Soho. But he hadn't taken the bait. Whatever they were up to, they had planned to use Reece – they *must* have – so what was going on? A change of plan perhaps. Did they know that he was on to them? 'Maybe they're just being careful. Maybe the whole Patterson thing has spooked them.'

Chase folded his arms across his chest, expelling one of his long bitter sighs. 'Or maybe they're just taking the fucking piss. We're wasting time,' he said. 'This is getting us nowhere. Let's go get her. The longer this goes on, the more chance there is of—'

'No. Not yet.' Joe waved away his protest with a sweep of his hand. 'She must be getting worried by now. She has to be. And the more worried she is, the more likely she is to panic, and when that happens – and it's going to be soon – she's going to start making mistakes.'

Eve took the call at half past three in the afternoon. It took her a moment to recognize the voice and a few further seconds to decipher the angry exclamations and translate them into any kind of sense.

'Everything . . . can't believe it . . . ruined . . .'

'Patrick?'

'The flat's been turned over. Jesus, I just got back and . . .'

She felt her heart sink. 'You've had a break-in?'

'More like a visit from a wrecking crew. It's been trashed, Evie. They've busted the door, ripped up the carpets, emptied all the cupboards, the fridge – shit, I've got three pizzas defrosting on the floor – they even slashed the mattress on the bed. It's a mess, a bloody disaster area . . .'

'God, I'm sorry.'

'It's not your fault,' he said. And then he paused. 'But please tell me it's just a coincidence that I met Jimmy Reece today.'

She frowned, her sympathy swiftly turning on its axis. Her voice lifted an octave. 'What? You met Jimmy Reece? Why? You promised me you wouldn't. You swore. You said—'

'Christ, please don't turn this back on me. I didn't *deliberately* meet him. I didn't make any arrangement. He met *me*, just turned up out of the blue and bought me lunch while—'

'While someone turned over your flat.'

'Yeah, but—'

'But nothing,' she said. 'Didn't you think that was odd

– Jimmy just turning up like that? Just a little bit too much of a coincidence?'

'No!' he snapped back. 'It's London. People are always just turning up.'

'And offering to buy you lunch?'

There was a long silence at the other end of the line. 'Fuck,' he eventually said.

And she knew that *he* knew that he'd been well and truly stitched up.

'Fuck!' he said again, and then sighed. 'The bastard was just keeping me out of the way, wasn't he?'

'It looks like that.'

There was another shorter silence. She heard him take a couple of deep frustrated breaths.

'Patrick?'

'I'm still here. So, do you want to tell me what the hell is going on? Because this really isn't making any sense or at least not the kind of sense that I want to think about – and as I'm standing in the ruins of what I used to call my home and—'

'I'm sorry,' she said.

'Is this to do with Cavelli?'

She paused. 'I don't know. Maybe. But why would it be? What would he have to gain by it?' Which reminded her that she hadn't opened those boxes yet. She felt an urge to run into the bedroom and drag them out from the bottom of the wardrobe but instead she rubbed her knuckles against her forehead, trying to decide what to tell and what not to. She hadn't wanted to involve Patrick in the first place – *he'd* been the one who'd insisted on meeting her in Soho – but it was too late to worry about that now. 'Was anything taken?'

'God knows,' he almost wailed. 'I haven't exactly taken an inventory.'

'Sorry,' she murmured again. 'Look, maybe you

371

should go away for a while, stay with a friend or something.'

'Sure,' he said. 'As soon as you tell me what's going on.'

'I can't. I mean, I would if I knew but I don't. But I'm going to find out. Just give me a few days.'

'Evie, for God's sake, if you're in trouble – I mean any *more* trouble than with this whole Terry business – then you have to tell me, you have to—'

'I'll call you. I promise.' And then before he had time to make any more demands she said a quick goodbye and put the receiver down. She stood for a moment, her mind racing, while she tried to slot the facts together. What was going on? First her own break-in, then the man in the alley, then Ivor Patterson – she shivered as she thought about what had happened to him – then the warning on the door, and now Patrick. But as hard as she thought, she couldn't make any sense of it. It was like a jigsaw puzzle with half the pieces of the sky missing.

She shook her head and glanced towards the bedroom. There was, however, *something* she could do: it was time to open those boxes, to find out what was really inside them. She'd put it off for long enough. And surely, if she explained, Cavelli would understand? She grimaced. Well, maybe not, but she'd cross that bridge when she came to it.

First, she went to the kitchen and found a sharp knife. If she opened them neatly enough it might be possible to disguise the fact she'd ever looked inside. All she'd have to do was buy some fresh dark red tape – if she could find any – and seal them up again.

Slowly, she crossed back to the room, the knife clenched tightly in her right hand like a nervous intruder. There was still time to change her mind . . . but no, she mustn't. There were men out there – impatient *angry* men – who believed she was hiding something, men who thought that she might have passed what they wanted on to Patrick. Wasn't that why his flat had been broken into? Her forehead crunched into a frown. But then how had Jimmy Reece got involved? Had he realized Cavelli was coming after him again and . . .

There was no point going over and over it. All she was doing was tangling her thoughts into knots. 'Actions, not words,' she murmured. Forcing herself to step into the bedroom, she knelt down and dragged out the two boxes. Which one first? The larger one. She lifted her hand but then hesitated. She could suddenly hear Paula saying, 'Whatever you do, don't open them. Martin's paranoid about his stuff.' Maybe she was making an almighty mistake. Well, sod it! Better that than being doomed to a state of perpetual ignorance. Then, before she could lose her nerve, she ran the point of the knife cleanly through the centre of the tape.

Eve sat back on her heels, stunned by the enormity of what she'd just done. Mutual trust – that had been her deal with Cavelli: he took care of Terry and in return she took care of his possessions. But it was too late now for regrets. What was done was done.

Tentatively pulling back the flaps she peered inside.

Her first impression, as she'd lugged it up the stairs, had been right – it *was* full of books. No gold bullion, drugs or diamonds. She wasn't sure what she felt. Disappointment or relief? If she'd been hoping for some kind of revelation, for any kind of lead, it certainly wasn't here. Lifting them out, one by one, piling them up beside her feet, she quickly flicked through the pages to make sure that nothing was hidden between the leaves. It was fiction mainly and not the type of stuff she'd expect Cavelli to read – Jackie Collins and Danielle Steele, a few mystery thrillers, along with some classics like *Little Women*, *Emma*, and *Pride and Prejudice*. Not his, she was certain, so they must have been someone else's.

Nadine's? That thought made her pause again. The notion that she was carelessly rustling through the books of a dead woman, a woman whose fingers must have touched the very same pages, a woman who had once lived and breathed and . . .

Eve packed them all back into the cardboard box and pushed it gently aside. Then, working on the age-old premise that you may as well be hanged for a sheep as a lamb, she took a deep breath and cut through the tape on the smaller box. As she reached inside, it didn't take her long to realize that the items in here were even more intimate, more personal, than the books she had just been rummaging through. There was a bundle of letters, about twenty, still in their original envelopes, fastened with an elastic band. They were all addressed to Martin Cavelli in the same sloping, slightly childish hand. She took them out and laid them carefully on the carpet. Next, she found a narrow hard-backed envelope containing his marriage certificate. Underneath that was a small glossy folder, the type you got from any photographic processing company. She opened it and took out the pictures. A woman in a striped bikini smiled brightly up at her. It had to be Nadine. She was smiling, laughing, sitting on a beach. She was slim, with long straight brown hair and expressive brown eyes. Her skin was the colour of honey. She was pretty, no, more than pretty: she had the kind of enviable good looks that didn't rely on make-up, that were natural rather than contrived.

Eve flicked quickly through the snaps, nearly all of Nadine, on the beach, by a pool, at a palm-fronted restaurant, only pausing when she found a few of Cavelli. She stopped briefly to stare at this man, this stranger in whom – either smartly or stupidly (only time would tell) – she had temporarily placed her faith. She tried to read his eyes. They were happier of course than the ones she had met in the prison but still dark, still faintly distrustful, as if the world was not a place in which it was ever safe to relax.

She moved on to the few remaining pieces: a cheap bead necklace, a charm bracelet and a couple of brooches, all carefully wrapped in tissue paper. She found the final, and possibly most important possession, in a tiny powder-blue box buried in the corner. Opening it, she discovered a simple gold band. Nadine's wedding ring? She took it out and held it up. Yes, it was too small to be his. She wondered if he'd taken it when he'd gone to see Jimmy Reece or if she had left it behind in one of those dreadful final gestures.

Why had Cavelli kept all this stuff? Out of love perhaps, nostalgia, sentiment, or because of some more disturbing obsession? And she tried to imagine what their relationship had been like, what had drawn them to each other, what kind of a woman Nadine had been and why she had chosen to leave him. Eve couldn't claim any fondness for Cavelli but she found Jimmy Reece equally, if not more, repugnant. The memory of Soho, of his predatory confidence, of his clammy hand snaking optimistically up her thigh, made her skin crawl. Although, perhaps, it wasn't fair to judge him too harshly; she'd only made his acquaintance after Cavelli had rearranged the contours of his face, and that, inevitably, was enough to mar any man's personality.

She carefully began to place everything back in the exact position she had found it. It was only as she picked up the bundle of letters again that her curiosity went into overdrive. Now that she'd taken the risk of opening the boxes, of completely pissing off Cavelli, wouldn't it be a wasted opportunity if she didn't grab the chance to find out what she could about him? And what better way than through the letters from Nadine.

She shouldn't read them, she knew she shouldn't but . . .

Eve sat down on the bed, removed the two folded

sheets from the first envelope, and started to read. She hadn't got further than the first line, *My darling Martin*, when the phone began to ring again. Should she leave it? It was probably Patrick, all geared up with another round of questions that she wouldn't be able to answer. But she felt too guilty to ignore him. It was her fault, after all, that he'd got home to find his flat in ruins.

Reluctantly, she walked back into the living room and picked it up. 'Hello.'

'Eve?'

And surprisingly, it wasn't Patrick's voice at all, but Henry's. 'Hey,' she said, relieved. 'Guess what?'

'Is everything all right?' Henry never had been good at guessing games.

'Yes, fine. But I've just opened the boxes and there's nothing in them. Well, I don't mean nothing exactly but nothing nasty, only personal stuff, letters and things.'

'That's good . . . isn't it?'

'Absolutely.'

'So?'

'So?'

'So what else has happened?'

Eve smiled. What Henry lacked in guesswork, he made up for with an uncanny instinct for reading her mood. She spent the next few minutes explaining about the latest incident with Patrick. After she'd finished there was a moment of quiet from the other end.

'Have you thought any more about what we discussed?'

'I don't want to go the police. Not yet.'

'I think you should. I know you're worried about Terry but you're not going to be much use to him if . . .'

He didn't need to finish the sentence. She knew exactly what he meant. *If she was lying in a hospital bed or, horror of horrors, somewhere much worse. The same place Ivor Patterson was languishing right now.* 'I just need a bit more time. A few days.'

'You won't have to talk to Shepherd,' he said, still trying to persuade her.

And Eve was glad of the opportunity to change the subject. 'I can't stand that man. He's such a creep. I'll be happy if I never have to set eyes on him again. The other day, when he was leaving, he said he was sorry to hear about my father – as if he really gave a damn.' She snorted. 'Then you know what else he said? That the way he'd died was *very Virginia Woolf* – whatever that's supposed to mean.'

She waited for him to respond with an equal measure of contempt and bafflement but instead, as if he was thinking about it, he paused for a few seconds and then murmured, 'I suppose he had a point.'

Eve frowned down the line. 'Did he?' she said, peevishly.

Fortunately, Henry was never quick to take offence. He heard the irritation in her tone but kept his own voice soft and patient. 'She put stones in her pockets too before she walked into a river and . . .'

'Oh, I didn't realize.' She felt instant remorse for having snapped at him. Her nerves were so frayed, it had become something of a habit recently. Then she barked out a laugh. 'How strange! You know, he couldn't *stand* Virginia Woolf. He was always going on about her. He used to say she was a self-important, arrogant prig.' Actually, he had used a set of far more colourful words but she didn't want to make Henry's ears turn pink. 'Although he still read her books. He claimed that you didn't have to like an author in order to respect their writing.'

'True enough.'

Eve rubbed at her temples again. 'Although it is odd, isn't it? I mean, that he should do that, choose to . . . to die that way, in exactly the same way as someone he so clearly disliked. As if . . .'

'As if?' Henry echoed.

'I don't know.' She felt a smile creep on to her lips as an idea occurred to her. 'Perhaps it was some kind of final gesture, putting up two fingers at the world, at *her*, of showing that there wasn't that much of a difference between them, that it didn't take a genius to die that way.' She stopped and laughed again. 'Or am I reading far too much into this?'

'Not necessarily. It was rather a love/hate relationship, perhaps.'

'Yeah,' she agreed. 'Perhaps it was.' She was still thinking about it when, in the background, she heard the knock on his door.

'Could you hold on,' he said.

She heard the door open. There was a female voice, slight and rather hesitant. Probably his new secretary. 'Mr Evans is here. Should I show him in?'

Henry must have placed his hand over the receiver because the rest of the conversation was muffled. Eve waited, faintly wishing that she was back in that office again, safe and unafraid, her only worry that she might not get all the typing done by the time the clock struck five. There was a lot to be said for the mundane routine of office life, especially when compared to her current situation. She had never really been a nine-to-five kind of person – a few years ago the idea would have thoroughly dismayed her – but was starting to appreciate its advantages: a monthly pay packet, a decent employer and a mighty slice of security. She wondered what the new secretary was like. Louise – wasn't that her name? She probably knew her by sight but couldn't bring her face to mind.

'Sorry,' Henry said, coming back on the line. 'I have to go. I've got a client waiting. Can I call you back later?'

'Sure. That's okay.'

'But promise me you'll think about it, about what we mentioned, about talking to someone.'

'Of course,' she replied, without committing herself to anything.

They said their goodbyes and she put down the phone. The letters were still lying on the bed but she wasn't certain now if she should read them. Perhaps there had been something fateful about Henry ringing when he did, a kind of divine intervention. They were private after all, a dead woman's thoughts and feelings, only meant for one other person's eyes – and that person wasn't her.

Anyway, she needed a coffee and a cigarette. She needed to get her head together. All this talk about her father, about the manner of his death, had sent her thoughts spiralling off in a completely different direction.

She went through to the kitchen, put some water in the kettle and sat down while she waited for it to boil.

The fact that Shepherd had made a connection that she hadn't, that *he* had been the one to tell her something she should have already realized, made her wince. How many times had she listened to her father going on about Virginia Woolf? Except that was precisely the point – she never really *had* listened. Groaning, she lowered her head into her hands. How often had she switched off while he was talking to her, choosing to think instead about some minor problem of her own? She covered her face. She couldn't describe how she felt, even to herself. It was something beyond guilt, beyond grief, beyond anything she'd experienced before.

Eve wiped her cheeks with the back of her hand. There was no point crying about it. What was done was done and could never be changed. She should have realized, should have picked up on the connection but she hadn't.

There *had* been something important about the way he had chosen to die – she was sure of it now – but she had been too preoccupied to see it.

In a hiss of steam, the kettle boiled and turned itself off. She got up, threw a teaspoon of instant coffee into a mug and poured hot water over it. She gave the contents a fast stir, added some milk, and sat down again. Lighting a cigarette, she looked around. She stared at the cupboards, at the walls, at the drab chipped paint. There was nothing inspiring about what she saw.

Had he hated living here? She didn't know. She'd never thought to ask. They'd lived in worse places but they'd lived in far better too – in smart Mayfair flats, in fancy hotels, even in the occasional country house. In her childhood, like a pair of exiles, they'd roamed from one place to another, sometimes welcome, often not. It couldn't have been easy for him to have ended up here – everything lost, all his dreams in ruins.

She should have spent more time with him. Especially after he'd found out about his illness. Even now, she could hardly bring herself to say the word out loud. It made her stomach twist. *Cancer.* God, she had so many regrets. There were so many things she should have done, should have said.

And why had he lied, pretending that it wasn't so bad, that there was still plenty of time for them to spend together? She could almost see him smiling back at her. *To try and make it easier, to spare her the trials of obligation – and to spare him the agonies of a pity he could bear neither to see nor to hear.*

And then, like a lightning hit, it suddenly came to her – the meaning of those tiny squares of paper, the letters and numbers on the notes she had found, one of which she'd thrown away, the other she had accidentally put through the washing machine and then rescued and hidden in the toe of her winter boots. W1 – wasn't that what he'd written? Not a reference to a London district, perhaps, but a surname. Woolf. Was it all to do with her? With the woman he loved to hate? W1. Not a postal district but a reference to her first book, perhaps. What *was* her first book? Eve didn't have a clue.

She jumped up and almost ran back into the living room. Quickly, she scoured the shelves, pulling the paperbacks out – *Night and Day*, *Jacob's Room*, *The Voyage Out*, *Orlando* – while she as smartly dropped them back down on to the desk. Picking one up at random, she examined the complete list of Virginia Woolf's works. *The Voyage Out* was at the top.

She hastily picked it up again. For a moment, as she held the novel in her hands, she tried to recall the numbers that came after W1. Two hundred and something. Two hundred and what? She thought she had memorized it but her mind was a blank. She flicked through the pages but nothing caught her attention. Dashing into the bedroom, still holding the book, she pulled out her brown leather boots, fumbled in their toes and eventually found the hidden scrap of paper. She quickly unfolded it. W1/267/32/BC/8PR.

Sitting down on the floor, code in one hand and book in the other, she turned to page 267 and began reading from the top of the page. There was something about vagueness, about dogs and a garden and a woman called Rachel. What? No, this didn't make any sense. She glanced at the note again. The number 32 came next. She counted through the first thirty-one words then found herself staring at the word *asked*. Well, it wasn't entirely inappropriate but it hardly helped. She put the book down and sighed in frustration. She'd got it all wrong. She must have. What was she doing? Just chasing after rainbows, searching for clues that didn't exist.

Unless it was thirty-two *lines* . . .

She closed her eyes and slowly opened them again.

And then, speaking aloud – as if the surrounding silence might be her witness – she carefully counted them off, her finger sliding down the page. One, two, three . . .

She expected the outcome to be as disappointing as the previous one but as her gaze rolled down, as it finally came to rest on the line she'd been searching for, she stared at it in shock and amazement.

Helen turned to her. 'Did you go to church?' she asked.

She ran her finger across the line, reading it again. A shiver ran the length of her spine. Helen – the name of her mother. Churches – her father's obsession. Was that just a coincidence? A pair of coincidences? She read the line again. No, it couldn't be. It had to mean something.

And there was only one church around here that he'd frequented. Although it wasn't a church so much as one almighty towering cathedral . . .

She could feel her heart start to race, her mouth turning dry, as the truth began to dawn. All the madness of the last few weeks had nothing to do with Martin Cavelli or Terry – and everything to do with her father.

Chapter Twenty-Six

Eve pushed the square of paper into her pocket, snatched up her jacket and rushed out of the door. She took the stairs two at a time, spinning round the corner of the banisters on the first floor, stumbling, almost falling until she reached the flat ground of the foyer, covered it in six fast steps and burst out breathless on to the street.

Turning right, she shrugged into her jacket as she walked. It had started to rain again, a fine but penetrating drizzle that soaked into her hair and clothes. If she kept up the speed she could make it in fifteen minutes. Or she could take the car. No, the evening traffic would be building up; quicker to go by foot.

She cursed herself as she headed towards Tombland. How had she been so bloody stupid? He had left the notes for her to find, confident in her ability to make the connection. Well, he'd overestimated her intelligence. If it hadn't been for that creep Shepherd, for Henry, she might never have caught on. But then she sighed with exasperation. Why had he left so much to chance? If there was something he had wanted her to know, something so essential, why hadn't he just told her? There was no doubt in her mind now that whatever was hidden in the cathedral was the cause of all her recent troubles. And not just hers – if Ivor Patterson *had* been the man in the car . . .

She tried not to think about it, about the way the private detective had died. Now wasn't the time to start losing her nerve. But even as she pushed the thought aside, it was instantly replaced by the image of the hangman's noose emblazoned on her door. Damn! What had her father got involved in? And whatever the object was, whatever he had found or taken, why hadn't he simply returned it? There was only one possible answer: that to return it would be as deadly as to keep it.

But that still didn't account for why he hadn't warned her. Not even a hint. Surely, he must have realized what would happen? Once he was gone, they'd come after her and then . . . A wave of resentment rose in her breast. He wasn't a fool, far from it, so why place her in such a position? But the moment the question formed in her head, she felt guilty about it. He would never put her in deliberate danger. Something must have gone wrong. Something must have occurred to make him change his plans, to act more quickly than he'd intended. Had he tried to call her? Perhaps he had. She frowned, pained by the idea that she might not have been there when he needed her. But he could still have left a letter. Then again, if he had, he might have been worried that someone else would find it first – the people who were pursuing him or even the police. It would have been too much of a risk. Although he could have posted it. Perhaps he hadn't had a stamp. Or perhaps, like her, he suspected he was being shadowed and that anything he mailed would be instantly recovered.

Which promptly reminded her: what if she was being followed again? She forced herself to stare straight ahead, to ignore the impulse to glance back over her shoulder. If there was someone there, and they realized she was on to them, it would be twice as hard to lose them later.

Although her mind was still racing, she slowed her

pace a fraction. She didn't want to look as if she was in too much of a hurry. Weaving her way along the busy pavement, she tried to figure out if she could feel another person's scrutiny, but wasn't sure one way or another. Her instincts, usually pretty good, had been thoroughly scrambled.

As she crossed the bridge, she paused to stare down towards the grey water and then casually glanced to her left. A group of laughing teenagers, three boys and two girls, cruised by her. Nothing even slightly suspicious there. Next came a solitary male, mid-fifties, in a suit and clutching a briefcase. She waited until he'd gone a few yards before turning her head to look at him again. But he was strolling on relentlessly, eager to get home. A young woman came next pushing a pram, and then two older women. She lingered for a few minutes more, waiting and watching, letting a steady stream of people pass her by until she was fairly certain that the only person interested in what she was doing was herself.

Eve checked her watch: it was going on four fifteen. Did cathedrals have a closing time? Not in the old days perhaps but these days were different. The world was full of irreverent thieves and unless there was a service going on, she was sure that they'd be locking the doors before the light began to fade. That deadline was enough to urge her on. She couldn't wait until tomorrow. If there was something to find, she had to find it today. She couldn't take another sleepless night.

Completing the rest of the bridge, she dodged the traffic on the road, and crossed over to Erpingham Gate. As she stood at the entrance and gazed up at the cathedral, at its towering and imposing spire, she tried to recall the last time she'd been here – six, nine months ago? She had stood here with her father and he had told her about the riots, about the thirteenth-century conflict between the church and the city. It had been something to do with tolls, with taxes, with the eternal battle between the rich and the poor. She couldn't recall the details, she hadn't been listening closely enough, but she knew there'd been fighting, violence, and that William de somebody had let his monks take their bloody retribution.

As she walked towards the entrance, she turned again to look behind her. The path was empty. If anyone was following they were keeping their distance. Or maybe her pursuers were all too busy trashing flats in London.

At the door she shook the rain from her hair and took a deep breath before advancing inside. Instantly, as if a heavy curtain had been drawn behind her, all the sounds of the city were silenced. Moving forward into the long narrow nave, she became immediately aware of the vaulted ceiling, of its immensity, its height, and of her own comparative smallness. She was flanked either side by a series of pale stone arches. Overwhelmed, she took a step back. How would she find anything in here?

It would help if she knew what it was. She could only take a guess: something small, easily hidden, slight enough not to be accidentally discovered. She dug into her pocket and glanced at the scrap of paper again. The remaining part of the code was BC/8PR. She pondered on the BC – Before Christ? Well, that wasn't going to make it any easier. There must be endless images of Christ in the building. It would be like searching for a needle in a haystack.

Trying to think back, to recall anything her father might have said, she slowly advanced again. She inhaled the smell, dense and musty. The air felt heavy as if it strained beneath the weight of too much history. She wasn't alone; other visitors, tourists, wandered here and there, constantly stopping to view some item of interest, to refer to their glossy guides, before shuffling on, their broken footsteps giving the impression of hesitancy, their voices reverentially low. Only the people who worked there moved with any speed, their briskness vaguely startling as they swept past.

Perhaps she should go back to the shop and buy a guidebook. It might give her some clues. She considered the idea and then rejected it. If all else failed, she'd pick one up on her way out, take it home and study it there. For now, she'd just follow her nose, and her instincts, and see what she came up with.

Ahead of her, in the centre of the nave, lay regular rows of pale brown wooden chairs. A vague idea that the letter P might be connected to pews dissolved before it had even begun to develop. She didn't remember the chairs from the last time she was here but anyway they looked too impermanent and were too clearly visible to provide safe shelter for her father's hidden treasure. In fact, now she thought of it, all this part of the cathedral was too open for any easy exploration. He would have chosen somewhere quieter, out of the way.

Accordingly, after strolling a few yards further, she veered to her right, passing under an arch and entering an adjacent old stone corridor. Not a corridor, she knew, it had another name. An aisle or an ambulatory perhaps? She smiled. There, she wasn't such a hopeless cause after all. A few facts must have lodged in her brain as she'd trudged reluctantly at her father's heels.

She looked around, immediately feeling the difference. Gloomy was the word she would have used to describe it (*he* would have said atmospheric), full of shadows, slightly sinister and indisputably mysterious. That *things* had happened here – and not all of them good – she had no doubt at all. It was enough to put her on edge again. Loitering by a pillar, she tried to access that sixth sense, to work out if she had unwanted company. She felt odd, shivery, but that could just be down to her surroundings.

Eve walked on, the sound of her heels clipping

unnaturally loud on the stone-flagged floor, an easy echo for anyone to follow. As she glanced over her shoulder, her eyes were drawn towards a small panel set in a recess in the wall. Now that was something she remembered. They had stopped here to examine it, to praise its almost luminous colours, its deep and penetrating shades of blue. She went over to look at it again.

The Limoges panel, a set of eighteen enamel-on-copper plaques, was a nineteenth-century copy but no less beautiful for that. It was as vibrant as a stained-glass window. This was the only occasion, when she'd last been here, that she had showed any interest in the tour and she could almost feel her father beside her again, his lips widening into a smile, glad to have discovered at least one object that pleased her.

Had he remembered that too?

Could he have hidden it here?

Her gaze swiftly roamed the recess but there was nothing apart from rough pale stone. She didn't dare touch the gold-framed panel in case it was alarmed – although *would* it be alarmed? Well, she didn't fancy finding out. The prospect of an army of demonic priestly figures, their black cassocks flapping like wings, was enough to keep her hands firmly by her sides.

Turning away, she found herself standing opposite St Luke's Chapel. She peered inside. It was a small room with a carved font and a dramatic painting on wood divided into five sections – all showing images of Christ. BC she thought again, her heart making a tiny leap, and she would have gone in if it hadn't already been occupied by a middle-aged American couple making the kind of intense scrutiny that suggested they'd be there for at least another fifteen minutes.

'Fourteenth-century,' the woman said, reciting from her guidebook. She was tall and rangy, athletic-looking, and her face wore the determined expression of someone who expected value for money. She extended a finger and pointed at each of the sections in turn: 'The Flagellation, the Way of the Cross, the Crucifixion, the Resurrection and the Ascension.'

Her partner, a shorter thickset man with wiry grey hair, tipped his head to one side and stared obediently at the images. 'Right,' he said.

Eve couldn't decide whether he was utterly bored or completely fascinated. Neither his face nor his tone of voice gave much away.

She could go inside too – that might be enough to discreetly move them on – but was concerned about the opposite happening, about getting pulled instead into a conversation she would not be able to escape from. And the last thing she needed was to get involved in some profound transatlantic discussion about the wonders of Norwich Cathedral.

She lowered her head and walked on. She'd come back later when they were gone, when she had the freedom to view the place in peace. In the meantime she'd just stroll around, acting like any other visitor, feigning interest, pretending to be absorbed. She took a few more steps and found herself in front of another chapel. This one was protected by an ornate ironwork grille. For a while she stared between the metal scrolls, playing the part, barely seeing, doing nothing more than killing time. She was vaguely aware of a religious painting on the wall, of a bearded man with a baby in his arms. Half her mind was still on the chapel she'd left behind – all those images of Christ, all those possibilities . . .

Impatiently she shifted from foot to foot. Peering through the gloom, she waited for the Americans to emerge, for the coast to be clear. It was only as her drifting gaze focused on the nameplate that she suddenly stopped short. She was standing right in front of the Bauchin Chapel. It took a moment for the initials to sink into her consciousness but when they did she gave a tiny jump. *BC*. God! Yes! For a second her heart seemed to stop. This was it. It had to be, didn't it?

She reached out a hand to fumble with the gate. Was it locked? No, it was just her fingers that were shaking, too tremulous to slip the latch. She tried again and this time it complied, the gate swinging open to allow her access. Stumbling inside, she took a moment to look around, her gaze briefly lifting to trace the vaulted curve of the ceiling before scanning everything at eye level.

All she had to find now was 8PR.

P was for painting? She stared at it and frowned. Well, not unless he'd managed to slide something behind it and she didn't intend to mess with that solid frame. It would be just her luck if the whole darn thing fell off the wall. And then she'd have some explaining to do . . . No, it couldn't be that. She swivelled round and focused on a statue. *Our Lady of Pity*. P for pity? She experienced a tiny jolt of anticipation but it was short-lived: a fast examination proved that there was no hiding place there either. What about the window – a pane of glass? A pulpit? She groaned with frustration. A priest? This was like one of those childhood games of I-spy where no matter how hard she tried, even when it was staring her straight in the face, she couldn't get the answer right.

'Come on, Dad,' she murmured. 'Give me a clue.'

But the surrounding silence only seemed to grow larger.

Eve tried to concentrate. P was for passion, for penance, for pain, for . . . she thought about the man in the alley and felt a chill creep over her . . . for psycho. She wrapped her arms tightly around her chest. P was for paranoia. She mustn't let her mind stray. What about the 8, the R? What did *they* mean?

There was a single bench running the length of the chapel. She thought of pews again. Was this a pew?

Another memory came to her, of the two of them moving forward through the nave and into the area where the choir did their stuff. She had stared at the seats there, at the decoration on their backs, at all the representations of human frailty and weakness, of greed and lust and violence, and said: 'Hey, check out those pews.'

'Stalls,' he had corrected her.

'Oh, pardon me.' And she had raised her eyebrows and laughed.

Had he remembered that, how she had mistakenly called them pews, suspected that she'd refer to any cathedral seating with the same word?

This particular bench was set back against the wall. Directly in front was a pale wooden unit split into three, a central block flanked by a pair of smaller ones, leaving enough space for two clear paths of entry. Each of the units was carved into sections. She counted them off. There were eleven in all. If she was standing at the door the bench would be on her right. 8PR – the eighth section in the pew to her right.

Was it possible?

She could feel her legs beginning to shake. Like the clichéd introduction to some momentous event, her heart was accelerating into a drum roll. She wasn't sure of the etiquette of actually sitting down in a place like this. Maybe it was only to be looked at, to be admired from an upright position. But she didn't have a choice. Anyway, if push came to shove she could always claim a fainting fit. It wasn't so far off the truth. She looked behind her – there was no one in sight – and slid quickly on to the slim wooden bench.

The back of the unit provided a shelf – for bibles and prayer books, she presumed, although it was currently empty. Leaning forward she placed her palm on the worn golden surface. This had to be it. She took a deep breath. *Please God.* Then, with her pulse racing, she half-closed her eyes and ran her fingers along the underside.

The smooth stretch of wood yielded precisely . . . nothing.

She made another more frantic series of sweeps from left to right, from right to left. What? Her breath escaped in a thin hiss of dismay. Perhaps she wasn't looking in the right spot. She tried again, feeling more carefully this time, but the result remained the same: nothing, a big fat zero. Her disappointment was profound, almost unbearable. Damn! As soon as the profanity touched on her lips she offered up a mental apology. *Sorry.* She didn't need to bring down the wrath of the Lord on top of everything else.

At her feet lay a couple of firm-looking hassocks, protection against the cold stone floor should she feel the urge to fall to her knees and pray. She was getting close to it. Another idea came to her. Maybe PR had stood for prayer, the number eight for the eighth position on the bench? Either way, it didn't matter now.

With a sigh she sat back, her hopes draining away. She'd been certain she was on the right track. But she'd been wrong. Either that or her father had changed his mind. Or she'd been so pathetically slow on the uptake that someone had beaten her to it.

At that final infuriating thought she lunged forward once more, exploring with both her hands. Her movements were reckless now, her groping rough and perfunctory. It wasn't as if she expected to find anything and she might still have missed it if one of her nails hadn't snagged on the slightest of obstructions, something small and sticky, a tiny piece of tape that suddenly came adrift and . . .

She paused, her heart beginning to pound again. There *was* something here.

But whatever it was, she couldn't afford to damage it.

Reining in her impatience, she picked at the corner gently, trying to peel it away from the wood. It would be easier if she could get down on her hands and knees, if she could actually see what she was doing, but the space was confined and scrabbling about on the floor, arse in the air, was guaranteed – should anyone be passing – to draw unnecessary attention to herself.

Whatever his final message was, it was flat and smooth, laid flush against the shelf and fastened so neatly, so securely, that any cursory sweep of a duster – should a cleaner be so dedicated – would pass easily over its surface. A letter perhaps? Yes, it must be. A letter explaining everything. That was what she wanted, what she needed.

'Yes,' she urged softly. 'Come on.' She had released one edge and was tugging at the next – he hadn't just secured the four sides but meticulously taped across the middle too – when she heard approaching footsteps. And not only footsteps but voices: the American couple, having finished their scrutiny of St Luke's, were about to descend on her.

'There's a painting,' the woman was saying, her guide-book rustling ominously. 'Behind the altar: *The Presentation of Christ in the Temple* by John Opie. He's an eighteenth-century Norwich artist. And there's a modern statue.' She paused. 'That could be interesting.'

'We could eat at the Italian place tonight,' the man said. 'Or we could go to that pub by the river.'

'Ah, and a window, the Benedictine Window.'

'Jerry says they do a darn good steak.'

Eve kept on picking at the tape, the click-clack of their shoes against the flagstones growing ever closer. She was almost done, just a little longer and she could be out of here. She was tempted to try and release it with one fast rip but was too scared of the damage she might cause. What if she tore it? She might have to leave with only half of what she had searched for. Time was ticking by. If they spent as long in this chapel as the last she might not get the chance to come back again today.

She had to stop them. But how? There was only one thing for it. Shifting forward, placing her elbows on her knees, she huddled down and assumed a stance of devout contemplation. Her hair fell like a curtain around her face. And no one could claim that she wasn't praying, although her pleas were perhaps of the kind the church would not entirely approve of. *Please make them go away. Please let them leave me alone. Please give me just a few more minutes.*

They stopped in front of the open ironwork gate. She could feel their gaze on her, their surprise and indecision. No one, at least no one decent, likes to interrupt a person bent in prayer. She could hear the soles of their shoes shuffling uncertainly. The woman, for once, was entirely speechless. Would they come in? She hoped not. If they did, she was jiggered.

She waited. She could feel them waiting too, their continuing presence like some devil on her shoulder. She pressed her knuckles hard against her mouth. *Please go away.* There was a shuffling, a whispering, before they eventually decided to move on.

'Should we take a look at the tombs?'

'If you like.'

Eve expelled her breath in a long and thankful exhalation of relief.

But there was no time to hang about. The tombs they were talking about were just across the aisle. She quickly reached down, tearing at the tape, finally managing to release the letter. Shaking off the sticky remnants, she triumphantly lifted it to the surface. Except it wasn't a letter at all – no final words, no explanations. It was just a photograph, a dull and slightly out of focus picture of a group of people sitting round a table. She stared down at it in baffled disappointment.

What did it mean?

She didn't have time to study it more closely. The Americans, clearly bored with the inscriptions of the dead, were already heading back. Shoving the picture into her pocket, she stood up, lowered her face and swept out of the chapel. As she brushed past them she was aware of their curiosity, of their inquisitive eyes boring into her.

Were they going to speak? She hoped not.

No.

Good. She walked on a few yards, gulped and caught her breath again. So she'd found it. But found what? She didn't dare take it out of her pocket again. Not here. As she was heading towards the exit, eager to get home, she thought again about how she might be being followed. Not by the American couple surely – unless they were deep undercover and had been trained by RADA – but there were other people around.

She had to act casual, act normal. Which was easier said than done. She felt unsteady on her feet. Veering back into the nave, she found a seat and slumped down. She should have rung Henry. She should have told him she was coming here. At least then she'd have had some insurance, someone to pick up the pieces if . . .

But she couldn't afford to think that way. And she could only have left a message. His phone would have been turned off; he would still have been talking to his client. The best thing she could do was to get home, to lock herself in, to examine the evidence and to take it from there.

She wished she'd brought the car. It wasn't a long walk back but it was an unprotected one. What if some-one was waiting for her? What if she was attacked, searched, the photograph taken? She shook her head.

How likely was that? It was busy outside, the end of a long working day. So long as she kept to the main streets, so long as she mingled with the crowds, she should be okay. And if anyone approached her, all she had to do was scream . . .

By the time Eve turned the corner on to Herbert Street her body was on red alert, her legs ready to sprint, her fists to lash out. Every nerve end was standing to attention. She felt like one of those vulnerable antelopes on the plains of Africa, nervously looking from left to right, aware that an invisible predator might be lurking, waiting to pounce, eager to tear her limb from limb.

She jogged the last few yards, pushed open the main door and ran up the stairs. As she hit the top landing, she already had her keys out. Excitement was starting to replace her anxiety. A few seconds later she was safely inside with the bolts pulled across.

It was done!

Next stop the kitchen. She reached into the cupboard and grabbed the bottle of cheap whisky she had bought to replace the brandy Sonia had finished off. Pouring a generous shot she drank it down in one and then replenished the glass.

Feeling marginally calmer, she returned to the living room, took the photograph from her pocket – there were still some strips of sticky tape attached to it – and placed it on the coffee table. She sat down on the sofa, lit a cigarette and stared at it. So this was the cause of all her troubles.

The picture showed five people sitting round a large table, two men and a woman facing the camera (although almost certainly unaware of it), a fourth man in profile, the fifth with his back turned. She examined the visible faces. The two men were in their late fifties or sixties, both grey-haired, one large, the other much leaner, their features a little blurry but probably still recognizable to anyone who knew them. The woman was younger, not more than twenty, with long fairish hair and a wide laughing mouth.

It had been taken in a whitewashed courtyard, somewhere abroad. How did she know that it was abroad? She picked up the photo and drew it closer. It was something to do with the feel of the place, the quality of the light, the luxuriance of the flowering plants that crept up the wall behind them.

So was her father the person who had secretly snapped it? And if so, why? There was only one other clue, a printed date in the left-hand corner: July 18, two years ago. It wasn't even recent. But important enough for him to hold on to, to hide in a place only she could find.

Eve took another swig of the whisky and drew on her cigarette. Her initial elation was starting to fade. She couldn't remember him having been away at that time. Although, when she tried to think back, she couldn't actually recall what *she'd* been doing at that time – probably some dubious scam involving a middle-aged man with more money than sense, a less than savoury experience that she'd conveniently forgotten. And she had to admit that there had been weeks, maybe longer when she hadn't got around to calling him. Guilt crawled across her conscience. Still, surely he'd have mentioned a holiday, a trip abroad? And she wouldn't have forgotten that.

She peered down at it again, frowning, searching for any details that might be useful. It would help if the image was clearer. He must have just picked the camera up and . . . Suddenly she recalled with a jolt the birthday gift she had bought for him, the phone that took pictures, the only item that had gone missing from the flat.

So that was what the break-in had been about. But if they already had the phone then . . .

He must have copied the photo and then wiped the memory.

It was only as her gaze skimmed across the man with his back turned, small, skinny, blond, that her eyes slowly widened. Why hadn't she noticed it before? There was something familiar about the stance, about the way he held himself . . .

It could be Terry.

Yes, she was certain that it was. There was no denying the thin hunch of his shoulders or that flick of fine blond hair around the nape of his neck. He was even wearing a shirt she recognized, a marine blue T-shirt with two white stripes running around the sleeves. She thought of the passport she had found in the bag Vince had brought round.

She sat back, astonished, confused. Having previously been dismissed from the equation, Terry was now right back at the centre of it. But how could he be? She'd only just been to see him – and given him every opportunity to talk. He'd admitted to a more serious part in the robbery but nothing else. And certainly nothing connecting him to a white courtyard and a photograph taken two years ago.

Had he lied to her? She wasn't sure. Perhaps she just hadn't asked the right questions. And it was too late now. She didn't want to mention the picture over the phone and she couldn't book another visit until next week. It was too long to wait.

There was someone else, however, who might be able to help.

She reached for her mobile and scrolled through the menu. Finding the name she wanted, she pressed down and held the phone to her ear. It took a few rings before she answered.

'Hello?'

'Lesley?'

'Oh, it's you,' she said, without even a cursory attempt at politeness. 'Look, I thought we'd agreed that—'

'Yes, don't worry, Vince's message came over loud and clear. I'm not . . . I mean, you won't hear from me again. I just need to ask you something. One last question and that's it. I swear.'

Eve could almost see her thinking about it, her sharp pink cheek pressed close against the receiver. She could also feel her desire to slam the phone down. But she didn't.

'What?' she said eventually, the desire to be rid of Eve forever clearly more tempting than the short-term satisfaction of a disconnection.

'Well, I was just wondering if you could help. You wouldn't happen to know where Dad and Terry went on holiday would you? A couple of years back. It would have been in July, I think.'

'Why?' Lesley asked suspiciously.

Eve raised her eyes to the ceiling but tried to keep her voice friendly. 'I just remember Terry saying how much he liked it there. I thought I might book us a couple of tickets – you know, a surprise for when he gets out.'

'I've no idea. Somewhere in Greece.'

Eve's fingers tightened round the phone. 'Yeah, I know it was Greece,' she lied. 'I was just hoping you might remember *where*. Perhaps he sent you a postcard?'

'You think I keep postcards from two years ago?'

Eve didn't bother to respond to that. If nothing else, she'd learned that the pair of them *had* been together, and in which country, which was more than she'd known a couple of minutes ago. 'Okay. Well, thanks anyway. Sorry to have bothered you.'

'So that's it? That's all you wanted?'

'That's it,' she said.

Lesley, perhaps relieved to discover that this was all she was calling about, that she wasn't being asked to visit Terry again, sent a small whispery sigh down the line. 'Right,' she said. She paused. Then, as if to reward her for not asking anything more awkward – or maybe just to alleviate what little remained of her maternal conscience – she suddenly threw her another scrap of information. 'Look, I'm not sure, it was a while ago but it may have been one of the islands, Corfu, somewhere like that.'

'Okay. Thanks.'

'Oh, and Eve?'

'Yes?'

There was another much longer pause. She waited for the expected *Please don't call here again* demand but instead all she heard was soft breathing and a slight clearing of the throat. The seconds ticked by. Whatever Lesley wanted to say, she clearly couldn't make up her mind about it. 'Was there—'

'It doesn't matter,' she said. And then abruptly put down the phone.

Chapter Twenty-Seven

Cavelli leaned forward on the bunk, swept his fingers through his hair and frowned. He was still undecided as to what to do next. Terry had been jumped twice in the last few days, nothing too serious, just a few cuts and bruises, but a worrying indication that the little runt's scalp was up for grabs again. He couldn't watch him 24/7. Someone, sometime, was going to catch him alone. And fuck knows how *that* would end. It was worryingly clear that the deal with George Bryant – if it had ever existed – was already history. Perhaps the Rowans had raised the ante, made him an offer he couldn't refuse.

'Shit!' he said aloud. How had he got himself involved in this? What had begun as a simple challenge from a provocative redhead, progressing to an opportunity for him to wreak some revenge on Jimmy Reece, had suddenly flipped into a major problem. He was starting to watch his own back now, had even thought about getting a tool. But tools led to killings and killings to life sentences. He was better off with his fists.

And okay, so he hadn't actually received any blatant threats himself but this wasn't paranoia. He wasn't overreacting. He was well aware of the whispering as he passed along the landing, of the averted eyes, of the unwillingness from certain parties to even acknowledge his presence. Sides were being taken, arguments weighed, decisions made. The whole wing was poised on the brink. He could feel the anticipation in the air, the thin tense straining, the warning as loud as a bloody air-raid siren that things were about to kick off.

He knew what Isaac would say: *Walk away, man.*

But since when had he listened to Isaac? Walking away was tantamount to cowardice. He might regret having ever agreed to protect Terry but that didn't mean he could abandon him. There was his pride to think about, his reputation. He might only have another year to serve but if he let himself be intimidated once, there'd be no end to it; they'd be queuing up to have a go. And any-way, he'd believed Evie when she'd said that her brother wasn't a grass. She might be good at lying, possibly even an expert, but her wide grey eyes had been indignant enough to convince him.

He stood up. It was time for another chat with Bryant.

Louise was starting to stress over Richard's presence. Yesterday, he'd come down with coffee for his father and now this morning, before Henry had even arrived, he was back again, hovering around her desk, smiling and oozing compliments like some lascivious Victorian heir trying to seduce the servant girl.

'So how are you?' he said. 'You're looking very pretty today.' He perched down on the corner of her desk and smiled at her.

'Thank you,' she murmured. She might have been less amicable if she hadn't been so terrified about what he might say next. She didn't trust that sly seductive gaze of his. Had he realized the photograph was missing? Did he suspect that she'd tampered with the surveillance report? If so, she was only a few minutes away from being well and truly fired. Shuffling the papers into a pile, she tried to look busy.

'Everything okay down here?'

'Fine,' she replied.

'Great,' he said. 'And how's the boss been treating you?'

She glanced up at him again. And this time she saw something that she hadn't noticed before. *Fear.* If she was worried it was nothing in comparison to the expression on *his* face. It gave her a confidence she hadn't been feeling before. 'Fine,' she said again.

'And no news from our mutual friend?'

She knew exactly who he meant. Eve. Eve Weston. The person who had sat right here, her predecessor, the woman who Henry was still seeing. 'No,' she said, more sharply than she intended. 'She hasn't been in touch.'

'Good,' he said. He hesitated. 'And, er . . . no other calls or anything that might have, er . . . distressed him?'

'Distressed him?' she repeated, a small furrow appearing between her eyes. She couldn't work out what Richard was after. Had he come down here just to ask about Eve? She didn't think so. However, unless he was playing some particularly perverse sort of game, he didn't seem about to start accusing her of interfering with his mail either.

'Upset him,' he said, as if by using a shorter word he might make himself clearer. 'I just thought he seemed a bit, well, jumpy, when I was here yesterday.'

'Did you? I didn't notice anything.'

He looked wearily around the office, a soft sigh sliding from his petulant mouth, before turning to face her again. 'My imagination then,' he said. 'I'm probably overreacting. I just get concerned about the old man.'

That would be a first, she thought but was smart enough to offer up a sympathetic smile. 'I'm sure there's nothing to worry about.'

'No, of course not,' he agreed. He hovered for a while longer before finally standing up and heading for the door. Then, like it was an afterthought, something of little importance, he stopped and said casually, 'I don't suppose the police have rung, have they?'

Louise, surprised, opened her lips to repeat the words, *The police?* But worried that she was beginning to sound like an echo she swiftly changed her mind. 'What about?'

'Either they have or they haven't,' he snapped back, the façade of benevolence slipping as surely as a skin sloughed off by a snake. 'It's a simple enough question.'

She stared at him.

'Well?'

'No, I don't think so.' She shook her head. 'Not while I've been here.'

He lifted a hand to his face, perhaps hoping to disguise the look of relief. When he removed it the smarmy smile was securely back in place. 'Sorry, sweetheart, I didn't mean to have a go. It's only that there might be a few follow-up queries to that unpleasant business we discussed before as regards . . .' Instead of saying the name, he glanced meaningfully towards her desk as if the spirit of Eve Weston might still be lurking there. 'It's nothing to worry about, minor details, but you know what the police are like. There's always one more tedious question that they feel obliged to ask and I don't want my father having to deal with it. He's been through enough already. I don't want him to get . . .'

'Upset?' she suggested.

Richard narrowed his eyes, momentarily suspecting sarcasm, but then as instantly dismissed the idea. His faith in his own persuasive charm was too entrenched to allow for it. 'Exactly!' he said. 'I knew you'd understand.'

'Of course.'

His smile grew wider. 'So if you do receive a call, you'll be sure to put it straight through to me?'

She nodded.

'Good girl,' he said.

Louise had the feeling that he'd have patted her on the head if he'd been standing closer. As it was he just threw her a bone.

'We should get together for a drink sometime.'

'Lovely,' she murmured.

It was only as the door closed behind him that she allowed her own smile to fade. She listened to his footsteps ascending confidently to the floor above. *How could she ever have fancied him?* He was about as attractive as bacteria. But that was a side issue. More essentially, she had to decide what she was going to do next, and top of the list was what she going to tell Henry.

For starters, there was the matter of how she was going to explain about removing the photo and altering the report. Okay, so she might have opened the envelope accidentally but that was no excuse for reading through its contents or, more importantly, *changing* them. Understanding as he was, she had the feeling Henry wouldn't be too pleased about the course of action she'd taken. Instead of confiding in him, of showing him what she'd found, of letting *him* decide what to do next, she'd chosen to take matters into her own hands.

When she came clean he was bound to be embarrassed, not to mention angry – men, in her experience, were always angry when they were caught cheating and there was no disputing that picture of him and Eve. She might have preserved his secret but at what cost? He certainly wouldn't be happy that she was privy to it. He might even think that she was trying to blackmail him. That thought made her wince.

And then there was the matter of the police – what if Eve *was* trying to rip him off? She didn't want to believe it but she couldn't be sure. More likely it was a ruse by Richard to try and get her on side, to prevent them from talking to his father . . . which meant that he was in an entirely different kind of trouble and didn't want Henry finding out about it.

Louise dropped her chin into her hands and groaned. Her head was starting to spin. Should she tell Henry about the photograph or shouldn't she? She couldn't decide. It seemed that she was doomed either way. If she did, he might feel that she had overstepped the mark, would possibly find a way to discreetly let her go. If she didn't he could easily get caught out by the next report. Unless Richard, satisfied by what he'd seen, had decided to drop the surveillance on Eve . . .

She gave the idea some consideration. If that was the case then she was better off keeping quiet. No one would ever need to know what she had done. Henry's affair would eventually fizzle out and everything would return to normal. Louise gave a tiny satisfied nod. Yes, all in all, that could be the best way forward.

Cavelli, keeping a close eye on the men around him, strolled along the landing and down the iron stairway. Dressed in jeans and a navy vest he flexed his biceps as he walked – a timely reminder to anyone who might think about taking him on that his hours in the gym had not been wasted.

Bryant's cell was guarded as usual but this time by a different pair of goons, two solid smug-looking guys in designer tracksuits and brand-new trainers. He made a quick assessment as he approached, weighing up the opposition in case things turned nasty. Plenty of brawn, he decided, but not too much brain. And judging by the size of their bellies neither was suffering from starvation. They were probably slow on their feet. Although he could be wrong. He'd made the same mistake once years ago and still had the scars to prove it.

It was the taller of the two, a thickset balding thug called Hales, who pulled away from the wall and blocked his path as he moved towards the door.

'You want somethin'?'

'Mr Bryant.'

Hales curled his lip contemptuously. 'He's busy, mate.'

'Tell him Cavelli wants to see him.'

The other minder, still leaning back with his arms across his chest, shifted a thick wad of gum from one corner of his mouth to the other. 'What's that, some kind of fuckin' dago name?'

Cavelli turned to look at him, letting a whisper of a smile alight on his face before replying softly, 'Sicilian actually.'

There was a long pause as he slowly absorbed the answer . . . and its implications. Then he produced a small tight laugh. 'Yeah, right.' But despite his bravado, he threw a wary glance towards Hales.

But Hales was the type who wouldn't have cared if a Mafia don had come to visit. In this prison George Bryant ruled the roost and he was paid to keep it that way. 'Fuck off,' he said.

Cavelli widened his smile. 'I only ask nicely once. Are you going to tell him that I'm here or am I going to have to step on your head and make the introductions myself?'

Hales took an aggressive step forward. 'Just who the fuck—'

But he didn't have time to finish what he was saying. Cavelli caught him with a fast clean right, an upper cut to the jaw, which sent him hurtling towards the railings. The barrier kept him upright – but not for long. With arms flailing he slid down to the floor with a satisfying grunt.

His mate, perhaps still pondering on his memories of *The Godfather*, was too slow to respond. By the time his brain had sent a message to his fists, Cavelli had swung around and was waiting for him. Punching hard into the soft flabby flesh of his gut, he saw the wad of gum come flying from his mouth. He punched again and heard the gasp like a balloon deflating as the man doubled up, sank to his knees and then keeled over on to his side.

Bryant came flying out of his cell. 'What the—'

He stared at his two minders lying on the ground.

'You shouldn't feed them so much,' Cavelli said. 'Makes them lazy.'

If Bryant was intimidated by what he saw, he didn't show it. He was too smart for that. Instead he reached out with the toe of his boot and, like a man investigating something vaguely repulsive, poked the winded one in the ribs. 'Get up, Morgan, you streak of piss!'

Morgan staggered, groaning, to his feet. As if in fear of the contents falling out, one hand was clamped tightly to his stomach. His face was the shade of wet clay and a thin stream of snot ran from his left nostril into his mouth. He swayed as he reached the upright position, holding on to the railing for support.

'Sort out Hales and get Liam over here.'

'Yes, boss,' he wheezed, wiping his nose on the sleeve of his tracksuit. But although the spirit might have been willing, the flesh was weak. His large body was still heaving, his lungs trying to retrieve the breath that they'd lost.

Bryant, who was not the sympathetic sort, let out a growl. 'Sometime before tomorrow would be good.'

Morgan nodded and forced his bulk unsteadily forward. Hales, who was sitting on the floor, was holding his jaw like it might be broken. As Morgan helped him up and led him away, he gave Cavelli a sideways vicious glare.

Reprisals were on the cards. There was no doubt about it.

Bryant finally turned his attention to the visitor. His eyes were cold, almost reptilian. 'You want to tell me what the fuck is going on?'

'You should be grateful.'

'And how do you work that one out?'

'I've shown you the flaws in your security. Whatever you're paying them, it's way too much.'

Bryant snorted and stepped back inside his cell. 'If you're looking for a job, you only had to ask.'

'Just a chat. Although naturally I'm flattered by the offer.'

Bryant sat down, crossed his legs, and then flapped a hand towards the other seat. 'So what's so important that it couldn't fucking wait?'

Cavelli shifted the chair round so that his back wasn't to the door. He didn't like surprises. 'I thought we had a deal.'

'I don't recall a deal.' Bryant paused, slowly stroking his thigh with his long narrow fingers. 'A conversation, yes, but not a deal.'

'An agreement then.'

'An agreement that I'd think about your proposition. Perhaps even, at a stretch, a *temporary* arrangement. But nothing more.' He sighed deeply as if the information he had to convey pained him more than it would Cavelli. 'Unfortunately, time moves on, things change. It's the way of the world.'

'What's changed?'

The only response he gave was a thin cruel smile.

Cavelli nodded. 'Okay. So how much are the Rowans paying you to keep out of it? Or are you just worried about what they might do if you don't go along with them?'

If he'd been hoping to goad the man into any kind of careless retort he was disappointed. Instead Bryant actually laughed, showing a row of white capped teeth. 'Oh, come on,' he said. 'Don't let me down. You can do better than that.'

'So you're telling me they have nothing to do with this?'

'Work it out for yourself.'

Cavelli tried to keep his cool. How he was supposed to work anything out when he was scrabbling in the dark was a mystery. If it wasn't the Rowan brothers then who *was* pulling George Bryant's strings? Someone influential, that was for sure. And someone he was prepared to take risks for. He was beginning to wonder just how much the sweet-talking Evie Weston hadn't told him. And getting any sense out of Terry was a hopeless prospect: the kid would just raise those soulful doped-up eyes of his and plead his usual bloody ignorance of anything and everything.

Cavelli shifted in his seat. His knuckles, where he had thumped Hales, were starting to throb. Resisting the urge to rub at them, he laid his hand in his lap and went back on the offensive. 'So what are you saying – that it's out of your control?' He gazed at Bryant, his dark eyebrows lifting. 'And here was me thinking you had a mind of your own.'

Bryant's expression barely wavered. There was only the slightest of reactions, a tiny pull at the corner of his mouth, but it was enough to reveal that he wasn't entirely at ease. 'We all have, how shall I put it – certain obligations?'

Recalling his conversation with Evie – her questions about the guy called Joe – and with nothing left to lose, Cavelli took a wild shot. 'I never realized you were Joe's dancing bear.'

And it hit the spot. A bloody hole in one! The words were barely out before Bryant visibly flinched, his eyes narrowing into two icy slits. His fingers curled into his thigh. 'Shall I give you a piece of advice, son?' He didn't wait for an answer. 'It's usually best to stay out of business that don't concern you.'

'Maybe it's too late for that.'

'It's never too late . . . and this isn't your argument.'

'It wasn't, but somehow it's becoming kind of personal.'

'Your choice,' Bryant said, menacingly, and as his gaze roamed over his head, Cavelli turned to see that they had company.

'Have you met Liam?'

Liam, leaning in the doorway, was built like a shit brickhouse – four inches taller, six inches wider, and with the kind of muscles that thrived off a regular dose of illegal steroids. As if that wasn't bad enough he also had the edgy dangerous look of a man whose crack habit frequently outran his income. Cavelli had seen him around, seen him in the gym. And that was about as close as he ever wanted to get. 'I don't believe we've been formally introduced.'

'Liam, this is Mr Cavelli. Be sure to remember him.'

The giant looked him up and down and then grunted a few incoherent syllables, probably the closest he got to any sort of speech.

'Mr Cavelli was just leaving,' Bryant said softly.

He got to his feet, not so fast as to show undue fear but fast enough to prevent Liam from having to prove how big and strong he was. 'Thanks for the chat.'

Bryant stared at him for a moment, before his gaze swept down to settle uncomfortably close to his groin. 'It's been a pleasure.' His cold eyes flickered up again. 'Be sure to tread carefully. I'd hate to hear that anything *unfortunate* had happened. I trust we understand each other?'

'Perfectly.'

Cavelli walked past the mountainous breadth of Liam and out into the corridor. With his fists clenched he was waiting for it, for the attack from behind, but it never came. He made his way along the landing and back up the staircase. And all the time, as the steel rattled noisily under his feet, he was thinking, thinking, thinking . . .

When he got to his cell, he sat down on the bunk and swore. *Shit!* This wasn't just a spot of trouble, it was grief of monumental proportions. There was only one Joe who could have this kind of influence and that was the man himself – Joe bloody gangster Silk. But Joe had a finger in half the pies of London so why was he concerning himself with the vengeful desires of a pair of dumb third-raters like the Rowans? What could possibly be in it for him?

Well, he wasn't going to get the answers sitting on his arse. He reached out for the visiting order on the table and picked up a pen. He was in a hole and the only possible way out was through the person who'd helped to dig it for him in the first place. If he was going to save his own skin, not to mention Terry's, he needed to see Evie Weston.

He was still scribbling her address on the envelope when Isaac hurried in. Cavelli glanced up at him and sighed. It was clear from his expression that Isaac had already heard about the 'incident' with Bryant's men. News travelled fast in Hillgrove. 'Don't say it,' he murmured. 'Don't even think about it.'

Isaac stared dolefully down at his grazed knuckles. 'Aw, fuck man. What you gone and done now?'

It was over twenty-four hours since Eve had found the photograph and she was still no closer to understanding its relevance. What was so significant, so vitally important about this image, that her father had gone to such pains to conceal it?

She drummed her fingers on the table. Terry must

know the answer. Damn, if only she'd found it before she'd gone on the visit. Could she risk putting a call through to the jail, leaving a message for him to call her urgently? But she knew it was pointless. He wouldn't be able to answer her questions over the phone. Anyway, she was better off seeing him face to face. It was probably smarter too, she grudgingly admitted, that she didn't provide any advance warning of what she wanted to talk about. If she took him by surprise she was more likely to get the truth.

As she bent her head to look at the picture again she heard familiar steps in the hall and the jangling of a bunch of keys. She jumped up and opened the door.

Sonia, with a small canvas bag at her feet, turned to smile at her. 'Hi, love. How are you?'

Eve stared at her, alarmed. 'More to the point, how are *you*?' She looked tired and worn, her make-up smudged as if she'd slept in it – and not just for one night. Only the red lipstick was fresh, bleeding softly into the deep grooves above her upper lip. 'Come inside. Come on. I'll put the kettle on.'

'I wouldn't say no.' Sonia stepped forward but then paused for a moment by the newly glossed door. 'You been decorating then?'

'Just a lick of paint. Thought I'd jazz the place up a bit. Grab a seat. I won't be a minute.' As Eve walked across the living room, she quickly bent to sweep up the picture. She might not have worked out what it meant but she knew it was important enough, and dangerous enough, not to leave lying around. She took it through to the kitchen and placed it on the shelf beside the pans.

But Sonia, forgoing the debatable comfort of the lumpy sofa, followed her in. 'What's that?' she asked curiously.

Eve turned to her, all wide-eyed innocence. 'What?'

'I might be getting on but I'm not senile yet. *That*.' She

indicated with her head towards the shelf. 'Whatever it is that you're trying to hide from me.'

'I'm not hiding anything,' she insisted. 'It's just a letter from a friend.' She didn't like lying to Sonia but what she didn't know couldn't hurt her. She busied herself with the mugs and the kettle and briskly changed the subject. 'So how's Val bearing up? How's she dealing with it all?'

'Not so bad. It's the shock that gets you, when it's sudden like. There's no time to prepare. He was hardly the best dad in the world but . . .'

'And the boys?'

Sonia pulled out a chair and slumped down into it. 'The little ones are too small to understand but Darren's pretty cut up – idolized his granddad he did, although God knows why. The stupid sod spent half his life in jail.' She gave a small bitter laugh. 'But then that's probably the reason. The kids today think it's cool to spend the best years of your life rotting behind bars.'

'Until they get there themselves,' Eve said. 'And realize what a shithole it is.' She thought of Terry again and hoped he was okay.

Sonia, as if reading her mind, raised a hand in apology. 'Oh, sorry, love. I didn't mean to—'

'Don't worry. He'll be out in a few months. I'm just hoping this'll be the first and last time.' Eve grinned, trying to wipe the worry from her face. 'He's hardly a criminal mastermind, is he? Although what he'll do when he does get out, God alone knows. He's never held down a job for more than five minutes.' She put a mug in front of Sonia and then placed a hand briefly on her shoulder. 'Lord, listen to me,' she said, 'droning on about my own troubles. I'm sure it's the last thing you need.'

'Oh, don't mind that. You carry on. Takes my mind off it all, to be honest. The world doesn't stop because

Peter Marshall has one too many and staggers into a river.' Despite the dismissive nature of the words there was a slight waver in her voice. She took a slurp of tea, her smudged eyes peering over the rim of the mug.

'Here,' Eve said, reaching for the bottle of Scotch. 'You want a strengthener in that?' She unscrewed the lid and poured out a generous splash. She supposed Sonia must have loved him once and no matter how sour those feelings might have turned, no matter how brutally they'd been stamped on, some flimsy remnant of affection still existed.

'Ta, love.' She licked her lips. 'Mm, that's hit the spot. I bet your Terry's looking forward to a decent pint. Worried sick he was, your poor old dad, when they arrested him. He was on the phone to that solicitor day and night. Didn't sleep for a week. Up and down, pacing the flat like a madman. I thought he'd tear his hair out.'

Eve glanced up in surprise. It was news to her. 'Was he really that bad?' Sonia, surely, was exaggerating. There had been no indication of that level of distress when she'd come up for the court case. In fact he'd been remarkably calm. Of course he'd not been happy, far from it, but he had been quietly resigned as if it was somehow inevitable, a fate decreed, that one day his only son would end up in jail. 'He was fine when I was here.'

'Well, it was sorted by then, all that hassle with the filth trying to stitch him up. That's what was preying on his mind. Couldn't bear to think of him stuck inside for years. Scared for him, you see. He's not exactly Mr Muscle, your Terry, is he? The bastards would have done him for that robbery and all if they'd got their way.'

And the bastards, Eve reflected, had been right. She wondered how much her father had known about the true extent of his involvement. Enough to give him a few

415

sleepless nights by the sound of it. So why hadn't he called her, shared his fears? Instead he had apparently chosen to confide in Sonia. Not for the first time, she pondered on just how involved they had been. Had their friendship progressed beyond the neighbourly? Had the two of them slept together? Inquisitive as she was, Sonia couldn't see through walls but still appeared to know an awful lot about her father's night-time activities. She frowned. Surely that implied . . . But then again, so what if it did? It was nothing but guilt that was fuelling her resentment. It was no one's lousy fault but her own that she hadn't been here when it mattered.

'At least he'll be home soon.'

Eve sighed. 'Yeah.' Leaning over to rummage through her bag, she came up with a crumpled pack of cigarettes. She needed a smoke. She shook one out and then slid the pack across the table. 'Help yourself.'

'Ta,' Sonia said.

As Eve was lighting up, her hand was less than steady. That awful niggling doubt was creeping back into her thoughts again, about how exactly Terry had managed to wriggle out of a twelve-year stretch without making some kind of a deal. That whole 'losing the evidence' tale had a whiff of fantasy about it. No one, not even her angel-faced brother, could be that lucky. She took a drag, inhaled and then breathed out a thin frustrated stream of smoke. 'That cop, Shepherd, was here again. He was looking for you.'

'What did *he* want?'

'I don't know. I told him you weren't here.'

'Maybe it was about the inquest.'

Eve, recalling his flu-ridden sneaky eyes and even sneakier questions, had the feeling that an inquest had been the last thing on his mind. 'Didn't he come round to see you at Val's?'

Sonia shook her head. 'No, I haven't seen him. Only

some slip of a girl. A PC, Moira Grey. She said it was being arranged. Said she'd let me know in a few days.'

'Oh, right.' A faint wave of relief washed over Eve. Whatever Shepherd had been after, and she was sure it wasn't to her advantage, he clearly hadn't followed up on it. With a bit of luck he was laid up in bed with enough germs to knock him out for a month.

But the relief was short-lived.

'So, are you going to tell me what's been going on?' There was a sudden sharpness to Sonia's voice which hadn't been there before.

Eve tried to look unconcerned. 'I'm sorry?'

Sonia flicked her cigarette towards the ashtray, missing by the usual inch. 'You might be your father's daughter, Eve Weston, but that innocent expression doesn't cut any ice with me. He could charm the birds from the bleedin' trees but I always knew when he was pulling a fast one.'

'I don't know what—'

'There's been more trouble, right? Something happened while I was away.'

'No, honestly. Everything's fine.'

Sonia's gaze drifted up towards the shelf again. 'So what's all *that* about?'

Eve might have known she wouldn't let it drop. When it came to tenacity Sonia was premier league. 'It's only something I came across when I was going through Dad's stuff.' And suddenly it seemed smarter to just show her than to go on feeding her voracious curiosity. Once she'd seen it, she'd as quickly forget about it. Eve stood up, picked it off the shelf and passed it over. 'Here, take a look if you want.'

Sonia placed it on the table and gazed down at it. After a while she let out a long soft sigh. Her eyes when she lifted them again were glistening. 'Oh, love. You didn't need to hide it from me. What were you thinking – that I'd get upset by some old picture?'

Eve shrugged, not having a clue what she was talking about, but sensing it was wiser to keep her mouth shut.

'He always did take a rotten photo.' Sonia placed her forefinger on the large man facing the camera. 'Usually too pissed to stay still, see? Bet he'd been on the hard stuff when this was taken.'

Eve's eyes flickered from the photo, to Sonia, and then back to the photo again. She stared at it in astonishment. My God, was she saying what she thought she was – that the big grey-haired man was Peter Marshall? That was the last thing she'd expected.

'I didn't know they were friends.'

'I wouldn't say that exactly. Had a common interest though, didn't they? Couldn't stay away from the cards. Just a whisper of a game and they'd be out the door like a pair of bleedin' greyhounds. That's what that little jaunt was all about. *I could do with some sun myself*, I told him for all the good it did. You know what he said? *It's business not pleasure!*' Sonia took another drag on her cigarette, pondered for a moment and then laughed. 'Came back looking like thunder, the three of them. Christ knows how much they lost. Couldn't get a civil word out of him for a month. Your dad wasn't much better.'

'Not like him to lose at poker.'

'Must have met an even bigger hustler than himself,' she said good-humouredly.

Eve forced her lips into the semblance of a smile. Her surprise was being superseded by a cold chill of dread. Peter Marshall was dead. An accident, allegedly. But had it been? She was starting to wonder. He was in the photograph and somebody badly wanted that photograph back, someone who was prepared to threaten, to bully, to maybe even . . . She remembered Sergeant

418

Shepherd showing her the picture of Ivor Patterson, the light that had come into his eyes when she had asked if there was a connection to Peter's death. The way he had sat forward and said: *Why should there be?*

'Do you recognize the others? I mean, apart from Terry.'

Eve had to squeeze the question out. Her throat had dried, choking her voice. Fortunately, Sonia was too distracted to notice.

'Nah, never seen them before. Some cardsharp mates of your dad's, I shouldn't wonder – and one of their tarts. Must have a few bob too by the looks of the place.' She gazed down wistfully at the sun-drenched courtyard. 'Who says cheats never prosper, huh?'

Eve drank her tea, glad of the restorative powers of the whisky. She cleared her throat. 'It does look nice. Do you remember where it was?'

'Not Southend,' Sonia grinned. 'That's for sure.'

'Did Peter not say?'

She shrugged. 'Oh, one of them hot foreign islands.'

'It was somewhere in Greece,' Eve prompted, trying to jog her memory. 'Dad always liked it there. I was just trying to think exactly *where*.'

But Sonia's train of thought had already drifted. 'You know, maybe I'll get our Darren to paint my front door too. They'd be matching then, wouldn't they? A splash of white always spruces things up.'

'Corfu maybe. Do you think that was it?'

Perhaps Sonia was finally picking up on her desperation because she lifted her gaze and said, 'What's wrong?'

'I'm fine.' Then, placing her elbows on the table Eve sank her chin into her hands. 'It's just . . . just that I hate forgetting things. It was only a couple of years ago. He told me and now I can't remember and . . .' She didn't even need to feign the emotion. Sheer frustration was bringing tears to her eyes.

Sonia reached out to pat her gently on the arm. 'Don't worry, love. Hey, don't get upset. It doesn't matter.'

Eve shook her head. Of course it mattered! She *had* to find out where this photo had been taken. Without that simple but essential piece of information all her father's efforts would have been in vain. He had left it for her to find, bequeathed it for a reason.

She had a sudden vivid image of him in the Bauchin Chapel, down on his hands and knees, carefully taping the picture to the underside of the shelf. What had he been feeling? Fear? Satisfaction? Hope? He must have been listening out, just as she had, for any unwelcome interruption, worried that someone might walk in on him. Not that he wouldn't have come up with some thoroughly convincing explanation – when it came to charm there never had, and never would be, anyone to surpass him. Thinking of his soft persuasive smile she almost smiled herself. It had barely touched on her lips before it faded again. She wondered if he had gone to the cathedral on the same day as he'd decided that he'd had enough, that whatever was left was not worth holding on to, and her mouth slid slowly back into despair.

Why hadn't he talked to her?

'You know,' Sonia said, 'I think it *was* Corfu.'

But Eve knew she was only trying to console her. Other than the country, she had no more idea of where the three of them had gone that summer than she had.

'Perhaps.'

'I could always ask Val. I could give her a ring. She might—'

'No!' The idea of Sonia even inadvertently broadcasting the existence of the photograph was enough to send Eve hurtling into panic. She gulped out her objection. 'No, don't. Please. It's not a problem.' Standing up,

420

she grabbed a couple of glasses off the draining board, and poured them both a large straight Scotch. It gave her a few seconds to get her thoughts together. 'Now I come to think of it you're right, it definitely *was* Corfu. I'm sure it was.'

Sonia nodded. 'Well, if he was staying with one of his mates, he probably wrote the address down some place.'

Eve's jaw fell open. God, how did she keep overlooking the obvious? She thought of the battered address book lying in the top drawer of her father's desk and her heart began to pound again.

Chapter Twenty-Eight

Going through the names one by one, Eve had almost given up hope by the time she hit the letter S. She ran her finger down the list: Smith, Stevens, Shipley, Silk, Sanderson. And she might have flipped over the page if an address hadn't leapt out at her. Under the name J. Silk were three entries, the first for an office in Docklands, the second for a house in Surrey, and the third for The Villa Marianne in a place called Elounda.

Her breath caught in her throat. Now *that* sounded Greek.

Jumping up, she dragged her father's atlas off the shelf. A quick thumb through the index gave her the information she needed. Elounda was in Crete. Yes! This had to be it. And if the J stood for Joe there was every chance that she had just identified her persecutor.

'The Villa Marianne,' she said out loud.

No sooner had she spoken, than a distant spark ignited in her memory. *Marianne*. That name meant something to her. She had a glimpse of a teenage girl with long dark wavy hair, deep-set coffee-coloured eyes, her skin tanned to an enviable shade of bronze. How could she have forgotten? Two or three years older, and all the more glamorous because of it, the beautiful Marianne had been the subject of her first ever adolescent crush. Eve had followed her round like a lovesick puppy, only tolerated because there was no one else to talk to.

It had been one of those summers, a long time ago, before her father married Lesley. They had spent three months in Europe, touring Spain and Italy and Greece (he must have been in the money, must have pulled off one of his better cons) – and had stayed a few leisurely weeks at a villa with high wrought-iron gates and a turquoise pool. She would have been about eleven, maybe twelve.

Had Marianne's father been called Joe? She couldn't remember.

She leaned over to examine the photo again. Maybe there was something familiar about the man sitting beside Peter Marshall . . . or maybe she was only imagining it. People could change a lot in twenty years. And the girl definitely wasn't Marianne although she might, at a stretch, be her daughter. It seemed unlikely with that fair hair but genetics could be unpredictable.

Eve racked her brains trying to think back, to resurrect her memories of that time, but they remained elusive. Like the faces in the photo, most of her recollections had blurred so that she couldn't even swear that the villa they had stayed in had actually been in Greece. The odds, however, were on her side.

So, what to do now?

If she wanted Mr Silk off her back all she had to do was pick up the phone and call him. His London number, if it hadn't been changed, was sitting right in front of her. But her father had gone to all that trouble for a reason – and until she knew what that reason was she couldn't afford to simply hand the picture over.

What she needed was more information.

She rang Patrick on his mobile. 'Hey, it's me. How are things?'

His voice sounded drowsy, as if he'd just woken up. 'Evie? God, do you have any idea what time it is?'

'Ten past seven,' she said, glancing at her watch. 'And it isn't even dark yet.'

423

'Oh,' he muttered. 'Is it? Hang on a sec.'

She heard the rustle of cotton sheets, the murmur of a woman's voice and then the rasp of a flint as he lit a cigarette.

'Sorry, babe. I must have dropped off. It's been a long day.'

Eve didn't bother to pursue the cause of his exhaustion. She had a pretty good idea that it was still lying naked next to him.

'How's the flat? Did you manage to get it sorted?'

'Not exactly. It's more . . . well, more of a work in progress. I've moved out for a while.'

'Oh, okay. So where are you staying at the moment?'

'Er . . . with a mate.'

She smiled at the evasion, not sure as to whether she should be flattered by his attempt to spare her feelings or offended that he thought she might actually *care*. She didn't. Not in the slightest. That pang she felt, that tiny stab deep down in her chest, was nothing more than a minor dose of heartburn.

'We've been divorced for years,' she said. 'You are allowed to sleep with other women now.'

'Seven years actually. Not that I'm counting but we may as well get the facts right.' He laughed. 'Thanks for the permission though.'

'It's a pleasure.'

'It always used to be,' he said provocatively.

'For you, perhaps,' she quipped straight back.

'Thanks, you sure know how to make a guy feel proud.' There was a slight pause while he took a drag on his cigarette. 'Okay, so assuming that you're not calling to beg me to take you back, I take it there's some other way I can enhance the quality of your life?'

'I could just be calling to see how you are.'

'You could,' he said, 'and I hate to sound hard done by, or even mildly cynical, but that would be a first. And there's a small voice in my head insisting that you're after more than a cosy chat about the state of my health.'

'A small voice huh? That's not encouraging. You should get that checked out.'

'Come on, babe. Spit it out.'

She grinned down the line. 'Well, as it happens I would appreciate some help. What do you know about a man called Joe Silk?'

'Christ,' he groaned. 'Please don't tell me he's the next on your prison pal's hit list.'

'This has nothing to do with Cavelli.'

'Good.'

'Why do you say that?' Her smile was beginning to fade.

'Because you do realize who Joe Silk is, right?'

'Yeah, of course. Well kind of, vaguely.'

'Then you know that he's trouble. The serious kind. He owns a load of property, runs a string of clubs in the West End, a couple of casinos, but that's just the legal side. He's into all sorts of shit: drugs, girls, illegals . . .'

Eve gripped the phone tight against her ear, her palms starting to leak. This was exactly what she *didn't* want to hear. That she might have been stepping on the toes of some minor thug was risky enough but deliberately crossing a major league gangster was heading towards the suicidal.

His voice became wary. 'What's the interest? Does this have anything to do with Jimmy Reece?'

'No, I told you. It's not connected to Cavelli.' She should have guessed she'd get an inquisition. Needing a cover story, and fast, she settled on a partial truth. 'I came across his name in Dad's address book. It rang a bell but I couldn't quite place him. I just wondered if they were close, if he'd heard, you know, about what happened . . .'

'Oh, right. I see.' Patrick seemed partly mollified by the answer. But then a hint of suspicion crept back into his voice. 'To be honest I'm surprised they even knew each other.'

'Well, it's not important. Perhaps their paths crossed sometime in the past.'

'Yeah, possibly. But I'd stay well away if I were you.'

'Don't worry, I will.'

She said her goodbyes, put the phone down and closed her eyes.

'Damn,' she murmured.

It was Saturday morning. A faint glimmer of sun broke through the clouds making the wet pavements shine. Eve was standing by the window waiting for the taxi to arrive. It was finally pulling up. At last! Grabbing her bag, she crossed the room, locked the door behind her and jogged down the stairs.

Now that she knew what she knew she had to act quickly.

The photograph was in the inside breast pocket of her jacket. Last night, on the pretext of sending some emails – an excuse that had permitted some temporary privacy – she had borrowed Darren's computer again, scanned in the photo, enlarged the image and printed out a reasonable copy. She had thought about sending it down line to Henry but decided against it. There was no saying whose prying eyes could be privy to his email.

As if the button might not be enough to keep it from accidentally falling out, she anxiously felt for the picture again. Was it safe to leave the copy behind? She had taped it to the middle of *The Collected Works of Shakespeare* so that if someone did break in (and the odds of them getting through that door, never mind past Sonia, were pretty slim) they'd still be hard pressed to find it.

Anyway, so what if they did. In a few hours, so long as

he agreed, the original would be securely stashed in Henry's safe.

Micky Porter checked the arrivals board, noted the platform number and then strolled over to the nearest café. He ordered a bacon roll and a coffee, sat down, and opened his newspaper. He still had fifteen minutes to wait.

For the past couple of days, due to more pressing matters, the surveillance on Eve Weston had been suspended. Joe had needed him here in London. There had been trouble at the clubs, three arson attacks and an unexpected drugs raid. One of the buildings was a write-off. Six of his girls had been arrested. The criminal world, for all its superficial secrecy, was a hotbed of gossip. Rumours were flying around: that Ritchie Frey was trying to muscle in, that the Empire was crumbling, that Joe was finally losing his grip . . .

Micky was keeping an open mind. He'd heard it all before. Recurring reports on the demise of Joe Silk had a tendency to be exaggerated. He was loyal to the boss – well, as loyal as any employee who continued to receive a healthy wage – and he wouldn't jump ship until he was sure it was actually sinking.

However, with the current crisis, he did find it odd that Joe was back on the redhead's case. He must have sent someone else up to Norwich to watch her. Weren't there more important things to worry about? He still didn't understand what she'd done, or maybe hadn't, to warrant such attention. And Gruber, unsurprisingly, hadn't shed any light on the mystery either. A few discreet inquiries about what he'd been asked to search for in the blond hustler's flat had drawn one almighty blank.

'You didn't find it then? No joy the other night?' (As if he knew what he'd been looking for.)

'No.'

'You must be losing your touch. Did you check under the bed?'

Gruber, unamused, had lifted his gaze and stared at him. 'It wasn't there.'

'Joe can't have been too pleased.'

He shrugged.

'So where do you think it might be?'

Taking a moment to think about it, he had finished his pint, pulled his shaggy brows together and frowned. 'Somewhere else?'

Micky still couldn't work out if Gruber was thick as shit or just deliberately obtuse.

The journey had felt interminable, more like five hours than two. Eve had spent them in a state of barely suppressed panic. Patrick's warning refused to stop spinning round her head. *I'd stay well away.* Which was exactly what she wanted to do – except the choice, she suspected, was not entirely hers.

She had moved places several times, starting off near the restaurant car (there was safety in numbers) and then changing her mind (wasn't it easier for a tail to hide in a crowd?) before finally retreating to a seat at the rear of the last carriage. The photograph, like a bright magnesium flare, was burning a hole in her pocket. She was convinced that everyone could see it.

As the train pulled into Liverpool Street she took her time getting off, making sure that no one was behind her. Her eyes cautiously scanned the crowd in front, searching for anyone who might be deliberately slowing their pace. She was so on edge, so nervy, that should some poor soul suffer the misfortune of having to bend and tie up his shoelaces she would probably scream blue murder and kick him where it hurt.

Fortunately, nobody stopped, stumbled or even briefly

hesitated, and she walked through the barrier and out on to the station forecourt with a sigh of relief.

As she mounted the steps to the upper level, she could see Henry already seated at a table outside the coffee shop. He was never just punctual, always early, for which she was grateful. The prospect of hanging around on her own, especially with what she was carrying, was not enticing. But it wasn't just that. She felt a genuine rush of affection on seeing his face, a reminder of how much she missed him.

In his usual gentlemanly fashion he got to his feet, leaned over and kissed her courteously on the cheek.

'How are you?'

She was tempted to tell the truth. Instead, reluctant to alarm him more than she had to, she delivered a smile, arched her eyebrows and said, 'Confused just about sums it up.'

'Let me get you a drink and you can tell me all about it.'

'Thanks. Shall we go inside?' It was too public out here, too many passengers milling about. And apart from her concerns about a possible tail she also had *his* position to worry about. The fewer people who saw them together the better. Celia, she was sure, would not have forgiven him yet. He had taken a huge risk last week in Soho; there was no point tempting providence.

She laid a hand on his arm. 'Oh, and Henry, thanks for coming today. I really appreciate it.'

'Why shouldn't I?' he replied.

Although they both knew the answer to that. After Richard's spiteful intervention – she felt a stab of anger at the thought of it – their meetings could only ever be surreptitious, stolen moments that would eventually, inevitably, fade away to nothing.

They went through to the back of the café and found

a quiet corner. In need of something sweet and comforting she ordered a hot chocolate and while she sipped at the froth went over the events of the past few days.

Henry's eyes grew ever wider as she explained about the hidden photograph. 'In the cathedral? Heavens!' Then, as if he had inadvertently made a bad pun, he pulled his lips into a fleeting grimace.

'Yes, and if it hadn't been for you, for what you said, I'd never have found it. Not in a month of Sundays. I just don't get it. I mean, he couldn't have guessed that I'd make the connection. Why should I? What have I ever known about Virginia Woolf?'

'Perhaps he realized that your curiosity about the notes would ultimately lead you to the answer.'

'Then he was taking an almighty risk. It's almost as if . . .' She stopped, frowning as she tried to sort out her thoughts. 'I don't know. As if he wasn't quite sure that he wanted me to find it. Does that make any sense? That he left all the clues but made them obscure enough to rely on an element of chance.'

'Leaving it in the hands of the gods?' he suggested.

She grinned. 'So now we're talking divine intervention?'

Henry raised his eyes to the ceiling and smiled back at her. 'And the gods, it appears, have spoken.'

'In which case free will has just flown out of the window and it's completely beyond my control.'

'That's one interpretation.'

Eve pondered on the notion. Then, undecided as to whether it was reassuring or not, she pushed it to the back of her mind and moved on to the revelations Sonia had provided. She told him about Peter Marshall, about the trip abroad, about her father's address book. By the time she had finished, she was even more certain of what she had to do next.

'So you see,' she said. 'Something must have happened

out there, something that makes this picture important. He travels all the way to a delightful Greek island, plays a few hands of poker, comes back and never talks about it again. That's weird, isn't it, Henry? Tell me that it isn't. I mean that he didn't even *mention* it to me.'

Never one to jump to hasty conclusions, Henry took off his glasses, gave them a polish with his handkerchief and returned them to the bridge of his nose. 'Unless Sonia was right. Perhaps he did lose heavily. Perhaps he just wanted to forget about it.'

'No,' she insisted, with a wave of impatience. 'He wasn't like that. Okay, he didn't like to lose – who does? – but he wouldn't go out of his way to hide it. Believe me, it wouldn't be the first time he'd come home with his pockets empty. He was a gambler, a serious one, and for him losing was just an occupational hazard, one of those twists of fate that hopefully didn't come around too often.'

She swirled the last few inches of chocolate around the bottom of her glass, her head gradually filling with those (fortunately not too frequent) childhood memories of her father's wry smile, of his promise that tomorrow he would find that winning streak again. *Don't worry, sweetheart. We'll soon be back on the road to riches.* And she had always understood what that meant – that it was time to move on, for their bags to be packed, for the landlady to be avoided, for a silent midnight creep, hand-in-hand, down the creaking stairs . . . And from nowhere Eve was hit by another of those fearsome crushing waves of grief: *she would never see him again.* A lump came into her throat. She lowered her eyes, fighting back the tears. 'No, it's something more. It has to be. Why else would he have done all that?'

'I don't know,' Henry said truthfully. Then, seeing in her expression an urgent need for consolation, he leaned

431

forward and placed his hand over hers. His voice was full of concern. 'Are you all right?'

She swallowed hard and forced a smile. 'I'm fine, really. Thanks. Sorry. I'm just . . . just . . .' Her lower lip was starting to tremble. She searched for a word that might describe what she was feeling but eventually gave up and resorted to a shrug.

'Eve?'

She shook her head.

For a while, as she fought to regain her composure, they sat in silence. And then, as if instinctively understanding that any continued sympathy might be more of a burden than a help, Henry gently removed his hand and returned the conversation to more practical matters. 'So what about this Joe Silk? Are you sure he's the man in the photograph?'

Eve's shoulders lifted a fraction. 'I couldn't swear to it but I'd say the odds are pretty good.'

'What do you know about him?'

'Not much,' she said, unwilling to repeat Patrick's damning description. 'He's a bit shady, runs a few clubs in the West End, has some other interests too, property and stuff, that kind of thing.'

'What kind of thing?'

She looked at him, slowly finding her smile again. Henry might be an innocent but he wasn't a fool. 'You know what I mean.'

'That he's an out-and-out villain?'

'Well, he's not what you'd call a pillar of society.'

Henry scratched his chin. He picked up his cup and drank the last of his coffee. 'How small a pillar exactly?'

She hesitated. Then, lifting her thumb and forefinger, she slowly drew them together. 'Quite. Very. In fact, all things considered, barely visible.'

'So you know what you have to do next.'

Eve nodded. They were clearly thinking along the same lines. She had to follow things up.

She had to go to Crete. It was her only chance of discovering the truth. 'I've not got much choice, have I?'

'No,' he agreed.

'So I'm going to do it,' she said with determination. 'I'm going to go there on Monday.' There were plenty of cheap flights on the internet. She could pick up a bargain, especially at short notice.

'Monday? Why wait. We can go right now.'

'What?' She burst out laughing. Henry wasn't usually the impulsive sort. 'What have you put in that coffee? It's a lovely idea but we can't.' He might be able to explain a few hours away to Celia but she might just notice if he went AWOL for a week and came home with a suntan. '*You* can't.'

'Why ever not? I might not be an expert in these matters but I'm still a solicitor.'

She stared at him, bemused. 'What on earth has being a solicitor got to do with it?'

'Well, someone should be with you when you give your statement to the police.'

'Ah,' she said, realization dawning. Another laugh bubbled on to her lips. 'Actually, I think we may have got our wires crossed. I was talking about going to Crete rather than the local cop shop.'

'Crete?' he echoed. And then, suddenly aware that what he suggested must have sounded like an indecent proposal, Henry blushed a deep shade of pink. 'Oh, I see.' He gave a small embarrassed cough and cleared his throat. 'I see, right.'

Eve couldn't resist the temptation to tease him a little. 'Although you're more than welcome to join me if you like.'

'Er, I'm not sure that—'

'I'm only joking,' she said, regretting the flippant invitation as soon as she had made it. Her relationship with Henry was so pure, so absolutely platonic, that even the most oblique reference to sex felt almost sordid. She straightened her face and swept any hint of innuendo from her voice. 'Honestly, I'll be fine on my own. I'll be there and back before you know it.'

Henry's cheeks, although still flushed, were gradually resuming their normal colour. 'But do you really think it's wise?' he said. 'If this man, this Joe Silk, is a criminal then wouldn't it be better to—'

'I'm not going to the cops!' she insisted. 'Not yet. I can't. Silk's not the only one in the photo, Terry's in it too, and until I understand what it means I can't afford to just hand it over.'

'Your father wouldn't have kept it if it implicated Terry.'

She nodded. 'That's true but it doesn't mean they won't try and stitch him up. He only escaped the robbery charge on a technicality and I don't suppose they're best pleased about that. No, the last thing I should do is bring him to their attention again – and especially in connection to Joe Silk. I can't. I can't take the risk.'

She gazed down at the table, sighed, and then lifted her eyes again. 'And anyway, even if that wasn't on the cards, what could I possibly say? *Hey, my father hid this photograph in Norwich Cathedral and I found it and yes, okay, so it's just a blurry picture of some people sitting round a table but I really think you should launch a major inquiry.* Come on, they're as likely to call for the men in white coats as to take me seriously.'

'You could tell them what's been happening,' Henry said, 'that you've been threatened, burgled, assaulted, followed – followed by a man who is possibly the same one as they found dead less than a week ago . . .'

'None of which I reported at the time.'

'You told them about the break-in.'

'No, I didn't. Sonia did that.'

'So?'

'So I'm hardly likely to come across as the most reliable of witnesses. At best I'm going to look suspicious for withholding evidence and at worst like some neurotic attention-seeking female. And by the time they've finished their interviews – that's if they haven't sectioned me by then – I could already have been to Crete and back.'

'But you could be in danger. Please, you *have* to think about it.'

She didn't need reminding. She *was* thinking about it. But, if anything, it only reinforced the decision she had already made. 'Well then, I'm probably safer out of the country for a while.'

As if confronted with an argument he couldn't win, Henry sank his face into his hands. A few seconds passed before he looked at her again. 'I don't know. I don't like it.'

'I don't either but I have to at least try and find out the truth. You understand that, don't you?'

'Why can't you just talk to Terry?'

'Because for one my visiting order isn't valid until the end of next week and it's not the kind of conversation I want to have over the phone, and for two, well, he hasn't exactly been honest with me recently. Even if he knows what the photo means, there's no guarantee that he'll tell me.'

'I thought you two were close.'

'We were . . . are. But God knows what else he's got himself involved in. First there was all that Rowan stuff and now . . . I just don't want to waste time hanging around and then find out that I have to go to Crete anyway.'

He nodded. 'So you're definitely leaving on Monday?'

435

'If I can get a flight.' She had to follow her instincts but the worry in his eyes was intolerable. And she realized that if she didn't say something to reassure him he might feel obliged to try and accompany her for real. The lie slipped easily from her lips. 'Look, if it helps, I won't go on my own. I'll ask Sonia to come with me.'

A brief flash of relief came into his eyes before caution crawled back in again. 'Are you sure that she's—'

'Are you kidding? If you're talking protection, she's perfect for the job. Have you ever seen Sonia when she's angry? There's not a man on earth who wouldn't think twice.'

He smiled.

'We'll be fine. I promise.' Then, before he had time to raise any more objections, she quickly changed the subject. 'But I could do with a favour, a big one. I've taken a copy of the photo but I need somewhere to put the original. Just until I get back. Is there any chance that you could keep it in the office safe?'

He didn't hesitate. 'Of course.'

'Thanks.' She glanced around. There were only a couple of other tables occupied, both by what looked like genuine travellers with suitcases at their feet, but she still shied on the side of caution. Waiting until she was sure that no one was looking, she slipped the brown envelope from her pocket and slid it across the table.

'Can I open it?'

'Best not,' she said. 'Not here.'

He glanced nervously over his shoulder. 'Why? Do you think we're—'

'No, I don't.' She laughed. 'But you'd make a lousy spy if we were.'

Henry's thoughts, as he ascended from the depths of Covent Garden tube, were mixed. After seeing Eve safely on to the train back to Norwich, he was still of a mind that he should have done more to dissuade her from what he considered a foolhardy and possibly even dangerous venture but was also, if being strictly honest, impressed by her refusal to follow any course of action that was even remotely sensible.

He couldn't help wishing that *he* had the opportunity to be getting on that plane on Monday. And he also couldn't help being faintly thrilled by his own role in this mystery. With the envelope safely transferred from her pocket to his, he felt like some secret agent or – and this was infinitely more appealing – like his fictional hero, Philip Marlowe, embarking on yet another of his wonderfully confusing cases.

Walking out into Long Acre, he was still trying to piece it all together – the latest turn of events, the list of names, all the possible connections – but without much success. The photograph was undoubtedly an integral part of the puzzle but the overall picture was no clearer. What was the link between Alex Weston and Joe Silk? Why had Patterson been following Eve? What did Cavelli have to do with it all?

He was so absorbed by these questions, so distracted, that he didn't even pause to consider the possibility that he might be being followed.

Had Louise plucked up the courage to tell Henry about the pictures she'd intercepted, about the surveillance, he would never have taken the risk of meeting Eve. And if he hadn't met Eve, Micky Porter wouldn't have been able to follow him back to the office in Covent Garden. And if Micky hadn't followed him he would never have had an address to pass on to Joe Silk. And Joe Silk, in turn, would not have been able to pass on those details to the psychopathic Keeler Chase.

Chapter Twenty-Nine

The Five Bells was situated halfway down an alley off the main square. It was either a pub suffering from an identity crisis or it had simply decided to hedge its bets. Old flock wallpaper clashed with brash chrome tables and art deco lamps. Even the jukebox, an eclectic mix of rock, hip hop, pop and Sinatra, couldn't quite decide where it was coming from. Frank was currently belting out 'For Once In My Life'.

The clientele was as confusing as the decor, a mix of the young and not so young, of noisy students, middle-aged professionals and a small group of pensioners who, as if there was safety in numbers, were huddled together in a corner by the bar.

'Is it that bad?' he said.

Eve's gaze, halting in its scrutiny, flicked quickly back towards him. 'What?'

'The pub, the beer, the company? Take your pick. You haven't said a word for the last five minutes.'

'Haven't I?' She picked up her glass and took a drink. 'Sorry, it's been a long day.'

'Want to share it with me?'

She didn't, she couldn't, but she took a moment to pretend to think about it before casually waving the request away. By now, hopefully, Henry would have the photograph secured in a box of solid steel. So long as *it* was safe she had one less thing to worry about. 'Oh, the usual stuff.'

Jack lifted his eyebrows. Then, when she didn't elaborate, he took hold of her hand and lifted it an inch above the table. 'And how's the injury?'

She gazed down at the scratches. After three days they had faded into thin pinkish stripes. The other damage wasn't so bad either; there weren't as many bruises as she'd expected after the assault by Cavelli's bunny-boiling girlfriend, only a few grey marks on her upper arms. It was her muscles that hurt more than anything, as if she'd been subjected to a vigorous ten-hour work-out in the gym.

'It's not good news,' she said. 'They might have to amputate.'

He grinned at her. 'Rotten luck. Still, not to worry, at least you've got the other one.'

'Thanks. It's your optimistic outlook that maintains my faith in the human spirit. What would I do without you?'

'Talking of which,' he said. 'Do you fancy a drive out on Monday? I've got the day off. We could find a country pub or go up to the coast. Be good to get out of the city for a while.'

'Ah.' She pulled a face. 'Actually, I'm going away next week.'

'Oh,' he said, disappointed.

'I just fancied a break.' She glanced towards the rain-spattered windows. 'I've had enough of grey days. I'm in need of some sun.'

'Where are you off to?'

She shrugged, thinking it wiser not to reveal the details. 'I haven't decided. And I'm not fussy. Anywhere where the sea is blue, the wine is cheap, and the sun manages to make a regular appearance.'

'So you haven't booked it yet?'

'No. I'll check out flights on the net, see what's on offer.'

'You know,' he said, sitting back and folding his arms across his chest. 'That sounds like a damn fine idea. I don't suppose you'd care for some company, would you?'

Eve hadn't been expecting that. She aimed for a smile while she scrabbled about for a suitable excuse. 'Er . . . wouldn't it be rather short notice for work and all?'

'I'm sure I could swing it. They owe me enough leave; I don't see why I shouldn't take some of it now.'

'Right,' she murmured, desperately searching for another way to put him off. She remembered the earlier misunderstanding with Henry. Sadly, there could be no confusion here; he had definitely invited himself.

'Sorry,' he said, seeing her expression which was probably bordering on horror. 'That wasn't fair. I shouldn't have asked. I didn't mean to put you on the spot.'

She relaxed a little. 'You haven't. It was just . . . well . . .'

'It's okay, I understand. I shouldn't have presumed . . . You're probably already going with someone, right?'

'No,' she said, the reply leaping out of her mouth before she could prevent it. 'It's not that.' She didn't want him thinking that she was jetting off with another man. Why it should matter she didn't know – it wasn't as if they were in a steady relationship – but for some reason it did. And then she inwardly cursed. Why hadn't she said yes, that she'd made plans with a girlfriend? That would have provided an easy get-out clause. 'It was just a bit of a surprise. I mean, we haven't really known each other that long, have we?'

'It's okay,' he said again. 'But if that's the only problem I give you my word that you won't be under any obligation to marry me just because we go on holiday together.'

She grinned back at him. 'Oh, please don't shatter all my dreams.'

'I'll leave it up to you,' he said. 'No pressure. Although I will, of course, be devastated if you turn me down.'

She looked into his blue eyes and then slowly lowered her gaze to that sensuous mouth. She had an irresistible urge to lean forward and kiss him. Instead she lifted her glass and took a few more sips of beer. Her resolve was beginning to waver. It might not be such a bad idea to take him with her. No, it was impossible. How could she ask around, find the information she needed, if he was always there? But what if Henry was right, if she was walking straight into danger? It would make sense to have Jack for protection. And she might not even discover anything, might draw a blank, in which case she'd still be stuck there on her own which seemed a shame when she could—

'I don't mean to rush you,' he said, 'but it has been almost a minute.'

'Are you as patient as this when you're in the interview room?'

'God no,' he said. 'The thumbscrews would be out by now.'

'Well, thank you for your patience, Inspector.'

Jack ran his fingers through his hair and stared plaintively at her. 'Come on, Weston, show some pity and put me out of my misery. A simple yes or no will do. I won't demand any explanations, I promise.'

Why was it that every time she looked at him he made her want to smile? And the trouble was that she wanted to make *him* smile too. Now that was a worry. She hadn't felt this way since . . . but look how that had ended. Even as she opened her mouth to reply she hadn't quite decided what to say. Yes or no. Fifty-fifty.

'No,' she said.

Seeing the disappointment flash into his eyes, she instantly regretted it.

'Fair enough,' he said.

Eve waited a couple of seconds, hoping the temptation might go away, but she finally gave in. 'What I meant is no, I *won't* turn you down.'

'What?' That dazzling smile made its appearance again. 'Are you sure?'

'Would you like me to think about it some more?'

'No!' he exclaimed. 'Your answer, I'm afraid, is legally binding. I wouldn't want to have to drag you through the courts.'

She shrugged. 'I guess I'll just have to make the best of it then.'

While he went for more drinks, Eve pondered on the wisdom of what she'd done. Although what was the point? She couldn't wriggle out of it now even if she wanted to. And did she? She glanced over at Jack, standing by the bar, and studied the back of his blond head, her gaze gradually descending over the curve of his neck, his shoulders, all the way down the length of his spine. She paused as she reached his peach of a butt. Well, even if she had made the wrong decision there were certain consolations . . .

He came back with a bottle of cava and a couple of wine glasses. 'Thought we may as well get in the mood,' he said. 'How do you fancy Spain?'

Ah yes, there was still the small problem of their destination. She shook her head. 'I don't think so, mister. You'll be suggesting the Costa del Sol next and I'm not sitting alone on a beach while you round up all the local gangsters.'

'As if,' he protested. 'I never mix business with pleasure.'

'Never? As I recall you attended a certain break-in not so long ago and—'

'Now that was different,' he said. 'And it was a one-off. That particular honey took advantage of my innocence and seduced me with her womanly wiles. I was powerless to resist.' Grinning, he poured out the sparkling cava and passed her a glass. 'So, if not Spain, then where?'

'Er . . . how about Greece?'

He didn't look too keen on the suggestion. 'Or there's always Portugal.'

'You know,' she said wistfully, 'whenever I go to Greece, I always have the urge to just rip off my clothes and swim naked in that warm blue sea.'

This snippet of information generated an enthusiasm that had previously been lacking. 'Come to think of it, Greece sounds like an excellent idea.'

'Good,' she said. 'I'll book the flights tomorrow.'

It was ten minutes to bang-up. Cavelli had already spent more of his precious free time trying to get some sense out of Terry Weston than he'd wanted but he was either too doped-up or too scared to talk.

'If I'm going to help you,' Cavelli said softly, 'I need to know about Joe.'

All he got out of him was a shrug.

'Terry?'

But still he wouldn't budge. He kept on sitting on the edge of his bunk, staring at him with those huge grey eyes, as if it all might go away if he just kept his sweet mouth shut.

'You're in the shit, mate. Surely you realize that?'

Terry lifted and dropped his skinny shoulders again.

Now patience wasn't Cavelli's strong point and anyway, he didn't see why he should play nursemaid to some uncooperative, ungrateful kid who barely had the grace to acknowledge his presence. The fact that he was going out of his way, putting *his* fucking arse on the line didn't seem to have registered. He rubbed on his knuckles, still aching from the day before, and tried another less diplomatic approach.

'For Christ's sake,' he said, raising his voice. 'This isn't just about you. Don't you ever think about anyone else? What about Evie?'

It was a smart move. The mention of her name prompted an instinctive response. Terry's eyes flickered, closed, and then swiftly opened again. 'What?'

Cavelli almost cheered. It was the first word he'd got out of him. 'You're not the only person involved in this. You want her to suffer too?'

'She's . . .' His brow crumpled into a frown. 'Evie's not . . . She's okay.'

'Oh yeah? Because from what I've heard Joe's making her life a fucking misery.'

Terry stared at him, the tip of his tongue sneaking out to dampen his lips. He took a good few seconds to think about it while his hands continued to wrestle on his thighs, a constant nervy tussle that made Cavelli want to shake him. Then suddenly his childlike mouth broke into a smile. 'Nah, you're just saying. She'd have told me. So I know, right? I don't need to worry about Evie. She's safe.'

'Jesus.'

Cavelli gave up. Perhaps she would have more luck. The visiting order and the letter telling her to come might have arrived by now. If not, it should reach her by Monday. He'd tried calling too but had only ever got that damned answering machine.

He returned to his cell. As he walked through the door Isaac glanced up, made a hasty appraisal of his mood, and went back to rolling his cigarette.

'Stupid little fucker!'

Isaac looked sharply up at him again. His voice sounded aggrieved. 'What, man? I ain't done nothing!'

'Not you,' Cavelli said, slumping down on his bunk. And then, because he wasn't in the best of moods, added sarcastically, 'Not *this* time.'

There was a short pause while Isaac debated whether it was prudent to proceed. He sealed his skinny cigarette, placed it between his lips and lit it. However, when no further slights to his character were forthcoming, he took the risk of speaking again. 'So you ain't got it sorted.'

'What do you think?'

Isaac decided it was a rhetorical question and smartly shut up again. What he thought wasn't anything Cavelli wanted to hear. He'd made that plain enough ever since his run-in with Bryant's boys. No point reminding him that he was headed for trouble. Anyhow, headed was hardly the word; he was already in it, right up to his neck. The moment he'd floored that bastard Hales, there was no going back. Rumour had it his jaw was broken. He hoped it was true.

'Well?' Cavelli asked.

Isaac raised his hands in protest. 'Hey, what did I say? Did I—'

'That's what I meant. You've usually got an opinion – what's so different about today?'

Isaac took a long drag on his cigarette, peered at him through the smoke and said, 'Thought you might be in need of some quiet contemplation.'

Cavelli grinned. For all his annoying habits, Isaac was one of the few people in this godforsaken place who could actually make him laugh. 'Oh yeah, and since when did you come over all considerate?'

'Since I learned what was good for me,' he said. 'And I figure you don't need no other fucker pissing you off right now.'

'I can't argue with that.'

Cavelli checked his watch. It was almost five. He didn't mind the early bang-up at the weekend. It was a long haul through to when the doors were opened again at eight but at least it gave him a break from watching Terry Weston's back – not to mention his own. He lay down, stretched out his long legs and put his hands behind his head.

By rights he should have been spending this time reflecting on the mid-week visit. Jesus, Kimberley was always good value for money – just wind her up and watch her go. He wasn't even sure why he'd done it. No, that wasn't true, he knew exactly why. He'd wanted to wind Evie up too, especially after that letter, to make her understand that she wasn't the one in control, that she couldn't take the piss, that *he* was the one who was pulling the strings. Except he wasn't – not any more. It had all gone pear-shaped.

He lowered a hand, wound his fingers around the coarse grey blanket and stared at the wall. There was no chance of seeing his plan through now. And it had all seemed so simple, so possible, the ideal opportunity to fit up Jimmy Reece. She would have done it too . . . with a little persuasion. He was sure of that. Anything to protect that runt of a brother. Once she'd got to know him, gained access to his house, she could have planted enough Class A drugs to send him down for a good long stretch. Intent to supply – that would have done the trick nicely. He felt the old familiar rage coursing through his veins. He might have disappointed Nadine but Jimmy Reece had destroyed her. That filthy bastard had promised her the earth and delivered her to hell. *He* was the one who deserved to be inside, to be counting the days, to be forever watching out for his precious aristocratic arse . . .

A breeze floated in from the window. From his position on the bunk Cavelli could see the sky, a filmy square

446

of grey. The rain had started to fall again, a fast patter against the glass, the drops gradually obscuring his view. He closed his eyes.

'So what do you reckon, Isaac?' He tried to keep his voice light. 'You think I'm fucked?'

'Nah,' he said. 'Not *fucked*, just . . .'

It was that sudden pause that confirmed all his worst fears.

Joe Silk was sure she would panic and he'd been right. It was the only good news he'd had all week. Lifting his glass, he sniffed at the whisky before tilting the glass and taking a large self-congratulatory swig. His decision to wait had been justified. The merchandise had changed hands; there was no doubt about it. Micky had seen an envelope passed discreetly across the café table at the station; too slim to contain cash, it had to be the photo. What else could possibly justify a four-hour round trip to London?

He hadn't really expected Gruber to find anything in Patrick Fielding's flat – the odds had been long – but the outcome remained more than satisfactory. This second break-in had been enough to shake her, to make her aware that the net was slowly closing, to provoke her into action. She must realize by now that time was running out.

Little Evie was well and truly on the ropes.

He smiled. He'd make her pay – and not just for her own treacherous ways. He felt a resurgence of anger at Alex Weston's betrayal. So much for friendship, for respect. That low-life grifter hadn't known the meaning of loyalty. If he hadn't already been six feet under . . .

'Please,' he had said, sitting across from this very desk, his palms laid open, his grey eyes earnestly beseeching.

'You do this for me, Joe – this *one* thing – and I swear that'll be it. The end. No one else will ever see it.'

He had stared at him in disbelief. 'You're threatening me?'

'No, not threatening, *asking*. You think I want to be here, to be doing this? I've got no choice. Terry's looking at ten years, maybe longer. I can't let that happen.'

'And what do you think I can do about it?'

'You can sort it. You'll find a way.'

Joe had shrugged, trying to hold his temper. When he spoke it was through gritted teeth. 'I wish that was true but I don't have that kind of influence. It's impossible.'

'If my son's going down, he's not going down alone.'

And there was something in Weston's expression, in the icy coldness of his voice, that told Joe he wasn't bluffing. And he only had to look at that photograph to understand how damning it was. 'And if I do as you ask, then you'll hand it over?'

He nodded. 'When it's done. I give you my word.'

'You've given me your word before. We made a pact, the five of us. You've already broken it.'

'I'm a father. What would you do in my position?'

Joe could have taken him out there and then – shit, he'd been tempted – but the risk was too great. Weston wasn't a fool; he would have made copies. Also, if Daddy met with an accident the kid might start squealing, the cops would be crawling all over the place and it would only be a matter of time before . . .

So he had grudgingly gone along with it, called in a few costly favours, and managed to get the major charges dropped. Then he'd sat back and waited for Weston to fulfil his side of the bargain.

And what had the bastard done? Joe's fingers tightened around the glass. Walked into a fucking river was what. Broken yet another of his empty worthless promises. And bequeathed the only item he had of value to his stinking bitch of a daughter.

He glared down into the whisky, his eyes narrowing into two thin slits. She should have known it was a legacy that could only destroy her. Didn't she realize who she was dealing with? He'd been patient, more than patient. He had even sent Peter Marshall round with a few gentle reminders as to where her obligations lay, giving her every opportunity to think things through, to make the *right* decision – but there had only been silence.

Was she completely mad? All she'd had to do was hand the damn thing over.

There had been a brief moment when he'd started to doubt if she even had the photograph, had wondered if Weston had maybe got rid of it. But then she'd hired that two-bit private eye and tried to blackmail him through Marshall. That told him all he needed to know.

No more second chances.

Evie Weston's time was up.

Chapter Thirty

Eve interrupted her packing for the third time, went through to the living room and without standing too close to the window peered down at the street. Her stomach took another dive. The car was still there, parked outside the café, a battered green Vauxhall with a crack running across one corner of the windscreen. And the driver was still inside, flicking idly through a newspaper. He was youngish, not much over twenty, but his face was hard, angular, unusually thin and sharp as if all his features had been sculpted by a razor blade. Occasionally he raised his head and glanced over at the door to the flats.

He was waiting for her. She was sure. Was he one of Joe Silk's men?

She drew quickly back, sheltering behind the curtains. He'd been there for the whole afternoon or maybe longer; she had only noticed him a few hours ago. Frowning, she looked at her watch. It was getting on for six. The plan had been for her to drive over to Jack's and for them to travel in his car to Stansted. She still had some time – the flight wasn't leaving until midnight and the Sunday evening traffic should be light – but how was she going to get herself, never mind her suitcase, safely across the road and into the Honda?

Maybe she should call Jack and get him to pick her up.

But that would only solve the most immediate of her problems. It might guarantee her safe passage out of Herbert Street but it wouldn't prevent her guard – if that's what he was – from informing Joe Silk that she was leaving. And if he realized what she was doing, and guessed where she was going then . . .

She was still turning over the dilemma, chewing on a fingernail, when the phone rang. Thinking it was Jack, she hurried over to pick it up. 'Hello.'

There was a short pause. 'Eve?'

At first she didn't recognize the soft female voice. 'Yes?'

'It's Lesley.'

'Oh!' she said, surprised.

'Can we talk?'

Talk? Lesley never wanted to talk – Eve's toes were still bruised from the last time she'd attempted a conversation. And there was something odd about her tone, something slightly off-key. She couldn't quite figure it out. 'Er, sure,' she said, glancing at her watch again. Eve waited but the line had gone quiet, not cut-off quiet, just a non-speaking pregnant kind of hush. She knew that Lesley was still there; she could hear her breathing. 'What is it?'

'Not now. Could you come over tomorrow? In the afternoon, about two.'

'I can't,' she said. 'I'm sorry.' Although even as she apologized she wondered why she was bothering. She frowned down the line. And it was typical of Lesley to ask *her* to drive over – couldn't she get in that fancy pink Mercedes and use a little petrol of her own? 'I'm going away for a few days. Well, a week in fact.'

'Away?' she repeated dully.

Eve, thinking she detected a faint slur in her voice, decided that she must have been on the booze, a few stiff cocktails to make a dull Sunday afternoon pass more swiftly. Life might be comfortable with Mr Player but she doubted he rated that highly in the excitement stakes. 'A holiday,' she said.

'Oh, right. I see.'

Lesley sounded disappointed, but kind of puzzled too, as if she couldn't quite see anything clearly.

'I'll be back in a week,' Eve told her again. She paused but no further comment was forthcoming. 'Look, is this about Terry?'

'Of *course* it's about Terry,' she snapped, instantly roused into her more usual irritability by the ludicrous notion of them having anything else to discuss.

'So can't you tell me now?'

Eve heard the rustle of her hair against the receiver as Lesley shook her head. 'No, I need to talk to you.'

You *are* talking to me, Eve wanted to snap back. She had the feeling this was more to do with Lesley's guilt than anything else, some alcohol-induced impulse to justify her behaviour and salve her dodgy conscience. Perhaps she had even changed her mind about going to see him. But Eve didn't have time to prise out the details. She still had her packing to finish and that other even thornier problem of a mean-looking stranger lurking just across the street . . .

'Will it keep?'

Lesley sighed. It was one of those sorrowful hard-done-by exhalations that she had honed to perfection through the years. 'I suppose it'll have to.'

'Okay, I'll call when I get back.'

No sooner had she put the phone down than she had second thoughts. What if it *was* important, something to do with Joe Silk or the Rowans or . . . Perhaps she shouldn't have been so quick to dismiss her. Her face scrunched into worry. But surely if it was anything urgent she'd have been more insistent. And she'd have sounded more concerned. No, Lesley was just after some sucker to dump her troubles on, anyone who was prepared to listen, to offer a sympathetic ear. Although if she imagined she'd ever get that from Eve she must have been drinking those cocktails since dawn.

Resisting the temptation to ring her back, she took another brief look through the window – damn it, he was still there – and headed for the bedroom. The case was open on the bed and she began checking through the contents, mentally ticking off the list in her head: two bikinis, shorts, T-shirts, a pair of light cotton trousers, three strappy dresses (did she really need three?), flip-flops, bras, pants, deodorant, toothbrush, shampoo, soap, sun cream, make-up. Should she take a cardigan? She couldn't decide. Her mind wasn't really on the job. Only a minor part was focused on the packing, a slightly larger part on Lesley's phone call, but most remained concentrated on the threat that lay outside.

How was she going to get out of here?

She was on her way back from the bathroom, a pair of towels draped over her arm, when the idea came to her. Of course! Why not? It was workable, wasn't it? She ran it a couple more times round her head, searching for flaws, as she dropped the towels carelessly on top of the T-shirts, squashed them down, and pulled the zipper round the case.

Taking it through to the living room, she placed it by the door. Then she flicked through the directory, found the number she wanted, and rang the local police station.

Eve was good at pretending; she'd had a lifetime of practice. When the call was answered she raised her voice an octave or two, her voice faltering between fear and disgust.

'There's a kerb crawler,' she said. 'He's been around all day and now he's parked up in Herbert Street, outside the café. Well, I'm saying that, but God knows *what* he

453

is. Some kind of pervert. Are you going to do anything about it? I'm sure it might not be a priority to you but some of us have daughters and . . .'

A calm-sounding man had asked for her name.

'What's my name got to do with it?' she said indignantly. 'You need to get someone round here. You need to get someone round *now*.'

She hung up before he got the chance to ask any more awkward questions. Could they trace the call? Her father had a withheld number, ex-directory, but they could probably bypass that. But so what if they did? By the time they'd traced it, if they even bothered, she'd be well gone.

While she was waiting she checked her bag to make sure she had her passport. Then she pulled on her cream jacket and went to stand by the window. She stared down at the man. He was smoking now, one skinny hand flicking the ash on to the street. His bony knuckles were stained with inky blue tattoos.

She stood impatiently shifting her weight from one foot to the other.

It was fifteen minutes before the patrol car arrived, cruising slowly into the street. From the shelter of the curtains, she watched, chewing on her lip. What if she'd been wrong? He might have a perfectly reasonable excuse for being here. He could be a cabbie, perhaps, waiting for a call, or just some bloke escaping from a row with his girlfriend. It was only her instincts told her otherwise.

One of the cops, a ruddy-faced thickset officer, got out and strolled across to the Vauxhall. He leaned over to talk to the driver. She didn't need to hear what was being said to understand the gist. The driver, clearly untrained in the skills of diplomacy, waved his arms around and embarked on an argument he was never going to win. When the questions continued, his thin mouth twisted into anger, spewing forth what could only be a stream of curses.

Not the smartest response in the world. And the cop, who didn't care too much for the attitude, was going to make him pay. He examined his driving licence, did a check on the registration, and then carefully circled the car meticulously searching for other ways to make his life a misery. These he appeared to find in abundance.

It was a while before the guy was finally allowed to leave. Eve watched the car, straining her neck to see whether it turned left or right, but it continued straight on towards the main road. She wondered what he'd do next. Pull in somewhere and return later? Well, he certainly wouldn't be back within the next ten minutes or so. The patrol car would probably do a circuit and then return to take a look.

Eve smiled. 'Thanks, boys,' she murmured. It seemed she was getting along a whole lot better with cops these days.

She hung on until they had moved off too and then picked up her luggage, locked the door behind her and headed down the stairs. On the first landing, suddenly remembering something she had meant to do, she put down the case and retraced her steps. Searching in her bag for a pen and scrap of paper, she hastily scribbled a note to Sonia explaining that she had gone to stay with friends for a week and pushed it under her door.

On the ground floor there was a small heap of letters lying in her box. Eve had forgotten all about the post yesterday. She was going to ignore it – it was bound to be bills – but then noticed Cavelli's spidery writing on the one on top. Oh God, another visiting order! Well, whatever gruesome experience he had planned for her next would have to wait. She shoved it, along with the rest of the unwanted mail, into the messy depths of her bag.

On the doorstep she paused, quickly scanning the

street. There was no sign of the Vauxhall. Lugging the case in her right hand she dashed across to her car, flung open the door and leapt inside.

By the time they reached the airport, Eve had developed a faintly hyper air. She had spent most of the journey glancing surreptitiously at the traffic behind, peering in the wing mirror and trying to figure out if they had a tail or not. It was possible, even probable, that Vauxhall man wasn't working alone. What if someone else had taken his place?

'Slow down,' she had said, when the same car had been behind them for a while. 'We're not in any rush. There's no point getting there too early.'

Jack had turned to grin at her. 'What's wrong,' he'd asked. 'My driving isn't that bad, is it?'

And she had inwardly sighed, only a murmur of breath escaping from her lips, as the car had accelerated, overtaken and disappeared into the distance. *Not that one at least.* For a moment she could relax again. 'Who said anything about your driving?'

'You just asked me to slow down.'

'That wasn't a criticism, Inspector. I was merely checking your responses.'

'And were they satisfactory?' He paused, grinning again. 'And are you going to call me Inspector for the next seven days?'

'I'll let you know,' she said. 'On both counts.'

Now, as they sat in a café sipping frothy cappuccinos and waiting for their flight to be called, she fought against the urge to look over her shoulder. If they'd been followed, so be it. There was nothing more she could do about it. Jack, blissfully unaware of her troubles, kept glancing at the departures board. His blue eyes were shining, his mouth constantly breaking into a smile.

Even his knees were dancing a jig beneath the table. Ever since they'd arrived, he'd been acting like a kid about to go on his first holiday abroad. Like a kid, she thought again, staring at him, and although she'd intended the observation to be cynical it somehow transformed into a warmer kind of feeling. There was something infectious about his enthusiasm. She found herself laughing instead.

'Haven't you ever been away before?'

'I love airports,' he said. 'Don't you? They're like a beginning, a starting point, everything fresh and new. All those places you could go to, all those possibilities.'

She tried not to think too hard about the possibilities that might be lurking in Crete. 'I guess that's one way of looking at it.'

He must have sensed her caution because a small frown appeared on his forehead. He kept his voice light and joky though. 'Are you okay? No last-minute regrets about your choice of travelling companion?'

'You bet,' she teased, transforming her real doubts into mock ones. 'Fact is, blondie, I'm still trying to figure out how to get rid of you. I was kind of hoping I might lose you in the crowd.' She felt a pang of guilt as his eyes brightened again. Perhaps it was time to confess, to tell him her real reason for wanting to visit Elounda. It was bound to come out sooner or later.

'Jack . . .' she began tentatively.

But he was already rooting through a carrier bag, pulling out the shades he had bought in the airport shop. He slid them on to his face. 'What do you think – pretty cool, huh?'

She didn't have the heart to break his mood. 'Yeah, pretty damn cool.'

* * *

457

They had made love as soon as they arrived, tumbling between the crisp white sheets, their bodies still dusty from the long coach ride. There had been an almost aching intensity about it, as if they had just been reunited after a long time apart, as if the journeys they had made to reach here had been quite separate.

She wasn't sure how long they had been asleep. From where she was lying she could see the window and a square of pale blue cloudless sky. Gently she disentangled her limbs from his, sat up and then bent again to kiss the smooth curve of his shoulder. He murmured, his lips parting for a second, but he didn't wake.

Eve slid carefully from the bed and pulled on his shirt. She walked around the room, her bare feet slapping softly against the tiles. It was nothing fancy, just a studio with a tiny kitchenette and bathroom, but it was clean and tidy. A small heap of tea and coffee sachets had been left in a bowl on the counter. There was even a pint of milk in the fridge.

While the kettle was boiling, she opened the slatted doors and stepped out on to the balcony. Instantly the warm air enveloped her and she stretched out her arms towards the sun. The room was on the upper floor of a wide white two-storey block and although there was no sea view – she had hardly expected it for the price – the balcony overlooked a pleasant semicircle of lawn bordered by a thick hedge of brightly flowering shrubs. Beyond it, hidden from sight, was the road that led into the centre of the village. She could hear the occasional car putter by and to her more immediate left and right the clatter of cups and plates, of footsteps and muffled voices.

Dreamily, she rubbed her eyes and yawned. The scent of Jack floated up from the collar of his shirt or perhaps it wasn't from his shirt at all. Perhaps his male, musky smell had sunk into the very pores of her skin. She should take a shower and get dressed, make coffee, get her clothes unpacked, start searching for the Villa Marianne . . .

But what was the hurry?

Whatever was out there could wait a few more hours.

She remembered gazing out of the window as the plane began its descent towards Iraklion, the sky a deep blue-grey, the runway sprinkled with tiny lights. It was as if the world had been turned upside down and all the stars deposited on the ground.

Chapter Thirty-One

Eddie Shepherd squeezed the car into a space twenty feet away from the offices of Clark & Able. He blew his nose hard and then leaned across the passenger seat, wound down the window and dropped the damp tissue into the gutter. A middle-aged woman, all twin set and pearls, pursed her lips and glared at him but Eddie glared right back and she passed on by without a word.

While he fumbled in his pockets for a cigarette, he kept his eyes firmly fixed on the building. Sandwiched between a building society and a firm of solicitors, the entrance to the first-floor office was through a freshly painted bottle-green door. It bore only a small silver plaque with the name of the company but not the nature of its business. Very nice. Very discreet. No need for the clients to go shouting their private affairs to the world.

He shouldn't really be here. Jack Raynor would blow a gasket but as he'd cleared off for the week (some kind of family emergency or so he claimed) what he didn't know couldn't bother him. And Eddie was sorely in need of another chat with Paul Clark. He didn't like being lied to. He didn't like it one little bit. It wasn't as if he was driven by any burning desire for the truth – those youthful ideals, had he ever possessed them, had receded as rapidly as his hairline – but more by a matter of principle. No one, and especially not some smarmy, over-dressed git like Clark, was going to make a fool of him.

There had been no progress on the Ivor Patterson case. MIT, he suspected, were already letting it slip down their list of priorities. With no witnesses to say otherwise, it looked like a straightforward mugging that had gone badly wrong. Eddie wasn't so sure. It would have taken one cool customer to go through the pockets of a corpse, remove his wallet and keys and then locate and calmly drive away his car. If it hadn't been for that, he might, just *might* have accepted it as the work of one of the city's addled crack addicts desperate for a fix.

He had been to Patterson's flat on the morning of his death. There was no sign of forced entry but then his attacker already had a convenient set of keys; he could have walked in bold as brass, searched the place from top to bottom, taken anything or nothing, and they wouldn't be any the wiser.

He frowned as he thought about the crummy basement rental in Chesterfield Close. It had been a pit, not fit for a dog to live in, but it was impossible to tell if the overlying mess had been made by an intruder or by Patterson himself. Old newspapers and magazines, butt ends, empty beer cans, used plates, mugs and socks had littered the floor. There were three overflowing ashtrays, two on the table and one still perched precariously on the arm of a battered old sofa. Even Eddie, who was not the most fastidious of men, had turned up his nose at the stink. The three small rooms Patterson had inhabited all contained that sour breath smell mingled with stale tobacco, sweat, rising damp and a few other odours that he preferred not to dwell on.

There had been no sign of a laptop or a camera or any of the usual paraphernalia that a private investigator might use. They had either been in his car, and gone up with the blaze on Mousehold Heath, or had been removed from the flat. There were a few old files and folders, the case notes inside parched and yellowy, but nothing of any interest. Well, apart from one thing: his bank statements. It had been clear from these, from the angry red print denoting the unacceptable level of his overdraft, that Patterson was already struggling to stay within the slim means of his salary – but this, in turn, didn't quite tally with the heap of glossy travel brochures strewn across the coffee table. The idle daydreams of a hopeful man or a sign that he was shortly expecting his luck to change? Eddie suspected the latter. And as the kind of cash injection that a trip to Florida required would hardly be found in his monthly pay packet – whatever profits Paul Clark made obviously didn't filter down into the pockets of his employees – it must have been expected from another source.

Talking of which, one of those employees was emerging from the door right now. Eddie watched as Charlie May stepped out on to the pavement. He was a slight, agile-looking man, in his late forties with a pointy fox-like face. A brush of thick tawny hair swept back from his forehead exposing a pair of dark gleaming eyes. To the outsider, Charlie always gave the misleading impression of a brisk, alert and reliable efficiency. In truth he was the laziest sod God had ever placed on earth. If there was a way to cut corners Charlie May would find it, and usually with his feet up on a couch somewhere. But for all that he wasn't stupid. He had a quick brain, a good intelligence, and Eddie had often thought that if he put half as much effort into *doing* work as he spent in avoiding it he'd probably be running Scotland Yard by now. As it was, he'd been kicked out of the Force before he'd even finished his first year on the beat.

He was halfway out of the car, hoping to grab a word with him, when an irate Paul Clark suddenly appeared on the threshold. His face was black as thunder. Eddie quickly withdrew, or at least as quickly as his bulk allowed, and after an uncomfortable collision with the steering wheel eventually manoeuvred back down into the seat. By the time he'd got his legs and arms into the positions they were intended to be he could see that a definite altercation was taking place outside the office. It wasn't so much a shouting match – Clark couldn't afford to be that indiscreet and Charlie would never make the effort – as an angry one-sided but softly spoken tirade. Paul Clark, his hands gesticulating, his mouth twisted, was virtually spitting in his face. Charlie, however, was doing what he always did when he was up to his neck in shit: he was nodding, shuffling, and trying his best to look contrite.

Clark turned his back and stomped back inside. Charlie glanced at the departing figure and then stared up at the sky, rolled his shoulders and smiled. He was still grinning as he strolled towards the car.

This time, instead of getting out, Eddie opened the window and leaned across the passenger seat. 'Hey,' he said.

Charlie leaned down to look at him. His lips parted, exposing his chipped creamy-coloured teeth. 'Eddie Shepherd. Nice to see you again.'

'Got time for a chat?'

Charlie thought about it for a moment. Then, scrunching his brows together, he glanced down at his watch. 'To be honest, I was thinking of grabbing some lunch.'

'It's ten past eleven,' Eddie said.

'What can I say? I missed breakfast. I'm hungry. You know what it's like when you're working nights. You never get time to catch up with your meals.'

More like *sleeping* nights, Eddie thought. He'd stumbled across Charlie's limp snoring body on many an occasion, curled up in the back of his car. Had the man ever done a whole night's surveillance awake? He doubted it. Still, this wasn't the time to start discussing his work ethic.

'Okay,' he said. 'Lunch it is. Get in.'

Eddie waited until he'd fastened his seatbelt and the car was edging out into the traffic before he laid down the conditions. 'Pizza okay for you?' And before Charlie had time to suggest a more expensive alternative, he added, 'Take it or leave it. It's too early for most places and the Chief Constable's on an economy drive.'

If Charlie was disappointed he didn't show it. 'I can live with pizza.'

Eddie drove past the office, hoping that Clark wasn't peering out through the window. Hopefully, judging by the state he'd been in, he'd still be pacing the floor, wearing a hole in that deep pile carpet.

'Couldn't help noticing,' he said.

Charlie glanced at him.

'Bit of strife,' Eddie continued, 'on the doorstep, there. You not getting along with that boss of yours?'

But Charlie May knew better than to give away even the smallest piece of information before he had his arse firmly seated on a chair and a menu in his hands. He turned his head and stared out through the window.

The restaurant Pizzeria was as bland as its name, a large anonymous space with regimented rows of formica-topped tables. A deep blue utility carpet covered the floor and splattered across the walls were the kind of framed pictures that looked like they'd been pulled from a free magazine. Its one redeeming feature – other than its cheapness – was that it was relatively quiet. Caught in that lull between morning coffee and lunch, only a few other tables were occupied.

Eddie chose a place well away from the window.

'So,' he said, after the food had been ordered. He leaned back and took a sip of his Coke, the ice cubes rattling uncomfortably against his dentures. 'What's going on then – the boss catch you sleeping on the job again?'

'Nah,' Charlie said, not even bothering to pretend to be indignant. 'Not supposed to be here, am I? Got packed off to the bright lights last week. Short-staffed at the London office, he said, everyone down with the flu, in need of some extra hands. So off I go, and the missus is none too pleased, I can tell you – she likes to know where I am on a night, even if I am on a job – and bugger me, when I get there . . .' He paused to take a long slurp of lager. 'Well, they don't look too short-staffed to me, in fact the very opposite and there's sod all to do except a pile of paperwork and you know me, Eddie, I don't like to be confined in four walls, I like to be out on the street and—'

'So you came back?' Eddie prompted. He had a feeling this might turn into a long story if he didn't nudge it along.

'Just for the weekend. I mean, where's the harm in that? I mean, yeah, I'm supposed to be on call in case anything urgent comes up but I got one of the other lads to cover for me. And so I'm planning on heading back this afternoon but first I nip into the office to see Janey – I've got some expenses due and I could do with the readies, you know, cause it ain't cheap in London and—'

Eddie interrupted again. 'And Paul Clark wasn't best pleased?'

'Threw a right old wobbler, didn't he? Said when he sent me someplace I was expected to stay there, not come sneaking back the minute his back was turned. *Sneaking*, that's what he called it. As if I don't have the right to grab a few hours with the wife and kids.' He swallowed half the pint in one aggrieved draught. And then, because even the effort of holding a grudge was too much for him, he put the glass back down on the table and laughed. 'Maybe he's got that executive whatsit – *stress*! Do you reckon?'

'More likely he just can't stand the sight of your ugly mug.'

Charlie laughed again.

The waiter arrived with the food and they both kept quiet until after he had left. Eddie stared at the monstrosity Charlie had ordered, some kind of giant meatfest piled high with spicy beef and pepperoni. He had gone for the more restrained ham and pineapple himself, a choice that made him feel faintly virtuous although he wasn't entirely convinced that it counted towards the five-a-day recommended intake of fruit and veg. Cholesterol levels, however, were the least of his problems. He was still trying to figure out why Paul Clark wanted to keep one of his employees out of the way – not to mention how another had ended up with his head caved in.

'How well did you know Ivor Patterson?'

'Ah, bad business that,' Charlie said. He made a sucking noise between his teeth and then took a large bite of his pizza and chewed on it purposefully. Although the tone of his voice was sorrowful, the event didn't seem to have affected his appetite. 'You caught the bastard yet?'

'We're working on it.' And as he hadn't directly answered the question, Eddie asked it again, rephrasing it slightly. 'You friendly with him then?'

'Nah, not friendly, I couldn't say that exactly. He was more of . . . well, a colleague I suppose you'd call it. Never saw him outside work. We didn't drink together, anything like that.'

Eddie sensed the evasion and pounced on it. 'You didn't like him?'

A wary gleam entered Charlie's eyes. He tilted his head to one side while he considered his response. 'Not especially,' he said. 'He kept himself to himself, didn't mix much. I didn't trust him. But in case you're asking what I think you're asking then no, I didn't kill the poor sod.'

'Well, that's a relief,' Eddie said drily. 'Or *I'd* be the one stuck with the paperwork all afternoon.' He took another sip of his Coke. 'You saying he was bent?'

'I'm not saying anything. The guy's dead, isn't he? Not down to me to cast aspersions.'

Charlie, for all his faults – sloth being only the prime example – had a strong moral streak. It might not extend to giving value for money in the workplace but it precluded many of the sleazier sidelines of his profession. Private investigators were paid to snoop and as a result often stumbled on information they could use as much to their own advantage as their client's. For an unscrupulous man, there were always opportunities.

'C'mon, Charlie, help me out here. I need some background.'

'What for?' he asked. 'I don't get it. It was a mugging, said so in the papers. The guy's walking down the street, minding his own business, and gets slammed from behind. Wrong time, wrong place. End of story. Unlucky but it happens. Why do you need to know about . . .' His inquiry rolled softly into silence. For the first time he paused in his ceaseless demolition of the pizza. Comprehension dawned on his face. 'Hey, hang on. Are you . . .? No, you're kidding me. You can't, you don't . . . God, you don't think it was deliberate, do you? You don't think someone took him out?'

Eddie shrugged. 'Maybe. That's why I'm here.'

Charlie opened his mouth, revealing an unpleasant

meaty mush, and then thankfully closed it again. 'Shit,' he murmured.

'I wouldn't be doing my job if I didn't explore *all* the avenues.' What Eddie failed to mention was that it wasn't actually his case any more but then, in his experience, it was always the minor details that tended to bog down an investigation. 'So if there's anything you can tell me . . .'

Charlie reached for his glass and downed the contents in one. 'Right,' he said. 'Okay.' But then he proceeded to stare silently at the empty glass as if his vocal cords, deprived of lubrication, had shrivelled into dust.

Eddie caught the attention of the waiter and ordered another round. This time he got a beer for himself. He'd intended to stay off the alcohol but decided that he needed something stronger than Coke if he was going to watch Charlie May speaking with his mouth full for the next ten minutes.

The place was still pretty empty and the drinks were promptly delivered. 'So?' he said. 'What can you tell me?'

Charlie speared a slice of pepperoni with his fork and gazed at it earnestly before sliding it between his lips. 'I don't know anything for sure.'

'You're not in the witness box. Rumour and gossip is just fine with me.'

As if this attitude was faintly reprehensible, Charlie shook his head and sighed. 'All I know is what I've *heard*, okay?'

Eddie nodded. 'What you've heard,' he repeated patiently.

'Okay, well there was a case, and we're talking several years ago, when it all went belly-up. It was a divorce, a real cut-and-dried, some rich geezer who was screwing every blonde in town. No names, okay? I'm not going there. But everyone knew about it. I mean we're not

468

talking any attempts at discretion here, the husband couldn't keep it in his pants, but when it came to getting evidence Patterson drew a blank. If his notes were anything to go by, the guy was leading a life that would lead him straight through the heavenly gates and into the arms of the Archangel Gabriel. Not a single photo, not one single scrap of evidence that pointed to the guy being anything but Mr Perfect.'

Eddie picked up a slice of pizza, the congealing cheese leaving a stringy trail behind it. He took a bite while he chewed over what he'd been told. 'There must be at least two of you though, working these cases? I mean no one can do twenty-four-hour surveillance. Even if he was covering then—'

'Yeah,' Charlie agreed. 'Absolutely. But if we're talking your standard divorce stuff then it's going to be the guy on the day shift who sees all the action, right? By six o'clock, by seven, the target – unless he/she is off on one of their business jaunts – is gonna be safely back home and tucked up within the loving bosom of the family.'

'So you think Patterson tipped him off?'

'That's the rumour,' Charlie said. 'And that he got one almighty thank you for his trouble. Believe me, the client was less than happy.'

Eddie nodded. It was interesting but flimsy. His nose was running again. He blew into a red serviette, screwed it into a ball, and dumped it on his side plate. 'Is that it?'

Charlie frowned at him. 'I told you. I don't have any hard facts. It's only rumour, right, supposition. Just that there were a few other cases that seemed nailed down and then suddenly went walkabout, insurance claims, fraud, nothing too big and never too often.'

'So why did Clark keep him on? He must have suspected.'

'Why do you think? It's always useful to have some-one who *owes* you – and who knows it.'

Eddie could see how that might be handy. 'But he wasn't working at the time he died, not for Clark anyway. He'd been sick and then he took leave, right?' Saying the word *leave* reminded him of Jack Raynor and how he shouldn't really be here, doing this. And what made it worse was that it looked like Raynor might be right. There was nothing to suggest that Patterson had been involved in anything seriously dodgy; taking the occasional backhander might not be strictly ethical but it was hardly the crime of the century.

'Yeah, Janey said he had the flu.'

Eddie took a large swig of beer, rinsing out the taste of the cheese. 'Right.' Would he go and see Paul Clark as he'd intended to? He wasn't so sure now.

'Must have come on sudden like.'

'Yeah?' He was only listening with half an ear. Maybe he'd skip Clark, save the aggro, and get back to the office.

'One minute we're working on a job together, not even a sniffle, he's absolutely fine. Next thing he's too sick to leave the house. And Janey, of course, she believes any old sob story. Never mind that I get stuck with covering his shift.'

To hear Charlie protesting about someone else swing-ing the lead made Eddie grin. 'Some people have no sense of responsibility.' Then, as a casual afterthought, he added, 'That the insurance job then? Butler, wasn't it?' He recalled Clark handing him the notes, the last case Patterson had worked on.

'Hell, no, that was weeks ago.'

Eddie had just taken another drink. He spluttered, a thin spurt of beer escaping from his lips and spraying across the table. 'What?' He wiped his mouth with the back of his hand.

Charlie didn't repeat it. His eyes immediately grew wary, his tawny brows shifting together in a frown.

'C'mon, don't go all dumb on me now! What are you talking about? What was the case you and Patterson were working on last?'

'What did Clark tell you?' he asked evasively.

'Fuck what Clark told me.' Eddie could feel a surge of adrenalin kicking into his bloodstream. Paul Clark had been lying. He'd known it all along. '*You* tell me!'

But for a man who normally loved the sound of his own voice, Charlie May wouldn't be drawn. He gave a tiny shake of his head and, as if searching for the nearest exit, glanced quickly around the room.

Eddie gave him an incentive. 'You want me on your back twenty-four hours a day, always looking over your shoulder?'

'You wouldn't do that, Mr Shepherd,' he said, perhaps hoping to ingratiate himself by adopting the more respectful title. His voice was wheedling, almost plaintive. 'You and me, we've always rubbed along okay.'

'Just give me a name.'

'You know I can't. That's stuff's confidential. Why don't you ask Clark?'

'Yeah, maybe I will. And maybe at the same time, just to improve that great mood he's in, I'll tell him how often I've caught you fast asleep in the back of that clapped-out Mondeo of yours.'

Charlie pulled a face, his mouth turning sulky. But it didn't take him long to make up his mind. 'You didn't hear it from me, right? I don't want this coming back like some bloody boomerang.' Then, as if to justify his decision to talk, he shrugged and said, 'It wasn't as if it was any big deal anyway, just a bog-standard surveillance. Divorce job, I reckon, the missus playing around while the old man's in the nick.'

'It was a woman then?' Eddie felt a jolt in his chest.

And he suddenly knew, even before he heard the name, what was coming. He breathed in deeply, a great gathering of air. He thought of the way the photograph of Patterson had fallen from her fingers. He thought of the file in his drawer, of all those slim threads waiting to be woven together.

'Weston,' Charlie muttered reluctantly. 'Eve Weston.'

Why wasn't he surprised? He slowly released the breath, a thin wheeze emanating from his lungs. Automatically he reached for his fags before realizing he couldn't smoke in the restaurant.

'The flats on Herbert Street,' Charlie added.

'And?' Eddie tried not to sound too interested while the cogs in his brain began to click and whirr. What had he told Raynor? Two men dead, three if you counted Alex Weston, and all in some way connected to *her*.

'Not much. I hardly saw her. There was only one time, a Saturday, she came out with some bloke early evening.' He screwed up his eyes as if trying to picture him clearly. 'An older geezer, grey hair, specs, suit. In his sixties. And they were friendly like, you know, very cosy.'

Henry Baxter, Eddie thought instantly. Unless she'd traded him in for a similar model. 'You get a photo?'

'In the file,' he said. 'You'll have to ask the boss.'

Eddie nodded. He recalled that office in Covent Garden, that other basement – tidier at least than Patterson's but no less claustrophobic – and the ageing solicitor who had employed Eve Weston. And not, he suspected, purely for her secretarial skills. If what the son had claimed was true, she'd been taking down more than his letters. Had Patterson found out and tried to screw him over? Had he blackmailed him, threatened to expose their continuing affair?

He wondered if Henry Baxter had an alibi for the early hours of last Monday morning.

There was no saying what some men would do to

472

protect their marriages – *or* their mistresses. Eddie turned the idea over but then dismissed it. It wasn't beyond the realms of possibility but somehow he couldn't quite envisage that silver-haired pedant creeping furtively along the street, wielding a cosh and caving in Ivor Patterson's skull.

Charlie, like a starving man, stuffed another slice of pizza into his mouth and mumbled, 'So you think . . . you think that what happened had something to do with that case?'

Eddie gave him a long hard look. 'I doubt it,' he said. 'But if I hear any rumours to the contrary I'll know exactly where they came from.'

Charlie's brows shot up. Then, still chewing, his greasy lips crawled into a smile. 'You know me, Mr Shepherd: the soul of discretion.'

Eddie pushed away his plate, half the food still uneaten, and looked at his watch. It was time to have a word with that lying git Paul Clark.

'Right,' he said, getting to his feet. 'I'd best be off.'

'But—'

He flapped a hand. 'Don't worry. I won't breathe a word about our little meeting.'

'But Mr Shepherd—'

'See you around.' Eddie swept up his jacket and, without a backward glance, strode out of the restaurant. It was only when he was in the car and halfway down the road that he realized he'd left Charlie May with the bill.

Chapter Thirty-Two

By the time Henry got back from his appointment it was after five and Louise had already gone home. He went through the list of messages she had left on his desk, checking to see if anything was important enough to merit his immediate attention. Only one caught his eye: A Mr Shepherd had called three times. It was urgent, she had written in her small neat hand, underlining the word twice. He winced at the unnecessary emphasis. Shepherd? He had no clients by that name.

It took a moment for it to register and when it did, finally nudged into place by the Norwich phone code, Henry felt a resurrection of the disgust he had experienced on first meeting him. *Sergeant* Shepherd, the policeman with attitude who had come asking about Eve. He recalled his thick splayed thighs, the ugly leer on his face, and the sly innuendo.

What did he want? Henry did not believe in the alleged urgency; men like Shepherd always assumed their business was more essential, more pressing than anyone else's. Well, whatever it was, it could wait. He wasn't going to call back today.

For the next hour Henry worked through his correspondence, dictating replies for Louise to deal with in the morning. He was aware of the floors above gradually emptying, of the clatter of high heels on the steps outside, the brief flurry of voices, of brittle laughter as the girls separated on the street and went their different ways.

Gradually, like a soft exhalation, a hush descended. Henry tilted his head and listened. It was as though the building breathed differently in the absence of its daytime occupants, its walls and floors relaxing, its heart beating to a gentler rhythm. Smiling, he returned to his work.

It was a further forty minutes before the peace was broken by the rough grating sound of the intercom buzzer. He looked up, surprised, and glanced at the clock. Twenty to seven – well outside office hours. No client surely would be calling at this time. He decided to ignore it. But seconds later, it came again, three longer more determined buzzes.

With a sigh, Henry got to his feet and padded up the stairs. It entered his mind as he crossed the foyer that Shepherd might have decided on a more direct approach. He paused, considering a discreet withdrawal, but the strident sound, far louder up here, propelled him forward again. He jerked opened the door and found, with some relief, that the stranger standing on the step bore no resemblance whatsoever to the disagreeable sergeant.

'Henry Baxter?' he asked politely.

'Yes,' he said.

'My name's Ian Allbright. I'm sorry to disturb you but I wonder if I might have a word.'

He had a faint but discernible American accent. Henry glanced at his watch. 'I'm afraid we're closed. Office hours are—'

'Oh, it's not about work, sir.'

That ingratiating use of the word *sir* made him suspect that Mr Allbright was about to try and sell him life insurance. Henry's gaze flickered over the man, taking in his light grey suit, smart but not too smart, the white shirt and blue striped tie. His hair was brown, cut short with a side parting. 'I see,' he said. 'So—'

'Actually, I'm a friend of Patrick Fielding. He asked me to drop by and talk to you.' Glancing furtively over his shoulder, he lowered his voice. 'It's about Eve. Perhaps if I could step inside for a minute?'

'Eve?' Henry said, but even as he spoke he automatically stood aside.

Allbright nodded and moved forward. 'Thank you.' He waited until Henry had closed the door before lifting his briefcase up towards his stomach and patting it with his left hand. 'I have some papers for you.'

Henry frowned. 'What papers?'

'Patrick thought they might be important. He thought you should take a look at them.' He glanced around the foyer and then up the flight of plush red-carpeted stairs as if concerned about being overheard. 'Er . . . perhaps there's somewhere a little more private?'

Henry wondered what the documents could be. A clue, perhaps, to what had been happening recently, something that might help shed light on the cause of all her problems. He felt a vague flutter of excitement.

'Of course.' He gestured towards the door to the basement and followed Allbright down the stairs. 'Take a seat,' he said, after they had passed through the outer room and into the inner sanctum of his office.

Allbright pulled up a chair, put the briefcase on the desk and opened it with a couple of clicks. There was a thin rustle as he rooted through the contents. Henry steepled his fingers and waited expectantly. However, when the lid came down again, it was not papers his visitor was holding in his hand but a gun.

Henry's jaw dropped, his heart skipping a beat. He didn't know what kind of gun it was or even if was real. All he was sure of was that it was pointing straight at him.

'What?' It came out as a strangulated gasp.

'You're an intelligent man, Mr Baxter. I know you won't do anything stupid.'

Henry stared down the barrel. It was pretty clear that he'd done the stupid bit already. The authenticity of the weapon no longer seemed in doubt. The gun, with what looked like a silencer attached, was aimed at his chest, just left of centre. He had a mental image – God, he hoped it wasn't a premonition – of a red rose blossoming in his breast, of the stain slowly spreading . . .

Allbright gave him a creepy smile. 'I think we have some business to attend to.'

'I don't . . . don't understand.' Henry's voice wavered. It sounded like an old man's voice, weak, slightly trembling. He slowly lowered his hands, taking care not to make any sudden movements. His gaze was firmly fixed on that finger on the trigger.

'I want the photograph.'

And Henry's pulse, as if it wasn't already racing, began to sprint. By now it was obvious that Allbright had nothing to do with Patrick Fielding. Which meant . . . Christ, he knew what it meant: he was dealing with some gangster's sidekick, the kind of scum who wouldn't think twice about killing someone old enough to be his father. 'The photograph?'

Allbright sighed, his smile fading. 'I'm sure your time is as precious as mine,' he said. 'I don't any see any point in either of us wasting it. Let's keep this simple. There are two things I want – first the photograph and then the whereabouts of Eve Weston. I know you're going to provide me with both – one way or another – so why don't we just skip the painful preliminaries and get on with it?'

Henry's first reaction was of pure relief. At least Eve

was still safe; they didn't realize where she was. The second, coming close behind, was of a cold eerie dread. It folded over him like a sheet of ice. He only had to look into those dead eyes to see what the man was capable of. He had to start thinking and thinking fast. Could he make some kind of trade-off, find a way of getting out of here alive without compromising Eve?

He swallowed hard and ran his tongue along his lips. 'Okay,' he said. 'I've got the picture, you can have it, but I don't know where she is. I swear. I haven't heard from her since Saturday.'

Allbright stared at him. He thought about it for a moment and then nodded. 'Okay,' he said. 'Just give me the photo.'

Henry, keeping his eyes on the gun, rose carefully to his feet. He could feel his legs shaking. 'It's in there,' he said. He gestured with his head towards the cabinet behind his desk. He didn't move until Allbright nodded again. Then, although reluctant to show his back, he slowly turned, opened the doors and revealed the safe. As he keyed in the electronic code, he thought again about what he was doing. But what choice did he have? Giving him the picture wasn't the end of the world; he knew Eve had a copy, maybe more than one, and as long as he could get to her before they did, so long as he could warn her . . .

He reached in, removed the brown envelope and shut the safe again. 'Here,' he said, offering it over.

'You open it,' Allbright said, waving the gun. 'Show me.'

Henry obediently opened the envelope and pulled out the photograph. He held it out for him to see.

Allbright scraped back his chair and stood up. 'Good,' he said. 'Very good.' But no sooner had he stepped forward and got it in his grasp than it fluttered to the floor. It landed slightly to the right of the desk.

For a few seconds they both stared at it.

'Pick it up!'

Henry wasn't going to argue. He bent down, scrabbling on the carpet. It was only as his fingers closed around the image that he realized what a bad mistake he had made. He almost sensed the intention before Allbright's booted foot, only inches away, lifted off the floor and stamped down on his hand with all the force of a ten-ton load of granite. Too late! He heard the bones snap, a slight brittle sound like the breaking of twigs, before he felt the pain scream through his body. The air rushed out of his lungs. Doubling over, he clutched at his hand but it was still trapped beneath the thick studded soles. *No!* But his shout, his plea, whatever emerged from his throat was stifled by a palm across his mouth.

'Shut it, okay? You make another sound and I'll break the other one.'

Henry groaned.

'You understand?'

His head was being forced back, the cold metal of the gun pressing hard against his temples. There were lights dancing in his brain. But from somewhere, somehow, he found the sense to grunt. The hold abruptly slackened and Henry fell in a limp sprawl across the carpet. The boot lifted and instantly he reached for his hand, holding it, cradling it.

Allbright snatched up the picture and put it in his pocket. 'Now tell me where the bitch is.'

Henry rocked his hand against his chest. 'I don't know, I swear.' He could hardly speak for the pain. Cold sweat was trickling down his spine.

'Come on, Henry. You know you want to help.'

For some reason Allbright's American accent was more pronounced now; in fact everything about him seemed exaggerated, his height, his smile, the colour of his eyes. He was like an actor playing a part, gradually

479

getting into character. *The psychopathic gangster.* And deep inside, like a gut instinct, Henry knew that this particular scene had been played out before – and that it always had the same ending.

Huddled on the ground, as helpless as a child, he was aware of his age, of his weakness. He thought about Celia waiting at home for him. He thought about the day they'd met, about the day Richard had been born. He wondered if it was true that your life flashed in front of your eyes just before . . . And he knew, knew absolutely, without any shadow of a doubt, that it didn't matter what he said, whether he lied or told the truth – without a miracle he was going to die here tonight.

Still, he could play for time at least. 'There are copies,' he said. 'Lots of them. She's been careful. She isn't a fool.' He had to squeeze the sentences out, short gasps between the waves of pain.

'She'll hand them over.'

'Why should she do that?' He had to keep him talking while he thought about what to do next.

Allbright smirked, his index finger gently stroking the trigger on the gun. 'Because she won't want to end up like you.'

'She'll go to the police,' Henry said. 'She'll tell them everything.' He was tempted to add *You won't get away with it* but it died on his lips, the threat like a bad piece of dialogue from a third-rate movie, too pathetic even to utter.

'Oh, I don't think so,' he drawled. 'She wouldn't want anything *untoward* to happen to that brother of hers.'

Henry's eyes grazed the carpet searching for a weapon, a handy metal bar left under the desk maybe, but of course there was nothing. Only dust. It was surprising how much dust there was. An unexpected calm was beginning to descend on him. It was as though he had used up his supply of adrenalin, his fear had peaked and like one of those hospital graphs was gradually on the descent again.

'Do you know, Henry, it's been nice to chat like this but I'm getting kind of bored. Perhaps you'd like to tell me where she is now.'

'All right.' Henry nodded weakly as if he might be about to comply. 'But can I get up first?'

Allbright took a moment to consider it. Then, rightly judging that the old man wasn't in any fit state to launch a counterattack, he waved the gun towards the chair. 'Sit over there.'

Henry staggered awkwardly to his feet, using his one good hand for leverage while the other hung limply at his side. He fell into the chair and pulled his damaged left hand up on to the desk. The movement intensified the throbbing pain. He stared down, feeling a curious sense of pity for it, as if it was not a part of him at all but something quite disconnected; limp and useless, it lay on the blotter like some battered piece of road kill.

'You want me to blow your bloody brains out, Henry?'

He looked slowly up. 'Aren't you going to do that anyway?'

Allbright sat down opposite him. His eyes were gleaming now. He appeared almost . . . Henry struggled to find an adequate description. Joyous was the nearest he could get. He was a man, quite clearly, who took pleasure from his work.

'Why should I?' he said. 'You tell me what I want to know, I've got no reason. I'll walk out of here and you won't call the Law. You won't call them because you don't want to see her get hurt. She won't call them because she doesn't want to see *him* get hurt. So she'll pass the rest of the photos over and keep her mouth shut. And that way, everyone's happy. You see?'

But Henry didn't believe him. 'You can't afford to kill

481

me,' he said with more confidence than he felt. He had nothing to lose now. He may as well go for it. He took a deep breath and rattled out the questions in quick-fire rapid succession: 'You think I haven't made arrangements? You think I don't know how important that photograph is? You think I don't know what it means to Joe Silk?'

He had the satisfaction of seeing a reaction on Allbright's face. It was fleeting, granted – the man was a professional – but he had found a weak spot. Now all he had to do was follow up on it.

'What are you saying, Henry?'

He was still trying to figure that one out when, suddenly, there was a noise from the top of the stairs, a small click like a door being opened.

Allbright, distracted, turned his head for a second – and Henry took his chance. Lunging across the desk he grabbed for the gun.

But he wasn't fast enough.

The last sound he heard was a soft muffled thud. And as the darkness enveloped him, dense as fog, he knew that it was over.

Chapter Thirty-Three

Eve had a problem. It was Wednesday already, their third day in Crete, and she was still no closer to finding the Villa Marianne. Her father's address book had only said Elounda; there had been no mention of a street name. Somehow she had imagined that once she was here she would know exactly where it was, but in fact the very opposite had happened. Apart from the clock tower in the square, and perhaps the harbour – although most harbours looked kind of similar – nothing seemed even remotely familiar.

On Monday afternoon, after a leisurely lunch, she had dragged Jack through the surrounding streets, claiming she was trying to get a feel for the place but privately hoping that something would come back to her. Every time they had stumbled on a villa, she had felt the fast thump of her heart – and every time she had been disappointed.

She had asked the rep, an over-smiley girl called Joanna, if she had ever come across it. 'It's white with wrought-iron gates at the front and, er . . . it's got a pool, a courtyard.' But she could have been describing any one of a hundred properties littered around the district. 'I'm sure it's not that far from the square.'

Joanna had continued to sort through her leaflets. 'It doesn't ring any bells but I'll ask around. Would you be interested in a trip to Knossos or the Samaria Gorge? They're both really worth seeing. I've got all the info here.'

And Eve had politely taken the leaflets, knowing even as she walked out of the door that the villa had already been forgotten. She had gone on to ask the maid who spoke no English, the man she bought her cigarettes off, three waiters and even a couple of German tourists but was met only by the same shrugs, the same shakes of the head.

There was no real reason why she shouldn't mention it to Jack. Had the two of them split up and searched separately they could have covered twice as much ground. All she would need to say – and she wouldn't even need to lie about it – was that she had stayed there once with her father, that she was curious to see it again. But something held her back. She wanted to keep Jack separate from the past, the photograph, from all the grief that was snapping at her heels. He was the only good thing in her life at the moment.

They were sitting near the harbour now, eating a breakfast of freshly grilled sardines and hot bread. Two tiny cups of thick Greek coffee cooled at their elbows.

'Eve?'

She looked up sharply, realizing he'd been speaking to her. 'Sorry.'

'Any ideas for today?'

'I don't mind,' she said. And then, aware of the blandness of the reply, quickly added, 'More of the same?'

He grinned back at her.

Yesterday, they had hired a car and driven out to the palm-fringed resort of Vai where, after finding the main beach covered by a swarm of towels and bronzing bodies, they had scrambled over rocks to a smaller, more secluded area. They had spent the whole day there talking, swimming, sprawling side by side on the sand. Had they been alone their roaming explorative hands might

484

have led to something more but their haven, sadly, was not completely deserted. Abiding by the laws of public decency, they had settled for some deep erotic kisses in the sea, whispered what they'd *like* to do and saved the best until later.

'How about a boat trip?' He had a pamphlet open on the table, one of those guides that Joanna had given her. 'Spinalonga – what do you think? Could be interesting.'

She gazed over his shoulder towards the distant smudge of the island.

'There's a tour boat leaves every half-hour,' he continued. 'Or you can hire one of the local guys. Hey, we could do that, try a bit of bartering.'

Despite the warmth of the sun, the flesh on her arms suddenly burst into goose bumps because now she *did* remember something, a flashback, a memory of sitting on an abandoned flight of steps while her father took her picture. 'The island of the living dead,' she said.

Jack raised his eyebrows.

'It's where they used to send the lepers. That's what they call it, the locals.'

He speared a sardine and put it in his mouth. 'Delightful.'

'Like *him*,' Marianne had said, when she'd told her where they'd been. She'd been lying on her back by the side of the pool, one hand trailing in the water like a glamorous movie star posing for a picture. Her loose wet hair flowed around her shoulders. She had raised the cigarette to her crimson lips and giggled. 'The living dead.' And Eve could clearly recall glancing over at the man she was talking about, the man standing under the arch of the doorway quietly watching them. She could feel him, sense the chill of his presence, but his face remained a blur.

'Eve?'

She shook her mind back into the present. 'Yeah, why not?' She picked up a piece of bread and shredded it between her fingers. 'We could go later, after lunch. I thought I might take a walk this morning, do some shopping. We can meet up later. Would you mind?'

Had he been a different kind of person, less secure, less confident, he might have objected but Jack wasn't the type to take offence. 'About midday?' he said.

She looked at her watch; it was only nine fifteen. That should give her plenty of time. 'Okay. What will *you* do?'

'Oh, go for a swim. Sit on the beach and top up my tan. Have a few beers. Don't worry, I'll keep myself occupied.'

He was wearing a simple white vest and a pair of black jeans. The vest showed off the muscles in his shoulders. With her eyes she traced the undulating contours down along his arms until she reached his strong long-fingered hands. His skin had already turned to a shade of dark honey, his hair lightened to an even paler blond. She felt a sudden impulse to abandon the project, to forget about the villa and join him on the beach.

Before she could give in to temptation, she jumped to her feet. 'I'll see you later then.'

Eve had been walking for over an hour and her legs were beginning to ache. Away from the breeze of the sea the heat was more intense. And it wasn't even June yet. What was it like in August? She could feel the tiny beads of perspiration forming on her face, on her temples and upper lip, as the sun beat down on the top of her head. She should have bought a hat. She should have worn her trainers too instead of the ridiculous flip-flops that were already chafing between her toes.

Starting from the harbour, she had worked her way systematically back through the village, crossing each street off her map as it was walked, examined and then dismissed. Only the main thoroughfares were marked, however, and she had frequently come across other minor nameless paths that sometimes led somewhere but more often than not petered out into a dusty nothingness.

Elounda was a spread-out, sprawling kind of place, the village constantly expanding to accommodate the increase in tourists. Perhaps that was why, after over twenty years, so little seemed familiar to her. If it wasn't for that clock tower, for the certainty of that one memory, she would doubt that she had ever been here before.

She was feeling somewhat dejected – the villa could be anywhere, tucked away in a corner she would never find – when she spotted the café up ahead. Five tables, two of them unoccupied, were huddled under a wide stripy awning casting a welcome block of shade. Yes, a drink was what she needed and a chance to rest her weary feet. She hurried forward and slumped down in one of the chairs with a sigh.

The waiter who came out to serve out her was tall, in his mid-twenties with a curly mop of black hair.

'*Kalimera*,' she said, drawing on her limited Greek.

He smiled broadly at her. 'Good morning,' he said. She didn't need to question how he knew that she was British; her pale skin and red hair were tantamount to a flashing neon sign. 'What may I get for you?'

'Something cold,' she said. She fancied a beer but settled on iced coffee. 'Frappé?'

'Frappé,' he repeated, still smiling as if she had made a perfect choice. 'Very good.'

He disappeared back inside. Eve stared down at the map. She had covered a fair bit of ground but it was starting to look like mission impossible. And what would she do if she did find it? Go and knock on the door, ask if this was Joe Silk's villa, ask if anyone knew anything about a photograph taken two years ago? She realized, with growing frustration, that she hadn't even got a plan.

The waiter returned with a long glass on a tray and with a dramatic flourish, like a magician producing a rabbit from a hat, set it down on the table in front of her.

'Lovely,' Eve said, thinking that maybe she should applaud. 'Thank you.'

'Ah,' he said, catching sight of the map with all its markings and squiggles and crossing outs. 'You search for somewhere?'

'Yes, a villa. The Villa Marianne.' Automatically, she repeated her hopeless description. 'White, tall gates, a courtyard, a pool.' She saw his bemused expression and smiled. 'I know. It's not much to go on, is it? But it's all I can remember. I stayed there once a long time ago.'

As if this information was an invitation for him to join her, he pulled up a chair and sat down. 'Marianne,' he repeated thoughtfully, scratching his ear. He turned the map around to look at it. 'Many villas in Elounda. Many rich persons.'

'I've noticed,' she said.

'Is not good.'

She glanced at him, trying to decide whether it was the buildings or the people he was objecting to. 'No?'

In the event it turned out to be neither. It was only the map. He prodded it with a finger and gave a sad resigned shake of his head. 'Many roads not here. Much wrongness. Is . . . how you say?'

'Useless?' she suggested.

He laughed, slapping a palm down on his thigh. 'Useless!' he repeated, his dark eyes shining like a child who has just been taught a naughty word. 'Is very useless!'

She found herself laughing too. It was a release as much as anything, an opportunity to free the tension from her body – and it was preferable to the other option of dropping her face into her hands and crying like a baby. She had been wasting her time. *Useless!* The word revolved mockingly around her head. *She* was useless.

This whole stupid search for the invisible villa was useless. But there was some kind of blessed relief in finally realizing it.

Eve was still smiling as an overweight middle-aged couple, their cheeks plump and shiny, staggered along the street and grabbed the last available table. With a series of grunts they lowered themselves on to the metal folding chairs. She watched as they gathered their overflowing beach bags closer to their ankles and then bent again to pat them anxiously as if a band of Cretan towel-robbers might be lurking just around the corner.

'Are you sure about this?' the woman said. Her whiny voice was loud enough to carry. 'Are you sure the food is *safe* to eat here?'

'As safe as anywhere round here,' the man replied curtly.

Eve stared at them, her smile fading into embarrassment. She hoped the waiter hadn't heard. She quickly turned, intending to say something, and to say it loudly enough to drown out their crass remarks, but he was already getting to his feet.

'Excuse, please.' He gestured towards the couple. 'I must . . .'

'That's okay,' she said. 'And thanks.' She threw him another smile, hoping to compensate by some small gesture for the incivility of her countrymen.

She watched as he presented a menu to the couple, nodded, smiled politely, and then walked back inside. She watched them peruse the contents, their eyes as suspicious as if they'd just been presented with a list of lethal poisons. What was the matter with them? She couldn't understand why people went abroad and then turned up their noses at the slightest hint of anything foreign.

Eve gave the frappé a stir and then picked up her glass and took a long welcome drink. She lit a cigarette and relaxed. A few minutes passed before she became aware of the heated debate taking place inside. Curious, she glanced in through the window. A group of elderly men, their faces as brown and wrinkled as walnuts, were waving their arms and shouting over each other. The waiter, standing with one hand splayed across his hip, was looking from one to the other.

After a while he broke away and put his head round the door. He looked at her and grinned. 'Yankee?' he said.

She looked back at him, confused. 'Pardon?'

'Americano?' he said. 'At the villa?'

So they were talking about the Villa Marianne! She felt a faint surge of hope. 'No,' she said. Then, wondering if it might have been sold since, that an American might have bought it, she shrugged. 'Oh, I don't know. Maybe.'

He said something in Greek to the men behind him. There was a volley of replies, another flurry of hands, a further outburst of views and opinions. By now everyone, inside and out, was staring at her – so much for discretion. Her business, it seemed, was the centre of attention.

The British couple, as if she was busy revealing the details of her sex life, were glaring at her open-mouthed. Their thin-lipped disapproval was as oppressive as the heat. She kept her gaze averted, refusing to meet their eyes. She had enough problems of her own without the additional burden of their suppressed outrage.

'The white paint,' he asked, relaying another question, 'not the pink?'

She smiled. 'It used to be white,' she said.

The talk inside continued for a while and then gradually grew quiet. The questions ceased and the men returned to their cards. The discussion, it appeared, had reached an impasse. Eve's brief flash of hope fizzled into disappointment. She finished her coffee, placed some euros on a saucer to cover the bill and prepared to leave.

The waiter hurried over to her table. 'Come,' he said, beckoning to her. 'I show you.'

She looked at him. 'Show me?' Then the light dawned and her eyes widened. 'You know where the Villa Marianne is?'

'Is possible,' he said.

Well, possible was better than nothing. It was worth a look at least. She got to her feet and picked up her bag. 'Thank you,' she said.

Within a few minutes she was starting to have doubts about the wisdom of her decision. As he weaved through the dusty side streets, leaving the café far behind, she quickly lost her bearings and began to feel uneasy. Was this an act of madness, wandering off with a total stranger? She had no real idea where he was taking her. To some lonely grove, perhaps, away from prying eyes, where no one would hear her cries and . . .

'Is it far?' she said. 'My boyfriend's waiting for me at the harbour. I promised I'd meet him at twelve. He'll worry if I'm late.'

She hoped by this statement to convey not just the fact that she'd be missed but also that she had a partner. What if he had misconstrued her friendliness? Perhaps by agreeing to come with him, he thought she was actually consenting to something else entirely. She felt the nerves flutter in her stomach as she shot him a sideways glance.

'Not so far now,' he said.

'This is very kind of you,' she said stiffly. 'Only I think that maybe—'

'Only little way,' he said. 'We see soon.'

And, not having a clue as to where she was, being utterly disorientated, she didn't have much choice other than to stay with him. If she just walked away she could be roaming these nameless paths for hours on end trying to find her way back. She was overly aware of how quiet it was, of the soft background thrum of insects, of the rhythmic slap of her flip-flops against the soles of her feet.

'I don't even know your name.'

'Christos,' he said. 'Christos Papageorgiou.'

There was something reassuring about the voluntary addition of his surname. And also in the casual way he loped along. His easy manner and soft brown eyes gave no hint of any evil intention.

'Eve Weston,' she replied. She relaxed a fraction. There were witnesses, weren't there? All those customers at the café for starters. And having hair this colour – she curled a damp strand behind her ear – meant that she was usually remembered. He'd have to be mad to try anything – well, either mad or reckless.

'You come from London, Eve?'

'Yes,' she said.

'I know London,' he said. 'I work Finchley. You know Finchley? My uncle he has restaurant there. I work six months in winter.' He grinned at her. 'Very cold, very rainy.' He shook his slender shoulders in a gross exaggeration of a shiver.

She smiled back. 'Not like Elounda.'

'You like?' he asked.

She hoped he was referring to the village and not himself. 'Sure,' she said. She spoke slowly and clearly, making sure there was no room for any kind of misunderstanding. 'It's a very pretty place.'

The road they had been following had gradually widened and now they were entering a more solid street, complete with a parade of shops and a gentle crush of people. Eve felt the remaining tension leave her body, her limbs loosening, her hunched shoulders rolling back, even her jaw relaxing as if she had been clenching her teeth together. She was secure here in the company of others. There was safety in numbers. She smiled again at Christos, feeling a need to compensate for her earlier suspicions.

They must be near the main square, only a short distance from the sea. A light breeze ruffled her hair and set the skirt of her dress dancing against her dusty ankles. She took time now to look around, gazing in the shop windows, absorbing the sights and smells, soaking up the atmosphere.

Like a jackdaw her eyes were drawn to a glittering display, an array of silver jewellery, of slender chains and rings and necklaces. She would buy a piece before she left, a memento to remind her of Crete. And something for Sonia too; she could do with a lift after everything she'd been through. She was still trying to decide what she might prefer – a bracelet perhaps – when she noticed the tattered poster on the wall, faded and peeling at its corners. *Missing*, it said in English across the top and directly underneath what she presumed was the Greek equivalent.

She might have thought no more of it, no more at least than of all the other similarly saddening posters displayed around London, if she hadn't come across another just a few yards further along. The picture on this one was clearer and the girl's face with its wide easy smile and long curtain of fair hair struck a chord. It took a second for Eve to process the information, for the features to translate themselves into someone she thought she recognized, and then . . .

Abruptly, she stopped, whirled around and walked back. There was a tightening in her chest, a squeezing sensation as if all the air was being forced from her lungs. Her lips moved as she quickly scanned the rest of the poster. *Andrea Banks, 17, disappeared* . . . Her heart skipped a beat, hoping for a different date, a different year, but there it was in black and white: the July of two years ago. It was the girl in her father's photograph! There was no question about it. Still she felt an urge to reach inside her bag and unfold the copy she had brought with her . . . but it was pointless. She had stared at that photo long enough and hard enough to be absolutely certain.

Eve could sense her knees starting to tremble. Despite the warmth of the air, she shivered. It didn't take a genius to add the parts together – it was a piece of arithmetic so simple that even a child could do the sums: a trip to Crete that was never mentioned, a girl that had gone missing, a photograph that had been secretly taken, a gangster called Joe Silk, all the threats that had been made . . . *Andrea Banks was dead!* She knew it as surely as if the teenage corpse was lying right in front of her.

God. No. Jesus!

She must have swayed a little because Christos suddenly took hold of her elbow. 'You okay?' he asked. His brown eyes were full of concern.

She turned towards him, flapping a hand in front of her face. 'Just the heat,' she mumbled. 'Sorry.' In truth what she felt was a vile clammy coldness. A wave of nausea rose up from her stomach. *Oh Christ, what had happened here? What had happened to that girl?* She tasted the sour bile in her mouth and hoped she wasn't about to throw up.

'You like water?' he asked.

She stared down at the ground. She stared at her feet, at the dirt between her toes. She did need water but what she needed more was to *think*. She needed to be alone, to get away from here. 'No,' she said. 'No, I'm okay. I'll be all right.' Her voice sounded odd, disconnected, like an alien sound that was coming from someone else's mouth.

Then she asked the question that she had to ask – although she already knew the answer.

'Did they find her?' she said, glancing again towards the picture.

He didn't respond directly. 'Elounda very safe,' he insisted. 'No worry. She meet people, she go away. Maybe not want to go home. Nothing bad happen in Elounda.'

Don't be so bloody stupid! she wanted to snap but she bit back the retort. He didn't know what she knew. He was only trying to reassure her – and perhaps himself too. No one wants a murderer on their doorstep.

'Not far now,' he said, tugging insistently on her elbow.

She didn't have the strength or the words to break away. Instead, unprotesting, she allowed him to lead her along the street. He made a sharp left turn along another winding lane. It seemed amazing that her legs were still carrying her along, moving one in front of the other as if they had nothing at all to do with her. Her head was filled with madness. There was a snatch of film running round, a short continuous reel that refused to stop and just kept playing over and over . . . four men sitting at a table with a blonde girl, four men sitting at a table with a blonde girl . . . four men . . .

They rounded a corner and covered a few more yards before Christos came to a halt.

'Ah,' he said.

She raised her eyes, belatedly aware that some response was expected. 'Huh?' It took a moment for her to focus on the pair of black wrought-iron gates pulled shut and secured by a thick length of chain and a heavy padlock. To either side stood a tall stone pillar, the white paint chipped and flaking. In fine italic script, engraved into the stone and picked out in black, was the name – Villa Marianne.

The breath caught in her throat. 'My God,' she murmured. If the choice had been hers she would have turned and fled but her legs, so compliant until now, had suddenly turned to jelly. She moved forward and wound her fingers round the intricate scrolls of the railings. If nothing else it was an effective method of keeping herself upright. She peered inside. She could only see the top left-hand corner of the villa, a flaking square of white, a part of the flat roof, a single blue shuttered window. The rest was obscured by a rampaging jungle of foliage.

'Is the place?' he asked.

She nodded. 'Yes.' The word emerged as a croak. She wanted to keep looking, couldn't help looking, but was aware of more pressing obligations. She could feel Christos behind her, along with the weight of his expectancy. He had gone out of his way to bring her here – the least she could do was to show him some gratitude.

Quickly she turned and smiled. 'Yes, thank you.' Then, immediately wondering if she had actually smiled or had only intended to, she lifted a hand to her face and laughed. 'Yes, wonderful! This is it. Thank you so much!'

The laugh sounded false, brittle and cracked, but he smiled back at her. 'Is good,' he said. 'Very glad.'

'Thank you,' she said again. Then, as he showed no immediate signs of leaving, she rummaged in her bag for her purse. 'Look, you've been so kind. Let me give you something . . . er, for a drink or . . .'

He quickly raised his hands. 'No no,' he said. 'Is fine. No problem.'

'Oh,' she said, worried now that she might have offended him. She had other far more serious concerns but somehow it was easier to concentrate on this one.

Fortunately he was still smiling. 'I go,' he said, tapping his watch with a finger. 'I go or very late for the work.'

'Sorry,' she said. 'Yes, you must. Okay.'

'This way,' he said, pointing along the lane. 'To the right and then on, on in the straight line – take you to harbour, yes?'

'To the harbour,' she repeated. 'Thanks.'

'You have good time in Elounda,' he said. 'Come back, have drink, yes, before you leave.'

'I'll try,' she said.

He set off down the path, glanced over his shoulder and gave her a cheery wave.

She waved back.

Leaning against the gate, Eve watched him walk away. What was that saying about the kindness of strangers? She had an odd lump in her throat as if she was about to cry. But the emotion wasn't just the result of a generous act. She knew that she had stumbled on something today, a secret that would change everything . . .

Andrea Banks.

What kind of legacy had her father bequeathed her? Most men of limited means were content with a senti-mental gesture or two – the gift of a watch perhaps or a signet ring. And what had she got? Her brow crumpled into a frown. *A photograph of a missing girl.*

Slowly she turned back towards the villa and gazed in through the gates again. She acknowledged, with a whis-per of relief, that there was no immediate danger here. The villa was not just locked up but abandoned; it had that air of utter neglect as if Nature was already reclaim-ing the land, preparing to swallow it up, to take back what was rightfully hers.

How long had it been empty?

But she didn't need to ask the question. Almost two years. She was sure of it. Ever since . . . ever since a girl with long fair hair had walked through these gates, had sat smiling in a courtyard, had . . .

That vile sick feeling rose up from her stomach again. She felt the spasm in her throat, a reflexive gagging action and swallowed hard. No, she wasn't going to throw up. Grasping the bars she closed her eyes and concentrated, willing the bile to retreat, trying to think of the sea, the cool clear crystal sea, of a long stretch of sand, of Jack, of anything but that girl's face.

A few minutes passed before it felt safe enough to loosen her hold. She blinked open her eyes and took a series of long deep breaths.

'You're all right now,' she murmured.

As if to prove the point, she straightened her shoulders, lifted her head and gave the gate a tentative shake. The padlock rattled against its chain. There was a brief flurry from inside, a thin scrabbling sound of insects disturbed, of air momentarily displaced. A bird rose up from the undergrowth, flapped its wings and soared above the roof of the villa.

She waited.

Nothing else happened.

Gradually, the heavy silence settled around her again.

Eve took a step back. She looked up at the blue shuttered window. It was as blank, as firmly closed, as the first time she'd looked at it but still she continued to stare; she had that odd, disturbing, prickling sensation of being watched. It was a feeling that was rapidly sliding into fear.

Walk away! a voice inside her warned. And for once she paid attention. Walking, however, seemed too cautious a response. Before she'd even reached the turn in the path she had started to run.

Chapter Thirty-Four

By the time Eve hit the harbour she was hot and sweating. Panting, she stopped to catch her breath and let the cool sea breeze float over her. She didn't know what she'd expected. For someone to come chasing after her perhaps? But of course they hadn't. There was no one at the villa – no one alive at least.

It was only a ghost that she'd been running from.

She started to walk again, trailing her fingers through her hair, trying to think of what she would tell Jack. Or maybe not so much *what* – there was no way of evading the truth now – as how. Would she be able to make him understand? She hoped so. What she needed was someone to talk to, someone she could trust, someone who could help her find a way through this nightmare . . .

Eve saw him before he saw her. He was sitting at the same table they'd shared breakfast at this morning, a newspaper laid out in front of him, a cold beer beside his elbow. She suddenly wished she'd never made that decision to go walkabout, that she'd never found out what she had, that she'd succumbed instead to more lustful temptations.

'Hi,' he said, glancing up, his mouth breaking into a smile.

God, he had such a beautiful smile. 'Hi.'

'You've got a pink nose,' he said.

'Have I?' She laughed, moving closer to the table, and then frowned. She stared down at her sore and dusty feet.

'Hey.'

She had that lump in her throat again.

'What's wrong?'

Eve shook her head. 'Nothing.' *Nothing?* What was she saying? She saw his confused blue eyes looking up at her. 'I mean, it's just that I think we need to talk.' She hesitated. 'Or . . . or rather *I* need to talk. I need to tell you something. But not here. Can we go to the apartment?'

The walk back had been a short one – but only in distance. In time, it had seemed to go on forever, every slow silent minute stretched and elongated. Even the final climb up the stairs had felt eternal.

She opened the fridge, got out a couple of beers and flipped off their caps before she sat down at the table. 'You might need a drink,' she said.

'What's going on, Eve?'

She reached into her bag and took out her cigarettes. She knew he hated the habit but her need for nicotine currently outweighed his disapproval. Her hand was shaking as she drew one from the pack and lit it.

'The thing is,' she said, 'well, it's what they call a long story and if I could just do it in one, you know, without any interruptions, then—'

'You're starting to worry me,' he said. And then, realizing that he'd just done exactly what she was asking him not to, he raised an apologetic hand. 'I'm sorry. Okay. Go on.'

And so she did. She told him about what had happened since she'd got the news of her father's death. Glossing over the break-in – he already knew about that – she told him about the man in the alley, about the assault, the threats, the phone calls. She told him about Terry, about her fears for him, about her arrangement with Cavelli and his boxes. She told him about being followed to Blakeney. 'I think it was him,' she said. 'Ivor Patterson.' She paused.

Jack's brows lifted but he didn't interrupt.

'And he's dead now.' She took a drag on the cigarette, pursed her lips and exhaled the smoke in a long thin stream. Frowning, she carried on. She told him about the Rowans, about the rumours. The only thing she didn't mention was the night in Soho when she'd gone searching for Jimmy Reece – for all Cavelli's faults, she knew now that he had no part in this. *Those* particular details were irrelevant. Instead, she told him about Henry's visit, about the missing phone, about the notes she had found, about where they had led her, about the discovery of the photograph. She told him about her conversation with Sonia, about the trip abroad she had never heard about. 'I found the address in his book and I wanted to come here. I wanted to see it again – the villa. I don't know why, it just seemed important.'

None of this, she realized, was exactly what he wanted to hear. He was gazing down at the table, his brows knotted, his hands clenched together.

'And was it?' he said eventually.

'What?'

'Important.'

Eve stubbed out her cigarette and immediately lit another. 'Yes,' she said. 'One of the men in the picture, the man who owns the villa – he's called Joe Silk.'

Jack's head jerked up. 'Jesus,' he said.

'I guess you've heard of him then.' She shrugged. 'Of course you have. He must be pretty well known in certain circles.'

He dropped his face back into his hands. 'Jesus,' he said again.

'Jack, I know this is one hell of a mess and I'm sorry, really sorry. I should have told you before. I wanted to but it was all so messy, so confused. You see that, don't you?' She looked at him pleadingly but he wouldn't meet her eyes. 'I didn't have a clue about Andrea Banks then. I didn't understand about the photo. And now I do, well, it changes everything. That girl's dead, she must be, and—'

'Are you sure it's the same girl?'

Eve got her wallet out of her bag and unfolded the copy of the picture. She passed it over to him. 'Go out, take a look for yourself if you want. There are posters all over the place.'

He stared at it for a long time.

'And that is Joe Silk, isn't it?'

'That's him all right.'

'With Peter Marshall and Terry. Do you know who the other guy is?'

He gave a reluctant nod. 'Yeah, Mr Psychopath him-self. The untouchable Keeler Chase.'

'Mr Psychopath?' she said nervously. She still couldn't tell from the picture whether it was the same man Marianne had held in such contempt. The man with the dead eyes. The man who had watched them from the archway.

'He's an evil bastard. Came over from the States years ago.' He scraped back his chair, jumped up and got another beer out of the fridge. 'You want one?'

'No. No thanks.' After all the sun, the alcohol was quickly going to her head. She could feel her thoughts beginning to blur at the edges and pushed the remains of her bottle aside. 'Evil as in . . .?'

'As in every definition you want to use. Joe Silk's

right-hand man, the one who sorts out all his little problems for him. The one who makes them disappear.'

She shivered at the last word. 'So he could have—'

'Let's just say he's more than capable.'

'Christ,' she said. 'Look, we've got to go home. Today, tonight – we'll take the first flight we can get. You've got to help me sort this out.'

There was a long silence.

'I can't.'

She looked at him, bewildered. 'You're a cop, Jack. What do you mean, you can't?'

'Exactly that,' he said. There was an edge of bitterness to his voice. 'Seeing as it's truth day, there are a few things I need to explain myself.'

Eve felt a sinking sensation in the pit of her stomach. Whatever was coming next, she was sure she wasn't going to like it. 'Go on,' she murmured.

His fingers tightened around the bottle. 'I know Joe Silk,' he said. 'And I don't just mean in a professional capacity.' He paused and cleared his throat. 'It was several years ago. Things weren't going well with Clare. Our relationship was on the rocks and I was gambling, big time. Or to be more accurate, I was *losing* big time. I was up to my stupid neck in it. By the time I came to my senses, Clare was gone, the house was gone and I owed Joe Silk over sixty grand.'

Eve stared at him, her eyes widening.

'Yeah, I really fucked up. Anyway, I moved out of London, I was trying to get myself straight when about six months ago Silk got in touch. Said he had a proposition for me. He said if I could get rid of some evidence – a couple of CCTV tapes – he'd clear the debt, wipe it completely.' He paused again, his eyes closing briefly. 'They were the tapes showing Terry at the robbery.'

She almost jumped out of her chair. 'What?'

He nodded.

As if subject to an information overload, her brain was starting to give off sparks. She was having trouble absorbing it all. 'I . . . I don't understand.'

'I didn't either at the time. I didn't get why he was going out of his way – and it was a pretty expensive way bearing in mind how much I owed him – to save the skin of some small-time—' He stopped, remembering that it was her brother he was talking about. 'Well, someone who wasn't exactly in his league.'

What had Sonia said? That her father had been pacing the floor, on the phone, tearing his hair out; scared witless that Terry would be going down for a long stretch. 'My dad was putting pressure on him.'

'Blackmailing him,' Jack said. He saw the indignation flash on to her face. 'Come on, we may as call it by its rightful name – seeing as we're both being so straight and honest with each other.' He had that bitterness in his voice again. He lifted the beer to his mouth and took another drink. 'And now we know how he did it. With a photograph Silk couldn't afford to have made public. A photograph he probably didn't even know existed until that moment.'

A flood of thoughts were washing through her head, about her father, the picture, about how he must have known what had happened to that girl . . . and how he had done *nothing*. That's what she couldn't grasp. Oh, he'd been a swindler, yes, a fraudster, but he hadn't a violent bone in his body. So what on earth had possessed him to keep quiet? Had he been threatened, forced into silence? She didn't have any answers. She couldn't make any sense of it. Instead she turned her attention back to Jack.

'So you agreed to do it – to lose the evidence.'

'Obviously. I'd like to claim I had a long hard battle with my conscience but it isn't true. I saw a way of getting out from under and I grabbed it with both hands.

And if that meant one unimportant little scrote – no offence – was going to walk then I wasn't going to lose too much sleep over it.'

But there was a hint of bravado now, as if he was trying to persuade himself as much as her. And she knew that Jack Raynor had sacrificed some essential part of himself on the day that he'd agreed to Joe Silk's deal – call it pride, integrity, whatever – and that it was something that was lost forever. Perhaps she should thank him for getting Terry off the hook but she knew that would only be rubbing salt in the wound.

'And did he stick to his side of the bargain?' she asked softly.

'More or less.'

And now, ludicrously late, she was struck by a thought so obvious that her knees, had she been standing, would have given way. She could feel the blood draining from her face. How it had taken her so long to see it she couldn't comprehend, too much else on her mind perhaps, but suddenly the truth was brightly illuminated. *She'd been wined and dined and thoroughly seduced by a man in Joe Silk's pocket!*

'Oh God,' she moaned.

'Eve?'

She shook her head. Jesus, what a fool she'd been. She'd walked straight into a honeytrap! Her, Eve Weston! And despite the fear, a part of her (granted a slightly hysterical part) felt a desperate urge to laugh. How often had she used her own womanly wiles to get what she wanted? This was karma perhaps, cosmic payback, some kind of divine retribution.

'You set this all up, didn't you? You and me, this whole—'

'No!' he said, moving swiftly to put his hand over hers.

'Don't!' She snatched her hand away. 'Don't insult me,

Jack. What are you saying – that this, us, is just a coincidence?' She was experiencing an odd internal tumbling sensation, like she was slowly falling. 'He knows, doesn't he? Your mate Joe Silk. He set this up. You're only here because—'

'Shit no!' He got to his feet, raking his fingers through his hair. 'I swear. I swear to God. It's not like that.' He paced over to the window, glared out for a second or two and then turned around to face her again. 'He doesn't know we're here. He doesn't know anything about us.'

He came and sat down beside her again, leaning forward across the table. 'I know what it looks like,' he said. 'And I know you've got every reason to doubt me but I swear, on my life, I'm not lying to you. I wouldn't. Eve, *please*.'

She stared back at him, deep into those pleading blue eyes. Almost instantly she had to shift her gaze. There was a fine film of sweat on his forehead, a thousand tiny beads. Did she believe him? She wasn't sure. He was certainly vehement enough but then so many easy lies had passed between them . . .

'Just hear me out,' he begged. 'Ten minutes, that's all I'm asking.'

She shrugged. It was easier than speaking.

Like a guilty man temporarily reprieved, he exhaled a small sigh of relief. 'Okay, you're right, of course it's not just a coincidence.' Then he saw her expression and quickly added, 'But it's not a set-up either. After I . . . after I did what Silk wanted, I thought it was over, the slate wiped clean, but then shortly after your father died he got in touch with me again. He said he needed some information on you. I told him we'd made a deal, that I'd kept to my side and that was it, finished, end of, but he wasn't having any of it. He said it wasn't finished until he said so. He said there were still some loose ends.'

She glanced at him. 'And I was one of them?'

'He said you were as much my problem as his, that you might cause trouble, might start digging up things that were better left buried and—' He stopped abruptly, as if an alternative interpretation of those words was just dawning on him. 'Oh Christ, I didn't know anything about this other stuff, Eve. About the girl, the photo. I promise you.'

Eve nodded. That, at least, was probably true.

'Anyway, he gave me the details of the place where you'd been working, Baxter & Baxter, and asked me to try and find out anything I could. I gave them a ring. I was just going through the motions, you know, doing what he asked. I didn't really expect to come up with anything but then I got through to Richard.'

'Oh great,' she said. 'My biggest fan. I'm sure he had plenty to tell you.'

'Enough to give me an excuse to go down there. He seemed mad as hell and from how he was sounding off I thought Joe Silk might be right, that you might be . . .'

'What, a threat?'

'No.' He frowned. 'I don't know. Maybe.'

'But you didn't even go in. Henry told me. It was Shepherd he saw.'

Jack didn't reply.

'So is he involved in this too?'

'No.' He reached out for his beer but it was empty.

Eve shoved the remains of her half-drunk bottle across the table. 'Here, have this.'

'Thanks.' He took a swig. And then another. He stared longingly at the cigarette between her fingers as if, just for a moment, he wished he could find a similar way of occupying his hands. 'I told Shepherd that there was a possible case of fraud. So far as he was concerned, that was all we were investigating.'

'And when Henry told him that wasn't true?'

Jack lifted his shoulders. 'People often lie, especially to cops.'

She sensed there was more. 'And Shepherd was happy with that?'

'I had to keep him quiet. I told him that it might be connected to something else, something bigger.'

'Bigger?'

'That this wasn't as straightforward as it looked, that there might be more to it, that you'd been visiting Martin Cavelli in prison.'

'How did you . . .' But she didn't even bother to finish the sentence. There wasn't much a cop couldn't discover if he put his mind to it. And Jack had clearly been putting his heart and soul, not to mention various other parts of his anatomy, into trying to solve his problems. 'So you already knew about that?'

'I had to tell him something,' he said.

'But why should it matter that I was visiting Cavelli?'

'He's got a record,' he said. 'He's violent. He's got connections.' He rolled the neck of the bottle between his fingers. 'It was just something to say, an excuse to have a root around.'

She took a drag on her latest cigarette. A heap of butts was already lying in the saucer. She nudged her way through the ash, creating a small empty circle. 'And then?'

'I told Joe Silk what I'd found out,' he said. 'And that was it.'

'Except it wasn't,' she said.

He laid his elbows on the table, lowered his gaze and then looked up at her again. 'No, it wasn't. I heard about the break-in, recognized the name and . . . and suspected Joe had to be connected. Too much to be a coincidence, right? I was worried about what he might be up to, about whether I was going to get dragged into it again, and so I made sure that I dealt with the call.'

Eve ground her latest cigarette into the grey ashy mess. 'And made sure that we met.'

'Hey,' he said. 'I'm not denying that. I wanted to see you, to meet you – I was curious apart from anything else – but I never pushed things further. You were the one who rang *me*, remember?'

Which was true, but then who was to say that he wouldn't have rung *her* eventually, that he wasn't just waiting to see if she made the first move? And most women probably did, drawn as she had been, towards those expressive blue eyes, the smooth handsome planes of his face, that soft seductive mouth that even now, perversely, still made her want to . . .

She shifted her chair back an inch. 'So you haven't been in touch with Silk since? You never heard from him again?'

He scowled and put his hand over his mouth.

'Oh, Jesus. Jack.' She was walking a thin line between love and hate, between sympathy and contempt.

'Only once more. It was the last time, he said. It was before we . . . I mean, it was just after the break-in. He asked me to leave Peter Marshall alone, to make sure he wasn't pulled in.'

'It was Peter who broke in?' She didn't know why that startled her so much. Perhaps it was his connection to Sonia. But when she thought about it she could see that it was logical; Marshall had been in Crete as well. In fact, with his violent background, it wasn't beyond the realms of possibility that *he* had something to do with the disappearance of the girl.

'Then Marshall suddenly turns up dead,' he said. His voice was low, no more than a whisper.

She stared at him. His face had gone a greyish shade, the pale bronze all washed out, and his hands were wrestling on the table top. She reached out, placing her fingers lightly on his arm.

He took a deep breath as if he was struggling to keep control. 'And I knew it couldn't be an accident. Not a chance in hell. It was down to Joe Silk. And then when Shepherd started sniffing around, checking out the forensics, I knew I was going to have to try and cover that up too because if it all started to unravel . . . well, it was only a matter of time before one of the threads would lead back to me.'

She was quiet for a while and then she said: 'When were you planning on telling me all this? I mean, if I hadn't recognized the girl and . . .'

'When were you planning on telling me?' He forced a smile, small and pained. 'We've both been less than free with the truth but I've never lied to you – not about . . . about *us*.'

Eve wasn't entirely sure of what 'us' consisted any more. For which, she accepted, he was only partly to blame. It took two to spin the kind of web they'd got entangled in. 'So what happens now?'

He expelled a long weary sigh, his shoulders sagging. 'I don't think we have much choice.'

She thought at first that he meant it would all have to come out, the whole sorry tale, but then she looked into his eyes and realized just how far off the mark she was. Her jaw fell open. 'Christ, you're not going back, are you?'

'You can't either. It's not safe.'

'Don't be crazy,' she said. 'We can't just go on the run.'

'You got a better idea? We're next on Silk's list of problems to be rid of. We both know too much.'

'Then *I'll* go back. I'll go to the cops. Don't worry, I won't mention you. I'll keep you out of it, I promise. I'll tell them about the photo, about the girl, about Joe Silk . . .'

'You're not thinking straight. You really want to open

510

that can of worms? Joe Silk's not the only person in that photograph, your brother's in it too.'

'He didn't have anything to do with it,' she snapped. 'Not Terry. It was Silk or that psycho or Marshall. Maybe all of them. What do I know? How else would my dad have been able to use it?'

He barked out a laugh, a harsh almost scornful sound. 'For God's sake, Eve. It still incriminates him. He was *there*, wasn't he, just like your father. What are you saying – that Terry didn't know what happened to her? How many years do you think you get for covering up that kind of crime?'

'Maybe he *didn't* know,' she said, desperately clutching at straws. 'It's possible, isn't it? Or maybe he was forced to keep quiet.'

'And I suppose he didn't know about the photo either – the photo your father so conveniently used to save him from a twelve-stretch inside?'

She dropped her head into her hands. He was right. Terry must have known. And she recalled, with a thin unpleasant shudder, the way he had begged her not to clear out the flat without him. *Please, Evie.* No, it had been nothing to do with sentiment – and everything to do with the fact he believed the photo was still hidden there.

'And apart from all that,' Jack said, pressing home his point, 'if you do go back, Joe Silk's going to be waiting. By now he's thinking that you're a chip off the old block, just dying for another chance to screw him like your father did. He can't take that risk. He's already killed Peter Marshall and . . .'

He didn't need to finish the sentence. There wasn't much doubt about what Silk would do if he caught up with her. She squeezed her eyes shut. Opened them again. Nothing had changed. God, this was all such a nightmare.

'But I can't just leave Terry, can I? I can't just abandon him.'

'He's not a child any more. He'll be out in a few months. Wherever we are, he can join us there.'

'And what if Joe Silk gets to him first? No, it's impossible. Anyway, I need to know. Do you understand? I have to talk to him, to find out what happened. That girl . . . Andrea . . .'

She shook her head, got to her feet and walked out on to the balcony. Leaning against the railings, she gazed down on to the neat square of lawn. Everything so tidy. So normal. Other couples were strolling up the path, returning from the beach for some lunch, for an afternoon siesta. How odd that while her own little universe was splintering, falling apart, this other world was still turning, regardless.

After a while he came to stand beside her and she felt the light brush of his arm against hers. 'Stay with me.'

'I'm sorry.'

She saw his mouth open as if to protest, to try and dissuade her, but then his lips slowly closed together again. There was nothing he could say. He knew that it was hopeless.

Chapter Thirty-Five

She had changed her mind a hundred times before she reached the airport, on each occasion shifting forward intending to tap the taxi driver on the shoulder, to ask him to turn around, and then slowly, silently, sinking back into her seat. Then there had been the long wait, over six hours before she'd finally managed to get on a flight. Although she shouldn't complain about that – it could have been days in peak season. But the hours had dragged on forever. How often she had looked up expectantly, a flash of pale fair hair appearing in the periphery of her vision, only to be disappointed yet again.

The plane was beginning its descent. Eve stared out at the grey misty dawn of Stansted. Almost home. Did she resent him for not coming with her? No. Well, only a bit. And in his position she suspected she'd have done exactly the same. He didn't just have Joe Silk to contend with, he had the Law as well – if one didn't get him, the other eventually would. And she knew what happened to cops in jail.

The worst part of leaving had been the pretence, the way they had both chosen to act as if it was only a temporary separation, that one day – not so far off perhaps – they would be together again. She could see it in his face, his expression a mirror image of her own, that it was only a way of getting through. Acknowledging the truth would have been even harder. So they had said their goodbyes quickly in a false light-hearted kind of manner and with one fleeting slight embrace. It was only then, holding him for the last time, that she realized the finality of it all. As she climbed into the taxi, tears had risen to her eyes. She had dug her nails into her palms and forced herself not to look back.

The plane jolted on to solid ground and cruised along the runway. Twenty-five minutes later, Eve found herself in the car park. Curiously, she had no memory of the time between landing and getting here, as if someone else, some benevolent stranger, had taken over the tedious proceedings of getting off the aircraft, collecting her luggage and clearing Customs. She dug into her bag and pulled out the car keys. A gift from Jack.

'Take them,' he'd said. 'They're not much use to me.'

'Thanks.'

'And promise me something.' He'd touched her chin then, forcing her to look up at him. 'Promise that you won't go back to your flat. Keep away from there – you understand? At least until . . . It isn't safe, okay? Go and see Terry, do whatever you have to do, but find somewhere else to stay.'

She stood on the tarmac, staring at the silver Peugeot. He was right – it *was* too risky to go to Herbert Street; Joe Silk's skinny spy had probably been replaced by someone with a few more brain cells. But she still had to head back to Norfolk. She had to see Terry as soon as she could. She took out her phone and turned it on. It gave a few angry beeps – missed calls – but she ignored them. She glanced at her watch. It was too early to ring the prison and book a visit; the lines didn't open until nine. And she still had to negotiate that tricky problem of how she was going to get to see him today – visits were supposed to be booked twenty-four hours in advance.

She unlocked the boot, threw in her case, and got into

514

the car. It was only as she turned the key in the ignition, as the engine purred swiftly and obediently into life, that the full force of what had happened, *everything* that had happened, seemed to suddenly descend on her. As if a lead weight had hit her squarely across the shoulders, she slumped down over the wheel, her lungs deflating, a sob rising in her throat.

She turned off the engine and cried for five solid minutes.

And then, still sniffling, she raised her head and scowled and glared at the damage in the rear-view mirror. It wasn't a pretty sight. Her eyes, a good match for her sunburnt nose, were liquid pink, her nose running, her mouth pinched. Even her hair was hanging in thin straggly strands around her face.

What's wrong with you?

But what was wrong, apart from the obvious, was that the whole car smelled of Jack. Or at least she thought it did. Maybe it was just her imagination. But even if it was, even if that warm musky scent had sprung purely from memory, there were still other reminders – a few blond hairs on the floor by her feet, a St Christopher on a silver chain hanging from the mirror . . .

Stop it!

He was gone. That was it. People came into your life and then slipped away again. She knew that better than anyone. There was no point getting too attached. Love, *that* kind of love, was nothing more than an illusion, a kind of madness, a freak wave rolling over you, something that took away your breath, swept you off your feet – and then left you well and truly stranded.

As she scrabbled in the depths of her bag for a comb and a lipstick her hand came across the mail she'd put in there and forgotten. She pulled it out, more as a way of clearing some space than with any intention of dealing with it, and dumped it on the passenger seat. It was only after she'd made some repairs to her face, when she was feeling vaguely human again, that she glanced down and saw the envelope with Cavelli's handwriting.

Certain that it contained no more than a visiting order, she carelessly tore it open. But there was also a note inside. She unfolded the flimsy sheet of paper and read it.

Evie, I need to see you. It's urgent. Please book a visit as soon as you can. You know what it's about. This is serious. Martin.

She read it again, her hands starting to tremble. It was postmarked last week, last Friday, almost a week ago. *Urgent.* Damn, why hadn't she opened it before she'd left? Starting the engine again, she put her foot down and sped as fast as she dared out of the car park and towards the motorway.

She didn't know why she was rushing – there was nothing she could do until this afternoon and even that was dependent on whether she could sweet talk her way into a visit. And now she had the additional problem of having to make a choice. Who was she going to try and see, Cavelli or Terry? She desperately wanted it to be the latter – she *had* to find out about Crete, about Andrea Banks – but that could wait another day. Perhaps Cavelli was more important. Also, she knew what Terry was like: if she started asking awkward questions there was every chance he'd withdraw into one of his sulks and she wouldn't get another word out of him.

Eve had demolished half a pack of cigarettes by the time she was on the winding country lanes that led towards Hillgrove. There was a village about a mile from the jail; she had noticed a couple of B&Bs there. Her plan was to book in, grab a shower and a change of clothes and then put a call through to the prison.

The sky was overcast and grey, a fine drizzle smattering the windscreen. She wondered if Jack was still in

Crete, if he would stay for the rest of the week, or whether he'd already packed up and moved on.

'What will you do?' she had asked. 'Where will you go?' But then had instantly raised her hand and said, 'No, don't tell me. I don't want to know.'

She was still considering whether she *really* didn't want to know – and if she didn't, why she was thinking so much about it – when her phone began to ring. Keeping one eye on the road, she dug down into her bag again. 'Hello?'

'Where the hell have you been?'

'Patrick?'

'Don't you ever check your bloody messages?'

'I've been away,' she sighed. 'I only just got back.' She could tell he was in a scratchy sort of mood and hoped he wasn't going to have another go about the break-in at his flat. 'What do you want?'

'Haven't you heard about Henry?'

'What?'

There was a short grotesque kind of silence. She clamped the phone closer to her ear. 'Patrick?' She could only hear him breathing, a thin uneasy kind of sound. Her heart began to pound. 'Patrick?'

'I'm sorry,' he said. 'There was some kind of burglary at the office. He was . . . he was shot. I'm sorry, he's—'

She must have let go of the wheel for a second and veered across the road. The driver behind her put his hand on the horn and held it there. She swerved back, mounted the bank, put her foot on the brake and screeched to a halt.

'Evie? Are you there?'

She couldn't speak. She could barely catch her breath.

He was almost yelling now. 'Evie?'

'Oh, Jesus,' she eventually murmured. 'Not Henry.' She had her head down over the steering wheel and could feel a scream slowly forming in her throat, an

517

agony of pain and guilt. *It was her fault. It was all her fault. She had given him the picture, dragged him into her mess, and now . . .*

'Will you just listen for a minute?'

But all she could hear were own recriminations. 'He's dead, isn't he?'

'He's not dead, okay? He was hurt pretty badly, shot in the stomach, but he's in hospital, right? They're taking care of him.' He paused again. 'Are you listening, Evie? Can you hear me?'

Gradually, as his words sank in, she felt the relief wash over her. She slowly raised her face. What he was saying seemed unbelievable, like the news of some modern-day resurrection. Only seconds ago Henry had been . . . and now he was alive again. 'Yeah,' she eventually managed to mumble. She wiped her eyes with the back of her hand. 'Are you sure? Are you sure he's okay?'

'They've operated and he's out of danger. I don't suppose he'll be dancing the tango in the near future but Sonia says he'll be fine.'

'Sonia?'

'She was the one who rang me. She read about it in the papers and recognized the name. She tried to get in touch but you've had your phone turned off.'

Eve was still trying to absorb it all. 'When did it happen? Where is he?'

'Monday evening,' he said. 'And he's in the hospital. I just told you.'

'*Which* hospital? I have to go and see him.'

'You can't,' he said. 'He's with his wife, his family. You think they're going to want you there?'

'I'm not his bloody mistress,' she snapped. But she knew he had a point; she was the last person that Celia would want to see. Come to that, she wouldn't be doing Henry any favours either. 'I'm sorry. You're right. I'm not thinking straight. It's just been such a shock, you know, hearing about—'

'Tell me something.' He paused.

'What?'

'Please tell me this had nothing to do with you – with the Jimmy Reece business, the break-ins, with all the weird shit you seem to have got yourself involved in.'

She hesitated for a fraction too long.

He expelled a long hissy breath down the line. 'Jesus, Evie. What the hell's going on?'

'I don't know,' she said. 'I mean, I don't know *all* of it.' She was tempted to tell him about the photo, the missing girl, to pour out all her suspicions, but decided against it. She had got Henry involved and look what had happened to him. Until things were clearer, she had to deal with this on her own. 'Just do me a favour, okay? Keep your head down for a few days and stay away from your flat.'

'I can't just leave you to—'

'I mean it,' she said. 'You can't help with this. A few days and then I'll tell you everything. I swear.'

'Where are you?'

She frowned out through the windscreen, at the prickly hedge that must have scratched a path across Jack's immaculate silver paintwork. 'I'll call you soon,' she said. 'I promise. Oh, and Patrick – please don't tell anyone you've heard from me.'

'Call me tonight,' he said.

'Tomorrow,' she bargained.

'At least send me a text, let me know you're okay.'

'All right,' she agreed.

'And call me, call me any time if . . .'

'I know,' she said. 'Thanks.'

Eve put down the phone and leaned her head back against the rest. 'Oh God, Henry,' she groaned. 'What have I done?' She had to fight against the urge to spin the car around and head back to London. Just to see him . . . just to walk past the room, even if she couldn't go in, just one quick glance to make sure that he truly was alive and breathing. But it wasn't possible. Sod's law dictated that she would run into Celia or Richard and some holy row in the middle of the hospital would hardly do much to aid his recovery. Or his marriage come to that.

She screwed her fist into the centre of her temple. Damn it! Why had she ever dragged him into this? For all her precautions last Saturday, she had not been careful enough; someone had seen her passing over the envelope and that someone was almost certainly connected to Joe Silk. And then another more gruesome thought occurred to her: Henry had not just been shot because he had the photograph but because they thought he knew what it meant. *What if they tried to finish the job?*

The idea shot a bolt of horror down her spine. Her head jerked forward again. Perhaps she should go to the police right now and tell them everything. Should she? Except she didn't have any actual proof, any solid evidence; there were only her own purely personal certainties and a crumpled copy of an old blurry photograph. And she was well aware of what such a step would entail: not only the trip back to London (there was no point dealing with the local cops) but further hours stuck in a stuffy interview room while she endlessly repeated her story, answered their questions, watched them raise their sceptical eyebrows and waited for them to make their phone calls to Crete.

No, it was all going to take too long. And surely, logically, if Silk had wanted to finish what he'd started, he'd have done it by now. It was already three days since the shooting. More likely he was taking a calculated gamble on Henry keeping his mouth shut. After all, what respectable lawyer would readily admit to withholding evidence of a murder? And, even worse, withholding evidence with the intention of blackmailing a major London gangster?

He was right, she thought, Henry wouldn't talk – although not for the reasons Silk imagined. Rather he would keep quiet until he understood exactly what was going on. He would not bring her name into it unless he had to. This was partly because he was a cautious man, partly because he would try to protect her, and partly, she decided with a wry smile, because it would save Celia the trouble of slapping both their faces.

Eve nodded. Right, so the choice was made. She would see Cavelli first before making any further decisions. Noticing a few curious glances from drivers passing by, she quickly leaned forward and turned the key in the ignition; she'd better get back on the road before some knight in shining armour decided to come to her rescue. The engine made a thin protesting rattling sound but eventually spluttered into life.

It was just after nine when she booked into Primrose Cottage. Why it was called by that particular name she had no idea; it was a three-storey grey brick house with a concrete forecourt and not a flower in sight. The owner, a small plump lady in her fifties, showed her to a single en suite room on the first floor.

'I'm sure you'll be very comfortable here,' she said, with the brisk confidence of a woman who was not used to being contradicted.

Eve smiled and gave the obligatory response. 'Oh, how lovely!'

It was only when she was alone again that she allowed the smile to fade. The room, barely big enough to swing the proverbial cat, was painted in a bright sickly pink with matching curtains and duvet cover. The carpet was pink. There were pink scatter cushions, a pink tasselled lamp and an endless array of dried pink flower arrangements. She stared at it with horror. Even Barbie, she suspected, would have felt the urge to scream.

A sudden yearning for a blank anonymous motel rose up in her. She longed for clear white walls, white sheets and space to think. Still, she would just have to put up with what she'd got. It was clean at least and she wasn't going to be spending much time here.

Putting her case on the floor, she sat down on the bed, took out her phone and dialled the jail. Engaged. She tried again. The same. It was always like this. Getting through entailed not just endurance but an infinite amount of patience too.

It took another six attempts before she was put on hold and then a further two minutes before she finally got through. However, as she'd expected, she had no joy trying to negotiate a same-day visit.

'Twenty-four hours in advance,' he kept repeating smugly. 'That's the rule.'

'But it's important, I have to see him.'

'Not without permission,' he said.

'And how do I get that?'

He gave one of those sneering half-laughs. 'You could try the Wing Governor, I suppose.'

'Okay.' But then, confident that she would think of something, she went ahead and booked a visit with Terry for the following day.

It was another twenty minutes before Eve was back on the phone again. In the meantime, she'd taken a quick shower, washed her hair and dressed in jeans and a T-shirt. There were still over four hours before visiting began – plenty of time, if she played her cards right, to get access to Cavelli.

She'd had an idea.

Ringing the main prison line – this one was picked up after a couple of rings – she asked for David Hammond.

'Who's calling, please?'

'Eve Weston.'

She'd expected more questions, at least a minor inter-rogation, but the line went directly to hold. There was only a thin buzzing sound, an emptiness that after a few minutes made her faintly wistful for a few reassuring bars of *The Four Seasons*. She was beginning to wonder if she'd been discreetly cut off when the phone suddenly sprang back into life.

'Hello?'

'Hi,' she said. 'Is that David Hammond?'

'That's right.'

'It's Eve, Eve Weston.' She paused, hoping that he remembered her, but when no sign of that was forth-coming quickly added: 'You helped me out a while ago – when my friend's car broke down?' It was more likely that he'd remember her wrestling in the car park with the frenzied Kimberley but she preferred not to mention that particular incident.

'Hi,' he said. 'What can I do for you?'

'Well, I've got a bit of a problem. I need to organize a visit for this afternoon. It's urgent and I'm not sure who I should be talking to. I know it's usually twenty-four hours in advance but I really need to see him.'

'Er, right . . . It's probably the Wing Governor you need to speak to.'

'You couldn't help?' she asked pleadingly, lowering her voice. 'I – I wouldn't ask but I'm worried, *really* worried. My boyfriend, Martin Cavelli . . . well, my ex really, it's kind of complicated – he sent me this letter and he just sounded so . . .' She allowed her voice to break, giving the tiniest of sobs. 'I don't want to wait until tomorrow. I'm concerned that he might . . . I've never

known him like this before. He's not the type to . . .
I mean . . . but you know when something's not right,
don't you?'

'What are you saying, that—'

'I just need to see him, to talk to him. *Please*. Is there
any way you can help?' She took another clearly audible
breath. 'The thing is, I don't want to have to explain all
this to someone else, to have to go through it all again
and . . .'

She waited, biting on the knuckle of her free hand.

'Look, do you want me to have a word with the
Governor?'

'Oh, would you? I'd be *so* grateful.'

'I can't promise anything,' he said.

'I understand – but thanks, thanks ever so much.'

She gave him her number, said goodbye, and then lay
back on the bed to wait.

Chapter Thirty-Six

DS Eddie Shepherd launched himself up from the plastic seat, grunted, yawned and stretched his arms. It was three days since Henry Baxter had been brought into the hospital and twenty-four hours since he'd been, theoretically, fit to talk. But Eddie hadn't got a word of sense out of him. He was claiming he couldn't remember anything about the intruder, about the breaking of his hand, about the shooting. Short-term memory loss, the doctors said.

Eddie wasn't convinced.

There's gratitude, he thought. Especially as he'd been the one who'd saved his bloody skin. Twenty minutes, that's all it had taken, to drag the truth out of a rattled Paul Clark on the Monday afternoon. And then it had all come pouring out: how Richard Baxter had hired them to follow Eve Weston, how the panic had set in when Ivor Patterson was murdered, how all the papers relating to the surveillance had been destroyed.

That was when Eddie had taken what he'd got to MIT.

Calls had been made and Richard Baxter had been picked up by the local cops in London. He had, by all accounts, gone quietly, still hoping perhaps to avoid any whiff of a scandal. By the time Eddie had arrived with DI Locke – a good three hours later – he was just about ready to spill his guts. Coming clean, he'd decided, was clearly a better option than being suspected of murder. So yes, he'd admitted, he *had* arranged the surveillance on Eve Weston but it was only to protect his father. He had followed this with a lengthy and colourful diatribe as regards her moral deficiencies. By the time he paused for breath his face had turned a dangerous shade of puce.

'She's a bitch, a gold digger. I was worried they might still be meeting,' he said. 'I just wanted to make sure that she didn't still have her claws in him.'

'So why not have *him* followed?' Shepherd asked. 'Why her?'

Baxter gave an angry shrug. 'Because she was probably at it with someone else, playing some other poor sod in the same way, taking him for every penny he had.'

'So you were looking for evidence to use against her?'

'I was trying to protect my father,' he said again.

Shepherd, recalling the first time they'd met, remained untouched by this sudden outburst of filial loyalty. Baxter, he was sure, had been driven by motives of a far sleazier nature; he had wanted a hold over Eve Weston and hadn't cared how he got it.

'Why the cover-up, then? Why ask Paul Clark to destroy the records?'

'I didn't,' he protested. He paused and stared at the two men in front of him. 'I simply suggested that as the surveillance was unconnected it could only muddy the waters.'

DI Locke leaned forward and smiled. 'Just trying to make our jobs easier for us, huh?' He glanced at Eddie. 'Isn't that nice? A good true citizen. Maybe we should give him a medal.'

Baxter squirmed in his seat. 'Look, I'm sorry, all right? It was a mistake, a big mistake, but I swear his death had *nothing* to do with me.'

They had let him go eventually, albeit with the prospect of a charge for obstructing a murder inquiry hanging over his impeccably coiffured head. Richard

Baxter was a Class A shit but, disregarding some of the more fanciful details, the kernel of his story was believable. He had no reason to kill Patterson.

The two detectives had sat in the interview room for a while contemplating this latest dead end. Eddie was the one who was most subdued. He was still convinced that Ivor Patterson had stumbled on something, something relating to the Weston girl, and had then been silenced for it. Which, if they discounted Richard, only left two immediate suspects – Eve Weston herself and her sugar daddy, Henry. The former, as Eddie had discovered earlier in the day, was away for the week. 'On holiday,' Sonia Marshall had said, appearing from the door across the hall and glaring at him. 'I don't know where so there's no point asking.'

So that only left Baxter senior.

'Why not?' he'd said to Locke. 'Seeing as we're here, it's worth a try.'

A call to his home had established that he was 'working late' at the office. They had gone to Covent Garden and found the front door closed but unlocked and instead of pressing the intercom had stepped into the foyer unannounced. Eddie had been sure as his feet sank into the deep pile carpet that Henry would be with the delectable Ms Weston – but whether they would still have their clothes on was another matter altogether. Working late? Well, that was one way of putting it. His mouth had slid into a grin.

Henry's office was in the basement. Eddie had quietly opened the door and peered down the steps. From below there were some muffled sounds, the faint murmur of voices. It was only as they began the descent and Locke let the door click shut behind him that all hell broke loose. There was a sudden scuffling noise, the beginnings of a shout and then . . .

The man had come flying out and hurtled up the steps between them. They had made no attempt to stop him – he had a gun in his hand. And while Locke had reached for his phone, Eddie had rushed through the outer office and into the next room.

Henry Baxter was lying on the floor and the door to the safe was open.

Eddie walked along the corridor and pushed a few coins into the drinks machine. He pressed a button, requesting coffee, and watched as the brown sludge poured into the cup. He was still thinking about that night. It had been a robbery but not for money, he suspected. There were no substantial amounts of cash kept on the premises and no reason why anyone should imagine there were. So what was of such importance that someone was prepared to kill for it?

Baxter wasn't saying.

Was that because he didn't dare or because he was protecting someone?

And that broken hand hadn't happened accidentally. He'd been 'persuaded' to open the safe and pass over whatever was inside. If he and Locke hadn't come along, Henry Baxter would be six foot under by now.

He sipped at the coffee and scowled. This whole business left a bad taste in the mouth. They were still waiting for the files on the surveillance to be retrieved from Paul Clark's computer but he wasn't holding out much hope; whatever Patterson had discovered he'd have kept to himself.

What in God's name was going on?

The one person who might have been able to answer that question had conveniently disappeared.

Did that make *her* the prime suspect – or yet another victim?

Chapter Thirty-Seven

She had never been on a Thursday before. The other visitors were strangers to her, not even one familiar face. Eve spread her arms and let the female officer pat down her body. She was so relieved to be here, so grateful that David Hammond had managed to secure a visit, that she almost thanked her when she'd finished.

Moving into the hall, she hesitated on the threshold and glanced around. It only took a few seconds to spot him. Cavelli was on his feet and waiting. He nodded, his mouth moving but not quite achieving a smile. As she walked towards him she tried to read his eyes but they were coldly blank.

There was a confusing moment as they came together in a bizarre shuffling dance – should they touch, shouldn't they? – before they side-stepped, separated and sank down awkwardly into their seats.

'I got your letter,' she said.

He looked at her, those dark eyes narrowing a little.

She stared back. 'You said it was urgent.' She had meant to play it cool but her resolve was slowly crumbling. She could hear the fear in her voice. 'It's about Terry, isn't it?'

Cavelli leaned forward, reached out and took her hands in his. To anyone who was watching, it would have seemed a loving gesture, but she was more than aware of the tightening crushing pressure. 'Seeing as this is supposed to be a heart-to-heart,' he said softly, 'and seeing as you took so much trouble to be here today, how about you tell me what's going on – and cut out all the bullshit.'

Trying not to flinch, she stared straight back at him. 'You were the one who wrote. Shouldn't you be—'

'Joe Silk,' he said.

'What?' Her heart gave a violent lurch.

His fingers tightened a fraction. 'So you've heard of him then?'

She didn't reply.

'Do you think I'm fucking stupid?'

She didn't reply to that either.

'Christ,' he said. 'Terry's not the only one in trouble here. You've landed me right in it, sweetheart, right up to my bloody neck. Either you tell me what's going on or all deals are off. You understand?'

She nodded and looked down. His hands were still wrapped around hers. For the first time she noticed the damage to his knuckles, the purple bruises and the swollen broken skin. Could she trust him? She didn't know. But she had come here for a reason, to try and get some help, and she was at the point where she didn't really have that much to lose.

'It's a long story,' she said.

He abruptly released her, sat back in his seat and folded his arms across his chest. 'Well, no rush,' he said. 'We've got two hours.'

And so she told him. She told him everything from beginning to end. It had only been twenty-four hours since she'd done the same with Jack but somehow that seemed a lifetime ago. By the time she finished his eyes were half-closed and he was slumped unhappily in the chair. He was looking like a man who wished he'd never asked.

'Fucking hell,' he murmured.

Which just about summed it up.

She kept her voice low, her body hunched forward, while she talked. 'So what do I do next – go to the cops? But if I do where does that leave Terry? He could be looking at another sentence and a far bigger one this time.'

'That's if it even gets to court. If Terry's a witness to murder Joe isn't going to let him give evidence.'

Eve shuddered. 'So what else can I do?'

What's it got to do with me? he would have had every right to say. But thankfully he didn't. Instead he raked his fingers through his thick black hair and frowned. 'Arrange a meet, make a deal? You've got something he wants.'

'You think I should give him the photo?'

'No, of course I bloody don't! So long as you've got a copy of that picture, you've got a hold over him. He might not like it but it's a fact. However, you could try and persuade him that his secret's safe, that you'll keep your silence if he stays away from you and Terry.'

'But he had Henry *shot*.'

'So do you have a better suggestion?'

She sank her face despairingly into her hands. 'I don't know. There's the girl too – she has a mother, a father somewhere. Someone killed her and—'

'And Terry's involved, one way or another. So I guess you just have to decide where your priorities lie.' He threw her a glance that might almost have been sympathetic. 'That father of yours has a lot to answer for.'

'And why's that?' she retorted defensively. 'Because he wanted to protect his son? That's not so very terrible.'

'Because he left you up to your neck in shit, darling. At least if he'd told you about it, you'd have understood what you were up against. You could have been prepared.'

He was right up to a point. Her father's actions had been odd, even reckless. 'I don't think he knew what he wanted. It's as if a part of him wanted me to find the picture and another part didn't. If Silk believed I didn't know about it, he'd probably leave me alone – but then there was the girl.' Her lips were dry and she ran her tongue along them. 'Andrea,' she murmured. Saying the name out loud suddenly brought the image of her laughing mouth, the long fair hair, flashing into her mind again. 'Perhaps he couldn't bear the thought of them getting away with it, of her lying out there somewhere . . .'

'Why didn't you see your brother today?' he asked. 'Why me?'

'Because you said it was urgent and it didn't take a brain surgeon to figure that it had to do with Terry. I suppose I wanted to make sure that he was still okay, that you hadn't pulled out.' She gave a small humourless laugh. 'Although I guess this isn't exactly the deal you signed up for.'

'Not one of my greatest negotiating moments.'

'Anyhow, Terry's not very good with the truth. I wasn't sure how much he'd actually tell me. I'm seeing him tomorrow.'

'You need to see Joe Silk tomorrow,' he said, as if her decision had already been made. 'You're running out of time, Evie. There's trouble on the wing and Terry's already been the target more than once. If this is coming from Silk, and I'm pretty sure it is, then you have to put a stop to it now. I can try and persuade him to go down the block, to go into solitary for a while, but I doubt if he will. I can't protect him on my own – do you understand?'

She nodded, her head feeling heavy as lead. The idea of meeting Joe Silk face to face was close to terrifying but there wasn't any choice. She could see that now. Even if she went to the cops, he would still find a way to destroy Terry. She would spend the rest of her own life too looking over her shoulder.

'So how do I find him?' she said. 'There's a number in my dad's address book but it's back at the flat. I don't really want to go there.'

'No, keep clear of the place. I'll get it – someone here will know – and call it through to you later. Arrange to meet him in public, somewhere busy. Don't go anywhere alone with him. Don't get in any cars, okay? And when you leave try and make sure that you're not followed.'

She forced her mouth into an uneasy smile. 'And do you think he'll go for it?'

'That depends on how persuasive you are.'

Eve was sitting on the bed in the pink room, her arms wrapped tightly around her knees, when Cavelli's call came through at seven o'clock. He gave her two numbers, neither of which were direct lines but rather places where a message was likely to get through. He didn't stay on the line for more than a couple of minutes. He didn't wish her good luck either – a subtle reminder, perhaps, that the success or failure of this enterprise lay entirely in her own hands.

She dialled quickly before she lost her nerve. They were both answering machines but she left her name and number, stressing that it was urgent.

Then she stood up and started to pace the floor. As the smallness of the room dictated that she had to change direction every few steps this did little to ease her frustration. An hour passed and then another. She was thinking about getting in the car and going for a drive – anything to escape the claustrophobia of pink – when her mobile suddenly sprang into life. She froze for a second and then snatched it up.

'Yes?'

'Eve Weston?'

'Speaking,' she said.

His voice was soft with a hint of an American accent. 'Mr Silk will see you tomorrow morning at his office, ten o'clock. The address is—'

'No,' she interrupted smartly. 'Not at his office. At Liverpool Street station. There's a café at the top of the steps near the exit. I'll meet him there at eight.'

There was a pause, the sound of a hand being placed over the receiver and then a faint murmuring as he conferred with someone else. What would she do if he refused? But she didn't have to worry; Joe Silk's need, apparently, was as great as hers.

'Very well,' he said. 'Eight o'clock.'

The line went dead.

Eve released the breath she had been holding and sank back down on to the bed. What now? She felt exhausted, in need of some sleep but there was too much to do. Should she go to London by train or by car? The former was quicker but would leave her more exposed – and if things went badly she could easily be followed. No, it was safer to drive.

She had chosen the time not only because the early morning crowds would provide her with protection but also in the hope that she could make it back for her visit with Terry.

By tomorrow afternoon, God willing, this nightmare could be over.

Chapter Thirty-Eight

She hadn't slept well and when she woke it was to a feeling of disorientation. For a moment, tangled in crisp white linen, she had no idea where she was. Alarm jerked her upright before the recollection of her journey down to London gradually filtered back. She sank down on to the pillows and reaching for her watch peered down at the face. Six twenty.

In less than two hours she'd be meeting Joe Silk.

The horror of that thought was enough to propel her out of bed. She stumbled to the shower and let the hot jets of water bring her fully back to consciousness. Slowly, it all came back to her. Abandoning the pink delights of Primrose Cottage for the greyer but more welcome surroundings of the motorway, she'd finally booked in well after midnight. The hotel hadn't been cheap, not much change from eighty quid, but had the advantage of being within walking distance of Liverpool Street and of having a place to park. She could have cadged a bed, or at least a sofa, from one of her friends but that would have come with a different price, and the prospect of 'catching up', of the inevitable question and answer routine, had been enough to deter her.

She had spent most of last night trying to think of what she'd say to him, of the best approach and the best arguments to use. Should she be aggressive or submissive, dictatorial or appeasing? Something in between seemed the most appropriate. *Appropriate?* She leaned back her head, letting the water run through her hair, and groaned. God, there was no response to this situation that could be termed even remotely appropriate.

Rubbing the sting of shampoo from her eyes, she tried to work out how afraid she actually was. Then wished that she hadn't. On a rising scale from one to ten, she had already bypassed the lower regions of anxiety and shot straight up into major terror. Joe Silk was a gangster, a killer . . . and she was about to try and make a deal with him.

Turning off the shower, she quickly dried herself and brushed her teeth. She ran a comb through her hair, made some minor repairs to her sunburnt nose, and frowned at the smattering of tiny freckles that had seemingly broken out overnight. Carefully, she applied foundation, blusher, eyeshadow and mascara, creating a kind of mask and the illusion – she hoped – of a woman of confidence.

Back in the bedroom she rooted through her suitcase. Her choice of clothes was limited to what she'd taken on holiday and what was still reasonably clean. She found fresh underwear and then, settling for the practical (best to pick something she could run in) she pulled on her jeans and trainers and a slightly crumpled white cotton jumper.

Eve looked at her watch. It was only five past seven. She dried her hair and then, still with time to spare, went down to the breakfast bar. She wasn't hungry – her guts were too churned up with fear – but she placed toast and coffee on her tray hoping to tempt her stomach into some small quota of nourishment.

The room was barely a quarter full. She sat down at an empty table well away from the window and set to work buttering the food she didn't want. She sipped the coffee, strong and black, and forced herself to nibble on a corner of the toast. Surreptitiously, she lifted her gaze to study the other guests; there was no reason why anyone should know that she was here – she had booked in under a different name and paid cash – but the tentacles of Joe Silk probably coiled into every corner of the city. It was interesting how many people could appear suspicious if you examined them closely enough – the way they glanced up from their newspapers, the way their eyes roamed idly over the room, even the way they ate their bacon.

Before she became too paranoid she turned her mind to other things. Where was Jack now? What was he doing? She gave a small shake of her head. No, she didn't want to think about him. She racked her brains for something else but other than her forthcoming appointment (and she really didn't want to think about that) it was the only subject capable of holding her attention for more than a few fleeting seconds.

She wondered if Jack would resign or simply disappear. The former, she thought, but quickly, before his sins caught up with him. By doing that, and if he came up with a good enough excuse, he might not arouse too much suspicion. And then she realized that if she was going to make this deal today then his connection to Joe Silk, his destruction of the evidence against Terry, might never be discovered. Perhaps she should call him before he made an irrevocable decision.

Or was she just searching for an excuse to contact him again?

She knew in her heart that he wouldn't change his mind. There was no going back now. And she understood that in some ways it had come as a relief to him, the constant dread of discovery being too great a burden to bear. For as long as he was a cop he would never be out of Joe Silk's clutches; there would always be one more favour asked of him.

Eve finished her coffee. She would need to go soon. She mustn't be late. A cold unsteadying dread was creeping through her body. She became aware that everything she was doing she could be doing for the last time – putting her cup down on the saucer, nudging aside the spoon, crushing her paper serviette into a small tight ball. It was as if the most mundane of actions were suddenly imbued with a new significance.

As she stood up her knees buckled and she had to hold on to the edge of the table, taking long deep breaths, until her legs steadied and she could make the journey across the room.

Cavelli had tried again that morning to get through to him. He had gone to his cell and put his head round the door. 'You got a minute?'

Terry had been perched on the edge of his bunk with a magazine in his hands. 'Huh?'

Taking that as a yes, he'd stepped inside. 'Look, have you thought any more about what I said? Maybe you should go down the block for a while, until things calm down.'

As usual his comments were met with that familiar casual shrug. 'I've got a visit.'

'You can still have your visit.'

'Why should I go down the block?'

'I've told you before. You're in trouble, mate. It might be best if you just . . . well, kept your head down for a bit.'

The block, although more often used for reasons of punishment – the cells were small and relatively bare – could also be entered voluntarily. If nothing else it would offer some temporary protection until Evie had sorted out a deal with Silk – that's if she *could* sort it out. But even if she did it might still take a few days for the news to filter through to Bryant.

'I'm not in trouble.'

Cavelli sighed in despair. 'Christ, Terry, Joe Silk's a dangerous man. You don't want to mess with him.'

'Joe won't hurt *me*.' Terry's tone was incredulous, as if the very idea was beyond the furthest limits of his comprehension.

Not for the first time, Cavelli wondered at the fact that this kid and Evie were related. The two of them didn't even *look* similar. Whatever part of Alex Weston's gene pool had been inherited, it clearly wasn't his intelligence or his charm. He was tempted to just walk away – banging his head against a brick wall had never been a favourite pastime – but gave it one last shot.

'Come on, your sister's worried. Can't you do this one small thing for her?' He thought about raising the subject of Crete or, even more dramatically, of Andrea Banks but to have done either would have ruined the chance of Evie getting any honest answers to her questions. He had to bite his tongue. Forewarned, as they said, was forearmed.

Terry grinned. 'I know why you're doing this.'

'Oh yeah?'

'Sure.' He glanced down at his magazine and then looked up again. 'But believe me, *mate*, whatever you may think, she's not interested in you. You're really not her type.'

'And what is her type exactly?'

'Good-looking guys,' he said smugly. 'Blonds.'

'What – like you?'

It took him a moment – he was hardly the sharpest knife in the drawer – before he finally grasped the meaning. Then he was up off his bunk like he had a rocket up his arse. 'What the fuck . . .'

Cavelli laughed. Having some tiny angry punk spitting in his face made a change from the vicious lumps of lards he'd been dealing with recently. He could have floored him in the time it took to raise his fists – but he didn't. There wasn't much satisfaction to be found in flattening a kid who barely came up to his chest and weighed as much as the sandwiches he ate for lunch. Instead he moved back and lifted his palms in a calming gesture. 'Hey, cool it,' he said.

And Terry had – although only to the extent of stepping forward, raising his sharp little elbow and providing a painful jab to the ribs. Pushing past, he'd bolted out on to the landing and headed for the stairs.

Cavelli called after him. 'Where are you going?'

But, unsurprisingly, he hadn't bothered to reply.

The station, firmly in the midst of rush hour, was heaving. As she forged a path through the mass of commuters, she had another brief flurry of panic – it was as easy, surely, to eliminate someone in a crowd as it was down a deserted alleyway. Her eyes flicked nervously across the faces of the people she passed. Perhaps she should have rung Patrick. He could have watched her back at least. But it was too late now.

Or was it? Her hand reached into her jacket pocket for the phone but then stopped. No, it wasn't fair to drag him into this. She couldn't fail to be reminded of the last time she'd been here or of the responsibility she felt for the attack on Henry. Her conscience, she decided, was already overloaded.

As she turned the corner, the café came into view and she would have stopped dead in her tracks if the force of the crowd hadn't continued to propel her forward. He was there already, sitting alone at a table on the outer edges. She recognized him instantly although whether it was from the photograph or the past she couldn't really say. She simply knew that it was him.

Another few yards and she would be standing right beside Joe Silk. Suddenly, as if a switch had been flicked, that fight or flight mechanism sprang into action, the adrenalin starting to surge through her blood. *There was still time to turn around and run!*

But she didn't.

'Evie!' he said, rising to greet her. As if they were old friends he smiled and stretched out a large mottled hand. 'How very nice to see you again.'

'Mr Silk,' she said.

'Oh, please, call me Joe.'

He gestured towards a chair and she sat down beside him.

'I hope coffee is all right?' he asked. There was a pot already on the table. 'I find I need at least three cups to face the mornings.'

'Coffee's fine,' she said. 'Thank you.'

While he poured, she took the opportunity to study him up close. He was the very picture of respectability, a mature silver-haired man, impeccably dressed, freshly shaven. His full mouth, the lips still widened in a smile, seemed kindly. Even the maze of tiny red thread veins, either side of his nose, gave him more of the look of a rosy-cheeked benevolent uncle than a murdering gangster. It was only the cunning in his eyes that betrayed him.

He lifted them now, aware of her scrutiny, and returned her gaze. 'Ah,' he said. 'How very like your mother you are.'

'Am I?' The comment, completely unexpected, caught her off guard. It had not occurred to her that he would have known her mother.

'She was very beautiful too.'

For a second, although she realized she was being

flattered, curiosity almost got the better of her – she wondered how well they had been acquainted, what she was like, if he had any idea of why she'd left – but then quickly pushed those thoughts aside. That was not why she was here. And it was only a ploy to get under her skin, to spin her off balance. She mustn't let him get the upper hand.

'Thank you for agreeing to see me,' she said briskly.

Something flickered in his face, irritation or amusement perhaps. His shoulders rose in the merest shadow of a shrug. Then he laid his palms flat on the table and gave a weary sigh. His head swung softly from side to side. 'Evie, my dear. How *has* it come to this?'

'How indeed,' she replied. Now that she was here, in the centre of it all, the terror had diluted into a more manageable kind of fear. True, her heart was still pounding but not as violently as it had been. She took a deep breath, swallowed hard, and looked him straight in the eye. 'I think there have been some . . . misunderstandings between us. That's why I wanted this meeting, in the hope that we could clear the air.'

'Really,' he said. 'Misunderstandings?'

'I'm trying to be straight with you.'

He stared silently back at her. The look, she imagined, was pretty similar to the one Little Red Riding Hood's granny must have seen when the Big Bad Wolf was sitting by her bed.

'Come on,' she said. 'Why else would I be here?'

'I've no idea. Perhaps you've brought some friends along.'

'What?' She frowned and then, belatedly, realized what he was suggesting. God, he suspected she might be working with the cops, all wired-up and waiting to record. And she thought *she* was paranoid. 'What?' she said again. 'For Christ's sake, I've got as much to lose as you have.' She pulled down her collar to reveal the

542

first few inches of her chest and then lifted the sweater from the hem to reveal a smooth slightly sun-reddened stomach. 'You want to check it out? You want to pat me down?'

Her voice must have risen because a couple at the next table turned to stare. Eve threw them a surly *mind your own business* glare before swiftly covering up and returning her attention to Silk. 'Since when did any member of the Weston family go running to the law?' she hissed.

He sat back, the smile slowly creeping back on to his lips. 'I was right,' he said. 'You *are* like your mother.'

She threw him a scowl. 'So do you want to talk or not?'

'As I recall, *you* were the one who asked for this meeting.'

'Okay. Fair enough.' She took a few sips of coffee, a delaying tactic while she calmed down and thought about how exactly she should proceed. A modicum of truth seemed in order. 'What you have to understand,' she began, 'is that until recently, until last week in fact, I knew nothing about the photograph. I didn't even know it existed.'

'And you expect me to believe that?'

'It's true,' she said. 'I swear.' She was able, on this point at least, to meet his eyes with a pure unwavering sincerity. 'We hadn't seen much of each other before he ... before he died, and there weren't any notes, any final messages. He just . . .' She paused, the memory still painfully raw, and her hand moved swiftly to her mouth. 'He didn't tell me anything.'

'So who did?'

'No one.'

'So why did you hire Ivor Patterson?'

Her jaw dropped open. She was as surprised as when

he'd first mentioned her mother. 'Patterson? I didn't hire Patterson. He was following *me*.'

There must have been something about the objection, about her righteously indignant tone, that was enough to question his assumptions. His forehead crunched into a frown.

'I only clocked him once,' she said. 'He tailed me out towards Blakeney but I managed to lose him.' Now she was confused too. 'I've been presuming it was down to you.'

He shook his head and gazed thoughtfully over the balcony.

From the upper level, they had a clear view of the forecourt and the platforms, of the trains coming in and out, quickly disgorging and then sucking up their next batch of human cargo. It was all faintly hypnotic. She wondered how many of Silk's men were lurking in the background. At least two, she reckoned, and probably more if he was as worried about this meeting as she was.

'Look,' she said, turning to him again. 'It doesn't matter where I found the photo or how, or who told me what or when. The point is that I've only just found out what happened in Crete.'

'Really,' he said.

She wasn't quite sure what reaction she'd expected but it certainly wasn't that. His face remained impassive. In fact he was so calm, so coolly indifferent, that she could hardly believe they were referring to a murder. Perhaps he thought she was bluffing. She lifted her chin and tried again. 'I know what happened to Andrea Banks.'

'Of course,' he said. 'Why else would you be here?' Then, as if they were discussing some minor business proposition, he casually lifted his cup to his lips and sipped at his coffee. 'So what do you want?'

His attitude, his whole demeanour, was enough to

chill her to the bone but there was no backing out now. The moment had arrived. Those final words of Cavelli's slid into her head: *It depends on how persuasive you are.*

'I want to make a deal. You think I need this mess in my life? I don't. All I want is to sort it out, to get back to normal. Naturally I've taken copies of the photograph but only for my own protection. I'm not trying to . . . to blackmail you. I don't *want* anything other than to be left alone – and for you to leave Terry alone. That's reasonable, isn't it? If we just stay away from each other, keep our distance, then surely we both benefit.'

'Until the next time your little brother lands himself in trouble.'

'No,' she said. 'I swear. If you keep to your side of the bargain, I'll keep to mine. I'll never contact you again.'

He appeared to give it some thought, his fingers lightly stroking his chin. 'I made a deal with your father. He let me down.'

'I know but this is different. I'm not claiming what he did was right but he was only looking out for his child. He couldn't bear the thought of Terry spending all those years in jail.' She paused and then, hoping to arouse some small element of paternal understanding, said: 'Dad was ill and he was desperate. You'd have done the same for Marianne.'

His brows lifted at the mention of his daughter. 'Perhaps,' he said softly. He leaned across the table until his mouth was almost touching her cheek. 'But then I doubt if Marianne will ever leave a corpse in the bedroom for me to tidy up.'

Eve jumped back as if she'd been slapped, her eyes widening in disbelief. 'What? Terry didn't—'

His shoulders lifted in another of those light indifferent shrugs.

'He *didn't*!' she insisted. 'And you know it!'

'Have you asked him?' he said.

'Why would I even bother to—'

His mouth slid into a thin cruel smile. 'Ah, then perhaps you ought to have a little chat before you dig too big a hole for yourself.'

'I don't need to have a little chat,' she snapped, trying to ignore the possible double meaning of what he'd just said. Her outrage was greater than her fear just now. 'I know what my brother is and isn't capable of. What is this – some feeble attempt to shift the blame? It's pathetic. Why would you have covered it up if it was down to Terry? Why would you have bothered?'

He sat back, calmly folding his hands into his lap. 'Because your father begged me to, my dear. Because we were friends – once upon a time. Because, to be quite honest, I was landed with a somewhat inconvenient situation and, all in all – although I have to admit it *was* a bad decision – that option seemed preferable to the others that were open to me. The Greek police are not especially *sympathetic* towards that kind of thing. Being the owner of the villa, I could foresee some rather awkward questions.'

'You're lying!'

He seemed amused by her continuing protestations. 'And so who exactly *do* you think was responsible?'

'How is Mr Chase these days?' she retorted.

'I'll tell him you were asking after him.' He smiled again. 'But no, I'm afraid you're off the mark. It's not Keeler's style. He's never been especially fond of women – not in *that* way, if you get my drift.'

Eve felt her stomach plummet. His drift was as clear as a thirty-foot tidal wave. Oh God, so Andrea Banks had been raped before—

She barely had time to complete the thought before Silk leaned in close to her again. A gleam of pure evil flickered in his eyes. 'Of course there is a simple way of establishing the truth.' His breath whispered hotly against her cheek. 'We could always dig her up, get the DNA checked out. You'll find that the results are quite conclusive.'

Eve felt suddenly paralysed, too terrified to move. The man was deranged, mad, sick in the head! Perhaps *he* was the one who had . . . Her guts heaved again and she was glad of the lack of food inside them.

He slowly sat back and sighed. 'But then if we have to go down that road, *everybody* loses.'

She could only think of escape, of getting away, of ending this nightmare. There was no safe deal that could be made with a lunatic like this. She should have listened to Henry. She should have gone to the cops or stayed with Jack or . . . Jesus, why had she been so stupid! Her eyes flicked sideways, trying to judge the time it would take her, if she could get her legs to move, to push through the crowds and sprint out on to the street.

'Before you make any rash decisions,' he said, 'perhaps you should have a word with his mother.'

Startled, her gaze flew back to him. 'Lesley?'

He saw the surprise on her face and was quick to take advantage. 'She hasn't mentioned anything to you?' He gave a low chuckle. 'Ah, but of course not. The two of you never really did hit it off, did you?'

'What's *she* got to do with it?'

'Terry has a history, my dear. Why do you think she was so desperate to get rid of him? Trouble is his middle name.'

'So he made some mistakes, got in with the wrong crowd. He's young. He's only twenty-one. It's not as if—'

'I don't mean *that* kind of trouble,' he said.

'What?' It was an instinctive response rather than a question. She already understood what he was implying. She felt a shiver run through her. But it wasn't true. It couldn't be. She'd have known. Surely she'd have known? And then she remembered the day she was at Blakeney, when Lesley had been about to tell her something but had then abruptly changed her mind. But that didn't mean . . . And then there had been the phone call, just before she had left for Crete. *I need to talk to you.*

'Poor old Vince,' he said. 'He's tried his best to keep things quiet but there's only so much silence money can buy.'

She shook her head.

'Ask him,' he said. 'Ask Lesley, ask Terry. Ask them about the other girl, the one who was lucky enough to survive.'

She swallowed hard. There was a hard weird lump in her throat. 'You're lying,' she said.

'Call Lesley,' he said.

'Why should I?'

'Why not?'

She didn't know why not. Why couldn't she just pick up the phone and prove what a gross stinking liar he was? Because for one it wasn't the kind of a call you could make at a busy station café and for two it would be like admitting that he *could* be right and that vile doubt was just too terrible to face. 'Because I don't need to question whether my brother's a goddamn killer or not.'

He nodded. 'Good,' he said, 'I respect loyalty, especially family loyalty. But there comes a time when . . . well, when you have to know where to draw the line.'

She glared at him.

'You're a smart girl, Evie, but they haven't been honest with you.'

'You think?' she said. She'd intended it to sound sarcastic, challenging, but it emerged as more of a defensive croak.

'I *know.*'

Under the cover of the table she ground a clenched fist

into her thigh. One half of her head was saying *He's just playing games; he's trying to psych you out*, while the other half was screaming *What if?* There were so many things her father hadn't told her – and she couldn't help wondering why. He hadn't even rung her after Terry was arrested. Not a word. He hadn't called her until the crisis was over, weeks later, until the armed robbery charge had been reduced to the lesser one of handling stolen goods. Why not? She wanted to believe that he'd meant to save her from the worry, from the stress – but that didn't quite ring true. He'd been sharing most of his problems since the day that she'd been born. So what had been so different about this one?

Joe Silk stared into her eyes. 'You know it too,' he said.

And what scared her the most was that he was right. She might not have been lied to but she hadn't been told the whole truth. Which didn't mean that she believed his accusations – how could she? – but she didn't have the evidence to refute them either.

'I realize this must all have come as . . . something of a shock. But I'm sure the implications are clear. Naturally, I'd prefer for the whole business to be sorted out in a civilized fashion but if it isn't then you – or rather Terry – have a lot more to lose than me.'

She gazed silently back at him.

A triumphant smile lifted the corners of his mouth. He glanced down at his watch. 'Well, I believe we've covered all the bases – apart from, perhaps, the rather tricky problem of Mr Baxter.'

'Henry doesn't know anything,' she said quickly. 'He has no idea of what the photo means. Don't you think if he did, you'd have had a visit from the cops by now? You can leave him alone. He isn't a threat to you.'

Silk gave her another of his interrogative stares and then softly nodded. 'Very well. And now the messy details are out of the way, now that we understand each other, I don't see why we can't reach an amicable agreement. The deal, if you still want it, is on the table: You stay away from me and I'll stay away from you and yours. You agree?'

'Yes,' she said. So she had got what she wanted. She should have been happy, relieved, but all she felt was an empty despair.

He got slowly to his feet and looked down on her. 'Take care, Evie,' he said.

And then he turned and walked away. She watched him slip into the crowd, one more grey suit merging with a hundred others, there for a second and then gone. At least he hadn't attempted to shake her hand again.

Chapter Thirty-Nine

Eve, after breaking all the speed limits, was already on the outskirts of Norwich. She had driven the whole way back with her mobile phone lying on the passenger seat. She was muttering as she drove. *Liar, liar.* Joe Silk was a liar and she was going to prove it. All she had to do was to make a single call. All she had to do was call Lesley.

So why didn't she?

She slapped her hand angrily against the wheel. How could she have let him wind her up like that? He had got her so mad that she hadn't even been afraid, not for a moment, when she made her way back to the hotel car park. She hadn't given a damn whether anyone had followed her or not. They either had a deal or they didn't and if they didn't then . . .

Well, it looked like they did. She was still alive, wasn't she – no unsightly bullet holes in the back of her head. Except it was hardly a deal to be proud of. The upside was that she'd got what she wanted – freedom from Joe Silk, safety for Terry – but at what price? The downside weighed heavily on her already overburdened conscience: there could be no retribution for Andrea Banks. Or for Henry either.

That couldn't be right.

She thought about her father and the dangerous fateful game he had embarked upon. Why had he even taken the picture? She would never know for sure. Just a casual snap, perhaps, a memento to remind him of the trip. But that still begged the question of why he hadn't wiped it from the memory. The presence of Andrea at the villa on the date she disappeared was a piece of evidence so damning that it was surely best destroyed. What had possessed him to keep it? Maybe, caught up in the horror of the moment, it had simply slipped his mind. And then later, well . . . maybe he had realized just how useful it might be.

Which was why, apart from her natural gut reaction, she was convinced Terry could have had nothing to do with it. If he was a killer – and that was a thought she could barely begin to contemplate – then her father would have wanted to ensure that the picture never saw the light of day.

However that didn't provide her with any clues as to who had actually committed the murder. If it wasn't Chase (and for some reason, although it could be one mighty red herring, she had believed Silk's denial) then it was either Joe himself or Peter Marshall. With their history of violence they could both quite easily fit the bill.

Would she ever discover the truth? It was doubtful. Eve couldn't fail to think about Andrea's parents or about the justice that poor girl would never get. As hard as she tried to justify the deal she had made, to claim that nothing she did now could bring Andrea back, a harsh accusing voice still whispered in her ear. A part of her hoped that it had been Marshall; at least she would know that he had paid for what he'd done.

She hit the ring road and joined a slow heavy stream of traffic. It was too early to go to the prison. She would head for the flat instead – there was no reason to avoid it now – and give herself some thinking time before the visit. What was she going to say to Terry? Would he speak about what had happened in Crete or would he refuse to? No, she wouldn't let him give her the silent treatment. Even if she had to turn him upside down and shake it out of him, she'd *make* him talk. In all likelihood he had only kept quiet because he was afraid of Joe Silk. Well, he didn't need to worry about that any more. One devilish pact had been made and then broken but another was now firmly in place.

She wondered whether she should drop off Jack's car and pick up her Honda but then decided against it. There was no point wasting petrol. She may as well empty the tank before doing the swap.

It was less than a week since she'd left Herbert Street but as she turned the corner she felt a faint flicker of surprise that it still looked the same. Quite what she'd expected she wasn't sure but it remained as dreary, as uniformly grey as always. Her usual parking spot was taken and so she drove fifty yards on and slid the Peugeot into a space by a boarded-up shop.

Eve locked the car, retrieved her suitcase from the boot, and walked back to the flats. In the lobby, she stopped briefly to pick up her mail – more bills, more circulars – before heading up the stairs. She had only taken a few steps when she became aware of a peculiar hissing noise. She paused and listened. It came again, more insistent this time. Leaning over the banister, she peered along the dim corridor and saw Dorothy Leonard beckoning her back down, urging silence by a finger raised to her lips. She was dressed in a pale pink trouser suit and frilly orange shirt. Oh God, this was all she needed! As if she hadn't endured enough madness today.

For a moment she considered the supremely rude option of just ignoring her but then, reminded of her current state of karma – any more bad deeds and she would probably be struck by lightning – she forced a smile on to her face and reluctantly retraced her steps.

Dorothy, still acting as if she was in the middle of a spy thriller, grabbed her by the elbow and pulled her smartly through the door.

'This way,' she whispered, leading her through into the living room without any further words of explanation.

Eve, trying to respond in a way that suggested such behaviour was perfectly normal, continued to smile. She had never been inside the flat before and found herself surprised by its brightness, its fresh white walls and lack of clutter. The furniture was simple but stylish and there were a couple of framed modern prints on the walls. Somehow she'd expected a quite different kind of room, not only rooted firmly in the past but perhaps more indicative of her neighbour's bizarre personality. Another timely example perhaps of just how flawed her judgement was.

'Would you like a cup of tea, dear? The kettle's just boiled.'

She put down her suitcase. 'Er, no thanks. I can't stay. I'm sorry. I mean, I'd love to of course, maybe another time, only I have to be somewhere.'

'That's all right,' she chirped. 'I know what it's like for you youngsters; you all lead such busy lives.'

Although neither of those descriptions came even close to being accurate, Eve nodded. Approaching thirty-five, she could hardly qualify for being a 'youngster', and 'busy' didn't begin to describe the hectic nightmare of the past few days. What was she doing here? Why had she been dragged down from the stairs? Shuffling from foot to foot, she waited to be enlightened.

Instead Dorothy said, 'Do you play poker?'

Eve stared at her. There was something decidedly surreal about all this. 'Occasionally,' she admitted. 'Do you?'

'Oh yes! We should organize a game sometime. Your father taught me how to play.'

'In that case, I'll pass. I won't be able to afford it.'

She threw back her head, her long silver earrings jangling, and laughed. 'Yes, he does have rather a tendency to cheat, doesn't he?'

Eve noted the present tense and inwardly sighed. She wondered how long it would be until she was asked how he was. She also wondered when it would be polite to raise the question of what exactly she was doing here. Suspecting that if she didn't approach the subject soon she could be here until the sun went down, she said: 'Was there something that you wanted to tell me?'

Dorothy looked confused, her forehead scrunching into a frown.

'Just before,' Eve reminded her. 'When I was going up the stairs and you came out and . . .'

'Oh yes,' she said. 'Your friend.'

'My friend?'

'Well, that's what he called himself.'

Eve shook her head. 'Are we talking today or—'

'He's waiting for you,' she said. 'Upstairs. He's been there for over an hour. He must be chatting to your father.'

Now it was Eve's turn to look confused. It was impossible to know whether this was just another of Dorothy's fantasies or whether she really had got an uninvited visitor. 'So what did he say?'

'I asked him who he wanted. I mean, you can't just have anyone wandering in off the street, can you? It's not right. I don't care if he is working for the government; this is supposed to be a democracy. There are those who have business here and those who don't and—'

'Yes, of course,' Eve agreed impatiently. 'But what did he say? What did he say *exactly*?'

'Why, that he was here to see you, dear. He stood there bold as brass and said, "I'm here to see Evie Weston."'

'What?' She could feel her lungs expanding, her

stomach tightening. 'Are you sure? I mean that he said Evie and not Eve?'

'Oh yes. I have an excellent memory.'

'What does he look like?' She was starting to sweat now, tiny prickles on the back of her neck, on her forehead. There was no one she knew, no one welcome at least, who would be expecting her to come here.

Dorothy narrowed her eyes in concentration. She took a while to think about it. 'Middle-aged,' she said eventually. 'Ordinary. Average height, short brown hair. He's wearing a suit, grey I think. Looks rather like a salesman, one of the travelling sort, except . . .'

'Except?' Eve prompted.

'He isn't,' Dorothy said, with a sudden brisk shake of her head. 'No, he's definitely not. He's one of *them*. That's why I thought I'd better mention it. Spies, dear, they're everywhere, you know, you can't get away from them. Just the other day I was—'

'And you're sure he's upstairs now?'

'Quite sure, dear.' She paused. 'Ah, and something else. I believe he had an accent, not a strong one but . . . American, I think.'

Eve covered her face with her hands and groaned. Oh God! Christ! Her heart had begun that relentless hammering again. She remembered the café in Elounda and Christos coming out to ask, 'Yankee?' She remembered Jack sitting in the apartment and telling her about the psychopathic Keeler Chase – Silk's sidekick, the crazy man who had come over from the States. Now her fear was growing into horror. Joe Silk was a liar and not only about Terry. There wasn't any deal. There never would be. He had only wanted to flush her out, to make her feel secure before . . .

She had to get away. And fast.

Had he heard her come in? Did he know that she was here? There was no view from the second-floor landing either down to the hallway or on to the street. The only way he could have seen her was if he'd come partly down the stairs and then he would have run the risk of being seen himself. No, the bastard would still be patiently waiting.

Dorothy stared at her quizzically. 'Are you all right, dear? Are you sure you wouldn't like to sit down?'

Eve was in danger of falling down but she had to make a move before whatever remained of her courage failed her. She had to get out, get back to the car, and drive over to the jail. Would they realize she had a visit this afternoon? Well, she'd just have to risk it. She had to see Terry before she decided what to do next. And that decision had to be made today.

'I'm sorry but I have to go.' She moved forward and touched Dorothy lightly on the arm. 'But look, thanks for letting me know. You were right about that man; he isn't any friend of mine.' She didn't want to alarm her but couldn't leave without providing some kind of a warning either. Although Keeler Chase was a professional – Dorothy should be perfectly safe if she kept out of his way – she didn't want to take any more chances. 'I think it might be best if you stay inside until he's gone.'

Dorothy, far from being worried, seemed to take it in her stride. Perhaps she had lived so long with her own conspiracy theories that this was all quite ordinary and natural to her. 'Don't worry. I'll bolt the door when you've gone.'

'Would you mind if I left my case here? Only I'm going to try and sneak out quietly.' Eve raised her eyes towards the ceiling. 'I don't want him to hear me.'

Dorothy nodded. 'Very wise, dear.'

Eve stepped softly into the lobby and listened for any sounds from above. Nothing. Even if he was much faster than her, he still had to negotiate two flights of stairs and so she should have enough of a head start to make it to the car. She squeezed the keys tightly in her hand and smiled at Dorothy. Then she took a deep breath, offered up a prayer and sprinted for the door.

It was only as she hit the street that it occurred to her that he might not be working alone. One upstairs and one keeping watch outside to warn him of her arrival. Jesus! But it was too late to worry about that. She ran as if she had the devil at her heels, her trainers pounding against the pavement and kicking up the dust. There were only two ways anyone could stop her now, either with a well-judged rugby tackle or . . . the thought of the perfect target her back was providing was enough to make her suddenly swerve and veer over to the other side. She passed the chippy, inwardly cursing the sod who had selfishly parked his car there. Another fifty yards to go. Was anyone behind her? She had no idea and she wasn't about to look back.

The Peugeot was only feet away. Her pulse was racing, her lungs squeezing out the last of her breath. She raised her hand and after pressing frantically down on the automatic button she saw the lights flash and heard the reassuring click. Leaping inside, she pulled the door shut and locked it. Shakily, she turned the keys in the ignition. It was only as the engine roared into life that she dared to glance over her shoulder.

The street was deserted.

But she wasn't taking any chances. Pulling out, she glanced manically around, constantly checking her rear-view mirror. Quickly, she put her foot down and accelerated down the road. At the next corner she took a sharp left without indicating and then a right and then another left. She was over a mile from Herbert Street before she remembered to fasten her seatbelt.

By the time she joined the bypass she was sure she didn't have a tail. In fact the more she considered it the more convinced she became that Keeler Chase would be working alone. He was the type, if what Jack had said was true, who would prefer to play the solo game. No loose ends to worry about. She flinched as she thought about what would have happened if she'd carried on up the stairs. 'God bless you, Dorothy,' she murmured.

'And to hell with you, Joe Silk,' she added, glaring through the windscreen. She thought of a thousand and one ways she'd like to destroy him, all long and slow and suitably painful, but although it made her feel marginally better it didn't come close to solving the problem of what she was going to do next. She was, as the saying went, well and truly fucked. Silk wasn't playing ball and so there were only two options – to call the cops or to go on the run. And it wasn't as if she had a lifetime to decide.

She had to talk to Terry.

It was twelve thirty-five when she saw the sign for Hillgrove and turned off on to that familiar winding country lane. But she didn't want to get there too early. If there was going to be a reception committee – and it wasn't beyond the realms of possibility that a few more of Silk's friends might be waiting for her – she'd prefer to have some witnesses to her untimely demise. Most visitors didn't roll up until well after one and that car park could be a lonely place.

Eve pulled in beside the muddy gateway to a farm. She turned off the engine, wound down the window and lit a cigarette. She leaned back. Her fear had been replaced by a more grievous sense of outrage. *Shit!* How had she been so stupid? Joe Silk had set the bait and smoothly reeled her in. *Bastard!* She should have seen it coming. All those years of experience and she'd still been suckered into believing exactly what he wanted her to believe. Her father would be turning in his grave.

She sat and smoked and simmered with rage.

Still, if Silk was currently beyond her reach there was someone else she could take her frustration out on. She grabbed the phone, scrolled down the menu and stabbed at Lesley's number. It rang five times before she eventually picked up.

'Hello?'

'Yeah, it's Eve.'

'Oh.' Lesley's tone contained the level of enthusiasm that was probably more usually reserved for cold callers trying to flog her double-glazing.

'You wanted to talk to me?'

'Did I?'

Eve glared down the phone. 'You rang me last week.'

'Oh yes, right. I suppose I did. To be honest, it's not really that convenient at the moment. I've got to—'

'I don't care, okay? I don't care what you've got to do. One minute, that's all I'm asking.' She dragged on her cigarette and gazed out at the wheat-coloured field beside her. She closed her eyes. There was no point trying to dance around the subject. Silk, for all his treachery, had told her something that couldn't be ignored, something about another girl, a different girl that Vince had paid off. She didn't, *couldn't* believe it . . . but she had to go there, just once, to make absolutely sure. 'I know about Terry and that girl.'

There was an audible gasp.

And then a dreadful silence.

Eve's eyes blinked open and her heart sank. She clutched the phone closer to her ear. She knew what she was wishing for – any of the normal responses, any normal reaction: *What? Who? What on earth are you talking about?* But none of them were forthcoming. She waited in vain. 'Lesley?'

The sound of her breath floated softly down the line. 'Lesley?'

Her voice, when she finally answered, was strained

and tight, no louder than a whisper. 'Who told you about that?'

Eve felt her whole body stiffen. She drew her hand to her mouth and stared up at the sky. 'It doesn't matter who.' She swallowed hard. 'I know all about it. And I know what Vince did too.'

Lesley didn't even try to deny it. 'He did what he thought was right.'

Oh God, yet another piece of information that she didn't want to hear. But Eve wasn't prepared to give up yet. Still clinging to a fine thread of hope and working on the premise that attack is the best form of defence she said, 'Yeah? And would that be right for you, right for Terry or right for her?'

There was another silence.

And then a ghastly gulping sound.

'For Christ's sake,' Lesley cried. 'You think I *want* a fucking rapist for a son?'

Eve hung up.

As her stomach turned over, her heart went into free fall. She wanted to scream but it was too late for histrionics. She flung open the door, staggered round the car and threw up in the ditch.

Chapter Forty

Cavelli stood by his door and gazed along the landing. It was all quiet. Too quiet. At this time, only fifteen minutes before bang-up, there was usually a flurry of activity from men making phone calls, collecting their lunches, and negotiating those furtive last-gasp deals that would see them through the next two hours in a blessed haze of oblivion.

The landing wasn't empty but those who were forced to walk along it did so in an odd scuttling manner and with their eyes fixed firmly on the floor. Hear no evil. See no evil. Something was brewing. He just hoped it wasn't going to blow today.

No sooner had that thought crossed his mind than Morgan, one of the fat bastards he had floored outside George Bryant's cell, came swaggering round the corner to his left. He had a posse in tow, half a dozen oversized bruisers. Shit! They stopped when they were about twenty feet away, spread their legs, folded their arms across their chests and gave him their tough guy glares.

In Cavelli's book there was a time for standing your ground and a time to use the sense you were born with. Seven against one, even at the highest limits of his optimism, wasn't the kind of odds he relished. He turned, intending to beat a hasty retreat to his right, but it was already too late. In a flanking movement the stairwell had been covered by the second battalion of Thugs Incorporated and his escape route effectively cut off. He recognized one of them as Dan Carter, the boyfriend of that girl Evie hung around with. She should choose her friends more carefully.

Unwilling to move back into his cell where he would quickly be trapped, he decided he would take his chances to the right. At least he would be out in the open and if he managed a few well-judged punches might just make it down the stairs. Unlikely, but it was a better option than standing still and waiting to be crushed in the stampede.

Morgan, however, must have anticipated his intention. A grin crept on to his round sweating face. 'Hey, Cavelli, aren't you going to say goodbye to your little pal before you leave?'

He gestured behind him and the massive bulk of Leroy appeared from a cell three doors down. His thick forearm was tight around Isaac's throat, squeezing on his windpipe.

'Fuck,' Cavelli murmured.

Isaac's skinny arms hung down limply and his eyes were bulging. There was a spreading blue bruise along the length of a cheekbone. His nose looked broken and his lower lip, split along its length, was bloody and swollen.

Cavelli stared up at Leroy. 'This has got nothing to do with him. Let him go. It's me you want, right?'

But Morgan was the one who replied. 'Not that easy,' he said.

Cavelli ignored him and continued to address Leroy. 'What's the matter? You such a woman you need a fucking kid for protection?'

Isaac made a grunting noise that roughly translated probably meant that this was not the best moment to start casting aspersions on the big man's masculinity.

'Mr Bryant sends his regards,' Morgan said. He moved his hands to his hips, looked Cavelli up and down, and laughed. 'He wanted to be here himself only he's kind of busy.'

'Yeah, busy getting you to do his dirty work for him.'

'Oh, no. This isn't work, shitface – this is pleasure.'

While Morgan was gloating, Cavelli was trying to work out how he could possibly get to Isaac. It wasn't looking good. Even if he managed to take Leroy out – and that would involve a minor miracle – he would still have the other seven to contend with. But then he guessed that was the point. As soon as he went for it, they'd be all over him, taking turns to shove his face in the concrete. And if he didn't go to them, then . . .

'Make your choice,' Morgan said.

Cavelli gazed along the landing. Not a bloody screw in sight of course although whether that was down to chance or design – men like Bryant had their ways – he didn't have time to ponder on. He heard a scuffling sound to his right and turned to glance in the direction of the other pack. His heart turned over. *Jesus!* Two of them were dragging Terry Weston out of his cell. He was kicking and struggling but was too small to put up any useful resistance. He had a gag in his mouth and those wide grey eyes were filled with terror. They pushed him to his knees and held him down.

It was only then that Cavelli fully understood the pure evil of Bryant's revenge. He could only save one of them. He had a choice – Isaac or Terry. Either way, he was going to get his own head kicked in but *one of them was going to die*.

Jesus Christ.

Morgan laughed again. 'Make your choice, shitface.'

Isaac or Terry.

Cavelli stared back at his cell mate, the blood in his

veins slowly turning to ice. Leroy tightened his stranglehold. Isaac grunted, gazing at him pleadingly, his lips moving as if in silent prayer. And then he quickly looked over at Terry again. He was weeping like a little boy, the tears running down his face, snot pouring from his nose. He thought of Evie and of all the ways she had tried to protect him. How could he make a fucking choice like this, how could he even begin to—

Cavelli launched himself across the space. The roar that came from his mouth was primitive, more animal than human, a sound that rose up from his soul. Instinct had taken over from reason. He was barely within reach of the group when Leroy pushed Isaac aside, throwing him against the railings. Morgan reached back and a weapon was placed into his hand. Cavelli felt the crunch, the agonizing pain as the length of wood, as solid as a baseball bat, swept his right leg from under him.

'That's for Hales,' Morgan yelled.

Cavelli writhed on the floor. Someone kicked him hard in the ribs. And then again. A boot smashed into his groin. He tried to curl into a ball but the blows kept coming, to his face, his chest, the base of his spine. He tried to crawl but his arms were kicked away. It could not be long now before . . .

Then, abruptly, like a door being slammed everything stopped. For a moment he thought it was over. Relief streamed through his body. He lay listening to his own groaning breath, to the murmur of voices around him. Then slowly, one by one, the voices fell quiet and an eerie silence descended.

Leroy leaned over, grabbed him by the hair and wrenched up his head. He clamped his palm across his mouth. 'Watch!' he demanded. It was the only word he had ever spoken to Cavelli. It was a word he would hear in his nightmares, over and over, from that day forth.

Along the landing, Terry was still on his knees. He

was staring straight at him, his liquid eyes as wide as saucers.

'And this is for Bryant,' Morgan whispered in his ear.

He must have given a signal because the man holding Terry put his left hand under his chin and jerked back his head. The blade was a glint in the light. It was there, hovering, just for a second – and then it sliced through his throat as cleanly as a razor.

Epilogue

The rain battered against the window, a fast brutal downpour that shook and rattled the panes. A miniature lake of water was pooling on the sill. As another fork of lightning split the thunder-dark sky, Eve put down the letter and frowned.

It was six months now since she'd left Norwich, over seven since she'd driven up the path to Hillgrove and seen the fleet of cop cars and the ambulances gathered ominously on the forecourt. Had she realized at that moment? Had a part of her known even before she entered the building that Terry was already dead?

What she had felt when they told her, when they had sat her down and were talking in those soft anxious tones, could not be described by a single word. Perhaps it could not be described by words at all. She had displayed all the natural responses, shock, horror, grief – and they had all been genuine – but hidden inside had been another emotion that she could not afford to show. It was so dark, so grossly shameful, that she could barely acknowledge it to herself. Buried deep within her soul was a small sprouting seed of relief. Now she would never have to ask him the question she was dreading – and would never have to hear him tell that terrible lie.

Sergeant Shepherd had been one of the cops who had interviewed her. The other was an inspector called

David Locke. By then she had had no choice other than to hand over the picture and to tell them *most* of what she knew.

This new version of the story – one that contained no mention of Jack or her conversation with Lesley and described Martin Cavelli only as an old friend she had called upon to help defend her brother – she had made up on the spot. It wasn't too hard; omission was less risky than the treacherous quicksand of detail.

'All I know,' she said, 'is that something awful happened to Andrea Banks at that villa, something that my father and Terry were forced to keep quiet about.'

Even then, even when Terry was lying cold in the morgue, when it no longer mattered any more, she had continued to protect him. Or was it her father she was trying to defend? The truth would come out eventually but she could not bear to be the one to speak it.

Eddie Shepherd placed the two pints on the table, sat down and glowered at the empty ashtray. It was over six months since he'd given up smoking and he was still reaching for his fags at least twenty times a day. That bloody Weston case had almost been the death of him: three weeks in hospital and enough drugs pumped into his veins to raise the envy of every Norwich junkie.

'Let it go,' Locke said. 'You want to give yourself another heart attack? What's the point?'

Eddie sighed into his pint. The point was that when he shut his eyes at night, he couldn't sleep; he went over the evidence over and over again, still trying to put the pieces together. Had Eve Weston been telling the truth? Only some of it, he suspected. And she was still sticking to her story. 'I don't like loose ends and I don't believe her about that picture. She knows more than she's saying.'

'But it makes sense that he'd keep it as protection. If they were witnesses to a murder, it's the one thing that would keep them safe. So what are you thinking – that he was using it to blackmail Silk?'

'It's possible,' he said. Although recalling the state of Alex Weston's flat it wasn't likely. And if Sonia Marshall was to be believed, he'd hardly been living the high life.

'Or maybe the daughter was the one trying to put the squeeze on Silk. He decides he's had enough, that he's going to hit her where it hurts and—' Locke made a fast cutting gesture to his throat.

Eddie wasn't sure about that either. He lifted his gaze to stare out of the window. The grey of the sky, the lashing rain and intermittent claps of thunder matched the darkness of his mood. 'We haven't even got a body.'

Locke snorted. 'Bodies are the one thing we haven't been short of.'

'But not Andrea's. If she was murdered at the villa, she must have been buried somewhere else. They turned that whole place over, inside and out – not a shred of evidence. Without the body, we'll never find out who killed her.'

'Well, whoever he was, the odds are he's past prosecution.'

Which was true. Of the five men at the villa, only one was still breathing. Alex and Terry Weston, Peter Marshall and Joe Silk were all dead. Yes, even the infamous Joe Silk had gone to meet his maker. He'd been found in the office of one of his clubs with a neat gunshot to the temple. A gangland execution perhaps – or a gift from someone closer to home. Had Keeler Chase decided to eliminate the last possible witness to his crime or had he simply done a bunk when he found out Silk was dead?

Eddie sipped his pint and frowned. The one person he never mentioned in these frequent and frustrating discussions was the bizarre resignation of Jack Raynor. 'Family problems' was the reason cited. Bullshit! He remembered Raynor's response to Peter Marshall's drowned corpse, his defensiveness over Eve Weston, his interest in Martin Cavelli. They were all loose threads that if pulled on hard enough might eventually . . . but he didn't want to go there. He had never liked the man but some dogs were best left sleeping.

Eve leaned her head against the window and felt the vibrations of the rain. Whenever she thought about that afternoon, it was always with a lingering sense of guilt. If she had gone straight to the cops when she found out about Andrea Banks, if she had seen Terry instead of Cavelli on that Thursday visit, if she had only found the time to speak to her father . . .

But what ifs didn't change anything. She understood now why he had taken that silent midnight stroll into the river. He had been too exhausted to go on, too tired of hiding such a dreadful secret. And yet, even at the end, he had still not been able to make a definitive decision. He was a father and Terry, whatever he had done, would always be his son. He could not be the one to condemn him to a life behind bars. So he had simply left the notes, hidden the photograph, and left the rest up to fate.

Simply? No, that didn't come close. There had been nothing simple about it. He must have struggled with a thousand angry demons. He must have thought about it, *lived* with it, for every waking minute of what had almost been two years. Someone else's daughter, someone else's misery and pain . . .

She wondered what Terry had said to him that night. Had he cried and pleaded, sworn it was an accident, begged for his help? She would never know. Perhaps her father would have acted differently if he had been aware of the previous assault but Lesley – more concerned with her own reputation than with the very real danger her son presented – had chosen to take matters into her own hands. Vince had been despatched with strict instructions and a wallet full of cash. Terry's first victim was a prostitute, an addict and probably a realist too; she had accepted their money rather than go to court.

How Joe Silk had found out about it was another matter altogether and he wasn't around to ask any more. Still, she supposed that if you dug deep enough you could always find some dirt. Was she glad that he was dead? More relieved perhaps than glad. She recalled him sitting in the café, slowly shaking his head. *Evie, my dear. How has it come to this?*

It was a question that continued to haunt her – along with so many others. What had made Terry like he was? Were monsters born or created? And if it was the latter, then had she played a part in what he had become? She wanted to grieve properly for him – he was her brother after all – but she could only shed tears for the child she had once loved; the grown man was a stranger to her.

She shivered, pulled away from the window and lit a cigarette. Perhaps coming back to London had not been such a great idea. Henry was right; she needed a fresh start, somewhere new, somewhere different.

'You have to look to the future,' he'd insisted the last time that she saw him.

That had been six weeks ago.

They had walked along the Embankment with their heads bowed low and a cold November wind whistling round their ears. Their meetings, since his recovery, had been infrequent. She knew she should not really see him at all – their friendship had already caused too much damage – but he remained the only constant in her life.

Henry was her anchor. He was her safety and security; he prevented her from drifting. Eventually, soon, she would have to let go but she was not quite ready yet.

'You have to stop feeling guilty for the things you had no control over.'

'But I *did* have control over getting you involved.'

'I made my own choices. Neither of us knew what was going to happen.'

She turned and leaned her elbows on the wall, staring out over the dark expanse of river. 'Doesn't it bother you that he's out there somewhere?' Keeler Chase still came to her at night, an uninvited visitor to her dreams. She saw him standing in an archway, watching and waiting, his blank eyes slowly brightening. 'Don't you want him to pay for what he did?'

But Henry only gazed into the water and sighed.

It was an ambiguous sort of sigh, not the kind that could easily be interpreted. She doubted if anyone could fully recover from such a violent encounter but it had produced one positive result. It had brought him closer to Celia. Extreme events provoke extreme emotions and ever since the shooting, ever since his life had hung so tenuously in the balance, they had managed not just to put their differences behind them but to rescue and revive their marriage. She felt a faint twinge inside her chest. Was it jealousy? Not exactly; she wanted him to be happy. It was more a pang of envy. She couldn't help wondering if she would ever experience even a fraction of that enduring kind of love.

'So does Celia believe you now – does she understand that you were never unfaithful?'

He had looked at her kindly, his eyes soft behind the lenses of his glasses. 'Oh Eve, there's more than one way to betray someone.'

And she couldn't argue with that.

With their shoulders hunched, they had walked

silently on. The traffic roared by beside them. For a while they were separate, lost to their own inner thoughts. It was only as they were approaching Waterloo Bridge that he had taken his hands from his pocket and linked his arm through hers.

'How's Sonia?' he said.

And for the first time she smiled. 'Still milking it for all it's worth. Eddie Shepherd's convinced she knows more than she's telling. He won't leave her alone. He thinks that if he buys her enough meals and plies her with enough booze she'll eventually give in.'

He laughed. 'He'll have a long wait.'

'And an expensive one.'

They stopped again to gaze out over the river. Huddling against the cold, they leaned in against each other. She felt the warmth of him, the security. How could she ever let him go? But then again how could she not? She half-closed her eyes. Her breath caught in her throat. She leaned a little closer and absorbed the feeling, the safety and the sweetness, and stored it up for some future lonely day when she would need it again.

'And how's Patrick?' he said.

'Yeah,' she murmured. 'He's fine. He's okay.'

'You don't think that you two might—'

'No,' she said. 'I don't.' Which wasn't to say that it hadn't crossed her mind; there was always comfort in familiarity. Only last week he'd rung again and asked her out. *Just for a drink, where's the harm in it?* And she'd been tempted but she knew that one drink would lead to another and then another and that in turn might lead to . . . 'No,' she said again. 'No going back, right?'

'The voyage out,' he said.

She nodded.

*   *   *

Eve glanced down at her watch. She had to be at work in less than an hour. The job wasn't the best in the world, serving cocktails to lecherous overpaid city slickers, but the tips were good. After Christmas, when she had enough money, she would go away – to Paris, to Rome, to anywhere her cash would take her.

She had to find a way to move on, to stop looking back. In a moment of weakness, brought on by too much wine, she had even tried to ring Jack. She had done that stupid drunken thing of sitting on the floor, curled up against the sofa, with the phone pressed to her ear. She had punched in his number, bitten down on her knuckles and waited . . . only to hear that flat relentless soul-destroying tone. His phone was disconnected. He was gone, out of touch, out of reach, out of her life.

She picked up the letter again and stared at it. Well, it wasn't really a letter. In fact it was barely a note; Martin Cavelli was a man of few words. *Evie, Come and see me.* And enclosed was a visiting order, not for Hillgrove but for an open prison in Surrey. So it couldn't be that long before he was due to be released.

What did he want?

She had written to him at the hospital, shortly after Terry's funeral, but he had never replied. No big surprise. A faltering apology was small reward for a broken leg, five cracked ribs and whatever else her hellish pact had inflicted on him.

Would she go? No, she couldn't see the point. There was nothing left to say.

But then again, her curiosity usually got the better of her – and at least she might finally get rid of those boxes . . .

The Debt

by Roberta Kray

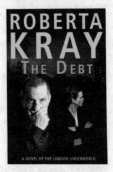

Johnny Frank's out – and the only thing on his mind is revenge

An anonymous police call was all it took to alert the police to a body at The Palace. Now, eighteen years on, Johnny Frank is out of prison and has only one thing on his mind – to kill the man who put him there. But first that man's going to suffer . . .

Jim Buckley has everything Johnny hasn't: a comfortable life, a family and a future. That is, until Johnny enters his life and sets about destroying the family from the inside out by planting suspicion, turning wife against husband and son against father.

But Johnny's plans soon go awry as his ugly past rears its head. A vicious murder and a kidnap force him back onto the streets of London. He could choose to disappear if it wasn't for Simone – Buckley's cool, classy daughter-in-law. As her husband's life hangs in the balance she might just be willing to do anything to persuade Johnny to help her.

£6.99 paperback

If you enjoyed *The Pact* why not order *The Debt*.

No. of copies	Order	Title	RRP	Total
		The Debt	£6.99	
		Free P&P		
		Grand Total		£

Please feel free to order any other titles that do not appear on this order form!

Name: _____

Address: _____

_____

_____ Postcode: _____

Daytime Tel. No./Email: _____
(in case of query)

Three ways to pay:

1. *For express service telephone the TBS order line on 01206 255 800 and quote 'PAC'. Order lines are open Monday–Friday, 8:30am–5:30pm*

2. I enclose a cheque made payable to **TBS Ltd** for £ _____

3. Please charge my ☐ Visa ☐ Mastercard ☐ Amex ☐ Switch

   (Switch issue no. _____)

   Card number: _____

   Expiry date: _____ Signature: _____
   (your signature is essential when paying by credit card)

Please return forms (*no stamp required*) to, FREEPOST RLUL-SJGC-SGKJ, Cash Sales/Direct Mail Dept, The Book Service, Colchester Road, Frating, Colchester CO7 7DW.

Enquiries to: readers@constablerobinson.com
www.constablerobinson.com

Constable and Robinson Ltd (directly or via its agents) may mail, email or phone you about promotions or products.

☐ Tick box if you do not want these from us ☐ or our subsidiaries